CHILDREN

The Ten Worlds – Book One

BJØRN LARSSEN

ISBN:
978-90-829985-6-6 (e-book edition)
978-90-829985-4-2 (paperback edition)
978-90-829985-5-9 (hardcover edition)

The Ten Worlds logo mark illustrated by Brad Bergman

Cover and type design: Ray Grant for josephtailor

FIRST EDITION

For Dad

NOTE

British English conventions, spelling, and grammar
were used in this book.
Anglicised spellings of names have been used, where available,
instead of Old Norse/Slavic originals.

This book includes depictions of sexual, physical, and emotional
violence, and is only suitable for adult audiences. For full list of
triggers, which may contain spoilers, see:
www.bjornlarssen.com/children-tw

You see, I'm afraid I'll always be still coming out of my mother
upside down.
Tori Amos, 'Upside Down'

Let's be realists, let's dream the impossible.
Ernesto 'Che' Guevara, 'Diaries'

INDEX

THE NINE WORLDS

Ásgard – The world of the Æsir, i.e. most of the Gods. Some of the Gods are not Æsir, which is their own fault and if they don't like it, they can go back to their worlds.

Midgard – The world of the humans, connected with Ásgard by Bifröst (Rainbow Bridge).

Jötunheim – The world of the ice giants. They prefer to be called jötnar (singular: jötunn), but no one else cares. Separated from Ásgard by the river Ifing.

Álfheim – The world of the elves. One day something interesting might happen there and we will be very surprised.

Müspelheim – The world of fire and lava. Separated from Niflheim by a void called the Ginnungagap.

Svartálfheim – The world of the dwarves. They prefer to be called dark elves. No one else cares either. A lot like Müspelheim, dry and hot, but more useful. Especially if one needs something forged.

Niflheim – The world of ice and snow. Separated from Müspelheim by a void called the Ginnungagap.

Helheim – The world of the dead. Ruled by Hel, the wonderful daughter of the witty and handsome Loki.

Vanaheim – The world of the Vanir. A lot of interesting things happened there a long time ago. We don't talk about it.

THE GODS

Loki – The Trickster, the Chaos-Bringer, the Mischief-Maker; present at every event that begins with the words "hold my tankard". Best friend of Thor. The most talented of shifters (shape-changers), Loki can be a man, a woman, an insect, a bird, a snake, in short – anything and anyone that can get him what he wants, which is everything. The wisest and most witty of the Gods. Also, the best looking, the most famous due to his endless talents, loving and beloved, golden-hearted, desired by men and women alike. An amazing lover, which goes without saying. All accusations against him are false. In his generosity, he has written this summary himself to ensure no mistakes were made, since he is as giving as he is modest.

Thor – The God of thunder and lightning, blacksmiths, farmers; the Friend of Men, the Redbeard, Ásgard's protector. Since he is too heavy to ride any horse or walk through Bifröst (that's the official version, *wink wink*), he travels in a flying chariot pulled by two easily confused goats and steered by his servant Thjálfi. He has been slaying jötnar for so long he can no longer remember why he even started. Often referred to as "Father" (in Midgard) or "Murderer" (in Jötunheim). Owner of the magical hammer Mjölnir. Good friend of the wise and scintillating Loki.

Odin – The All-Father, the Furious, the Mad, the Inspired, the Wise, the Old Bastard; the God of battle, kinship, death, courage. Father of Thor. The ruler of Valhalla – the Hall of the Slain. Possesses all the wisdom of the Universe, which he paid for with his eye. Unlike Loki, who was simply born perfect. Very fond of wine, especially when the Gods' resident bard, Bragi, opens his mouth. Two ravens, Huginn and Muninn ("thought" and "memory") allow him to see and hear everything everywhere a large raven can reach.

Frigg – The Beloved, the Protectress, the wife of Odin, the Silent Prophetess. Knows everything about the future, which is exactly why she spends her days baking, cooking, feasting, and avoiding her husband. Dwells in a hall named Fensalir. You haven't lived until you've tried her cherry pie. Is not the mother of Thor. Or anybody else. An awkward topic that is better left unmentioned, at least until you're finished with your pie.

Heimdall – The Sentinel, the Watcher, the Owner of Beautiful Eyelashes, the All-Knowing, the Boring, the Who Cares. Guards the Rainbow Bridge connecting Ásgard with Midgard, ensuring that the undesirables don't make it through. In other words, stands there and does nothing. Those with poor taste call him "good-looking". Enjoys *special massages* if you know what Loki means. A spoilsport. Knows nothing about fun or humour. Has it been mentioned how boring he is, especially in comparison to Loki?

Freya ("Lady") – The Mistress of Magic, the Goddess of love and war, the lover of gold and of her twin brother, Freyr. Her holy animal is a cat, her favourite flower a rose – both beautiful and capable of drawing blood from anyone who dares to hold them too tight. Dwells in the hall Sessrúmnir. Believed to possess a falcon cloak allowing her to become a bird (not true) and be the most beautiful of women (true).

Freyr ("Lord") – The God of fertility, prosperity, sex, battle, cycles of nature, and most enjoyable things. Also known as the Peace-Bringer, since having sex, smoking interesting herbs, and drinking makes most battles stop. Does not understand the word "moderation". Easily recognised by the constant erection entering the room before the rest of him. According to legend, owner of the magical ship Skídbladnir, which some believe can be folded and carried in a pocket. Others believe that this legend has been made up to explain what the always-present bulge in his trousers might be. The answer remains a mystery to everyone except for those who've had a chance to check (i.e. practically everyone).

Eir – The Healer (of the Gods), the Carer (for the Gods), the Helper (of the Gods).

Týr – The God of justice and sacrifice, the Judge, bringer of victory in war. Stupidly impartial, even when finding himself on the losing side. Rarely accused of possessing a sense of humour or any other emotion, unless boring listeners to death counts as an emotion.

Can be incredibly irritating when he decides, incorrectly, that Loki is wrong about something.

Thrud – The daughter of Thor and Sif; the Worker, the Strong, the Feeder. Freya's housekeeper.

Hel – The Goddess of the Dead, the ruler of the Underworld (Helheim). Daughter of Loki. A wonderful young lady, especially if you're looking at her non-decomposed half and if you don't try to leave Helheim once you've entered it. Sister to Fenrir wolf and the serpent of Midgard. Long story.

Bragi – The God of poetry, the best among skalds, the husband of Idunn, the headache of Odin. Any story told by Bragi has the power to replace reality or create a new one, and his words spread everywhere like rats in Midgard. Has most probably not written this book.

Idunn – The Life-Bringer, the keeper and grower of the fruit of youth, the wife of Bragi. Rarely seen anywhere but in her garden. It is not recommended to hurt any plant in front of Idunn. The remains of those who've tried make for a great fertiliser.

Sif – The Golden-Haired, the Blossom-Bringer, the wife of Thor. Possesses hidden depths, hidden so deeply that nobody has ever seen any proof of their existence. Is probably useful for something, although it's hard to say what.

Magni – The son of Thor and Járnsaxa.

Módi – The son of Thor and Járnsaxa.

Maya – Freya's foster daughter. Has some qualities. Apparently.

Loki – The most witty and wise of all Gods. Very handsome. Just in case you missed it.

CHAPTER 1

MAYA

I STARED INTO THE DARKNESS, waiting for the impossible to happen. I tried to hide in my fur coat, but it wasn't the cold that made my teeth chatter. I stood on the shore of river Ifing, its current savage enough to tear limbs off any fool who'd try to dip a toe in. Ifing served as a barrier between the world of Gods, Ásgard, and the one where I now dwelled, Jötunheim. It could never be breached – that was the very reason for its existence. Yet I was ordered to wait for someone who would cross the river that couldn't be crossed, bringing along the only thing that was more dangerous than Ifing, and who would make me responsible for it.

I had tried and tried to come up with an explanation that would convince King Thrymr that his demand could never be fulfilled. When his voice had become quieter, nearly a whisper, I had known to stop. The cargo *would* arrive on the shore this night, he had said, and it *would* be better if I didn't return empty-handed. If only he knew how many times I had stood here wishing that this river could be crossed, that I could go back to Ásgard, to my clean, warm chambers—

I blinked, then rubbed my eyes.

No.

The blue light flickering in the darkness grew brighter with each blink, gently rocking left and right as it approached me. I wanted to scream, but my lips seemed to have been sewn shut; I couldn't run away, as terror nailed my feet to the ground. *No.* I could only watch as the moonlight, grey rather than silver, cut a man's silhouette out of the darkness. At first I thought that he was walking on water, perhaps even on the rocks that Ifing's roaring current turned into sharp blades. Once he got closer I saw a small boat that rocked as it floated in the air just above the river, never touching the water. The impossible was happening in front of me, yet I remained unable to come up with a thought more elaborate than "no".

The eerie blue light grew into an orb made of tiny, glowing particles that moved like scared flies stuck inside a jar, bouncing within invisible barriers that held them together. It radiated so much mana that I was forced to take a few steps back and cover my eyes with my hand. I could never command so much power. The boat slowly lowered itself to the shore, the orb hovering over the man's wide-brimmed hat, its shadow completely obscuring the man's face. He was holding a large bag. My skin was burning, my stomach was protesting, grey and white flakes obscured my vision. I needed to lie down. I was feeling sick. *No.*

"My lady," said the man and I winced, as if I had woken up from a nightmare to find myself in the middle of an even worse one.

"Is th-this M-Mjölnir?"

"The one and only. Do you have the letter?"

He gingerly placed his cargo on the ground, letting the fabric unfold. It was less of a bag, more of a blanket, in the middle of which lay...

The onslaught of power felt like a sudden kick in the belly, so brutal that even the man recoiled. Thor's hammer hated me, it hated being here, away from its owner.

"Letter," urged the man. I handed him the parchment, unable to tear my gaze away from the hammer. My skin was burning, yet I was shivering. *No.* I didn't – I couldn't—

"Lift it."

Help me, Gods, I prayed, then felt the blood drain from my face.

The Gods were no longer on my side. Their fury, once they discovered that I'd helped with Mjölnir's theft, made jumping into the river and letting the rapid current tear me into pieces sound tempting. I felt dizzy, stumbling under the weight of the expectations placed upon me. This man was some sort of incredibly powerful mage. He could achieve the impossible and float over Ifing. I was a nobody, a human with some minuscule powers...

"I'm in a hurry, little lady."

Please help me, I prayed silently to nobody in particular, then clenched my teeth and felt drops of sweat emerge on my forehead. Mjölnir slowly rose into the air, hovering just over the surface of the blanket. I wasn't lifting the hammer so much as wrestling with it. Without a word of warning, the man squatted and pulled the fabric out from under the hammer in one swift motion.

I let out a little cry and the weapon wobbled in the air.

"Don't drop it and don't move too fast," warned the man, "or it will return to him. Goodbye."

I didn't watch his departure, afraid to tear my gaze away from the hammer. The fierce heat of the orb's power gradually weakened and so did the courage I'd never had in the first place. I was the King's sorceress. I'd spent the last twelve winters building my position in court, guarding it, ensuring that nobody could replace me. They called me the witch, feared and hated my magic, believing me to have God-like powers. I had to deliver Mjölnir to the King and it was all I could do not to let it fall to the ground.

I have often wondered why a road led from the City of Light to the shore of Ifing, as if a harbour had once stood there. Now I didn't care, only wishing that the road had been shorter. The City was built on a reservoir of mana. In Ásgard mana overflowed everywhere, as present as air, still nowhere as intense as the power that the orb nearly killed me with. Here I could only tap into puddles or trickles of it and I needed every drop to do this.

My body stiff with exertion, I took the first step, then another. The hammer's movement was irregular, stopping and starting as it fought against my magic. I didn't know an object could hate a person. I only realised that I was biting my lip when I felt the taste of salty, silky blood in my mouth. I was forced to carefully lower the hammer to the road's surface every now and then to take a breath and find another spot with a bit of mana. I looked back at the river, then towards the City. At this speed I'd reach it in time for the summer festival.

King Thrymr didn't like waiting and didn't care how difficult this was. To him or anybody else with no magical powers this hammer would look commonplace, a chunk of darkened iron, the handle too short to comfortably use. Those people wouldn't feel the resistance and the power I was wrestling, until they tried to touch the hammer. I was taking air in and letting it out in small, rapid pants, breathing as if I were sprinting uphill. I made it another few steps, paused, lowered the hammer onto the road and leaned against a tree, trying to force my breath to slow down. I wiped cold sweat off my forehead and tears from my eyes. I groaned as I lifted Mjölnir again.

I was raised in Ásgard by Freya, the Goddess of love and war. When she sent me here on my sixteenth birthday, promising me a great adventure, I was bursting with excitement. Freya was sending me on a special mission to Jötunheim, a whole new world where the jötnar lived! "Thjálfi will take Thor's chariot and bring you where you need to be," she said. "You will go to the jarl, show him your powers, then offer to become his sorceress. They will love you like they love me. And in case something goes wrong, you can always fly away!"

I had taken this as a promise that I could fly back to Ásgard. I hadn't questioned why Thjálfi had to take me over to Jötunheim. I never realised that I needed mana to fly and that the flow of water blocked it – just one of the many reasons why Ifing couldn't be crossed. Once the chariot had disappeared on the horizon, so had my excitement, replaced by a fear as strong as that which was gripping my innards right now. The whole new world, cold and cloudy, seemed much less exciting now that I was actually in it. And this was before it dawned on me that Freya had never told me why she was sending me here, for how long, or how – if – I would return...

The hammer's handle scraped the road and I squealed in fear, but nothing happened. I lowered it again, then sat down, wishing I could make my heart beat slower. I was drenched in sweat. At least I could already see the gate open wide, unguarded. For a blink I was taken aback by the walls not glowing, before remembering that I had been the one to turn the City of Light dark again. The King's orders were clear: nobody would leave their houses that night to disturb me, not one guard would stop me inside the castle. Most of the City's dwellers knew better than to even try and peek through their windows.

"You can do it," I groaned, lifting myself and the hammer again. It felt like its weight added to mine, my feet so heavy they seemed to leave tracks in the road. I was nearly there, I encouraged myself, before barely stifling a frustrated cry. Getting to the gate wasn't enough. I still had to get through the streets, into the castle, up the stairs...! My hands hurt, folded into fists so tight that my fingernails would soon draw blood. Every muscle I had strained to carry the hammer one step after another. The reservoir of mana under the castle was large – I had placed the castle here for a reason. I just had to reach it first.

It took me an eternity and a day to reach the gate, then drag my feet through the dark streets of the City. On any other night, the walls I had built would glow faintly with a light I had given them. Now everything seemed dead and I shuddered in the eerie silence, nearly losing the hammer. *Don't think about death, the hammer, or the King*, I told myself. *Just the warm bed ahead. Almost there.*

The heavy iron and hardwood door of the castle stood open wide, as I had left it. I needed to conjure glow around myself now, as I couldn't take the moonlight inside with me. I had enough mana to draw from now and that allowed me to see the wide, marble staircase in front of me. I stumbled on the first step. Something was obscuring my vision. Was it snowing inside? Exhaustion, I realised. Was it possible to die from magical exhaustion?

Mezzanine. The warmth of tears rolling down my face. I rested against the balustrade, staring down at the giant feasting space that the King intended to use soon. My knees suddenly attempted to fold and I barely managed to keep myself standing. There were twelve more steps, but it felt more like twelve thousand. I'd just rest for a moment.

"Hurry up," hissed the King, standing in the doorway of my own chambers, gesturing impatiently.

The hammer rose into the air again, scraping across the floor once, then again. The screeching sound echoed from the marble walls. My legs, my calves, my feet, my neck, everything hurt, but I was almost done. I leaned against a column, lowering Mjölnir to the ground, next to the King. There. I'd done my task. Let me sleep.

"Inside," he whispered feverishly. "Into your private chambers, nobody can see it!"

One last time I lifted the hammer. He had enough courtesy to let me in, shut the door behind me, and pull open the curtain that hid my bed chamber. I couldn't tell whether it was my glow or sheer depletion that turned everything into fog. The King pulled at the drapery over my bed and I just let the weapon drop onto the soft duvet before collapsing in a heap on the floor.

"Bring back the light," King Thrymr commanded. "I want to see."

My hand sought the crystal pendant on my neck. One touch was enough for the glow surrounding me to seep into the walls, causing them to shine a pale light again. Normally I'd mutter some nonsense, pretend that I was performing special rituals. I was so desperate to get out of the task I thought impossible, though, that I had told the King all my deceptions. I could never do it, he should find someone with much more talent, I pleaded. The runes on my door were just for show, the potions he suggested I use were fake. He listened, nodded, then told me to hurry up. Why wouldn't he just take the hammer now and go? I'd done his bidding.

My own stupidity slapped me in the face, just like Freya used to do back in Ásgard. If he could just "take" the hammer, he wouldn't have needed me. He wouldn't go away until he got whatever it was that he wanted.

"Is this really Mjölnir?" he asked and I opened my eyes to see him bent over the bed, much closer to the hammer than I would consider safe. "You wouldn't be trying to deceive me, hmm?"

"Don't touch it, Your Grace," I croaked. Even from here I could feel the hammer's anger. King Thrymr couldn't see the chunk of black iron for what it really was. "It's very dangerous..."

"You'll see 'dangerous' when I wield it," huffed the King. In one swift motion, he grabbed the handle, or rather, he tried to. The lightning blinded me, followed by thunder so deafening that the thud afterwards barely registered. The room was filled with the metallic smell of a storm, the bed miraculously un-scorched. The King was gone. My mind went blank for a moment until I heard a quiet groan. The impact had hurled him at the wall so hard that his body bounced back, lying in a weird, contorted position. I'd be charged with murdering the King.

Blood pulsated faster in my veins, only instead of blood it felt like ice. "Your Grace," I cried. "Please...please be alive!"

"You've hurt me."

"No, it wasn't me, I'm sorry, I'll bring the healer, Your Grace, it wasn't—"

"Be quiet. Come here. My head...hurts."

I crawled towards him. I was as good as dead if I didn't find a way to placate him without telling him it was his own fault. King Thrymr made no mistakes. "Please let me check your head," I pleaded. I took the indeterminate sound as a permission and, as gently as possible, I lifted his head to check for blood. The King let out a quick hiss, but my fingers were dry and the relief was instantaneous.

"You truly have great power, Your Grace...somebody weaker would have died... but a healer should..."

"No healer. Nobody can know." He groaned. "Put me to bed. I need to lie down, that's all."

"The hammer—"

"Move it elsewhere."

"I can't, Your Grace, I truly can't. I need rest."

He sighed. "Then lie down next to me and tell me how it all went, hmm? We'll rest together. It was very difficult, mhm?"

"Yes." I stretched myself on the floor next to him. He sounded calm. I might live to see the morning. "First, the man—"

My eyes popped out in shock. We were lying next to each other, yet suddenly the King was on top of me, his hand covering my mouth. It took me another blink to understand he *still* wanted more from me.

"You planned it," he muttered slowly, the way he spoke when sentencing people to death. His long, greasy hair hung down the sides of his face, tickling me, his breath reeked of onions, his hand was dry, warm, big, his body flattening mine. "You wanted Mjölnir for yourself so badly that you used magical powers against your King." A slight smirk appeared on his face. "I can't blame you. Power is such a turn-on, isn't it?"

I could barely hear him over the pounding of my heart. This was not happening, I knew it was impossible. I was having a bad dream. Someone must have put acacia in my food. I was poisoned, this was nothing but a vision...

"Once Freya is mine, I will bed her every night," mused the King. The stench of onion was unbearable. "I will be invincible, untouchable. The Gods themselves will fear me. What would a nobody like you have done with Mjölnir? Was it Thor you wanted to bed? Hmm?" His hand was still covering my mouth. Now his thumb and index finger briefly shut my nose, suffocating me. I tried to let out a sound, any sound, but only managed a quiet, muffled "mmm".

The King's crotch rubbed against mine. "What should I do with you, my sorceress? You have been useful so far. Shall I reward you with your King's child? Oh yes... your King is feeling as merciful as he is powerful. He will make your dream come true, reward you generously." His hand released my mouth. He fought with his belt while his weight still pinned me down, then growled in discontent. His knee forced my legs apart as he cursed, lifting himself up, the belt resisting.

I jerked my head towards the bed where Mjölnir lay. I could never move the hammer now. Under the bed... I didn't think. No time. I gathered all the mana I could draw and flung the thing at the King's head with all the power I could muster. He didn't even grunt. The full chamber pot didn't strike so much as it smashed into the side of the King's head, tearing him off me and throwing him at the wall again. I rolled away and lifted myself to my hands and knees, breathing heavily through my mouth.

Some of the excrement had splashed over my hair, not reaching my face. The King wasn't so lucky. His face, hair, chest, the clothing that cost more than some families earned in their lifetime were all soiled. He was breathing; I saw the excrement bubble on his lips and a whole new level of terror inside me emerged, squeezing my stomach like a vice, pushing out vomit. Most of it landed on the floor, but not all.

"C-cunt," I heard, or thought I heard. King Thrymr's skull must have been made of iron. It would have been better for me if the blow had killed him. I knew some of what would be done to me. I'd done it to others as he watched.

I didn't really so much as get up, as the vision lifted me off the ground. Leaning against the wall, I couldn't stop looking at his chest moving up and down until his lips started moving too, bringing me back into the nightmarish reality. I rolled against the wall rather than walked. If I were to fall now, I wouldn't be able to get up again.

I made it back into the "magic room". I glared at the vaguely magical-looking tchotchkes. If only a potion of strength actually existed! Most of the dusted bottles contained mud, the rune-covered books – nonsense, all produced to scare off potential burglars or spies. I carried all my power inside me and currently I had little left. Although the smallest berry from Idunn's garden back in Ásgard would have restored my strength. Ásgard was very far from here.

I had no weapons and I didn't know how to use any, as I'd always relied on magic. The idea of taking Mjölnir was laughable. The castle and the streets were empty, though; the gate – unguarded. Even slowly and carefully I should make it out of the City before the King could drag himself out of here and alert his men.

I opened the door and froze in surprise before taking one step. So did the wide-eyed man with a very sharp looking knife in his hand.

My instinct kicked in before he composed himself. I sent him flying, screaming, until he hit the ground of the feasting hall with a thud, cutting the scream short.

The silence barely lasted a blink before an arrow whizzed so near my face I would have sworn the feathers touched my skin. I only didn't shriek because air seemed to have gotten stuck in my throat. *That could have killed me*, I thought in disbelief. I had never been shot at. "The witch!" someone yelled. "Get the witch!"

This is real.

Everything turned dark again when I grabbed the crystal. What now? *Whizz*, then the *bonk* of an arrow hitting marble. I squealed and ducked. How did they know, who were they, and...why? I was useful, I wanted to cry, important, I brought him Mjölnir, I was the King's...

Shouting. Words I couldn't decipher. I couldn't understand... An orange, flickering light, first a dot, then growing. Another power orb, my confused mind screamed, no, a burning torch, they had torches! More flickering lights on the other side of the gallery. Growing, moving closer. *Run!* My legs failed me and I fell off the stairs, yelping in pain as my body hit each step in turn, trying to cover my head, until I reached the mezzanine. It took me a blink or two to decide that I wasn't dead. It hurt too much. I had no time to be in pain, no time to be tired, I needed light, I needed *sleep*. Shouting, questions, "where is she?" Door, get out of here, think later, but how did they know?

I didn't even try to lift myself up anymore. I blindly found the top step, sat on it and bumped down the stairs – *ow* – *ow* – my buttocks hitting one step after the other – more bruises, each bringing me closer to the door, closer to freedom. Being alive hurt so bad now... eleven... twelve. Now I just had to run down the streets until I reached the gate, escape the heavy boots slamming the floor, shouting, sounds reflecting from the cold marble, coming at me from all directions. I couldn't even walk, much less shift and fly away.

A sob blocked my throat. When I'd thought that I would die I didn't *really* think that I would.

"Get the witch!" tore through the ruckus and something like peace poured over me.

There were no words that would make King Thrymr forgive me. I wouldn't die for this, oh no. I would live a very long, excruciating life. Unless they "got the witch". With the chaotic running, shouting, darkness they'd shoot at any target the moment they saw one. I wondered how dying felt.

I propped myself up for the last time. "Aim well," I whispered. I would join the other dead in Helheim soon. My hand wrapped itself around the crystal, ready to conjure the glow. Suddenly a horrible suspicion arose that Odin might declare this a death in battle and make me go to Valhalla. I hesitated just long enough for Mjölnir to strike me and end everything.

~

Pain. Wood smoke. Heat. Light breaking in through my eyelids. Flames so bright they didn't even flicker. They were burning me alive. My back felt really cold, though. My tormentors weren't burning me correctly. Amateurs.

Ready to scold them, I opened my eyes with a quiet groan. Even my eyelids were aching. There were no flames, even though I could still smell the smoke. Only warm sunshine, blue sky, trees... and a heavy hand that landed on my mouth, pinning me to the ground. "Again...?" I tried to groan, but it came out more like "mgw?"

"Quiet," whispered a bearded giant above me. The sun illuminating him from behind turned his curly red hair into fire. "They're near. Promise you'll be quiet and I'll take my hand away. Okay?" He paused. "Well?"

"Mwh."

"Oh," he said, then withdrew his hand. "Sorry. Okay then? Because if you're going to scream, I have to kill you. And don't turn me into a toad, or I'll have to kill you too."

My confusion was complete. I'd been hit with Mjölnir, so I was dead, but the last time I saw Helheim it was surrounded by ice and snow. Had they changed something while I was away? I lifted myself up and looked around. We were in some sort of circular clearing in a forest. Half of it was surrounded by massive boulders. There was a fire pit in the middle. The boulders were nearly as tall as the trees, five, six times taller than me. Very strong magic must have been used here, I thought with a mixture of fear and awe. I bit my lip, immediately letting go when it responded with pain. I was dead, my body had no right to ache! I squinted at the blinding sun, wanting to complain, when doubt crept in.

"Is this Helheim?" I whispered.

The giant glared at me, put a finger on his lips and hissed so loud that the sound nearly drowned out Ifing's roar. Ifing? I listened more attentively. Voices, men shouting at each other, to my right – the road. If I got up now and started walking, I'd reach the river. The boulders hid us from the City of Light – from now on known as the City That Suddenly Needs a Lot of Candles – and the road. We were in the Haunted Forest, alive.

I glanced at my companion and stopped breathing. The giant's hair and beard were so red they looked unnatural. Like his father's. He glared at me again and I felt even smaller than before. Why hadn't I just thrown myself in the river? Being alive seemed very overrated compared to what Thor's son here would do once he found out what I'd done.

His arms were as thick as my waist. My gaze moved to his hands and I bit my lip again. This pain was nothing compared to the son of Thor breaking my bones one by one, starting with the fingers, or perhaps toes... Would he agree to break my neck and kill me fast if I answered all his questions about Mjölnir's whereabouts and my role in its disappearance? *Dear Gods*, I started praying, then I abruptly stopped. The Gods were not my friends anymore. Still, an answer arrived in the form of a bird's cry.

My pulse quickened. I sat up despite my muscles' protests, shifted into a swallow and...

...no, I hadn't. I couldn't shift any more than I could run right now. I had never experienced this before, and I felt my already dry throat constrict. Was it possible to just use up powers? What if they would never return? I told myself off for thinking such negative thoughts when I should instead focus on the various forms of torture Thor's son would subject me to soon.

The beard confused me. When I had arrived here, Járnsaxa, his mother, had either still been pregnant or had just given birth. That was quite a beard for twelve or thirteen, or even thirty. It contrasted with his undeniably childish features. Like a kid with a fake beard, a man-child with the literal body of a God. He'd look so sweet while killing me.

"They're gone," he said in a normal voice. I'd have jumped out of my skin, but I was too tired, so I just flinched half-heartedly. "You can leave. Oh. No. You can't. You'll tell them where I am."

"Who's 'them' and why can't I tell them?" I asked weakly. I had nowhere to go, nothing to eat, no strength to move, no powers. I couldn't leave any more than I could stay.

"Because I'm hiding," he said in a tone that suggested my question was stupid.

"So am I." I rested my back against one of the boulders and sighed in contentment. "How did I get here?"

He looked sheepish. "I ran into you, but not on... I didn't see you, and then... They wanted to kill you and I don't like it when people die. I took you with me. Sorry."

I nearly scolded him for ruining my chances of dying quickly. "So, you just grabbed my..." I stopped myself from saying "body" "...me, then ran away? They didn't catch you?"

"The gate was open and everything was dark. I hid in the forest, then brought you here, I can find this place with my eyes closed. I've been coming here for a long time."

"You're the son of Thor. Why would you be hiding?"

"Don't call me that. I'm just Magni. A blacksmith."

My gaze landed on a hammer secured to Magni's belt and I failed to contain a little gasp. I could imagine many sorts of torture involving fire and a heavy hammer, magical or not.

"What's wrong?"

"I was just...wondering if this place is safe."

"Nobody enters the Haunted Forest."

"How come you're not afraid?"

His eyes seemed tired, blank. "Nothing's more scary than people."

I'd been warned against the Haunted Forest the moment I had arrived here. Once I had heard about the monstrosities awaiting me there, I couldn't resist combing through it in search of them. I had been very disappointed to find out it was only haunted by mosquitoes and spiders. Back then those boulders had not been here, though. They were not my work. Until yesterday I hadn't encountered a mage powerful enough to build this construction.

Magni didn't like it when people died? What a weird thing to say. His wary stare and a muscle twitching in his cheek made it clear that he was afraid of me. Perhaps I should remind him that he could simply break my spine with two fingers and leave me paralysed. Greatly reassured by this thought, I briskly produced a friendly smile to make him feel more at ease. Magni reacted with a sharp intake of breath, recoiling from me and wrapping his arms around his knees. The trousers, too short, revealed boots worn out to the point where they barely had soles. They were dirty, same as his tunic. The belt his hammer hung from looked like it could break at any moment. Thor's son looked...poor.

"Tell me what you've done," he demanded in a slightly muffled voice. "My mother came to the forge and said that horrible things would happen at night, so I should steal some food and go to Midgard. She said there would be no guards once the lights went down. Once *your* lights went down. But when the lights did go down, I couldn't see anything, so I had to wait for the lights to come back, then the guards came out... Why did you do that? Then it became dark again—"

"Wait," I interrupted. "I have to think." I shouldn't have gestured at him with my hand, because his eyes nearly popped out of their sockets. I let my hand drop in as un-witchy a way as possible. Even that hurt. I must have been one massive bruise underneath my clothes. It was a miracle that nothing seemed broken.

Magni's confusion dispelled mine. It was I who unknowingly gave the signal that it was time to kill the witch by bringing the light back. Aside from the King, I was the only one who knew where the hammer was, and I'd become a liability rather than an asset. I would have died quickly and silently, once the King had finished "rewarding" me. The man with the knife, the guards with the torches and bows were just an extra precaution. I couldn't even pretend that I'd outwitted them. I was saved by the chamber pot, Magni, and the legends that kept both the young and the old away from the Haunted Forest.

"Are you still thinking?"

I shook my head, then nodded. "I need to get away from here."

"But why would the King want his witch killed?"

"It's not 'witch', it's 'sorceress'."

"That means witch," Magni explained. "Why would the…"

My hair was glued with something. Absentmindedly, I reached to remove it from my face. I grimaced. Now my hair *and* my fingers would stink. "I hit the King on the head with a chamber pot. A full one. If they catch me, I'll spend the rest of my life dying. Do you have some water, by the way?"

"Why did you do that? You're his witch."

"Stop calling me that! I have a name. Maya. He was forcing himself upon me."

"Forcing himself?"

"He tried to rape me." I cast another look at Magni's arms, hoping I wasn't giving him ideas. If this giant man-child threw himself on me, he'd simply crush me to death.

"And then?"

"And then I hit him on the head with a full chamber pot."

"Why?"

"It was the first thing I saw."

"But why? It's his right as the King. The law says…"

"First of all," I interrupted, "he made that law up. Second, it also states I've got the right to make sure I'm safe."

"Wouldn't it be safer to just let him? Then they wouldn't want to kill you."

Magni's eyes were innocent, expression full of concern. The man-child thought he was helping. He must have inherited his father's intellect.

"At least you know why you're running away," he sighed. "I just know that Mother told me to steal food and go to Midgard. I don't want to. They have humans there. They are covered in scales and they breathe fire. Then they kill and eat each other for the amusement of Odin the Death-Bringer…"

"He prefers 'All-Father'," I muttered, tuning him out. I had to come up with a version of events that made me look innocent.

One of the few things the Gods feared were jötnar invading Ásgard. Thor regularly descended upon Jötunheim, using his hammer to destroy towns, cities, settlements seemingly at random. Jötnar couldn't unite against Thor any more than sheep could unite against wolves. There was, however, one place that had an advantage over all other parts of Jötunheim...

"Absolutely," I nodded, interrupting him. "Tails, horns, fire. I'm human, by the way, so that's what humans look like. Magni, do you know why so many people come to the City of Light?"

His face immediately darkened and I regretted the quip. "B-because it's safe."

"Correct, and the reason it's safe is that you and your mother live here," I continued carefully. "Do you know that the taxes here are three times as high as everywhere else and that other cities don't have laws that permit the kings to sleep with any woman they want?"

"How's that our fault?"

"It's not your fault, it's..." I paused, searching for a word. "Convenient. For the King. People will pay or sacrifice a lot for safety. But sometimes... sometimes men get...bored of women, so... just in case of that... suppose there was a..."

"What's that have to do with me and my mother? Just say it!"

"You know what would keep the City safe forever? If King Thrymr could steal Mjölnir, then..."

"Hogwash," Magni interrupted. "Nobody can touch Mjölnir, only Thor, Loki, the dwarves who made it, and me."

"Oh, you too?"

"I played with it when I was little. Then he took it away. Thor, I mean, not the King. He'll never have it."

I grimaced. "He does. And he won't give it back until Freya agrees to marry him. Once Freya is here – not that it's going to happen – your mother and you will be... ah..." *Good Gods, how do I say this nicely?!* "...unnecessary."

"Ooo," said Magni, instead of erupting with fury. "Lady Freya will come here? When? Will we all get to see her?"

It felt as if someone slapped the tiredness out of me. "No," I spat. "She won't. Ever."

"No," he agreed. "Because you're lying, witch. Come up with something else."

"I'm not lying! Somebody stole it, brought it to Jötunheim, and now King Thrymr has it. I had to die, because I knew about it. That's all." I congratulated myself. Perfect.

"How do you know that?"

He pressed his lips flat and crossed his arms on his chest, sending me into panic. That was a *lot* of arms and chest. Since I couldn't shift, could I cause one of the boulders to fall on him?

"Talk, witch!"

"It – it had nothing to do with me, someone else did it, you said it yourself, I can't touch it!"

"Witchery!"

Please remember you don't like it when people die, I pleaded quietly. "Magni, it came from Ásgard! Do you think I'd be hiding here if I could just go back to Ásgard?"

His eyebrows wandered up. "Back? You are a Goddess?"

"I – no. I'm human, I just have some powers others don't have."

"How did you make the City glow?"

"Ah, that's easy."

"A whole city is easy?" His tone was no longer accusatory, but full of wonder.

"Do you know what mana is...? Of course you don't. Mana means 'life power', it's the fuel for magic. Like wood for this fire. When you put wood in this fire, it disappears and turns to heat and light."

"You put wood into the city?"

"Good Gods, Magni, it's a metaphor..."

"Why do you say 'good Gods'? It's 'dread Gods'. They're not good, except Lady Freya."

I ground my teeth. Their obsession with "Lady Freya" made me sick. I had turned this pile of turf into the City of Light and an illiterate jarl into an illiterate King, and that made me "the evil witch". Yet every single jötunn, man or woman, loved "Lady Freya", who had never set a foot in Jötunheim. "As I was *saying*, mana is invisible. It's even here, right under your feet... don't look so alarmed, it's not going to bite you, it's been there all the time! There's quite a lot under the castle. You see this crystal on my neck? It can only have one function at a time, but once I tell it what to do it just does it by itself. I told it to take the mana from under the castle and turn it into light. It's really quite simple."

Magni seemed unimpressed. "Simple? So that's it?"

"It's not just 'it', I'll have you know! Very few have those powers. You see those boulders around us? They didn't come here by themselves, did they?"

"No," he agreed. "I put them here."

"You see, with magic I – I'm sorry, you did what?"

"I built this."

I gawked. "With your...hands?"

"Mostly with my back."

"But they are so big," I said, bewildered, looking at the rocks. "Nobody could move them without magic."

Magni shrugged. "I'm strong. If I can do it, others can as well."

I stood up, noticing I was already less sore, and knocked on one of the rocks. Could it have been empty inside? It definitely wasn't an illusion. I looked at Magni in awe. He was observing me with a smug grin. "And you can wield his hammer," I mused, biting my tongue a blink too late.

"Not now that it's gone! You went to Ásgard and stole it!"

"It wasn't me! What can I do to make you believe me? Someone brought it here to the shore, I just used my powers to bring it to the King. The hammer is now on my bed."

"Your bed...!"

"Good Gods, Magni, I didn't intend to sleep with it! You have no idea how difficult it is to carry Mjölnir without touching it and if you drop it, it's just going to fly straight back to your father."

"Back to Thor. I don't have a father."

I took in his mended clothes, the dirty, calloused hands, the gaze stuck in his lap, and I sat down. "I'm sorry," I said quietly. "All I want you to know is that yes, I can move things around without touching them, I can make the City walls glow, I can shift into animals, but no,

I did not steal the hammer by myself. I don't know how it got here, I don't know what's going to happen now, I don't know what I am supposed to do."

"What would you do if you could do anything you wanted?"

I silenced. "Eat," I finally said. "Did you say you stole food? What do we have? I mean, if you're willing to share, of course."

"I've got onions and potatoes. Cheese, bread. Sausage."

"Is that all?" I asked when it became clear that he didn't just pause to think.

"Why, what do you want then?"

"Don't you have...apples?"

"Apples?" he echoed.

"Apples, carrots, pears... Am I supposed to eat raw potatoes?"

"You don't have to eat anything," said Magni, as he turned away from me, dug out an onion, peeled it with a few swift moves and bit into it as if it were an apple.

I waited just long enough for him to know I was deeply offended, then helped myself to some of the bread. It looked like Magni wasn't speaking to me. I resisted the urge to tell him that I wasn't speaking to him either and decided to look for a place where I could wash myself. Without thinking twice, I shifted into a swallow, pleased to hear a shocked shriek. I clambered out of the fur coat – not all of my clothes shifted with me – then flew up. Only then did I realise that I hadn't lost my ability after all. I moved clumsily, my bird muscles as stiff as the human ones and my wing glued with the same substance as my hair before, but it didn't matter.

I found a shallow stream and dove into it, only to emerge half-drowned and disappointed. I had no intention of using my beak to clean myself and the cold water alone wasn't enough. I certainly wasn't going to shift into a cat and lick myself clean either. The last form available to me, a horse, required help. I got out of the water, cold and still dirty, and to my surprise inadvertently shifted back into my human form. My black leather trousers and black woollen tunic were completely soaked, but that wasn't why I shivered. What if it had happened mid-flight? I needed more rest. I wrapped my arms around myself, rocking back and forth, clenching my teeth to stop them from chattering. A blink later the self-pity turned into the cold burn of fury. I'd done everything for this mediocre jarl who would never have become King without me. My reward? Losing everything, nearly getting raped, then discarded. And they'd shot at me!

I tried to shake the water out of my hair like a dog would, but when it hit me on the mouth I lost control.

I shifted into a bird, then back into a human, shrieking, squawking, flapping the wings of a small, powerless animal that ate insects and a small, powerless human that deluded herself she'd be the "revered and adored sorceress". My whirrs and chirps sounded neither human nor bird-like as I screamed in anger, pain, frustration, fear, not caring whether someone could hear me, until I ran out of all the energy I'd been trying so hard to save.

Still wet, but no longer cold, I lay there on the yellow, dead grass, panting. My hair still stank. Who knew your own shit was so hard to wash off? A perfect metaphor for everything. Too exhausted to shift again, I was forced to walk through the trees instead, avoiding the branches that tried to poke my eyes out. I decided that I still wasn't speaking to Magni, which would allow me to avoid further interrogation. Not a word, I promised myself, then sniffed the air. This wasn't just wood smoke.

"Are you baking potatoes? Can I have one? Please?"

Magni jumped to his feet. "I thought you left me! You just did a bird... became... flying... somewhere! Then I heard this horrible scream, it was a troll, the Haunted Forest is really haunted! I was so scared...!"

"Please give me a potato," I begged. "I'm sorry, I won't do it again if you just give me one. Please." I loved potatoes. Just not raw.

He harrumphed, muttered something, picked up one of the thin metal pokers and handed it to me. Somehow it didn't occur to me that the other end of the poker was nicely heated up by the fire and I dropped the thing with a surprised yelp, only stopping it from hitting the ground at the last moment. Carefully keeping my lovely, lovely baked potato in the air I pulled out the poker, making sure not to touch the hot part. I looked around for something to scrape the burnt bits off with and noticed Magni's open mouth and huge, unblinking eyes.

"What's wrong?" I asked, immediately concerned, then lowered my voice to a whisper. "Guards?"

"Don't – you – don't do witch things in front of me!"

"Do you have a knife?"

"Flying potatoes are unnatural!"

"It's hot, I can't hold it..."

"Stop it!"

I sighed. "Dropping it now. There. In the dirt now. I can't even see it. Pleased?"

I got no answer. Cursing under my breath, I patted the ground blindly in search for the potato, not daring to use the glow. I scraped the worst of the dirt off with my fingernails, hissing every now and then. Stupid Freya, stupid King, stupid half-God afraid of flying potatoes. I *told* him I could do it. As I ate the half-burnt, half-raw vegetable I had a feeling that this wasn't how one cooked potatoes on a bonfire, but said nothing. He could have kept them for himself, killed me, or just left me behind. When I was finished with the last cold bits and spitting out dirt, I began to feel guilty.

"I don't think witches even exist," I said, trying to sound as though I were talking to myself. "Neither do trolls. What you've heard was, uh, not a troll. I told you I could move things with magic, that's how the potato stayed in the air. I... I'm sorry I didn't warn you I was going to shift, I should have. For me it's normal."

"I'm not listening to witches." Magni paused. "What's shift?"

"It means changing shapes, like I did earlier. A swallow, a cat, a horse, that's all I can do. I'm really not dangerous."

"You've tortured people."

"Ah," I answered nervously. "I...didn't enjoy it."

He didn't answer.

"The King made me do it, I did it in his chambers, he... he liked to watch, please understand, I couldn't say no, or I would have to swap places with..."

Magni spat into the fire, ending my blabbering. Probably for the best. Exhausted, my stomach unhappy with the "meal", I curled on the cold ground and immediately fell asleep.

I woke up stiff, cold, wet, yet much less sore. Then I saw Magni, staring into his small fire, and I shivered, not daring to get closer. He could still change his mind about not killing me.

What would you do if you could do anything you wanted? he'd asked me yesterday. Oh, I knew the answer to that. I wanted to go back home to Ásgard, soak in my hot tub, Granny Frigg's cherry scone in one hand, Idunn's pear or peach in the other. Once I washed my hair, of course.

"I was raised in Ásgard," I said when the air became thick from Magni's efforts to avoid looking at me. "By Freya. In her hall, Sessrúmnir." I sighed. "You can ask me anything you want, about Freya or Sessrúmnir or anything else."

Predictably, Magni immediately became my friend again. "Ooo... is she so beautiful?"

"That she is," I admitted, moving closer to the fire.

"And good, and loving..."

"Mmm. I don't know about those."

"She *is* good," Magni informed me and even his freckles seemed indignant, then his eyes narrowed again. "Have you met Odin the Murderer?"

"Many times. Why?"

"Are you friends?"

I snorted. "Odin has no friends."

"Does he enjoy killing so much that he has undead warriors fighting in Valhalla for his amusement every day?"

"That's true, but—"

"Does he tell humans to die for him and they do that?"

"Yes, but—"

"How can you be human? You don't look human. You look like... like a person."

"This is what humans look like, Magni. I used to believe you were ice giants and I called dark elves 'dwarves'."

"They are dwarves."

I rolled my eyes. "Sure, and they all start forging from the moment they fall out of the womb. I was born to human parents in Midgard, but I had those, um, powers. When I was a toddler I didn't understand that it wasn't good to make cows fly. Or roofs. Or parents. So, Freya took me away and raised me."

"Lady Freya is so kind."

"Magni, she didn't ask my parents' permission. She stole me."

"She was just helping," Magni insisted and I noticed his lip starting to quiver. I rolled my eyes, but only on the inside. I'd bet Bragi had something to do with it, the skáld whose words were so powerful they could replace the truth in everyone's minds. Freya had probably paid him with her own body to spread her cult here... but no, Bragi would never cheat on Idunn.

I cleared my throat. "Now that they know Mjölnir has been stolen," I said, "the Gods will gather in the Great Hall. This is called an Assembly. Odin sends his ravens out when he calls an Assembly and the Gods have three days to arrive, then they discuss the matters and come up with solutions or ideas, until Odin approves of something and Týr declares it just."

"Týr?"

"Týr is the God of justice. You don't know him?"

"Justice," muttered Magni. "The King is a monster and you tortured people for his fun. Was that justice?"

"Magni, I...regret that. Sometimes you have to kill or be killed and that's all the choice you've got."

"I will never kill anybody," he said resolutely. Involuntarily, I snorted and the boyish, challenging gaze immediately turned wounded.

"I'm sorry," I said, surprised that seeing it hurt me. I'd never met someone so...transparent. "I didn't mean to upset you, but how do you imagine that? Going through life without killing anybody?"

"I saved you. I didn't let them kill you."

"What if it was your life or someone else's?"

"I'm strong. I can fight. I won't let that happen. I'm not like Thor."

"What if it was your life or someone else's?" I repeated.

Magni picked up a stick and started drawing in the dust. "So, Lady Freya will come here in two days?" he asked, not looking at me.

"Freya's never going to come here to marry King Thrymr. Never. Get that out of your head. Freya only loves one man and that's her twin brother." Now I spat on the ground. "They sleep together. In that way. Man, woman, naked way." I paused. "You know, like Thor and—"

"I know what you mean. She knows it's wrong and she will stop and come here. She loves us and we would do anything for her."

I didn't bother answering that. Freya would never exchange buggering her own brother for the company of a jötunn king who smelled of onions. Even if Magni was right, she wouldn't need to involve Mjölnir in that.

I leaned over to look at Magni's wonderfully elaborate drawing of what was probably a hinge. Whoever stole Mjölnir and sent it to King Thrymr either didn't know or didn't care that there was a sad man-child blacksmith God somewhere who wanted to make pretty things and save lives, even those of witches. If I could do anything I'd take him to Ásgard with me and find him a forge where he could make that hinge, while wearing clean clothes that were actually his size...

"Maya?"

"Hmm?"

"Mother told me to go to Midgard. How do I get there?"

"Why not Ásgard?"

Magni gave me a disbelieving look. "Me? In Ásgard?"

"You belong there. Much more than I do. You're the son of a God." Even if that God picked his nose while eating. "I came here, because Freya told me to. I can only hope that one day I'll find a way to go back and even then they might not let me in. Nobody has the right to stop you..." My voice died out when I realised that one day I might have to ask *his* permission to enter Ásgard.

"No. Thor lives there."

"You don't have to see him, if you don't want to. True, Ásgard is the smallest of all the worlds, but there's enough space. For instance, Heimdall and Loki can't stand each other..."

"I can't stand Loki either and Heimdall only waits to kill those who try to enter."

I rolled my eyes. "It's a world, not a settlement. You wouldn't have to see any of them, no Loki, no Heimdall. You could visit Lady Freya..." *As if*, I thought, nearly choking on my own hypocrisy.

Magni didn't answer with "ooo" this time, just scowled. "What would I do there?"

"You could be a blacksmith."

"Are there many blacksmiths in Ásgard?"

"Um... well... I haven't actually met any, but that only means you'd be even more in demand."

He pshawed. "I don't want to be in demand from those creatures. You go to your Ásgard, I'll take my chances with the humans, if you're not lying and they're really like people."

Peace in Midgard. Good luck with that, kid.

Magni noticed my interest in his drawing and quickly destroyed it, spreading the dirt around with his hand. I had nothing more to say to him, so I turned to dig into our food supplies and swallowed loudly. We didn't have supplies, just remains. I shifted and flew towards the City of Not Much Light at All Due to the Day Being Cloudy.

"I think he's preparing for the wedding," I said in disbelief upon my return, once Magni had stopped hyperventilating at the sight of me shifting back. "Flags everywhere, carts full of food and whatnot. Some guests are already arriving, nobles, jarls. The invitations must have gone many days ago! What is he going to do when it doesn't happen? He will be humiliated beyond belief in front of everyone who matters. And he won't even have you and your mo-" *Oh bugger. Bugger, bugger, bugger!*

"Have you seen her? Is she okay?"

"Oh, I, ah," I said nervously, thinking as fast as I could. "I suppose she must be somewhere indoors."

"Where?"

I pretended to cough, giving inspiration time to strike, but nothing came to mind. "Dungeons," I finally mumbled, unable to look him in the eye.

The King was illiterate. I took care of his correspondence. I had written the letter that I had handed to the man with the blue orb. I hadn't written those invitations, somebody else had. Magni's mother, Járnsaxa, was King Thrymr's advisor – or "advisor" – and could write. I knew about Mjölnir, so I had to die. If she had known about the wedding, warning her son was probably the last thing she had done before she had died.

I felt my throat tighten, and I hadn't even liked Járnsaxa.

"Have some bread," said Magni, his voice slightly broken. "It's getting dry."

"Ah, no, thanks. The food is all yours. I ate as a bird."

"You ate bread as a bird?"

I squirmed, my hand instinctively wrapped around my belly. "No, not bread. Leave it, please."

"Then what did you eat as a bird?"

"Good Gods, what do you think birds eat? I ate insects, Magni, that's what I ate. Can we not talk about it?"

"What do they eat in Ásgard? The Gods," he quickly added, "not the birds or insects."

"Everything they wish for," I muttered.

"Ásgard has good crops, aye?"

"Mhm."

"You miss it?"

"Mhm."

"I should be quiet, right?"

"Mhm."

Sometimes my dreams showed me the future. This one brought back the recent past. King Thrymr's face above mine again, the stench of onion unbearable. A chamber pot, I thought, but couldn't move or even make a sound... Then the King grabbed my shoulder and I yelped, brutally transported from my own chambers into cold darkness.

"Wake up! Maya! She's here!"

The onion-scented breath was almost painful, but the bearded face belonged to Magni. The silver moon illuminated him from behind. His hair turned to something I couldn't even name. He looked like...a God. A scary one.

"What's going on?"

"Lady Freya has arrived!"

I sat up so rapidly that I nearly head-butted him. "What? Where? When? Now?"

"I saw the chariot. First, I heard the goats, then the breaking branches. It can't fly high, it rubs against the trees. Normally it goes from the shore, then over the road," Magni explained and I finally understood why the road leading from the castle to the shores of Ifing existed. "I thought Thor came here to destroy everything, but he would have gone straight into the City. There," he said, pointing somewhere into the darkness. "Can you go and check?"

"How do you know Freya was in it?" I rubbed my eyes, one of which seemed more awake than the other.

"Who else? She came to marry the King!"

"It's too early, unless I slept through three nights," I muttered. "The Assembly? Remember? You must have dreamt it."

"I'm going to see Lady Freya!"

"If Freya comes here at all, she will not come alone. She will bring more maids than there are jötnar in the City. Bridesmaids, servants, gold, jewels, her gowns alone would never fit in Thor's chariot... Magni? Are you singing?"

"Her face shines liiiike a thooousand suns, her hair is made of goooold, the Briiisingaaaamen on her neck is aaaalso maaaade of goooold..."

I demonstratively stuck my fingers in my ears. *She's a Goddess of war too*, I wanted to scream, *and a coward! She's someone who would steal Thor's hammer, send it here to start a war and get all of you killed without getting her hands dirty. She hardly remembers Jötunheim exists! She hardly remembers I exist, if she remembers me at all!* The shriek that burst out from me earlier by the stream threatened to return. I bit my lip and the metallic taste filled my mouth again. *Dread Gods.*

Magni tapped me on the shoulder.

"Are you done?" My lip was thick and sore now. I blamed Freya.

"Maybe it's Thor. He came to take my mother to Ásgard. I'm not going."

"It's the middle of the night," I groaned. "Please let me sleep."

"I'm never going to fall asleep," he muttered. A moment later the first snore echoed through the forest.

If there were two Gods who absolutely wouldn't come here now, they were Thor and Freya. He was missing his weapon and could hardly be accused of having any wits. As for Freya, even if Odin found a way to force her, the Assembly never happened in fewer than three days. Magni must have dreamt it. Still, in case someone had come here, perhaps I could convince them to take me back. I used to have friends in Ásgard. Maybe Granny Frigg would take me under her wing. I could probably learn to bake. Oh, her pastries...

I gave up on sleep when the sun began to rise. It was time for breakfast, which would contain some delicious insects and absolutely no pastries. I glanced in the direction where Magni pointed last night. My breakfast was everywhere, so to speak. I might as well look for the non-existent chariot.

I returned hungry and had no qualms about waking Magni from his slumber with a kick in the butt. "Wake up," I croaked, my throat dry from excitement. "I've found them. You were right." I cackled. "Your Lady Freya is here. She and King Thrymr will make a beautiful pair."

"Whmh," said Magni, rubbing his eyes and lifting himself up. "And all the jewels and maids and everything?"

"She only brought one maid. Except it's not Freya and it's not a maid. It's your fa– Thor in a wedding gown and the maid is Loki."

The dreamy lustre in Magni's eyes disappeared. "Thor in a wedding gown?" he repeated slowly.

I nodded. "He's not pleased. Loki shaved his beard off. He looks terrible. You'll love it."

"The beard will be back in a week, mine does the same. Why is he wearing a gown? What is Loki doing there? They know Loki."

"Not like that. I can shift into a bird, Loki can shift into anything and anybody, an animal, a man, a woman. She's a maid right now. Even Odin can't do that. They're preparing to go to the City."

"So...Lady Freya isn't here?"

I rolled my eyes. "I'm going to watch," I said. "If I see your mother, I will let you know." Hope lit up his face and I immediately regretted my words. Now he would ask and I would have to answer.

I flew in circles around the City, surprised by the crowds of workers, guards and soldiers I'd never known the City even had, all of them clad in crimson uniforms. My bird self kept being drawn towards the bakery. I told myself the bakery was closed, even though I couldn't help but notice multiple times that it wasn't. Instead, I perched on top of the sentry tower and tilted my head. The way birds looked to the sides always made me somewhat nauseated and I'd never figured out how Odin managed to see with five eyes all at once... also, there was fresh bread nearby... maybe I could just really quickly... then I noticed the weirdest thing.

One of the crimson-clad guards had a big belly, a red nose, and was chewing on a sandwich. Bastard. One that I knew. It was Finn, the treasurer. I couldn't decide what was more shocking – Finn getting out of bed so early or the uniform fitting him perfectly. With his belly it must have been made to measure. I did another quick look around the City and saw more familiar faces. Even though only the important ones' uniforms fit so well, the City was a wave of crimson and gold. This had been prepared behind my back for a very long time.

King Thrymr could barely count his fingers without help. He clearly hadn't come up with all this. Only Gods planned things many winters in advance, hundreds of winters, sometimes. Freya sent me here long ago. Why? So she could see Thor wear a wedding gown?

The crimson-clad guard manning the sentry tower leaned out so far, I worried for his safety. I couldn't blame him, though. I had never seen anything like it either.

Thor was a sight to behold. The veil covered his face and hair, tens of golden rings hid his hairy fingers, but there was nothing that could have been done about the massive shoulders or his height. I'd have given a lot to look under that veil and I was certain King Thrymr would as well. He seemed taken aback by the fact that the top of his head barely reached where I expected the bride's stubbly chin to be. I heard the not-quite-rhythmical steps of boots hitting the ground, then a brief bleat of the fanfares' cacophony. Despite all the preparations the surprise was complete, especially as the ladies arrived in time to break the fast, rather than sup.

The bride tried to cross her arms on her chest and the maid elbowed her in the ribs. The sickly feeling that all this would end badly mixed in my stomach with the urge to hysterically cackle.

"My lady," said the King, looking up at the thick veil, taking a step forward, then a step back. He cleared his throat. "My lady..."

"Your Grace," squeaked Loki. She looked perfect. Her dress was nice, but not too nice. She was pretty, but not beautiful, in a way that suggested she came from a good family, but not one that would be invited to a royal wedding. The modest, tight braids and slightly pouty lips made her noticeable, but not breathtaking. "It is our great pleasure to arrive here. Her Grace, Lady Freya, is not allowed to speak until the vows are exchanged."

Loki. Nobody else would have come up with this. Playing a cruel, elaborate, and, frankly, hilarious prank on someone who saw Loki as his best friend.

"She will have to speak to exchange our vows," said the King, his eyes fixed on Freya's very well-padded bosom.

"That is exactly what I meant, Your Majesty."

"She's very..." The King paused. "Wide."

"Lady Freya is... a... wearing the latest fashions from Ásgard. Layers. Very popular among the Gods."

"I see. And you are?"

"I am Lady Freya's maid. Just a humble and unimportant woman, me. O-overjoyed to be chosen by the Goddess herself."

Nothing about the genius of Loki, the wisest and wittiest of the Gods? I tried to stare straight and cross my eyes. It hurt.

"And what is your name?"

"My name – is – ah – ah, I am so excited I almost forgot my own name, Your Excellency, your presence strikes me so strongly! Sigyn, that's it, yes, my name is Si-sigyn."

"Good," said the King, his eyes nervously wandering between "Sigyn" and the multi-layered mountain. "Would my lady like to refresh herself after the journey? How did you get over here so fast? Hmm?"

"In Freyr's magical ship," croaked Loki. I could almost hear her sweating. "He brought us here, said his goodbyes, then departed. He will not be returning, since Freya and I are staying here, in the beautiful City of Light that we've heard so much about."

"Sigyn," said the King, "spare me your beautiful words. Neither of you would be here if Mjölnir didn't make it into my hands. Does she want a bath or not? Hmm?"

"Ah, no, it is a custom among the Gods that nobody can see the bride without her gown and veil on before the vows—"

"Is it? I would still like to see the face so beautiful a thousand poets can't find words to describe it."

If he'd addressed the real Freya this way, he'd be reduced to minced meat by now.

Loki's back straightened up, as if she grew a bit, and everyone including the King inadvertently took a step back. "Your Grace. Lady Freya can look like any woman. That's why the poets can't describe her. Once you are married, you will be bedding a different woman every night, if such is your wish, yet she will always be the same Goddess, always yours, untouched by anybody else. You will see every side of Her Grace. *After* the vows are exchanged." Loki cleared her throat, then her shoulders dropped, so did her eyes, fingers modestly steepled in her lap. "Your Excellent Majesty," she finished in near-whisper, and everyone seemed to start breathing again.

The King gawked, as did everyone else including me, then returned to the immobile bride. "Freya, my love, let us feast. What could I possibly please you with?"

"Oh no, no," exclaimed Loki. "It is a custom among the Gods not to speak, drink, or eat for seven days..."

The growl of thunder made everyone wince, including me. Some of the crimson-clad men looked doubtfully at the cloudless sky.

"Except," Loki continued almost without a break, "for the feast right before the wedding. Today marks six days of Her Grace's preparations. She is ready to be wed any time."

"I believe our letter only reached you two days ago."

Loki's hands were shaking. Fortunately, I was the only one who wasn't looking at the bride. "Frigg, the wife of Odin, predicted the future. Regretfully, it is not up to me to reveal anything else, your Royal Highness. So, I've already said too much, please excuse me, I am not the wisest..."

I nearly fell off the windowsill. If swallows could laugh, I was yet to discover how, so instead I mildly shat on the roof. Loki's gaze shot up for just a blink and the slight grin that crossed her face was for me. It was neither a friendly nor a threatening expression, just an acknowledgement. Shifters knew shifters. She wouldn't know who I was, but she knew I was not a bird.

"Drinking and eating is perfectly fine before the wedding, as long as Lady Freya's modesty remains covered until the vows are exchanged, and then you shall kiss the sweetest lips in the Nine Worlds, caress the most wonderful hair, look into the eyes that are like..."

"Eyes, yes," interrupted King Thrymr. "I would like to at least look into her eyes. Once. Even the most modest of women don't hide their eyes from their betrothed. How do I know this isn't a magical trick, hmm? It might be a golem for all I know."

"A go-go-golem?! Your Majestic Highness!"

"I want to look into her eyes, or Mjölnir stays here forever."

Loki nervously licked her lips before turning towards the mountainous bride, who hadn't moved since they arrived. "Lady Freya, Your Grace, would you agree – even though it is breaking all of the customs that the Gods have ever agreed on – to look into the King's eyes with all the love and affection that you can muster?"

"Muster?" asked the King, but Loki was already standing on the tips of her toes to reach the veil. The King recoiled so rapidly he nearly fell on his royal backside. "Dread Gods!" he roared. "I mean... by Freya... what... her eyes... such anger, I swear..."

"It is not anger at all, it is the light of love and fire of her desire, your... High Royalness. Freya has loved and desired you for many years."

One of the highly royal eyebrows wandered up. "Really?" the King asked, almost lazily. Loki was in trouble.

"Oh, yes, yes yes yes! In fact! This is why Mjölnir found its way into your hands!"

"Is she grinding her teeth?"

"In excitement! She has confided in me for a long time that it was her dream to become the queen of Jötunheim. Freya and Loki, the trickster, the wisest of the Gods, the wittiest, the..."

"I know who Loki is."

In the brief silence I heard Loki swallow loudly before the blabbering commenced. "Ah, of course, everybody knows who Loki is... what was I... So, Loki and Freya, or perhaps the other way round, they came up with a perfect plan to ensure that Thor would never bother the beautiful Jötunheim again. Loki stole Thor's hammer..."

Lady Freya cleared her throat, causing the ground to shake slightly.

"A-a-and gave it to Lady Freya, so that she could send it over to you, knowing that you would understand the gift comes from her heart... from her love..."

"Hmm. I did not see love in those eyes."

The gown seemed to tighten even more around the bride's shoulders.

"You will see it very soon, Your Excellent Royalness, you will see everything and more, once the vows are exchanged between the two of you. I hope you don't mind, but we are very tired after the journey, especially Her Grace Freya, who had no sleep and no food and not even a drop of mead – I mean water – before coming here. Can you imagine her excitement to finally meet His Grace King Thrymr himself in person? Her Grace is de-*lir*-ious with happiness and desire, she's been dreaming about this moment for..."

"Delirious," muttered the King. "I can believe that. Let us feast, then. I will sit next to my beloved and make sure that—"

"Oh! How could I have forgotten!" cried Loki. "That will not be possible, since the Gods' custom is to not even accidentally touch their beloved before the vows are exchanged. We have already broken the universal law by allowing you to look into Lady Freya's eyes, and, Your Very Highly Excellent Grace, it is dangerous even for someone as powerful as you to meddle with the laws of the Universe. It is not just some woman you are about to marry, she is the most important of all the Goddesses. And she will be yours very soon – in fact, er, how soon?"

"Soon. Before I allow you inside, I gather you have no weapons?"

The bride growled.

"Poor Lady Freya," gasped Loki. "She is so tired, even her voice is different, her throat must be so dry! Soon she will be sleeping in your royal bed, which I have obviously never seen, but I am certain someone as powerful as you must have the most luxurious bed in the Nine Worlds... We have no weapons of any sort, we have full trust in your hospitality, your Royal Highness. You may search me, but I must deny you the right to search Her Grace. I swear on Odin's staff and Freya's own golden hair that you will find no w-weapons whatsoever."

Loki was clearly terrified. Could this be someone else's plan that she hadn't been made aware of? Now she stood, unprepared, between Thor, who was undergoing a very public humiliation, and the King, who used his reputation and wealth to show the whole of Jötunheim he was powerful enough to marry Freya. This made even me feel uneasy. Who was that man with the blue orb? Could it have been Odin? Why?!

As the bride sailed majestically towards the entrance, I decided I knew enough for the time being. Magni must be shitting rocks by now and I had nothing more to gain by sitting here.

～

"Are they dead?" asked Magni flatly, not even flinching when I shifted in front of him.

"Nobody's dead yet. The King is extremely suspicious, though. Your father looks ridiculous and Loki is dying of nerves. Apparently, they're going to have a feast. I wonder how Thor is going to eat and keep the veil on?"

"Have you seen my mother?"

"I haven't been... no, I mean, not yet."

"Go inside and look for her in the dungeons. Please."

"Magni," I groaned. "I'd be recognised."

"Then go as a cat," he said. "They are holy to Lady Freya."

My eyes opened wide. Stories told about Freya ranged from half-true to utter nonsense. My attempts to explain to the jötnar that Freya didn't own a "magical falcon cloak" but was simply a shifter were one of the reasons I was unpopular. Since then I just nodded and smiled. Of *course* she owned a chariot pulled by cats, animals that divided their days equally between sleeping, eating, and shedding all over her gowns. Now that they believed she was here, though? I would be carried inside on a silken pillow. "Great idea," I said and meant it. "Stay here and wait for me," I ordered, shifted back into a swallow and flew away.

I did not expect a battle in front of the castle. Everyone wanted to witness the event, from the crimson-clad fat men to the children. As a cat I would get trampled to death before I reached the entrance. I couldn't fly into the feasting hall over their heads and get caught shifting. The castle's windows were hardly ever open, the fires burning bright even in the summer, the thick marble walls always ice cold. One window always stayed a bit open, though. Mine.

I never shut my windows. I couldn't sleep in a place without fresh air, cold or not, or I felt like I was suffocating. Also, I wanted to be able to shift and escape if I needed to. Which I would have done when the King tried to force himself upon me, had I not been so tired. Maybe it was for the best, as I had gotten to meet Magni and now I was doing something useful.

My window was still open, but the opening was narrow, and I couldn't fly sideways. It had never occurred to me that I could want to fly in, rather than out. I deliberately hit the window with my head a few times, wishing I was a bird heavier than a swallow or at least that I had oiled the hinges sometimes. When I finally made it inside and shifted back into a panting human with bumps on her head all I wanted was to spend the rest of the day in bed. Bed...! The hammer was still there. So were the smell and the stains.

Now what?

I moved into the main room, filled with the cobwebs I cultivated with great devotion and the books that I had dirtied to make them look ancient and vaguely threatening. I pressed my ear to the door and heard what sounded like a crowd gathered right outside.

"What in the Nine," I muttered to myself. I purposefully built the gallery surrounding the feasting hall in such a way that the stair-case led straight towards my own door, covered in nonsensical combinations of runes. People were supposed to be scared and disperse, not hang around. I'd never expected that half of Jötunheim would be pushing up the stairs at once. The witch couldn't be seen here. I had to open the door, shift into a cat, then somehow make it down the stairs without getting trampled. Which meant that the door would remain unlocked and open, with that hammer just sitting there on my bed. Then again, did it matter when the only ones who could wield the hammer were currently busy looking pretty next to the King?

I looked around in a quick goodbye to almost half of my life. I needed nothing from here. As a cat I couldn't carry anything anyway. I took a deep breath and opened the door, slowly and quietly, just enough to push through. When I shifted I saw feet and calves. Lots of them. Luckily, cats were acrobats, unnoticed unless they wanted to be.

"Something touched me!" someone yelled. "There are rats here!"

"Magical rats," someone cried. The feet briskly changed position. I meowed, barely avoided getting crushed, and panic began to suffo-cate me. I needed air.

"Stop pushing!"

"You're pushing! I don't want to stand by that door!"

"Then go further!"

"You go further!"

"What is she wearing? What is she wearing?"

"Go to the back, you're too tall!"

"I'm not standing there!"

"What is she wearing?" a particularly unpleasant voice kept repeating. "What is she wearing? What is she wearing?"

"Layers," I heard just as I managed to find the stairs. The feet kept moving in what seemed to be all directions at once. My attempts to avoid getting kicked were futile, people were kicking each other not to miss anything. I needed air, I was choking – OW! My tail! I screeched in protest, instinctively bolting forward.

The countless calves and feet parted suddenly, as if on purpose, leading me into one of the openings in the balustrade. I shot into the air. If I were human, the fall would have killed me. Since I was a cat, I landed on my feet, right in front of the table housing the most important guests. I was completely fine except for being in shock.

"It's a cat!" someone particularly observant yelled.

Indeed, I thought, very pleased with myself for not having instinctively shifted into a swallow mid-flight. What worried me was noticing that the exhaustion had begun to creep in again. They'd better hurry with my silken pillow.

"How wonderful!" exclaimed Loki. "Cats are holy to Lady Freya! They are one of the reasons she wanted to come here. We heard that cats are adored in Jötunheim. Revered. Fed scraps from the royal table. Unless we have been...misled?"

I looked up just in time to see "Sigyn" wink at me. Did she know who I— A bowl of delicious smelling food appeared in front of me and I lost interest in anything else. I loved being the guest of honour. I moved my tail, checking its state. It didn't seem permanently harmed. Once I had eaten, I'd make someone trip over me.

"Lady Freya seems very hungry," I heard, a sudden reminder why I was here. I looked up, curious, and saw the many-ringed hands of the bride lifting what looked like an ox, then attempting to stuff it under the veil. If I had hands, I'd be hiding my face in them. "Sit back, maid. I want to look at my betrothed. What is she wearing underneath, hmm?"

"Your Royal Highness...!"

"Ah! That's not what I meant. It's just that I thought I saw... it looked like her chin needs plucking."

"Absolutely not," said Loki, 'accidentally' leaning forward just when the King did the same. "It's a... a special... I'm afraid I can't talk about it, Your Graceful Excellence. You shall find out very soon."

"I'm not used to waiting," King Thrymr murmured and my fur puffed. No. He wasn't.

"Very few people get to marry a Goddess. In fact, I can't even think of one."

"True. Very true. Tell me, Sigyn, how do I know that she will not return the hammer to Thor?"

"Oh, she will, Your High...Royalness. Just as agreed. He will be able to defend Ásgard, and she will be here to ensure the safety of Jötunheim."

The bride was munching loudly, and Loki cleared her throat equally loudly to make a point, then succumbed to a coughing fit. I might have despised Loki, but if I were sitting in her place right now I'd have already run away screaming.

"Just as agreed. Mhmmm. Is she wearing the Brisingamen? I would love to see it."

"Your Excellency! Her Grace Freya would never go anywhere without the Brisingamen! Once the vows—"

"I'd like to see it *now*," said the King lazily. This was how Odin spoke at the Assembly when he wanted something very badly.

Loki gasped in shock. "There is no such possibility. She would have to nearly undress. That cannot possibly happen in the presence of your subjects!"

"I'm willing to take a break and go to our chambers. She can even have a nap on my royal bed."

"Your Highness," said Loki, her tone suddenly very serious. "You are not dealing with some 'she'. That barbarian Thor wants nothing more than a reason, even the smallest one, to declare this marriage null and void, so that he can tear Lady Freya away from you and destroy every chance of your future happiness. I am sure you can imagine his fury at the disappearance of Mjölnir! He is so strong that even the Gods found it difficult to restrain him. He only calmed down once he was promised that as soon as Freya received the hammer, it would be sent back to Ásgard, carried by his son and his mistress. I can only applaud the wisdom that made you ensure the safety of this awful brute's mistress and her son, keeping the City of Light protected. Are they here?"

"Not at the feast," the King answered. "Once the vows are exchanged, you will get to meet them. They are safe and sound here in the castle."

Liar, I thought, before my body stiffened, crouching, my tail wrapped around it. I couldn't force my cat self to calm down. What if he wasn't lying? I had assumed that Járnsaxa was dead. What if I was wrong and she actually was somewhere in the dungeons? The guards had more than enough time to find Magni in his hideaway. One threat against Járnsaxa, and Magni would plead to be thrown into a cell just to protect her. What was I even doing lazing here and gawking at the mountain clad in grease-stained white fabric?

I forced myself to stretch my spine, meow softly, then stroll towards the door that stood ajar. The crowd thinned and I managed to make it outside safely, without getting trampled or kicked. The cat body kept trying to trip someone, not really listening to the human part's commands. It was time to find a nice, deserted spot, sit there and shift into a bird.

It didn't work. Instead, I returned to my human form. Flakes of ash and snow appeared in front of my face and I tried to wave them away. The exhaustion was back, I hardly had time to rest in comfort and warmth. My breath became fast and shallow, my heart slamming against my ribs. I was so cold, but not physically, it felt like my mind was cold. I had achieved nothing.

I wrapped my arms around my knees, letting my hair fall on my face, ignoring the reek. Then I jerked my head up, realising this made me look even more suspicious. I was the witch, everybody knew the witch. *Come on*, I pleaded with my own body, *shift for just a bit*. The snowflakes were gone, or almost gone. My magic might have been depleted, but physically I felt strong enough to run, or at least walk briskly.

I'd never seen the streets so empty. Still... what if someone tried to stop me, would I be able to cast them aside? Was I capable of moving anything at all right now? Maybe I should try. Something small. A pebble. I stared at one, concentrated, drew a bit of mana, not too much, just enough. *You can do it*, I told myself, and sent the energy into the pebble.

The castle walls exploded.

I was so shocked by the enormous power I suddenly had that I made no sound, my breath stuck in my lungs. Rocks rained around me, giant, white, sharp pieces of stone. The ground shook and more marble erupted in the air, marble and dust and – oh good Gods, all those people inside. Lightning shot through a sky that had been blue a blink earlier. A thunderstorm. Inside the castle. A crack more deafening than thunder. The castle's walls were breaking apart. Only now I screamed and jumped to my feet. I no longer wanted a quick death. I had things to do.

Covering my head with my hands I ran away from the castle, not paying attention where I was going. Instead of stopping at the gate I reached the city walls. I had no thoughts, just instinct. I jumped as high as I could and shifted for just long enough to fly over the wall. I was back to my human form while still in the air. My body smashed into the ground.

It must have been Thor who had done all this. Somehow, he'd found the hammer. Loki's fear. All those people inside. Was I hearing their screams? Or my own? Salty tears burnt my bleeding face. It was dark, as if night had suddenly fallen over Jötunheim. Lightning struck, then again. Explosions shook the air, again, again. I crawled through the dead grass, dirt, stones. Snow and ash, ash and snow. I rubbed my eyes. Wet. Tears and blood on my face, my hand. It hurt. The chariot. I needed to find the chariot. Beg. Back home. I pulled myself forward with my hands through the ash and snow and dirt. In the darkness the snow and ash fell around me. I could see nothing else. The chariot would take me back home. Find...the...chariot.

CHAPTER 2
MAGNI

"GREAT IDEA. Stay here and wait for me," said Maya. A blink later and a small black bird flew into the sky, disappearing almost immediately.

"Sure," I said to the air. The idea was stupid. I was stupid. Even if she did turn into a cat and find my mother, what would she do to set her free? Meow at the guards? I was the one who could open doors without needing keys. I was wasting time sitting here when I had to be there instead.

I took a deep breath. I pulled my hammer out of my belt and held it tight. I wasn't going to hit anyone, but they didn't know that. I began my ascent towards the City, reminding myself that I was big and strong, when a twig cracked somewhere. I yelped in alarm. I wasn't afraid at all. I just wished I felt a bit more brave.

The dungeons, Maya said. If there were stairs going up to the gallery there were probably also stairs going down to the dungeons. Maya didn't seem certain, though. They could have locked Mother anywhere. Even in the witch rooms, with Mjölnir... Mjölnir! The witch rooms were easy to find, covered in magical runes! I just had to get to the servants' entrance, let myself in, make my way up to the gallery without being seen, find the witch rooms, enter despite the magical runes, and not let the spells kill me. Once I had Mjölnir, I would threaten them until they told me where Mother was.

The closer to the gate I got, the colder it seemed to be. My teeth even started chattering. I started doubting my plan. I was easy to notice on the stairs or anywhere else and I didn't know how to not die from runes and spells and I didn't know whom to threaten to find the dungeons. Maybe Mother wasn't even there and only the King knew where to find her. My hammer's handle got slippery. My hands were sweating. My feet turned heavier and heavier as I saw the gate. That meant they could see me as well. What if they had bows and arrows? One step at a time, Gunnar told me when he started teaching me how to forge, take it slow and you'll avoid mistakes. It's just that if I slowed down any more, I'd stop moving. Maybe nobody was guarding the gate and they were all feasting...

"Sshh! Magni! You can't come in! Go away."

My jaw dropped. Even though he was wearing red clothes I'd never seen on him before, I'd recognise Gunnar anywhere and anytime. "What are you doing up there? If they find out, they'll kill you! You go away."

Gunnar chuckled. "They sent the blacksmith to guard the gate from you and the witch girl, while everyone who really knows one end of an axe from the other is feasting. Have you heard? Lady Freya has arrived to marry the King!" He paused. "But you still can't come in."

"I'm just looking for Mother."

"No, Magni, I... you really can't come in." Gunnar's voice sounded stilted. "I could tell you about Lady Freya. As long as you stay outside. I've been ordered... You're not allowed in here and I don't want to hurt you, son, I can't. Please. Go."

"Just tell me where the dungeons are..." I swallowed. "That's why they put you here. I can't hurt you either. Come with me," I pleaded. "We'll find her and leave. Nobody will know."

"Wait. I'm coming down."

A door in the wall opened and Gunnar appeared, panting, a steep ladder behind him. His red clothes looked completely new. The buttons were golden, shiny. "Ah, son. I'd be doing the same. Now punch me."

I gawked. Gunnar looked around, then tried to hand me some rope I refused to take. "I'm not hitting you! What's this?"

"Hit me in the nose, make me bleed. In case someone finds me, they'll see that I fought hard. Or hit me in the head, so there's a bump. Hurry up!"

"Gunnar..."

"Go, son, find your mother, then come back here. I'll join you and all three of us will go away. We'll start a forge somewhere." He produced a stiff grin that was missing a few teeth. "It will be alright. I... just wanted you to... nah. Never mind. Go on."

I felt an instant chill. He was hiding something from me. "What? Tell me, what is it?"

"Just go on," he groaned, then sighed and looked down. "It's just that if something happens... you... ah, son, just do it already. Make it look real."

"Tell me," I pleaded. I almost forgot that I was scared and now the fear was building again.

Gunnar half-smiled, half-grimaced, his nose wrinkled as if it was itching. I tensed, but he still surprised me when his hands shot forward and arms wrapped around me. He patted my back clumsily. Clean red uniform or not, he smelled of iron and smoke and sweat and Gunnar. "Love you, son, I guess," he said, his voice muffled. "Be careful." As abruptly as he hugged me he withdrew, then punched my chest. "Now hit me, tie me up, go get your mother. Let's hope she and I get along. Go!"

I was so dumbfounded that I could only say "thanks". There must have been something better to say, but I didn't know what. I would say it later, when I knew more words, maybe.

I dealt him a clumsy blow, changing my mind at the last moment and hitting him in the temple, slowing my fist at the last moment, afraid I would kill him. When Gunnar fell, I yelped out in pain. I dropped to my knees to check. He was breathing. I didn't want to tighten the rope too much, but couldn't leave it too loose either, in case... if something happens... my fingers kept trembling. I'd lived with Gunnar, the master smith, for the last hand of winters. He'd taught me about the craft and about how to be. He was... my... if I could pick a father for myself, it would have been Gunnar.

"You there!"

I jerked my head up. A man I didn't know was running towards me, a wood-chopping axe I'd made in his hand. For the shortest of blinks I didn't understand what he was doing. Bringing it to me? Then he roared like some sort of animal, raising the axe above his head with both his hands. Faster and faster, louder and louder. I could already see his face when his body just – just flew away, the axe bouncing from the ground, the scream ending in a grunt. I looked at my hand, then back at his immobile body. The hammer had escaped my hand and struck the man's chest.

Run. Wait, I have to check, I could have killed him. Just run, stupid, find your mother. But he might need help...

I stuck fingers in my ears, even though the shouting was inside my mind. I'll check on my way back. I grabbed the hammer. I didn't even know him and he wanted to... with an axe that I had forged myself.

I tried to blend with the walls, glancing around, when two people flew past me, yelling at each other.

"Lady Freya!"

"I know, fool, wait for me!"

"Lady Freya...!"

The man's clothes were red too. The woman following him was panting, her stomping heavier than the axe man's. They were headed towards the castle and I almost ran after them, instinctively, forgetting to blend into walls, excited about Lady Freya. When three children bolted past me, screaming at the top of their lungs, nearly drowning out the yelling from the castle's main entrance, it occurred to me that right now I really was as good as invisible. The entrance was besieged by a growing crowd of people yelling angrily, demanding to be let in. A few excited dogs added to the noise. I heard "Lady Freya" over and over, same as "bugger off" and some other words. The stupid people hadn't thought about going around to the servants' entrance.

My smugness didn't last. The crowd there was just slightly smaller and a whole lot angrier. Banging on the locked door, shouting threats, cursing. I cursed too.

I hid behind one of the big houses the rich people lived in and tried to think up another new plan. If there were other entrances, I didn't know them. There might be more men with axes running around. What if my mother was in the King's chambers? He might want to hurt her and watch. No, Lady Freya would nev—

Nausea punched me in the belly. Thor couldn't marry the King for obvious reasons. He'd free himself from that gown sooner or later. Then – what? What was the King going to do with Mjölnir, hallow the marriage with it? He couldn't touch it. Thor didn't know where it was. I was the only one who could help him out. Even better, I could go to the wi– to Maya's chambers, take the hammer, tell Thor that I would give it to him if he promised to leave us alone. I could hide it so that nobody would find it and tell the King that I wouldn't return it until Mother was freed.

If I couldn't make myself blend in, I had to make sure I stood out.

"Witch lair," I shouted, pushing through the crowd, trying to throw people away as politely as I could. "I must find the witch lair! King's orders!"

The last two words made everyone quieten. Even those who were already on the stairs heading up turned to stare at me. Suddenly nervous, I prayed to the real Lady Freya that nobody in the feasting hall had heard me.

"Up," someone said uncertainly.

I pushed forward, but it was harder now, the crowd denser. I didn't want to throw people off the stairs. "The bloody blacksmith," I still heard, then "Thor's bastard". They kicked me in the shins, elbowed me, on purpose or not, hurting mostly themselves. I got stuck on some sort of balcony, pressed to the balustrade by the crowd. Without wanting to I took a brief look at the mountain of white fabric and immediately wished I hadn't.

"I can't see! Get out of here!"

"Let me out!" I yelled in response. "Witch lair, King's orders!"

"Magical rats!" someone shouted straight into my ear. I let out a little yelp. Spells and poisons were bad enough. Nobody told me there would be rats!

"What is she wearing? What is she wearing?"

"Layers!" I heard, then stepped on something soft and I cried in alarm. The response was an inhuman shriek. I tried to shake the magical rat off my foot and people cried in protest as I accidentally kicked them in the shins and ankles instead. Or maybe the rat bit them.

"He's going into the witch's lair!" a breaking, boyish voice pierced the air. I knew who that was. Björn, the baker's son, whose arm I once broke, but it was by accident and he'd started it. "Let him pass!"

The crowd split in front of me, giving me free passage, muttering something and gawking at me. I gulped nervously. If Björn wanted me to go there, it meant I shouldn't. Magical rats could be just the beginning. I looked up and stopped breathing when I faced the rune-covered door. Maya said that she wasn't a real witch, it's just that maybe she'd lied and the red paint looked like fresh blood and I didn't want to die.

I ascended the stairs, my feet leaden, the crowd around me quiet. The door stood ajar and my blood curdled. That's how the magical rats must have escaped. She had lied to me, there *were* witch things in there. I couldn't enter this place.

"Don't just stand there like that," a woman's voice croaked, "some of us want to see Lady Freya!"

"Go, Thor's bastard!"

"Get in," Björn's voice urged.

"King's orders," I mumbled, not knowing what to do, afraid to get caught before reaching the door I didn't want to reach anymore.

"Well come on then, lad," an older woman hurried me, gesturing impatiently. Someone pushed me hard enough for me to trip. Flapping my hands around, trying not to fall, I smashed straight into the bloody runes on the door, and a chorus of screams accompanied the sudden darkness around me when I fell in.

"He's dead," someone shouted. He didn't sound upset.

When I opened my eyes it became less dark. I lifted myself up and shut the door with my foot before remembering the magical rats. I only didn't open it again because I didn't dare to touch the handle. Every single hair on my skin seemed to stand up, tickling.

There were rows of glass jars with things in them. I couldn't read the runes, but I knew what witches kept in their lairs. Voice of fish and dragon's bathwater and the noise of a cat's footsteps. I couldn't go near those things. I carefully stepped away, my gaze glued to the jars, knowing that each breath could be my last. Something wrapped itself around my head and I squealed. I didn't die a gruesome death, though. There was only the disgusting feeling that there was something slimy on my hair. Every beat of my heart seemed to shake my hands, which I slowly raised before crying out in disgust. Thick cobwebs! Venomous spiders all over me! I leapt towards the desk, about to lean on it, stopping abruptly right before I touched it. If anything was protected it would be the witch desk! Parchments covered with spells and drawings! Why did I ever agree to come here?

Oh. It was my own idea. I shouldn't be allowed to have ideas.

As I waited for my heart to stop trying to jump out through my mouth, suspicion slowly arose inside me. So far nothing had really happened. That door covered in bleeding runes didn't kill me. The jars were covered in dust, clearly untouched, same as everything else except the desk. I was only attacked by a spider web. I slowly extended a finger and touched a witch-book gathering dust on the desk.

Nothing happened.

This was a *decoy* witch room. Somewhere there was another one with the real runes and magical rats and spiders and fish voices in jars. Unless I was already dying or even dead. I felt quite alive, though, especially my bowels and my bladder.

What if it was a *decoy decoy* room and it just pretended that there were no traps, but if I touched something that didn't look like a trap... Aye, I liked it that the walls glowed at night and that Maya could fly to the City and back and tell me things, but still, magic was not natural and I didn't want any of it near me. A blade soaked with poison could suddenly jump out of nowhere and pierce my hand. Or my foot. When the idea of *decoy decoy decoy* traps appeared in my mind I shook my head and reminded myself why I was here.

There was no bed in this room. A red curtain hung next to the shelf with the frogs' claws and fish breaths. I looked for a stick I could push it aside with, then realised an inconspicuous stick would certainly be a magical weapon. I nearly screamed in frustration. My heart started doing that thing again where it beat so fast that it was as if the blood pulsing in my veins made the hair on my head stand up.

The red curtain was dyed with blood. I just knew that. And it was also a trap. That hid Mjölnir.

With a yelp I tore the curtain off and threw it on the ground. Everything turned dark and stayed like that until I opened my eyes again. I was suffocating, clearly dying from magic, then remembered to breathe and I felt better. I was still seeing red, though, and it really was there, a red canopy hanging over the... My eyes opened wide. All of this bed was for *one* person?

Maya and I were not the same and not just because she was a witch. Sorceress.

A chamber pot lay on the ground. The piss and shit may have mostly dried, but I could smell why the window had been left open, cold or not. Could she have been telling the truth after all? An icy stream of sweat flowing down my spine made me shudder.

I inhaled sharply.

It just lay there like it was nothing. A darkened, hammer-shaped chunk of iron forged by the dwarves at Loki's request, so that Thor could kill jötnar with it. No decoration marred its ugly perfection. I'd had all sorts of ideas earlier, what to do once I had it, but I forgot them all. Even if the runes and books and jars were all fake, Mjölnir was real. A faint memory appeared, Thor yelling, snatching the hammer away from me. I was small then. Now I was a grown-up, and he and Mother needed my help. He would thank me. Maybe even hug me.

I carefully secured my own hammer on the belt, then grabbed Mjölnir's handle and the magic smote me.

The walls, the bed, the floor, everything was on fire. I roared in surprise and shock, ran out, jumping over the burning curtain heaped on the floor. Everything was burning here too, the desk, the shelves, jars full of poisons! People outside, the fire would cause the jars to explode, send the evil magic everywhere, I had to run, we all had to run! I kicked the door open, sending it up into the air. It slammed into some people, but they were not real people, blood pouring out of their black eye sockets, their hair and clothes on fire. Heat. Burning flesh. My lips were wet and I licked them. Metallic, salty. Blood was everywhere, the runes, I slipped when the not-real people attacked me, snarling. Red and black and black and red, and suddenly I had no eyes either, just blood pouring out, the marble stairs were burning too, I took a swing with Mjölnir and sent the not real people's bodies flying, then again, I needed space, I needed to escape, reach the stairs, find Mother, my hand was slippery from the blood and the hammer slipped out and flew into the air, through the crowd, then through the balustrade rather than over it, then dove towards Thor—

—there was no blood and no fire and my hand was just sweaty like all the rest of me. Everything was silent and still. I seemed to fly with Mjölnir. A many-ringed hand shot up, grabbing the handle and immediately the hammer flew again, right into the crowd, right towards me. The blood pouring from the walls wasn't real, now it would be, this was not supposed to—

The staircase produced a crack that almost sounded surprised. The marble shook under my feet and when the mass of people started running down, tripping, falling, getting trampled, I ran too, I trampled too, the gallery that no longer had a balustrade, a scream, mine, a turn, saving myself at the cost of others who fell. *Crak-crak-crak* sang the hammer as it flew in a circle, smashing each of the columns that supported the roof over the gallery, every strike punctuated by lightning. I fell off the stairs and others fell over me. I shook them off, lifting myself up. We all had the same goal, outside, away from – not yet!

"Dungeons!" I roared, turning back. Bodies slammed into me, crazed, carried by the fear I also felt, but *Mother*, the many screams that turned into one drowned by the bellowing storm. Lightning, fog, nay, dust. Rocks, rocks flew towards me, towards us all. One hit my forehead. My hand shot up to cover my face. The taste of blood was real now, and the dust, and the sound of thunder that lasted forever, I stumbled again, I had to go back, didn't they know? People, their clothes red, faces red, pushing me out. I pushed against them, forcing them back inside. Thor went berserk. He'd destroy the castle even though all of it would fall on his head, all our heads. I'd done this. I had tossed Mjölnir into the air and the hammer had done exactly what it was supposed to do.

Sudden weakness befell me.

I was outside somehow, or maybe not, there was no sun and no moon. Lightning showed me countless eyes that bulged out, mouths open in soundless screams. One big mass, no longer men and women, *something* the hammer and the rocks turned into meat. I kept coughing and screaming too and couldn't hear myself either, deafened by the endless triumphant roar of thunder. I didn't want to, stop, not this, never this—

A rock had taken a slice off my scalp, no, it was the hammer, no, it was a *bird* pulling at my hair, tearing the skin off my head. "Mother!" I yelled through the excruciating pain, flapping my hands in the air, trying to hit the thing. Maya said she was a swallow, a small one. This bird was giant, strong enough to pull me away from the castle.

"Run!" shrieked the bird, how? "Stand up! Run!" It grew further, pulled harder, lifted me from the ground when I stumbled, dragged me. Half-kicking, half-running, backwards, then sideways, I ran, wanting nothing but to stop, ran past what used to be the gate. There was no sentry tower anymore. Gunnar. Gunnar was in there. Tied up. By me. My legs gave in and the bird pulled me up by my hair. The sky was black. I wished I could pass out, stop feeling and seeing and hearing, lightning, many lightnings all at once split the sky into pieces, thunder and thunder and thunder, dust and blood and the white of the marble and the red blood on red uniforms. No air. Insane bird's claws digging into the skin on my skull. I had never known pain like this, not from hot iron or any wound. My head exploded with each deafening thunderclap. I'd lost. *Let me die. Let me die. Let me not feel and not hear and not know it was I who did this.* Lightning and lightning. Not a drop of rain. Just black until it turned lighter. *Please end*, I screamed, or maybe just thought it, still, the bird listened. I fell when it let go of me. It was lighter here, the bird gone when I tried to catch it and tear in half, Loki kicking my hand away.

"Get in the chariot!" he shouted. "Thjálfi! Get him to Ásgard, then come back, fast!"

"No!" I yelled, "Midgard!"

"What then?" asked Thjálfi and his bored voice drilled into me harder than the eagle-Loki's claws ever could. The black sky and the endless thunderclap and the white lightning were inside me, not around.

"Get in!" urged Loki.

"Midgard," I repeated. It was the last thing Mother had said to me. "Get to Midgard."

My hands were slippery with the blood and the dust, clutching the sides of the chariot. Something kept shrieking, a sound I knew, the goats. My scalp hurt and so did my ears and the sun blinded me when the chariot shot into the blue sky and the clouds and lightning and the death and my mother all stayed behind us.

When the chariot slammed into the sand, Thjálfi yelling curses at the frantic goats, I half-crawled out, half-fell out. Thjálfi shouted again, the chariot and the goats sent a wave of sand my way, and a blink later it was...

...quiet.

I spat out some sand and rubbed it out of my eyes.

Gentle waves petted the shore and I gawked at them. I had never seen anything like this, stretching towards the horizon, calm and lazy. Breathing. It whispered. Ifing screamed. I kept listening for the thunder that wasn't here, but there. On my knees, I covered my eyes with my hand and strained my eyes. I couldn't even see Jötunheim from here at all. Like all of it never happened.

Gunnar had hugged me and said he loved me. He'd been calling me "son" for a long time now. I never understood. Someone who had never... who didn't even... I should have died instead. I was too weak to control Mjölnir. Thor was right not to let me touch it. I'd sent the hungry hammer to feast. I only had myself to hate for this.

I crawled towards the water and fell, face down. Didn't last long until I lifted myself to all fours, coughing, spitting out all that I hadn't left behind. I didn't know death had a taste. I vomited into the water, tormented by the thought that the blood I was tasting wasn't mine. The water tasted like tears and I couldn't drink it. I rinsed my mouth again and again. The pain in my scalp was a dull burn now, except where the salty water bit into the skin. With hands that seemed to belong to someone else I removed my belt, my boots, then the tunic that had death splashed all over it. I lay in the tepid water, letting it wash over me.

The sun was setting, golden and red, over the edge of a quiet world where humans murdered each other all the time to please Odin the Slayer. Everything was in reverse. Mother hadn't told me she loved me and it was fine, Gunnar said "love you, son," and I'd never known. He seemed so ashamed to admit it. I wished I had told him that I loved him too, it was true, but he died and he never knew. It would have been easier if he hadn't said anything... The guilt smashed into me as if Mjölnir had remembered there was one victim still left. I wanted to weep, my throat tight, tears stuck inside me.

I scratched the wounds on my scalp open and when the salty water bit into them, the piercing pain seemed to bring relief. I still couldn't make myself cry. I'd forgotten to check if that man with the axe was alive, I suddenly remembered, and a dry snigger shook my body in a violent shudder before another punch in the belly pushed all the air out. Some of those who had died might have stood a chance if I hadn't pushed back when they tried to escape.

I rolled to my side, curled, my cheek against the sand of the shore. The sun was going down and it was getting cooler. Another shiver went through me. I had to find some humans. They would kill me for Odin's amusement. I couldn't really remember how to walk, though, I just sat up and rocked back and forth, staring at the horizon. The position of the sun told me nothing. I couldn't tell which way home used to be.

"Thor?"

I turned into stone. He couldn't be here, he was busy destroying... I had a *human* behind me. It saw a giant with the red hair I hated, because it was his, and could only come up with one conclusion. They would envy him if they knew he took so many lives just... just now – *it was probably still happening.*

"Father Thor?" repeated the voice. The human sounded like a woman. I was naked except for my soaked trousers. Half of me just wanted to die, so I could rest. The other half was afraid of what I would see once I faced the human. I forced myself to turn, knowing I had no real choice, and the shock sent a shudder through my body again. The human looked like a normal person as well, no scales or claws or even horns. Was this a trap or merely bait to lead me into one?

"Are you a jötunn?" I asked, unsure.

"Do I look like an ice giant?" The human chuckled. No flames came out of its nose or mouth. "Do you need..." Its gaze slid to my chest for a blink or two before returning to my face, then down to my chest again. I felt my cheeks becoming hotter, although I didn't know why. "Do you need help, Father Thor?"

"I am not Thor," I said. "He just...destroyed the City of Light."

The human looked so much like a person that it was disturbing. Her eyebrows went up. "Where is that?"

When I swallowed, I tasted salt and dust. I couldn't understand. Thjálfi had brought me to Ásgard after all, but first Loki had found a jötunn woman who would welcome me and delude me into thinking humans looked like people. Or maybe it was another witch, hiding behind spells. Or a jötunn that was trapped in Ásgard against her will. Or an evil Goddess of some sort...

"You lost your clothes," said the woman-human, then she licked her lips and winked at me. She wasn't really looking at my face, though. Just at my... It made me more uncomfortable than the idea of putting the bloodied tunic back on. I was wet and got stuck in the fabric. The human helped me out, even though it was a perfect opportunity to kill me. When my head finally emerged and I could see the world again, she was right next to me, practically leaning over my chest, her eyes half-shut, lips half-open.

"Are you unwell?" I asked, worried. She winced and withdrew, crossing her arms, then asked me in a rather dry manner who I was and where I had come from.

"I'm just a blacksmith," I said.

"You sure look like one. What's your name?"

My mind went blank. Maybe they knew Thor had a son, although I wasn't sure he knew that himself. If they did, they might have heard my name. I would go from one place where I was nothing but his son to another.

"Did a dog eat your tongue?"

I forgot all the names I'd ever heard until "Gunnar" came back from the depths of my memory. I was already answering when I decided it wasn't mine to say, but it was too late and I ended up mumbling something like "Dnnr".

"Dobrosława is my name," said the woman. "Let's get you to the jarl, Donar. He'll decide what to do with you." Her hand wrapped around my arm, or rather my elbow. I winced, but there were no claws or hidden blades. Either she was a jötunn and not a human, or she was disguising herself. She looked up and smiled, then slowly licked her lips again and I understood. I did it all the time when my lips were dry and cracking. Instinctively, I licked my lips too, tasting salt and a bit of dust. Her hand slid up, grabbing as much of my arm as she could.

She took me down a path through the forest before reaching a wide dust road and gesturing towards some odd construction. It looked as though someone had chopped a lot of trees, sharpened them all as if they were sticks, then built a wall out of that. Like a very big shed without a roof, but with a sentry tower that looked just the same as back in the City of Light. A moat surrounded all of that and a bridge over it led inside.

"This is the great gord of Jomsborg," said the woman and she sounded like she wasn't joking.

The great gord, surrounded by a wooden palisade, was larger than I expected. I had little else to say about it. The bridge could be lifted and serve as a gate that I could probably break by blowing at it. Thor would wipe it all out within a blink if it didn't belong to "humans". There were more around, but they must have all been jötnar or witches in disguise, because there were no scales and the only fires were logs burning in iron braziers. The houses were more like shacks. There was no castle, not even a small one. Dobro-su-ava was leading me towards a brick building with a pointed wooden roof. They were very backward here.

She told me to wait and went to confer with two armed men guarding the entrance. She pointed at me, saying something I couldn't hear. One of the men glared at me as the other disappeared inside with Dobro...something-or-other. I had already forgotten her name. A bad feeling overwhelmed me. *I want to go back*, I thought, then shrank. There was nothing to go back to.

A loud noise made me flinch and I jerked my head back to see a child trying to catch a hen, both barely avoiding running into a brazier. Dogs barked, one after another, as if passing a message. The whole scene felt both familiar and odd. Could I have been wrong about the scales and the fire? I still wasn't completely certain that this was Midgard.

"I took care of everything," said the woman. I hadn't noticed her approaching and I nearly jumped out of my skin. "Look humble, don't talk too much." She stood on her toes and gave me a little peck on the cheek "for courage". The corner of my lips lifted uncertainly. It wasn't until I stood in front of a long table inside the dark, smoky hall, lit mostly by candles, that I noticed the walls weren't glowing.

Jarl Myesh-kow stared at me without a word until I became uncomfortable, then exchanged a few whispers with two others sitting next to him. I tried to make myself look smaller and less Thor-like, almost missing the jarl's announcement. I was more than welcome, he informed me, since their blacksmith was just about to depart.

"Down a ditch," muttered another man.

"You will spend the night in my guest chamber, Donar," said the jarl, then he clapped his hands twice. "Guards will be placed outside for your safety. My daughter Niedomira will take care of your needs."

Everything about the room was too small for me. I had to be careful when standing up so as not to hit my head on the ceiling. The bed was only half as long as me. The tiny window didn't open. All of that ceased to matter when Niedomira brought me thick soup with various things floating in it. I recognised meat of some sort and carrots, which were small, orange, flat and round, just like the ones we ate back home on special days. Everything tasted good, except some leaves that floated on top. I thought that maybe I wasn't supposed to eat them and I blushed. I was happy that nobody saw me. I sucked the soup off them and put the leaves under the bed, then cleaned the bowl with bread fresher than anything I had eaten in the last few days.

The dark drink that came in a clay mug was both sweet and sour, another thing I had never tried before and I didn't dare ask whether it was supposed to taste like this or whether it had gone bad. The guilt and shame chewing on my insides didn't stop me from enjoying the hot meal.

"You need a bath," said Niedomira when she came to take away the dishes. It occurred to me that I was being welcomed like a guest of honour if the jarl's own daughter was taking care of me. Maybe the guards outside my door really were for my safety, to keep humans away. "I'll arrange one for you in the morning."

"Thank you."

"Is it true that you are a jötunn, Donar? You're definitely a giant. More fire than ice, though." She messed up my hair, chuckled and left me wondering who she was talking about, until I remembered it was me. I was now Donar, a jötunn blacksmith, a nobody that had no home, no Mother and no Gunnar.

"Lady Freya," I whispered. "I swear on the hem of your holy dress. I swear on your holy necklace, Brisingamen. I swear on your holy falcon cloak. I will stop Thor from killing any jötnar ever again. This is my oath and I…"

My voice died out. Nobody asked about the blood all over my clothes. Only humans could have been so used to it that they didn't think it strange. I was definitely in Midgard.

~

Clad in white, a silver headband holding her hair as if she were some sort of princess, Niedomira walked slowly, holding my arm. It didn't feel like she was taking the new arrival to his smithy, more like a procession. People formed something of a path for us to walk through. Some touched my shoulder, making me wince. I always blushed easily and I soon grew dizzy from all the blood rushing towards my face.

"Thor," someone whispered.

"Father Thor."

"It's him."

"Look at the hammer."

"It's him."

"His name is Donar," said Niedomira loudly, staring in front of her, as if speaking to herself. "You will leave him alone." The voices quieted, but didn't stop.

I couldn't stop glancing around at the humans. I towered over everyone, same as back home. If they thought all the jötnar were like me, I could see why they believed us to be giants. One or two humans smiled. A few women gawked, their mouths open, as if they'd never seen anything so interesting. Others scowled. A man let out an angry hiss, making sure I was looking, then wrapped his hand around the hilt of a short sword and bared his teeth. I put my hand on the hammer's head, as if by accident, and heard a few gasps. Then I looked away, because I remembered it was a human and I felt afraid again.

"It's him."

How was it that everything and everyone I had ever known was gone, yet Thor found a way to follow me here?

"Here we are," announced Niedomira, as she opened the door and let out a frustrated cry. "By Odin, why is he still here?" She looked around, her lips pursed. "Wojciech! Come here and get him out!"

Wojciech, a slim, bearded man, bowed towards me before disappearing inside. I didn't like the bow any better than the hiss. As

Niedomira waited, tapping her foot, I examined the equipment. The fire and the anvil stood outside, under a roof that was just high enough for me not to have to bend down while working. The anvil was placed higher than I was used to and the fire – lower; I would have to learn to work in a different way. Some of the people followed us and now gawked at me from a distance, whispering to each other. My face must have been redder than my beard.

Wojciech dragged someone outside, puffing with effort. It was a man who was sleeping so soundly that he continued to snore even as his breeches fell off, and his buttocks and his legs rubbed against the ground.

"My apologies," said Niedomira, waving her hand in front of her face, scowling. "I thought he was taken care of last night. You will have to air this place out, one spark might set it on fire. Throw him somewhere outside, Wojciech."

"Yes, my lady. Anywhere in particular?"

She smiled. "Somewhere he won't come back from. Donar..." Niedomira's gaze measured me from head to toe. "You look like someone who knows how to work hard. Am I right?"

I nodded.

"I'll try to keep those people away from you," she said quietly and I instinctively leaned closer. "If they bother you too much, just let me know and I'll take care of it. Still, it might be good if you went to the tavern tonight and bought some drinks." She placed something in my hand. "Have a nice time, make some friends. Be careful, though. Some of those men are brawlers, especially when there is drink."

"Thank you for your kindness," I muttered, rubbing the coin she placed in my hand. I had never been inside a tavern in my entire life. Maybe instead of the clean tunic she had given me I should have kept the bloodied one, to impress the *brawlers*.

"It's our pleasure, my father's and mine. We need someone like you, badly. You've seen what a mess Kowal was."

"Kowal?"

She gestured in the direction of the drunken man, who was now kicking the air, his trousers wrapped around his knees and ankles, clumsily trying to free himself from Wojciech.

"We need horses shod, tools sharpened, we need axes, swords... You won't run out of work. Keep your head down and don't let anybody mess with you. And remember, if you need anything, come straight to me." A peck on the cheek and she was gone. I touched my cheek, straightened my back, and noticed that one of the people staring at me was the man with the sword.

I retreated into my new dwelling, shut the door, then immediately opened it again before I passed out from the smell. I promised myself that I would scrub this place from top to bottom every day until it stopped reeking and that I would never, ever touch strong liquor.

I did not enjoy myself. The innkeeper kept staring at me. So did the few patrons. I said nothing, unable to figure out what was expected of me. Wojciech, whom I already knew, smiled kindly. Before I had a chance to ask about Kowal, someone else demanded to arm-wrestle with me. I slammed his hand against the table and he let out a surprised grunt of pain. The others began to laugh and tease him. His eyes met mine and I realised I hadn't made a friend, although I wasn't sure why. It had been his idea.

When the jeers ended, someone else – I couldn't keep up with the names – showed me his sword, which I hastily complimented. He then explained to me that he had never lost a fight, his tone suggesting that he was actually talking about something else. I promptly swore that I believed every word and that I was very impressed. This made the arm-wrestler snort, which made me blush. I had said something wrong again.

I hadn't realised the sword-man I saw earlier was even inside until he slammed his mug on the table, making me wince. He sat in the farthest corner with his legs spread, the fingers of his right hand tapping the sword's hilt. "You're not Thor," he said.

"I never said I was," I answered, shaky, wondering whether I was too sober to deal with humans, then I remembered. "Can I buy you a..."

"I'll be watching you."

"Go to sleep, Dalebor," said Wojciech. "You're drunk enough."

"You're not my wife to tell me what to do."

"Stop this," demanded the innkeeper and for some reason everyone's eyes turned towards me. Again. I said nothing at all this time, how was that also wrong? I left the coin on the table, having absolutely no idea how much it was worth, and escaped. If I had to become a "brawler" to make friends, I was happy to be on my own.

Once I found the forge again, a lit oil lamp and some food awaited me. The stinking rags that Kowal probably slept on were gone, replaced with some fresh straw and a blanket. There was even a jug of the same sweet and sour drink I'd had before. I had no idea how I would have managed without Niedomira's help. I was so lucky that she was taking care of me. I wondered what Gunnar would have made of all this. He visited me in my sleep, and we laughed like we always had when one of us accidentally set himself on fire and didn't notice. He gave me a hug, patting me on the back again. Neither of us said anything, but we knew. I woke up feeling almost cheerful until I remembered.

My back and shoulders hurt from the strange placing of the anvil. My leg was bruised from bumping into it and even though the bruises would be gone before the day was over, they were painful. I struggled with the tools as well, but not as much as with the humans.

"I'd like to see you shoe my horse," one said. I had only shod a horse two or three times before. My hands were shaking under the man's fixed stare, his arms crossed on his chest. I prayed to Lady Freya that the horse wouldn't kick me in the face. I could tell the owner was disappointed when all went well and he had to part with his coin.

"My plough doesn't plough like it used to," sighed Dobrosława, fiddling with her hair, and I had to point out that she hadn't brought it. She stomped off in a huff, followed by children's laughter.

Having the fire and the anvil placed outside allowed people to constantly just "ask something". "What is the biggest sword you have ever made? Can you fight with a sword? A double-handed one?" More than one man's eyes narrowed as he stared at my hammer and I decided never to leave it unattended. If I wasn't using it, it returned to its place on my belt.

Dobrosława aside, there seemed to be an endless stream of ploughs, scythes, axes, knives needing sharpening. There were more horses needing to be shod, their owners no longer testing me, just impatient to go back to work. Pitchforks and scythes. Swords, daggers, double-handed axes, more questions about my fighting abilities. When a trader arrived, needing his tooth pulled, I couldn't tell which of us was more terrified. In the evenings I'd fall on the straw and fall asleep, exhausted. I could see why the jarl seemed so pleased to see me.

If it weren't for Niedomira, I would have probably starved to death. She brought me food and kvass, the brown drink, then reminded me to actually eat and drink it. When the pointing and whispering became unbearable, she'd appear and suddenly everyone would find something important to do. Her visits were the brightest point of my day. I liked the kisses on the cheek and having a friend I didn't have to go to a tavern to see.

Someone else – Dalebor – paid me daily visits and I wished he'd just stayed in the tavern if he had nothing else to do. At times he'd just stand nearby and smirk, distracting me. Other days he'd ask me questions that I could tell were not what they appeared to be. Did I use the hammer to fight? How far could I throw it? Were there horses big enough to handle my weight in Jötunheim? I almost waited for him to ask whether I preferred thunder to lightning or the other way round.

"Can I hold your hammer? Just to see."

There was nothing that someone like Dalebor could "just see" in my hammer. "No," I said. "It's a special hammer. I don't like it when others touch it."

"Why?"

I considered that. "It's bad luck for a blacksmith."

"Really? I didn't hear Kowal complaining."

"Kowal isn't here anymore."

"No," said Dalebor, stepping closer towards me and leaning on his fists, resting his weight on top of the anvil. I shouldn't have recoiled, but I did. "He isn't. He was a good friend of mine. A God or a man, nobody has the right to come here and get my friends killed."

"Out," snapped a woman's voice. Niedomira was marching towards us, shooting daggers.

"We're just talking like the friends we are," said Dalebor, not moving. "Right, Donar?"

"Not anymore," said Niedomira before I had a chance to answer. "I suggest you leave Donar alone. Unlike you, he's working."

"He looks so big and still needs a lady to defend him, eh? Hey, Thor, is it true what they say about you getting wed to a jötunn king? Did you like the wedding night?"

"Out," Niedomira repeated.

He didn't deign to give me another glance, just strode away. I stood completely frozen. They knew about the City of Light and everything else. Faking a smile had never been harder.

"My dear Donar, you really should have told me this was happening. Dalebor talks a lot and does little, and I don't like that he's interrupting you. I will make sure he keeps to himself. Have you made any other friends?"

I could tell that I was being gently scolded. "Uhm. Not really." I paused, unsure whether it was right to add, "Just you."

"You must feel so sad and lonely, far away from home," she sighed. "You look like you need a hug."

She stood on her toes, but I still had to practically bow so that she could wrap her arms around my neck. I didn't know what to do with my blackened hands, worried that I'd dirty her dress, so I stood stiffly in the uncomfortable position. When she let go, though, I felt disappointed. Niedomira was warm and soft and smelled nice. She laughed sweetly, saying something about how big I was, and I laughed too. Still feeling somewhat flushed, I leaned out discreetly to follow her with my gaze as she departed. I rested my fists on the anvil and nearly toppled over. Dalebor awaited her, leaning against a building. She wrapped her hand around his arm. He put his hand on her buttock.

"Father."

I only remained quiet because the shock had taken my breath away. "Wojciech," I managed when I could speak again.

"May we talk? Inside," he added.

I had replaced everything I could, scrubbed the walls and removed the top layer of dirt from the floor, but the smell of vomit and alcohol seemed to have soaked into everything. I started apologising and Wojciech shook his head. "It's not right," he said. "You should not be living in these conditions. Father, we do not know why you are attempting to hide your identity..."

"I'm nobody's father. Just Donar, nothing and nobody else."

"Many of us are proud that you have chosen Jomsborg out of all places, but others..." Wojciech cleared his throat. "There is talk. Some men want nothing more than to be known as godslayers, some women want to bear a God's child."

"I'm not Thor! What do I have to do or say for you to believe me?!"

He shook his head. "Those who believe you may pose the greatest danger. Jomsborg is not safe for you. When I told you that some wish you ill... not all of us do. You do have friends here, real ones who don't want anything from you."

"Niedomira," I nodded.

Wojciech said nothing for a while. "When the time comes, please remember it was I who warned you, Father," he finally uttered. He bowed deeply before leaving.

I sat on the floor and hid my face in my hands. I was a red-head, taller and stronger than anybody else I had ever met, here or in Jötunheim. I was a blacksmith and carried a hammer with me at all times. What was I supposed to do? Hide the hammer, shrink, lose my hair? If Wojciech meant what I thought he did, as he also seemed incapable of just saying what he meant, it didn't matter whether humans believed that I was Thor or not. I was at risk "when the time comes". They really were something else, something I didn't understand. We might have used the same words, but we spoke different languages.

The bloodshed and the destruction and my mother's death were now another story about Thor's adventures. Perhaps more amusing than most. The ending never changed. Thor killed some ice giants and won. If I went to the tavern, someone would probably start telling it and there would be much laughter, just not mine—

Goosebumps covered my skin. Was that what the people whispered among themselves, pointing at me as if they thought me blind? Were they laughing at *me* in a wedding gown, worse, were they admiring how ruthlessly I destroyed that jötunn city and killed them all?

Wojciech's warning came too late, his talk about my "friends" and "Jomsborg not being safe" was no less frightening than Dalebor's posturing. Next time, possibly even tomorrow, Dalebor would ask to hold the hammer again, but he'd bring a few brawlers along. Did Niedomira sound *happy* when I said I had no other friends? Was she my friend when she let Dalebor touch her like that?

I picked up the first thing within reach, a copper razor, fiddling with it nervously. When someone knocked on the door, I dropped the razor. The knocking repeated, louder. I made no sound, overcome by dread. What if the intruder tried to come inside? I quietly picked the razor up. It was very sharp. An image of the razor at Dalebor's throat made me gasp. I was becoming like them. Like humans.

Another image replaced it, that of me – bare-faced, bald-headed, rubbing ash onto my eyebrows. I now knew that the "great gord" of Jomsborg was just one settlement, neither large nor important. I knew why Dalebor was asking about horses. Neither Thor nor I could ride one, we were too tall and too heavy. The winter was coming, did the ships still sail in the winter? I could travel somewhere, start again. A big, bald jötunn blacksmith named... named... not Donar, not Magni... Kowal. The faster I left, the better. Maybe it was a brawler who knocked on the door. I'd leave at night, this night. I had coin now. There was nothing unusual about buying food or warm clothes for the winter.

Whistling, I wandered around, looking relaxed and not at all suspicious, side-eyeing the bridge that was also a gate. I could send it flying with a kick, but I couldn't swim. This was not the City of Light and the sentry tower wasn't there just because cities were supposed to have them. The watchmen here had swords, axes, bows. *Some wanted to be known as godslayers.* I left the gate alone and walked past the palisade, trying to assess its height. I leaned against it as if by accident and heard the wood cracking. One harder push with my shoulder and the wooden poles would fall. They should be long enough to let me get over the moat. How many would I need to handle my weight?

"What are you doing?"

The watchmen's captain, the one who lost the arm-wrestling match, stood right next to me, glaring. "Just looking," I squeaked, then cleared my throat. "Aye. Just...looking."

"At what?"

I desperately searched for something to say. "All the...wood."

He raised an eyebrow and I started sweating.

"All those braziers," I improvised, "and you know, it's all... the houses, even the hall's roof, it's all wood and straw..."

"And your point is?"

"Just worried that something might burn," I said lamely.

"Go back to your forge and watch your own fire," suggested the captain. "We'll worry about the fortifications."

I bent my shoulders, nodded and thanked him. His stare weighed heavy on my back as I inconspicuously strolled towards the market, stumbling a bit, unused to inconspicuous strolling. I bought a sack, then filled it with food, barely paying attention to what I was buying and how much I was paying. Were they giving me strange looks? The laughing woman on the right, was she laughing at me? Was I hearing whispers? I pushed the coin into the baffled seller's hand and hurried to see the seamstresses.

"We don't have anything...your size," the daughter said as she did that now-familiar up-and-down look. I'd thought I knew what it meant. Now I wondered. Was she thinking of the wedding gown?

"We'd need some time," added the mother. "And some coin, for materials. Now."

"I'll pay whatever it takes for you to hurry up," I burst out, then bit my lip. "I mean, just because I'm cold. Working outside and all that." Were their eyes widening? Did they glance at each other? "Say, how much time?"

"A few days," said the mother, observing both me and her daughter, who started taking measurements by squeezing my arm. The cape I wanted would have no sleeves. They wanted to bear a God's child, said Wojciech. I forced a smile-like grimace on my face. Being a God's child was not something I'd wish on anyone.

I returned to the smithy in a foul mood. The realisation that I had no winter clothes seemed to have made me feel cold. I slapped and picked at my arms, protected only by a thin, tight tunic. The leather apron hardly helped. The goosebumps wouldn't go away, neither would the mild nausea. Hopefully I wasn't getting ill. A few days... I could only pray to Lady Freya that Niedomira was simply placating Dalebor, so that he'd leave me alone. She was trying so hard to calm him down that she let him grab her buttock without asking.

I dropped the sack on the ground and wrapped myself in my blanket, then lay down to rest just a bit. I dozed off before I knew it and woke with a start when someone touched my arm.

"It's me," whispered Niedomira. "Let's talk."

"It's night," I mumbled. "Can't it wait?"

"Now is the time. There are men waiting outside."

"Waiting for what?"

She knelt next to me, holding a candle. The flame flickered and when Niedomira grinned, her face turned into a skull. "For us, you and me. My father is weak and a coward. You are Thor, big and strong..."

"I am *not* Thor," I cried.

"Of course not," said Niedomira politely, as if talking to a child. "But people don't know that. If something were to happen to my father, I would not be allowed to take his place, I'm a woman. You, on the other hand? If you married me, we'd be able to do anything."

"Nothing is going to happen," I murmured, feeling sick. There were men waiting outside.

Niedomira chuckled. "When I lay here in your strong arms, someone killed my father, a cowardly attack on the gord of Jomsborg. It will be clear to everyone that we need a defender. Who would be better than Thor and the jarl's daughter? We will wash the kingdom in blood to avenge my father."

"Avenge," I groaned.

"I'll tell you what to do, you'll just sit there being..." That all-too familiar pause. "Big. You will never lack anything. A warm bed, the best food, your own guard, then, soon, an army. And you'll have..." She put the candle away, then shook off the cloak she was wearing. "This."

I recoiled. It wasn't a dream, but it was still a nightmare.

"It's so cold in here," she whispered. "Oh, Donar, hold me in your arms. I know you're lonely, so am I. You don't belong in this reeking hole. You and I..."

I pushed her away, a bit harder than I intended, and Niedomira landed on her butt. "I'm– I'm not– no! I will not kill your father! What kind of monster are you?"

I heard her sharp intake of breath. "Monster," spat Niedomira, a sound like the crack of a whip. I tried to curl up against the wall. "Monster, Donar? I offer you everything, even myself, this is how you repay me, with violence?" She paused. "Jomsborg might be unimportant now, but it won't be once the harbour is ours," she hissed. "We won't be paying anymore for using it, we will be paid. One word and all this is ours. Say it."

"Get out of here, you – you traitor!"

Only the candle's occasional sizzle interrupted the silence.

"Very well," said Niedomira slowly. "Then I will go." She wrapped herself in the cloak, picked up the candle and left me in complete darkness. I barely had a chance to blink before the door slammed against the wall. There were men waiting outside.

"You are arrested for treason," announced Dalebor. "Niedomira told us about your plans," he added. I could tell he was delighted.

Inside the dark, smoky hall, behind the familiar long table sat the jarl and four more men. None of them looked surprised. They had been waiting.

"Here is the traitor," said Niedomira, taking a seat between her father and the watchmen's captain. Dalebor's torch moved so close to my hair that I hissed in surprise and tried to move away, only to feel an arrowhead touch my temple. My hands were tied behind my back. My mind was blank.

Jarl Mieszko steepled his fingers. His eyes were tired. "Who are you?"

"You know... it's... Donar, the blacksmith..."

Dalebor sniggered.

My eyes met Niedomira's. A light grimace on her face and a little gesture with her head made me understand. It was still up to me to decide whether it would be me or the jarl who would leave this place alive.

I straightened my back. She was taking me for a human.

"Have you come here off your own accord, Donar the blacksmith, or were you sent to murder me?" asked the jarl. He sounded old, frail. A strange feeling overcame me. He didn't care. He just wanted to go back to bed.

The briefest of blinks. Light. Heat. A sharp arrowhead piercing my skin. The man with the crossbow gasping, withdrawing. A slap. The familiar stink. It was over before I understood what was done to me. Dalebor set fire to my hair. I knew the smell from the forge, where I'd regularly lose some of the hair covering my forearms. Not my face. Never my face.

"Answer," suggested Dalebor.

"D-D-Donar, that's all, you all know me, I haven't done anything wrong, please!"

The watchmen's captain raised his hand and I silenced.

"He threatened to burn Jomsborg just today."

The jarl's eyes closed. "Is it true?"

"No!" I couldn't stop side-eyeing the torch. My cheek felt hot and I didn't even know whether it was real heat or imagined. Never before had I felt afraid of fire.

"Be honest," sighed the jarl. "I might still spare your life."

"I wouldn't," said Niedomira, her voice anything but friendly. "Whatever he says will be a lie anyway."

"He planned to kill you, Your Grace, isn't it enough?" asked Dalebor.

"How do you know?" asked Wojciech. I hadn't noticed him, sitting to the side, in half-darkness. My heart didn't beat faster, but a bit harder, like it was reminding me that it was still there.

"Surely you don't think I went there alone?" cried Niedomira. "All I needed was the final proof, and he hurt me, he pushed me! I was so afraid, Father, for my life, but mostly for yours..."

"Enough," interrupted Jarl Mieszko and Niedomira froze, mouth open. "I know the truth," he continued. His frail voice and tired expression were gone. Niedomira glanced at Dalebor. Wojciech's eyes met mine. They did it again. One thing was being said, another was happening.

"We opened our doors and our hearts—" Niedomira started, her voice slightly shaky.

"Quiet! You have said and done more than enough, *daughter*. Donar, the work you have done for us is appreciated. Our tools are fixed, our weapons sharp and replenished, horses shod. Therefore, I will show you my mercy and instead of sentencing you to death, I shall outlaw you."

"So that means I'm... I'm going to leave," I said, trying not to make it sound like a question.

Dalebor's snigger was cut short with one look from the jarl. No word was said, but the dreaded torch finally moved away from my face. I exhaled, my tense muscles relaxing. It was going to be fine. I could leave, as I wanted to.

"I outlaw you," repeated the jarl. He was looking down, at his own steepled fingers, avoiding my eyes. "You will be led outside. All you can take is what you have on you."

"Not the hammer," said Niedomira. "That's dangerous. Take it off him."

Silence befell the room. I felt rather than saw the crossbow drop. The watchmen's captain was studying his fingernails.

They were not certain.

"Are you sure you want to touch it?" I asked, trying to elongate the words in that threatening way, but unable to stop the trembling.

"He is allowed to take everything he has on him," said Wojciech.

"Outlaws own nothing," started Niedomira, but she didn't finish. Without the slightest hint of warning, the jarl's hand shot towards her throat. Her eyes bulged out, lips moving soundlessly. None of the men made a sound, not even Dalebor, only I inhaled sharply. The jarl let go and returned to his previous position so quickly, his shoulders sloping, head hung, that if Niedomira didn't still look like a fish pulled out of water I would have thought I'd imagined it.

"With power come choices," he said, sounding even older and more tired than before. "Some are harder than others. This law was imposed by the King and will be fully observed. Donar can keep the hammer and everything else he has on him. Wojciech, Dalebor, you will lead him out and ensure the law is observed *exactly* as imposed by the King." The jarl paused. "I had no choice," he said to me and it sounded as if I were the judge and he were pleading.

Niedomira stopped massaging her throat and smirked.

There were no stars in the sky. Some of the watchmen stood by the braziers that glowed rather than burned, massaging their hands, talking quietly with each other. There was just enough light for me to see snowflakes lazily drifting towards the ground. Wojciech gently squeezed my arm and my fake bravery broke.

"What does it mean that I am an outlaw?" I cried. "I haven't done anything! Let me just go to the forge and take my things, I was going to leave anyway, please!"

Dalebor snorted. "You don't own any 'things'. An outlaw is not allowed to have any possessions, whether it is a piece of wood or a farm."

"Except for what you've got on you," said Wojciech, his voice flat, wooden.

"If you were married, your marriage is now null and void," continued Dalebor, sounding very pleased. "Your children no longer have a father. Any attempt to hide your identity is punished with death. Do you understand me, or should I repeat it? Some have fallen under your spell, but not me. Once you're out of the gate, you are fair game. Am I missing something, Wojciech, or is that the law as imposed by the King?" He cackled.

"The rope," said Wojciech. "His hands are tied with rope that does not belong to him. He can't take it with him. Free his hands."

"What? We never free their hands!"

"Lower the bridge!" yelled Wojciech, then lowered his voice again. "I outrank you. Free his hands."

Dalebor's curse snapped at the same moment as the rope. I didn't even have to try hard, just moved my wrists a bit. Fortunately, the rope was thick. A thinner one would have bitten into the skin.

"Thank you, Wojciech," I said, trying to keep the shakiness out of my voice. "I will remember that. I will remember you too, Dalebor."

I wanted them to remember me as marching into the darkness straight and proud, but shivers kept running up and down my body. The bridge was lifted and I just stood there, massaging my arms, thinking. The lights of Jomsborg didn't reach far, there was no moon, the road was covered with snow. What was I supposed to—

Twang – woosh – thunk!

I leapt with a surprised squeal. The jarl said I was outlawed, that they wouldn't kill me! He lied! The bow string sang again and I yelped loudly when another invisible *woosh – thunk* cut through the silent darkness. Whooping. Cheering. Shouting.

"Run!" someone yelled. "You're no fun!"

Thunk and I wrapped my arms around me, running into darkness, screaming, *thunk* I was a big target, they could still see me, they were missing on purpose, playing with me. "Fair game"! I couldn't tell the road from the trees, I couldn't breathe, wheezing, panting, the air burning inside my lungs, I was not made for running, I was too heavy, *thunk* I stumbled, flapping my hands to stop myself from falling, my weight carrying me until I caught my footing again. I didn't know anymore if I was still hearing their laughter, or if it was just ringing in my ears with my own wheezing. I couldn't go on but I had to, away from this cursed place full of humans Thor loved so much.

I tripped over something again, instinctively extending my arms to stop the fall, hurting my wrist, crying out in pain and surprise, and then just crying, crawling through the snow, my heart bouncing inside my ribs. I lifted myself to my feet. My legs were so weak now I stumbled rather than walked. I didn't know where I was or where to go. I had never seen blacker sky in my life. One huge sob gathered inside my chest and erupted with the thought that if I had known then what I knew now, maybe I would have killed Thor after all.

How could I even try to pass for someone else? It was possible to describe me with one word, the dreaded name that followed me wherever I went. I had no razor, no food, not even a blanket. I had my hammer and a pouch with what little coin I had left, both equally useless right now. I could light a fire even in the pouring rain, but not without flint and kindling – *fire* – Dalebor's torch burning my face again, a vision gone in a flash.

"At least give me lightning!" I screamed at the frozen sky and the darkness answered. A white flash of pain exploded in my shoulder. I listened to my own cries dying out, feeling indifferent, as if it were someone else who wouldn't be cold any longer.

CHAPTER 3
MAYA

I BANGED on the door until it opened, which took exactly one bang.

"Your Grace," gasped Thrud.

"Thrud," I gasped in response. She looked the same as she had the day I left, the messy mop of blonde curls that didn't dare to shine as golden as Freya's, her eyes wide in surprise, complexion rosy. She radiated youth, freshness, and *cleanness*. When she looked me up and down her completely polite, neutral look caused each body part in turn to blush.

"Please come inside, Your Grace," she said, already perfectly composed, unlike me. "I will be back shortly."

The white and golden hall, the statues of naked men and women were both familiar and strange, like a dream. I shuddered. I was filthy and here, of all places, appearances mattered. I glanced back at the door. Had Thrud not already gone to notify Freya, I would have escaped.

Calm down, I told myself. I was addressed as "Your Grace", meaning that I was still considered a guest of honour. I was not offered food or drink, though, nor a chair to sit on. A guest who wasn't staying long. At least as far as the housekeeper was concerned.

On our way here from Jötunheim I had been too busy not falling out of the chariot and too exhausted to think about my arrival. Should I act indignant? Pleading? Had I sealed my fate by coming here like this? Good Gods, what if Freya knew that I had helped steal the hammer?!

"Is this really you, Maya? What are you doing here?"

The gown wrapped around Freya's waist was a bit loose. Her waist-long auburn hair was slightly messy. Early afternoon or not, she'd come here straight from bed. Her twin brother's. Her tone alone nearly reduced me to tears. I just nodded.

"Don't touch anything. Your hands are dirtier than Idunn's. And your hair! How dare you enter my hall looking like this? You *stink*. Get out of here!"

I would have cried if I'd had it in me. "I apologise," I said flatly. "It was a mistake. Um. Goodbye."

"Where do you think you're going?"

"You just told me to get out of here."

"Out of here where someone could see you! Go to your chambers, foolish girl, and wash yourself. Let's pretend this *arrival* never happened." Freya smiled sourly. "As long as you and I live, you have a place in Sessrúmnir. I expect you not to look like this when you join me for breakfast." I was still processing the words and putting them together into sentences as she turned on her heel and departed.

Thrud led me down the hallway I both remembered and forgot. Mirrors hung everywhere. Every time I caught a glimpse of myself I felt shame mixed with anger, sadness, hunger, confusion, all sorts of pain. When the door opened my mouth opened too, forming a perfect "O". My chambers looked exactly the same as they had the day I had left, and tears gathered in my eyes. Nothing had changed; the statues in the hallway, the glowing jewels serving as lamps, Thrud's girlish face, Freya's perfect lips slightly skewed by irritation that someone dared to interrupt her...entertainment. The only thing out of place was me.

"If you need anything, Your Grace, please call on me."

"Thank you so much, Thrud. I'm... I'm just back from Jötunheim."

"We know, Your Grace." Thrud nodded politely and left me with an itchy feeling that maybe I wasn't entirely welcome.

The chaos and destruction I'd escaped, the grime covering me, the feeling that underneath my clothes I was one big bruise made the warm silence of my old drawing room seem unreal. I still stood in place, looking around, wondering whether I was having one of my dreams, when gentle knocking sounded.

"Her Grace Freya sends this with her compliments," said Thrud, as she placed a small bowl in front of me, nodded and left without another word. I grabbed the pear and swallowed it in three bites. I'd admire the golden sheen and the aroma some other time.

The effect was immediate. My blood seemed to simultaneously become warmer and flow slower through my body. The exhaustion turned into relaxed tiredness, the sort I would have felt after a long hike on a warm, sunny afternoon. The destruction, massacre, screams faded into irrelevance. The pressure in my forehead, the aching between my shoulder blades, the sharp pain in my hands and the dull ache in my ribs all disappeared. My lips opened and a small groan escaped with some saliva. Ohhhhh, it had been so long since I'd tasted Idunn's fruit.

I was floating in dreamy pleasure. I could *feel* myself becoming younger and happier. The layer of sticky fear that covered my mind for so long dissolved. Everything would be right, it already was.

I used to take it for granted, like everything else. Every moon-turn I would visit Aunt Idunn in her garden and leave with enough fruit for everyone in Sessrúmnir, pears, peaches, cherries, nuts, bananas; I had never forgotten my first and last avocado, because I thought it would be sweet and fruity like everything else. My thoughts became lazy, disconnected and I continued to float in the memories until I remembered my hot tub and wafted towards the bathing room.

When I slipped into the hot water another quiet groan escaped my lips. I lay there with my eyes closed for a while, floating, feeling the freeze deep inside my bones melt away. I massaged my scalp with soap until my hair felt like silk and smelled like flowers in the spring. I lifted my hand lazily and watched the steam raising from my now bruise-free skin. A long time ago I stood by the blazing fire in my old chamber and kept seeing my own breath. Not so long... a while... a few days.

I would never need to check my dubious-smelling food for poison again. I would not have to fear whispers, glances, jibes, the King's guttural growl, the healers' muttering about witches coming from abroad to steal their posts. I would never have to deal with them again, because they were dead.

The happy bubble wobbled uncomfortably before another wave of happiness engulfed me. It seemed cracked at first, like there was a scratch on my bliss, but the sensation didn't last. I couldn't hold on to the dark thoughts even if I tried. They would be back tomorrow for me to worry over. I wouldn't be able to eat any more fruit before the moon turned − the sickness was real. I could visit Aunt Idunn, though, just because I missed her. My eyes closed and I saw her, radiating warm charm that was nothing like Freya's icy beauty. The memories that emerged wrapped me in happiness. I knew that Idunn's wrath could destroy Ásgard, but all I could think of was the dazzling smile that shone like the sun in her dark brown face, the happy wrinkles carved by joy rather than age, the colourful head-scarves and dresses that made *her* look like a bursting garden, like life itself...

I spat out water, coughing, startled. I'd dozed off. Once out of the bath, I wrapped myself with the soft, fluffy gown. My body immediately dried, even my hair, which the gown wasn't touching. I ran my fingers through my hair just because I could. Everything was so lovely, but nothing more so than my bed and the softest of duvets on top of it.

When I woke I was completely disoriented. The white walls glowed with a warm light and I briefly tensed up before I remembered where I was. I dropped back onto the pillows, relieved. Thanks to Idunn's pear and its soothing power, the exhaustion was gone, as though wiped off. Now I'd feel a bit tired and heavy for a few days, but it was a price worth paying. The air, the fabrics caressed each hair on my body. I had no idea how long I had slept, but it was enough. I wouldn't be hungry for a while either.

I could go for an actual walk, I thought in disbelief. No shivering in the cold or watching my back, just the peace of Ásgardian night. Wrapped in the gown I let my forehead rest against the glass doors, my fingers gently tapping on its surface. I could stand here and wait for the magnificent sunrise, so different from yesterday's pale sun on the blue-tinted grey sky. I couldn't wait to hear what Magni would say once—

This time the happy bubble didn't wobble. Thor's hammer smashed it into shards that cut into my heart.

When I had found the spot where I saw the chariot earlier it was just landing, or rather smashing onto the ground, empty, the goats bleating. Or had I dreamt it? I had slept for a while... The one thing I remembered clearly was Thor's return. When I saw the remains of the gown hanging off his body, blood and dust mixing on his hands and on the hammer, I shuddered. Loki wrapped his arm around me. Thor said nothing, just growled. Even the bleating of the goats and Thjálfi's shouting couldn't drown out the constant, bear-like *rrrrrrmmmrrrrrrr* of fury still unsatisfied. With his head hung low, Thor looked shockingly like Magni, staring at the bloodied hammer he held with both hands. I shuddered. Did he care or even realise he had killed his lover? His son? *Rrrrrrrrrmmr-rrrrrrr.*

I shook my head and the soft hair caressed my face rather than slapped it. All this was past now. I was back and Freya swore in the presence of a witness that I could stay. I was home.

I stepped outside. The smooth rocks under my feet, the birch-wood benches covered with white sheepskins, the table covered with a blindingly white cloth, the soft chairs where we'd break our fast soon. I continued, stepping onto the warm, dewy grass, knowing that nothing wriggly or dirty would be hiding there. Daisies and chamomile flowers were strewn about, looking like they had just popped up in random spots. Four gardeners spent days tending to them under Freya's gaze. The tulips around me always bloomed. I knelt in the grass, touched one and the flower opened in my fingers. As far as I could tell in the silver light of the moon, the tulip was either white or pale yellow. Mana surrounding me here was nothing like the fierce fire of the blue orb, it was like a soft blanket. I lay down in the grass and inhaled the sweet air.

Last night I slept on the ground, surrounded by rocks, next to a snoring giant who wanted to make beautiful iron hinges. Dead grass had been my pillow. We had been surrounded by trees so gloomy I could see why they called the forest "haunted". That was all. The City stood proud, seemingly indestructible, no longer aglow, but still white and imposing. Magni shook me awake to tell me excitedly about Lady Freya's arrival.

The last traces of the ecstasy of Idunn's pear had left in a great hurry.

I had to be polite towards Freya if I wanted to get anywhere, perhaps even apologetic, but all I wanted to do was to punch her in the throat. Yes, it was very nice of her to let me stay here, since I was homeless due to a massacre that had torn down an entire city. The anger began to bubble inside me again. I had to squash it, be like Magni, not like Thor.

"Calm down," I said to myself through clenched teeth. It wasn't working.

If it weren't for her own cult that she somehow spread among the jötnar, none of this would have happened. Would it really have killed her to come over? She could have just gazed around and the other jötnar would tear King Thrymr into very small pieces, then beg her to be their queen! That would mean, of course, taking a break from buggering her brother. Such sacrifice! Hundreds, perhaps a thousand or more people had died with her name on their lips! They travelled to their death just to see Lady Freya once in their lives! And Magni?!

"Calm down," I repeated aloud. It came out as "call-don". My jaw was hurting.

I'd had enough of the garden and lost interest in the sunrise that I couldn't share. Stomping as angrily as it was possible while barefoot in the grass, I returned to my chambers. My leather trousers and black cotton tunic hung from a chair, looking as if a seamstress had just finished working on them. My boots were polished and shiny. But there was more. I was taken aback for a moment, before letting out a frustrated half-sigh, half-cry. A gown was placed "invitingly" on the bed. It was blood red – how tactful – embellished with what I knew were real rubies. She still hadn't given up. At least she knew better than to take my normal clothes away.

I got dressed, noticing that the leather was soft again, all the cracks and tears simply gone. There was no trace of dust or mud on anything either. The fake fullness of Idunn's pear had worn off long ago. Hungry, I paced around the room, trying to will the sun to go up faster. No matter how many times I repeated "calm down" under my breath, the anger kept simmering. Once I couldn't imagine staying inside any longer, I stormed out to discover breakfast was already waiting. That was even worse. I had to wait. If I touched so much as the smallest berry I'd get scolded for my bad manners.

So I turned away from the table and waited.

And waited.

Freya was not an early riser.

"Darling," I finally heard after an eternity and a day had passed. "You look...neater."

Freya's hair was still auburn, complexion smooth and milky, both her eyes and her velvet dress the colour of leaves in the spring. Birds sang, flowers bloomed, the sun was just warm enough, the breeze fresh. Silent, I stared at her, watching her half-smile fade. She was clearly waiting for something. A long time ago I would have been terrified, knowing that if I took too long to guess there would be consequences. Now the best I could do was not snarl.

"And a very good morning to you too, I suppose," she said, her voice hurt and resigned.

"Good morning," I mumbled.

"I," she said, placing her perfect hand on her perfect chest, her eyes widening in fake surprise, "am in a state of *shock*, darling. After all this time you appear here completely out of the blue, dishevelled, filthy. Uninvited. Is there a reason?"

It felt as if a hundred people inside my mind stood up and simultaneously began to yell over each other, but I only had one voice to lend to them. "They're dead!" I screamed. "Because of you! A whole city and all its people! Gone!"

Freya raised her finger and I instinctively quieted. She became distracted by her own sparkling fingernail before answering. "People? Jötnar, honey," she said, and the three words punched the air out of my lungs. Her stare returned to me, curious in that blank way perfected by cats.

"They love you," I finally managed, panting between words, "loved you, they, they…"

She almost imperceptibly shrugged. "You seem to be very distressed, petal. All I have done was say that I had no intention of marrying that jötunn. Not even for a hundred hammers. Darling, did you have dinner last night? You must be starving. Why aren't you wearing the dress I prepared for you?"

"Do you know how many people died there?"

"I bet you haven't even tried it on. What's wrong with my choice this time? The red would really suit your hair. So many colours, fabrics…"

"You're still talking about that dress," I gasped in disbelief.

Her sigh dripped with disapproval and I felt like a child again. "If you insist on trousers, maybe you could humour me and try some that are not like…" She cast a heavy look. "Those."

I ground my teeth. "I like leather and these are very comfortable."

"A different colour?"

"I like black."

"You can't say I haven't tried," said the long-suffering victim of my inability to dress up to her standards. "I hope you will permit Thrud to take care of your fingernails at the very least. It would be very impolite of you to refuse even that."

"What's wrong with my fingernails?! They're clean!"

"Honey," said Freya, her sharp teeth making a brief appearance that had nothing to do with a smile, "you and your jötunn friends might have shouted at each other, but here the rules are different."

The tiny hairs on my forearms stood up in warning.

"The prophecy," she demanded.

"Now? Are you joking?"

All of a sudden my cheek stung. She'd slapped me, just like when I was a child, and the words began to roll off my tongue. I had forgotten the prophecy ever existed, yet apparently every word patiently waited to be uttered again. For the first time it occurred to me that the long, boring poem I was reciting might really be the key to the future.

One day, Freya told me when I was a child, I would have to recite the prophecy to Odin. I felt afraid and said so. Odin's morose face and fierce one-eyed gaze scared me. *Don't worry*, said Freya reassuringly, *you will be dead by then.* That didn't help at all, so she added more detail. It would be a long time, she said. *You will die in Midgard one day a very long time from now, then one day even later Odin will find you and you will tell him the prophecy...* I was too young to realise that "a very long time" could have meant either ten winters or ten thousand of them.

Did Freya ask Bragi to come up with this? Bragi's words had the power to alter the past and the present, replacing the truth in people's minds. Was this "prophecy" an attempt to alter the *future*?

"That was wonderful, petal. Have a bun."

I hadn't even realised that I'd finished. The surprise was briskly swept away by the return of fury. "A bun? Petal? How old do you think I am?!"

Freya raised her hand again and I winced, but all she did was admire her fingernails – blue like the sky, shimmering in the sun. Why would someone need blue fingernails? She smiled at me. I forced the corners of my mouth to move upwards, trying not to show my teeth too much, still feeling the sting of her slap. *Be careful, or else*, said her smile. *I hate your guts*, said my grimace. *I don't mind*, said hers. *I know*, brooded mine.

Hunched over the plate like an animal afraid that the food would be snatched away I raised my eyes, chewing and swallowing as fast as I could, watching Freya. She was staring into space. Her fingers caressed Brisingamen, the most elaborate golden necklace that had ever existed, at once enormous and delicate, ostentatious and discreet. I only had a crystal on a worn-out leather strap on my neck. No king or jarl would have bothered stealing even a regular hammer from a smithy in order to marry me. That beautiful neckline of hers, half-shut eyes, blue fingernails and red lips brought countless deaths. And she *shrugged*.

Yesterday around this time I was probably sitting atop the sentry tower, watching Thor in a wedding dress.

"You have become so rude, darling," sighed Freya. My jaw stopped moving. "You've been away for so long, only to descend upon my hall without so much as a warning. Or taking a bath. You don't even ask how I am doing. Yet here I am, opening my door to you and sharing everything that I have. I invite you to stay here any time you like. I give you presents and you eschew them, again, not a word of gratitude. So? What do you have to say for yourself?"

I slightly choked on the half-chewed piece of bun, which was probably for the best, because I had a *lot* to say to that.

"I have not killed anybody," Freya continued, pouring me a goblet of wine and handing it to me. "Please don't eat so fast. It's very uncouth."

"You got an entire city destroyed on your whim," I wheezed between coughs, dropped the rest of the bun and gulped the sweet wine. "All those people—"

"Sweetie, I have no idea what you are talking about. What whim? Are you unwell?"

"You've turned Jötunheim into your toy! They believed you to be the Goddess of all that is good!" My voice was gruff and sounded as though I were crying. I cleared my throat. "They died with your name on their lips!" Strangely, I still sounded as if I were crying. "Whose plan was it?"

"What plan?"

Had I still been drinking, I would have bitten through the crystal goblet. "Dressing Thor in a bridal dress. Sending him over to the City of Light. You knew he would destroy it. And don't pretend you have no idea what I am talking about."

"But, sweetheart, you seem to have a very bad opinion of me. I would have never suggested anything like that!" Freya paused, tilting her head, as if curious to see my reaction. "It was Sif's idea. Thor didn't wait for the Assembly, he just grabbed Loki and off they went."

The shock nearly strangled me. "S-S—"

"You must remember Sif, darling. The wife of Thor, mother of Thrud, flowers grow where she—"

"I know who Sif is! She would never come up with something like that! She's too stupid!"

"She did, petal. Have you met that jötunn lover of his and their son?"

"Oh yes," I said. *Stay calm.* "Especially the son."

"As you can imagine, Sif hates them. Please don't bite your fingernails."

"I'm not biting... Why would she humiliate Thor in front of everyone?"

"In the very unlikely case I were to find that a man cheated on me," said Freya dreamily, her eyes widening in amusement, "I would ensure that he would get *thoroughly* humiliated, as publicly as possible. I would then ask Bragi to make sure that the stories and questions about the event would never end. You will understand one day, when you find a man of your own. Was there a special someone in—"

"I remember Sif better than you think and I got to know the King. Neither of them were smart enough to come up with this. If it wasn't you either, then it must have been that man."

"What man, dear?"

"The one who brought Mjölnir," I said, rolling my eyes, but only on the inside. I'd already gotten slapped once. "Please stop making that surprised face, it doesn't work on me."

"But, darling, I really don't understand. A man brought the hammer to Jötunheim? Who, how? According to Sif, a large woman came through the window and took the hammer. Sif woke up just in time for the woman to threaten her with death if she made so much as a sound."

I snorted. "Bull's bollocks. No 'large woman' could touch that hammer. It was a man with a blue orb filled with light hovering above his head. Some sort of container of mana."

"Oh, sweetie pie. Haven't we discussed this before? It's not possible to contain mana."

"He crossed Ifing in a boat that hovered over the water. Where did he get mana from?"

"You must have made a mistake."

I closed my eyes and counted to five. My teeth hurt from my attempts to grind them to dust. "I know what I saw. There was a man. He wore a large hat, I didn't see his face. An orb – maybe it was something else, but that was what it looked like, like a crystal ball full of small blue lights – hung over his head. So much mana came out of it that it was almost too much for me to withstand. Who was that man? He wrapped the hammer in some sort of fabric that blocked its magic. Then I had to carry it to the City..."

I ran out of breath and watched as she failed to control her face. I saw quick flashes of fear, excitement, surprise, anger... and relief. "I have no idea," Freya exhaled. She didn't even bother to fake surprise again. "I believe it might have been deception," she said right before I threw the table in her face. "Don't you think that would explain everything?"

It took me a blink to understand what she was saying. I slowly exhaled, feeling the fury pour out of me as if someone had made a hole in a wine skin.

Deception was the most powerful form of magic. It didn't work on me, but only when I knew I was being deceived. Since I didn't know, then maybe the orb was a product of deception... No, the other way round, if the orb was a product of deception, then I didn't know... "I don't think so," I said reluctantly. "A part of it, maybe, but I carried Mjölnir from the shore into the City and trust me when I say it was real. Someone, somehow, brought it there."

"Maybe someone threw it very far?"

I snorted. "Even Thor couldn't throw it over Ifing and, if he tried, the hammer would just return to him. I saw it with my own eyes in the City. It feels angry, it radiates angry magic... I know! The dark elves! Dark elves made the hammer and trapped mana in it. They did it with the orb now. This orb comes from Svartálfheim."

"No, darling. Mjölnir and Brisingamen are objects. Each of them only has one purpose, like a dog that only knows one trick. A bit like a crystal. You can't take energy out of Mjölnir and use it for something else any more than you could take a flame of a candle and store it for later use. Sweetie, it's just not possible."

I gawked at her, my mind blank, because despite what I had seen, I actually agreed with her.

"Did you say it was someone with a great magical power and a big hat? Sounds like Odin to me."

"I thought about that. But if it were Odin, he would have obscured himself in a way that would have made him look... not like Odin."

"Or," mused Freya, "he would not obscure himself, so that you would think it's not him, because..." She sipped on wine, then wrinkled her eyebrows. "Deception," she sighed. "It was definitely a man? Not a large woman?"

"Sif didn't see any man or woman stealing the hammer, because she and Thor don't sleep together," I snarled. "I told you, she's too stupid to come up with this plan or any other. I saw a man and I saw an orb."

"This man, was he a shifter?"

I opened my mouth, then closed it. "I didn't notice," I said lamely. "The orb distracted me."

"And there you go, petal," sighed Freya. "It's not that important, honey. I truly am very sorry about your jötnar friends, but it is in the past now. Mjölnir is back, you are back. All is well, isn't it? Let's focus on the future. What would you like to do next?"

"I am going to find out who is behind this," I threatened, watching her face for signs of alarm or at least a scowl.

"Please let me know when you do," she smiled, which meant either that she would do everything in her power to stop me or that she genuinely didn't care.

"Just stop playing and tell me what *you* want," I said. "We both know I have no say in what happens to me."

"Honey!"

"I did not send myself to Jötunheim or decide on a whim to become a sorceress for King Thrymr."

"You were a child. Now you are a woman. Despite" – she cast a heavy look at me – "your choice in outfits. But don't listen to me, what do I know? You should do whatever you want, whatever makes you happy."

I made a face and she laughed. "Now you look like a child again. Have you really worn those things the whole time? Not even a new pair of boots?"

"Yes," I said dryly. "I mean, no."

"Have you found yourself a nice man? Or woman?"

"No."

"But why not, honey? You're pretty enough in your own special way. Except for your clothes. And fingernails. Nobody at all, really? Are all jötnar that ugly?"

"No. Can we not—"

"Have you tried an orgy? You can meet very nice people at orgies."

"An orgy!?"

"Don't dismiss it unless you've tried it, that's all I am saying, pumpkin. I care for you, you know, all I want is your happiness."

"Then never say the word 'orgy' in front of me again," I groaned. "Why did you send me there? Because of the hammer? You predicted that?"

Freya rolled her eyes. "What have you been up to all that time, sweetie? Have you learned something new? Tell me all about it."

I stared at her. "Um, how to survive?"

"That's it?" she asked, after an uncomfortably long pause.

"It wasn't as easy as you might think! I had to be constantly aware of everything, watch my back, front, and sides, I—"

"So, you haven't learned anything? And you haven't found yourself a—"

"No, I haven't found myself a nice anyone and I have no such intention."

"Any new form of magic?" she probed.

"What new form of magic? Are you saying that you sent me away so that I would meet someone nice at an or– so that I would learn something n-new...?"

Freya's lips were pursed. She wasn't even looking in my direction, just waiting.

"Oh," I said, looking down, examining my apparently unacceptable fingernails.

I'd spent so many nights as a child crying myself to sleep, then waking up in the morning excited about what might happen next, until I was told that I was going away and my curiosity changed direction. Since then I had been so focused on what I already knew that it never occurred to me that there could have been even more. "You should have told me," I said weakly. "I would have tried harder."

Freya shook her head. "You've always been a contrarian. Why would this time be different? If I were to tell you to learn, you wouldn't, just out of spite. Yes, I sent you to a place where I expected you to be in danger, because I wanted you to return stronger and wiser. And this is all you come back with? Filthy hair, bitten finger-nails, complaints?"

"I... I built a city..."

"Do you know who doesn't feel the need to learn anything, pumpkin? Your friend Sif. Many, many winters ago Idunn helped Sif discover that wherever she walked flowers grew, crops improved, trees became greener and taller. She then never once felt the need to learn anything else. She got confirmation that she was a Goddess and her ambitions were all fulfilled. For all we know, Sif might be powerful enough to rule Ásgard if she tried. But she doesn't. Still, when she gets jealous, cities must fall to placate her. How about you?" Freya leaned back on her chair and crossed her arms on her chest.

I had nothing to say to that. All I came up with was "that's unfair".

"I see I'm wasting my breath." She spread her arms, as if admitting defeat. "Get some more rest. Think of what you want to do. I have no plans for you, no orders, I didn't expect to see you here at all. You are lucky to have caught me here, as I am leaving later today, and I will be away for a while. Thrud will be taking care of you. I wish you a nice day."

"How did she do that?" I muttered to myself, angrily chewing on a piece of candy I hated, the selection of foods appropriate for a child to show me my place without saying a word. I had never once managed to control the conversation back then and now, twelve winters later, she still steered it wherever she wanted. She knew exactly when I was about to explode and how to stop me. She was supposed to admit, for once, that she had made mistakes. Instead here I was, ungratefully complaining and being compared to *Sif*.

After the chewy candy the pink wine tasted bitter and I spat it into the grass, fighting the urge to bite through the crystal goblet and chew it to dust. So, she'd sent me away for my own good, like everything she'd done to me. I hadn't found the answers, because I didn't know that there were questions. I hadn't found Magni or his mother either, I hadn't helped anybody, and I wouldn't have made it back here without Loki's help. The more times I repeated that I'd built a city and made it glow, the less I impressed myself. I didn't even have enough imagination to make it look like anything other than Sessrúmnir's white marble. *I didn't ask for any of this*, I wanted to screech. *You sent me to do your bidding, didn't tell me what it is, now you're angry that I didn't succeed?!*

"Your Grace," said Thrud, jerking me back into the present. "Would it be possible for me to take care of your fingernails?"

It took me a blink to fold my face into something resembling a smile. I followed her to my chambers, where a small table with various utensils was already waiting. She sat next to me and took my hand. I looked away and let her massage my fingers with something greasy that smelled and felt quite nice. I closed my eyes and breathed slowly. I would *not* take my anger out on Thrud.

Could Freya have both lied and told the truth? I was too preoccupied with the blue orb to notice whether the man was a shifter or not. How could she know his identity when I could tell she truly didn't believe in the orb's existence? Deception, a shifter... I was almost certain it wasn't Loki and didn't believe it could have been Odin. Odin had a dark sense of humour that appeared at the most unexpected of moments, but he would never have risked disarming Ásgard's protector. Unless the same "wisdom" that made him do things like hang off The Tree with a spear in his side for days at a time told him to do that...

"Good Gods!" I cried, tearing my hand away from Thrud's. "What are you doing?!"

"I'm sorry, Your Grace, it's hot wax. I should have warned you."

"You should have," I barked, then stopped paying attention again.

This was not Sif's plan. Somebody came to her and suggested that it would be great revenge over Thor. That would be something Loki would come up with, but Loki's fear suggested it wasn't. At this point I could only reiterate that this couldn't have been Sif's plan. I was running in circles.

Once the wax solidified, Thrud removed it, then started picking at my cuticles with some sort of tool. I looked at her out of the corner of my eye, then bit my lip and told myself that if I had survived a rape attempt and the destruction of a city, I could survive hot wax and—

"Aw!"

"I'm sorry, Your Grace. Would you prefer that I stop?"

"Please continue," I said, defeated.

I had learned something in Jötunheim after all. The rules were different for those who had power. Yes, I could tell Thrud to stop, which she would report to Freya. I would then have to explain why I was "being ungrateful" again. Freya told me I always had a place to stay here, but she did not make an oath. Only one of us could throw the other out, same as only one was allowed to roll her eyes openly. Since I wouldn't wear that dress, my fingernails needed altering. If I refused that, perhaps my feet would prove to be flawed, or ears...

"Your other hand, Your Grace."

"Do I have to?"

"It would look strange if I only did one, Your Grace."

I had lived in the City for so long and I was so busy with my "position" in the "court" that I had only made some sort of friend two days before everything ended. If I so much as hinted to Freya that I was sad about Magni, I would never stop hearing about a special man in my life. He was special in a way she would never understand. I sniffled. I didn't believe in deaths that I hadn't witnessed myself, but it hurt.

If you could do anything, anything at all, what would you do? he'd asked. I would turn back time and find a way to change everything.

"Glimmer, Your Grace?"

"Do I have to?"

"Perhaps take a look, Your Grace?"

It wasn't Thrud's fault, I reminded myself, then perfunctorily glanced at my hand. My heart started beating faster. I lifted my hand to look closer, the way Freya looked at hers. "That's... unexpected," I finally said. My voice shook a bit. She had taken my hands away and replaced them with much nicer ones. "I don't know what to say. Thank you."

"Should I do your feet too, Your Grace?"

I immediately tensed. "Would that involve wax again?"

"Yes, Your Grace."

"Maybe not today. Sometime later. Yes. Much later."

"Her Grace Freya sent you a pair of boots," said Thrud.

I immediately bristled. "And why is that?"

"I think she wants to give you a present, Your Grace." She looked just as innocent and neutral as she sounded.

"You can have them."

"They wouldn't fit, Your Grace. Is there anything else that I could do for you?"

The memory of Magni's words poked me in the ribs again. Thrud was the daughter of Thor and Sif, a God and a Goddess. Why was she Freya's housekeeper? I examined her sweet face, looking for resentment, but if she was hiding something, she did it extremely well. I would resent me if we swapped roles.

"Tell me, Thrud, if you could do anything at all, what would you do?"

"Exactly what I am doing, Your Grace," she responded immediately. "I am very happy here."

"That will be all," I sighed, resigned.

I slept without dreams that night and when I woke up the boots stood by the door, where I left them.

I had to admit that I liked the gift. I could even imagine thanking her for it properly. Black, polished leather with just a hint of purple to it, the decoration present but minimal, fur lining... They could be my winter boots in the unlikely case I was exposed to winter again. She had never given me boots before. Imagining her joy and the piles of footwear that I would soon discover in the room made me chuckle. I liked them enough to try one on.

I yelped in pain. The boot flew across the room and hit the wall. I bent my leg and blew on my toes, examining them. They were red and itchy. I could have just as well wrapped them with stinging nettles. There were no blisters, thankfully. Back in the days when she'd forced me to try on various garments I hated, I'd spend days crying in pain as maids put ointments on my skin. Only my old clothes, the ones Freya disapproved of, never hurt me. They even grew with me as I got older. What I couldn't understand was that I detested the gowns, but I really liked those boots, I wanted them. Apparently that made no difference.

As I was lacing up the old boots, swearing under my breath, I noticed my fingernails and what I saw gave me a pause. They looked exactly like they had before Thrud had done the wax thing – raw, red skin, cuticles sticking out, bitten unevenly.

I hadn't bitten my fingernails since I was a child.

My hair was always the same length. When I tried to cut it, I woke up with the same hairstyle as always, the cut-off strands having mysteriously reappeared. Too bad it didn't wash itself instead. My fingernails, apparently, were always going to be the same as well. I couldn't wear other clothes any more than I could bathe in lava. Other than the crystal pendant, I could stand no jewellery. Once it got cold, I could put on a coat, gloves, or a cloak, as long as my normal clothes were underneath. After a bath I could wear a gown. I scratched my chin, thinking, but couldn't come up with anything more.

Freya never wore the same dress twice. She had her favourite form, like all shifters, but seemed to constantly be on the lookout for an even prettier one. Her hair, the colour of her skin and her eyes, her figure, even her height kept changing. I couldn't even put on a lovely pair of boots or have nice fingernails that I now wanted. I could only be me. Thrud's work and my suffering were for naught.

I must have been such a disappointment to Freya. She'd picked the wrong child to raise. Long ago I decided not to search for my real, human parents. What would the point be? Would it be worse if they loved me and begged that I stay, or if they hated me and called me a witch? I had told Freya I didn't want to know, and she hadn't tried to change my mind. It would have been nice, though, to be accepted exactly as I was. Even Granny Frigg kept telling me I was too thin.

I hid my hands in my lap when Thrud served a small breakfast, but she lingered, no doubt eager to see the effects of her work. With a heavy heart I reached for sliced mango and Thrud's face dropped.

"It's not my fault, please believe me," I pleaded. "They did it by themselves."

"Your Grace," she said darkly, bowed, then left me with a heaping serving of guilt. A blink later I realised Thrud probably went straight to Freya. I jumped to my feet, grabbed an apple and escaped.

It was perhaps unjust of me to think of Magni as the only friend I'd ever had. Granny Frigg would give me her hugs, as warm as her smile. She'd say I was looking too thin and "force" me to eat delicious pastries or pies. I could live with that. I strolled towards her hall, Fensalir, jumping over crystal clear streams, nearly tripping over an overexcited rabbit. A giggle escaped me, an odd, teeth-clenching giggle. Like I was trying to make myself furiously happy.

Frigg welcomed me as though I'd never left. She'd just finished making cherry pie, which she insisted I try just in case it hadn't come out so well, especially as I was looking so thin. I laughed, trying not to salivate all over the familiar kitchen, but something bothered me. It had been twelve winters since I last saw her, and Frigg was behaving as though I'd really never left. Not a thing had changed, except new recipes. I could guess the next thing she would say. Like time stood still here.

I shifted in my seat, feeling pinpricks of sweat on my skin. "Granny Frigg," I said, putting the fork down so gingerly as to make absolutely no sound. "May I ask you a question?"

"Only if you promise you'll finish your pie, dear, you look so thin. You can ask me anything, I just might not answer. Is it a personal question?"

"It's about the future..." I paused. *The prophecy*, my thoughts screamed, *tell her about the prophecy*. "Is it true that you can see it?"

I might as well have thrown a bucket of cold water at her.

Frigg sat down, wiping her hands on her apron, her face stony. She stiffly nodded towards my plate and I was afraid not to take another bite of the pie. "Why do you ask?"

"S-something happened and... if I knew... I wish I could turn back time and change it all, so if I could have seen it..."

Frigg shook her head slowly. "A very long time ago I used to look into the future for frivolous reasons. I always learned things that I didn't want to know. Once you know something bad is going to happen, you want to fix it, yet it's impossible, because it *is* the future. When I tried, I found myself causing those bad things." She was now rocking rhythmically in her chair, staring through me, clearly seeing something or somebody else. "I was punished by the Norns once, dear, for using my gift to find out how to sew pretty dresses and make boots. Afterwards I couldn't speak for a year and a day. It turned out that I needed one more lesson. I looked into the future for the last time. I wanted to see my children. There were none. Not after a winter and a summer had passed, not after a hundred, nor a thousand, as I sought in despair, until I reached the very end of everything. All I saw was death, pain, destruction, all of them inevitable."

"But Odin..."

"When Odin drank from the Mimir's well, he acquired all of the wisdom in the Universe, dear. This wisdom tells him that one day everything will end. And it will. I know what, how, when it will happen, and I would have given everything not to have found out." She shook her head and sighed. "When Odin stirs up wars, then sends his Valkyries to bring the strongest of the warriors to Valhalla before the rest are sent to Helheim, he is not doing it out of boredom, dear. He's afraid. He constantly replaces his warriors with even stronger or more agile ones, in the belief that he can postpone or change the fate of the Universe."

"Can't he?"

Frigg shook her head again. "The fate is set in stone, dear. Yours, mine, his, everyone's. He can't do anything about it. He's building up to it, and each of his deeds leads us closer to the final day when there will be no more winners or losers."

The prophecy. "I... I've got a secret," I said. My voice was little, broken.

"Please keep it. I've got enough to carry and I don't want any more. I stay away from Odin, because he only wants one thing from me. He wants to know what and when it will happen. If he knew of someone else..." Frigg paused, her stare so penetrating I felt as if it was burning holes into my face. "He *would* find a way to make that someone tell him. Odin is not allowed in here."

"But he is your h-husband."

"His hall is the largest of all," continued Frigg, as if she hadn't heard me, "mine is the smallest. I have all I need. The worst thing that can happen to me is that I will burn my pie just before someone visits. Why don't you try some cherry pie, dear? You look so thin. We all look for our place. I've found mine. Nobody's making me stay here or do what I do. I know when and how everyone I've ever loved and will love is going to die. Odin thinks of this knowledge as a weapon, but it's an unbearable weight. He doesn't understand that there is no army large and powerful enough to postpone the inevitable."

"But maybe...?"

"Dear, you said that something happened and if you'd known, you would have done things differently. Perhaps you would, contributing to the very same things happening. Our choices are not as free as we imagine, because their outcome has already been woven by the Norns, and you can't negotiate with the Norns, for they are time itself." Frigg's voice became unforgiving, dark, just like Odin's, and I shivered. "Everything. Everything would end up the same. Only now you'd be at fault."

"I've had dreams," I muttered, once I could speak again. "Premonitions. They come to pass."

Frigg's wrinkled face paled. "I don't want to know."

"I just wondered—"

"Dear, it was wonderful to have you here, but I'm afraid you must go."

"Just one more thing, Granny Frigg...!"

She seemed to soften at the word "granny". "Yes, dear."

"Do you know how and when...I will die?"

The face of a Valkyrie returned. "No," she said.

I thanked her profusely, apologised, thanked her a few more times, finally bid her a good day. I didn't get a hug.

The prophecy, which Freya had carved inside my mind, was meant for Odin. She had told me that I would die in Midgard, which I didn't think about when I was being shot at in Jötunheim. But the dead didn't stay in Midgard. Those not picked for Valhalla found themselves in Helheim, under the care of Hel. She was truly wonderful and loved her "guests" so much that once they set one foot in, they were never allowed to leave or receive visitors, not even Odin. Most, especially men, wanted to spend their afterlife in Valhalla. I once snuck into Valhalla and couldn't see myself out fast enough.

If Frigg was right and the future couldn't be altered no matter what, telling Odin the prophecy would be an act of inconceivable cruelty. It listed all the ways in which he would fail. It could also be a long list of lies, designed to pull him away from what he should actually do to avoid the real end. If Frigg was right, and I knew she was, knowing when and how I would die would cause me to do all I could to avoid it – and fail. My stomach was suddenly squeezed in a vice and the feeling had nothing to do with the cherry pie. I didn't want to know. I also now understood why Frigg never attended the Assembly.

Nevertheless, it was so hard to understand. If it didn't matter what I'd done back in Jötunheim, I could have stayed home. Thor had already met Járnsaxa. The City would just have been smaller. And Mjölnir would have to be delivered to the King by someone else who had the powers I had. Wasn't it I who made jarl Thrymr the

King, though? How would that work? I would have never met Magni, but the future, in which I had met Magni, was the real future, because I was in it...

Bugger!

Odin believed that he was contributing to the future, building it. Frigg was just baking, yet she, too, was building that future. It just had more pie in it. The future was nothing but creating the past I could look back on, on my death bed. That meant I could either work and make my life worthwhile, or spend the rest of my days taking hot baths. Odin had all the wisdom and chose the former. Frigg had all the knowledge and chose the latter. I had none of those things. *If you could do anything, but anything at all...*

When I cleared my throat Idunn raised her head and beamed with pleasure. As always, she was an explosion of colours. She was the spring rain and the sunshine, the fresh buds and the ripe fruit, the most powerful of all the Gods and Goddesses. Idunn's produce was what kept Ásgardians alive and as young or as old as they wanted. Ásgard would manage without Thor, Loki, Freya, maybe even Odin, but Auntie Idunn's dirty hands held the future of everything and everyone.

She was not named in the prophecy.

"It's been so long," Idunn said, lifting herself up with a little groan, then giving me a hug. She smelled of dewy grass at sunrise. "I missed you."

"I missed you too," I said, delighted. Someone had noticed my absence after all. "How is the garden doing?"

"Not too bad, not too bad. Have you tried my watermelons yet?"

"Water...melons? I'm not sure. Do they grow in water?"

"I'll send you one," she laughed. "To Sessrúmnir, is that right?"

"Word gets around fast," I smiled. "That's right. I already ate a pear, though... mmm... The watermelon will have to wait until the moon turns."

"There will always be more," she said and the strange feeling accompanying me since my return seemed to raise its head.

"Auntie Idunn, what do you do with all..." I gestured around. "All this?"

"What do you mean, Maya?"

"All the fruit, vegetables, everything that grows here. Isn't it too much for Ásgard?"

Idunn's laughter was like song with one false note. "Most of the grapes go into Odin's wine."

"And the rest?"

"The watermelons take a lot of space. I'm very proud of them."

"Yes, but the rest?"

"Do you know, I grew a whole new sort of walnut. I put much less power into them than I usually would, and Frigg bakes them into cake. Eating it won't cause you harm... as long as you know when to stop." The smile was still there, but steel flickered in her eyes. I was about to cross *Goddess* Idunn, rather than my auntie.

"I had cherry pie," I said, my voice slightly choked. "Way too much. I don't have space left for anything."

Idunn wiped sweat from her forehead. "Is there something else you need?" She cast a meaningful glance at her leek.

"No, I just wanted to see you. Looking forward to the watermelon. Have a wonderful day!"

"You too," said Idunn, squatting again, immediately forgetting about me. I stood still, listening to her apologising to her vegetables for the interruption. It was true, as long as she was here there would always be more, and even more than that. Since Bragi brought her from Svartálfheim, Idunn never left Ásgard. Even if every lowly servant, every horse or cow in Ásgard was being fed Idunn's apples, pears, cherries, and watermelons, there would have been too much. The dandelions made me think of Jötunheim's dead grass, the warm baths – of the chills of summer, the dry bread that was crunchy inside rather than outside, and the City of Light turning to rubble, because Thor thought with his cock and Sif was jealous.

It wasn't only Freya who saw all mortals as replaceable. Others would just phrase it differently, or, like Idunn, say nothing.

Eir, the Goddess of healing, only ever used her powers to help the Gods. Never the humans, jötnar, or elves. I found out it was a rule when I'd cried to her once, covered in blisters from another one of Freya's attempts to dress me. King Thrymr also had rules that were convenient to him alone. I questioned neither. Heimdall, Ásgard's sentinel, could see all the death and suffering in Midgard, but never did anything about it. His task was to wait endlessly for those foolish enough to try and cross the Rainbow Bridge. Crying babies could be slain right in front of him and he wouldn't even move. The roof of his hall was made of enough gold to buy half of Jötunheim, yet for all I knew Heimdall never set a foot inside. Thor... enough said. Freyr brought people ecstasy and joy and life, because he fed on them, bringing them to a point where they would die from too much pleasure.

I used to think of Ásgard as my home, but it was just a place I was allowed to be in. Nothing here was up to me. Gods remained Gods and kings remained kings precisely because they had everything and didn't have to share. If Idunn were to make all people forever young and Eir – to help with their ailments, they might begin to see themselves as equal to the Gods. They could start getting ideas...

Deep in thought, I tripped over something and strong hands caught me before I hit the ground. I let out a little surprised gasp.

"Hello," said a slender, muscular man in clothes that were way tighter than they needed to be. Loki. His hair was so long and shiny mine almost curled in embarrassment. "You need a mother, so she can tell you to watch your steps. How do you like being back? Enjoying yourself?"

Uncertain how to react, I produced a dutiful smile. He made my skin crawl, nevertheless the last time I saw him he'd saved my life. "I'm having a walk. On my own."

"A walk! Great for your health. I noticed you've been paying visits to old friends."

"Have you been following me?"

"Not at all! I just thought it would be nice to accidentally bump into you. My favourite thing about coincidences is that once you spend enough time helping them happen, they do. Why so serious, my little sorceress?"

"Maybe you could turn around," I suggested, "then bugger off, and bugger off until you can't bugger off anymore, then bugger off a bit further?"

"Your language! I am shocked! What a sharp tongue you've gotten all of a sudden! You must have learned a lot in the last years indeed, hanging around all those soldiers and whatnot."

"King Thrymr had no soldiers."

"Some men can be poets, yet still behave like soldiers when they see a woman."

I decided that I had done enough smiling for the day.

"I am not talking about myself!" he protested. "I am an intellectual, a delicate creature that would never hurt a fly. My specialties are wit, wisdom, and advice. And I happen to have some advice for you."

"Do you now," I said flatly.

"Stop being so angry, so serious about everything. Why not try and have fun for once? It's just a life, just a Universe or two. Our time will come to an end, blah blah, so what? Even we, the Gods, are mortals, just for a longer span of time, if you understand what I am saying. Your long face is not going to change anything. We are what we are, all of us. My lovely self, Thor, Odin, King Thrymr – well, that one's decomposed by now, but I know you are just wise enough to understand my elaborate metaphors." Loki grinned.

"I liked you better as Sigyn," I said.

"Aaah, Sigyn. I am courting a Sigyn right now, can you believe it? Me, in love, at my age! She is a wonderful creature; you will adore her when you meet."

I raised an eyebrow. "Don't you have enough, eh... children?"

"Never! A man has to spread his seed. The more, the merrier. If I had a thousand, I would have wanted a thousand and one."

"Thor doesn't even seem to remember his own," I said.

"Oh no, my dear, there's the sad face again. I didn't say a man has to take care of the wheat that grows from his seed, did I? Yet I would, with my sweet, sweet Sigyn. A bunch of little Lokis, running around, causing mischief..."

I shivered. "Does she know that before Angrboda died, she gave birth to a wolf, a serpent, and to Hel? Hardly a bunch of little Lokis."

"One day a woman will give me a beautiful child, whether it will be Sigyn or somebody else. There are many women in the Nine. One has to keep trying," said Loki.

I'd had enough. "Keep 'trying' somewhere far away from me. Goodbye, Loki, thank you for your sage advice... actually, I'd like to ask you a question. Why *did* you bring me back here?"

"Because I like having you where I can see you."

His mocking laughter followed me as I strode away. Once I could no longer see him, I sat on a rock and stared at a bunch of hyacinths, beautiful in their eternal bloom. Unlike Jötunheim's yellow, dead grass.

I frowned.

The hammer was back, some jötunn city had fallen, Sif clearly got away with Mjölnir's theft. So did I, even though she was a Goddess and I – Freya's foster daughter, a human that happened to have some magical powers, one who plodded around scowling at hyacinths. All I wanted back in Jötunheim was my hot tub, Frigg's pie, Idunn's fruit. My wishes had come true. I couldn't change the past, I never could, Frigg made it more than clear. Why wasn't I "having fun for once"? What *was* my problem?

If you could do anything at all... Thor murdered, Frigg baked, Idunn gardened, Bragi composed his sagas. I found Freyr repulsive, but Freya spent each summer in his arms, delirious with happiness. There had to be something that would make me happy too.

Instead of being suspicious and questioning why Freya invited me to stay in Sessrúmnir, I should just appreciate it.

My teeth clenched. My happiness would not be found in thoughts about Freya. Now, of course, it was as if I'd uncorked a jar filled with nothing else. The childhood she had given me was not something easily forgotten; she owed me a *lot* for that alone. She kept trying to pay her debts towards me in gowns, boots, necklaces, things to put on your ears. Nothing would make her happier than making me who she felt I should be, someone with long, sparkly fingernails wrapped around the arm of a nice man or a woman. She'd have what she wanted and she could argue that she owed me nothing more.

Oh, but she did, a little voice inside me whispered. *Much, much more.*

For...a reason. I pushed that thought away, but failed to return to my ruminations.

What could I ask of the Goddess of love and war, though? I wanted nothing to do with war, love, or men like Loki, who "had to keep trying". Far away from me, I'd answered. It made him laugh. Loki didn't listen to pleas or respect wishes. Just like King Thrymr, or Odin, or Thor. Men who courted a woman for a shorter or longer time, depending on their position. If the results didn't come quickly enough, eventually they just took what they wanted. Come to think of it, I couldn't only blame men, because Freya was the same. I shivered as the echo of Loki's last words, "I like having you where I can see you" returned. Now Freya also had me where she could see me. But in Loki's words hid more than one meaning.

It was as if lightning struck me. I jumped to my feet, shifted and soared towards Sessrúmnir, hurrying as if the idea was a bee chasing me. I knew what I wanted and I wanted it now.

CHAPTER 4

MAGNI

"...CAN'T SEE IN THE DARK," I heard. "And I pulled a muscle."

"Don't make me laugh..."

It was dark in the dream. Yes. In the dream, something seemed to be holding me. The hot, dull ache radiating from my shoulder felt real. Nightmare. The dream stopped in a white flash of pain when I tried to move and I had to stop existing for a bit before the voices came back.

"Hillevi?"

Silence.

"It's up to you."

The pain became fuzzy, as if it were spreading, turning into heat. It was still pitch black. I remembered I'd yelled at the sky and lightning struck me. It wasn't a dream. I could now tell that I was sitting with my back against a tree, my hands tied behind it, disembodied voices saying things I didn't understand. The hot pressure in my arm made me shudder and I nearly passed out again, or maybe I had.

"...two days," I heard. It was a woman's voice. "It's not my fault."

"Do you think he was right?" A man.

She snorted. "When I shot him he was crying his eyes out. If he's Thor, I'm a Valkyrie."

"You'd eat a Valkyrie for breakfast..."

The voices seemed to arrive from different directions. I could smell wood smoke but couldn't see a fire. I was blind. She shot me? *Fair game.* My body shook violently again, from the cold and the fear and the pain, my tongue got caught between my teeth, and I yelped.

A hissing sound, an intake of breath between the teeth.

"Two days," said a man's voice. "Two. Days. Really?"

I smacked my mouth. Those were my lips? Dust, my tongue stiff, swollen. Dry. I moved my wrists behind my back, trying to free myself from the bonds. The pain was not so bad anymore, still a flash of light blinded me. In a different way. I saw things now. People. I was blindfolded, the woman tore a blindfold off. She seemed angry. She also kept moving in front of my eyes, like everything else. I kept blinking, but it wouldn't stop. Exhausting. My eyes kept closing.

"How are you awake?" she asked sharply. "I know what I shot you with."

I tried to shrug. More dull pain washed over me. Did she want me to apologise?

"Maybe you don't," said someone I couldn't see.

She disappeared and something blocked my view. A face.

"Who are you?" the man asked softly. A hand patted my cheek. All I could see now were eyes, dark, brown. Couldn't he see my mouth was made of sand? I couldn't answer. Dizzy again. Cold.

"Wine," said the woman. A mug touched my lips. I nearly choked when the first sip made it through. The wine was hot and smelled sharply of alcohol and spices. Like standing by the fire, only from the inside. I could almost feel my bones unfreezing, as if my blood had been replaced by heat. The slab that was my tongue started to move reluctantly again. I didn't know wine could do that.

"More," I groaned when they took the mug away.

Someone laughed. "Likes his wine, this one."

I could now see better. Still, everything remained confusing. I saw a lot of legs and didn't know which ones belonged to who. There was a fire burning and I was too far and seeing it made me feel cold. A shiver sent another jolt of pain through my shoulder, radiating through my chest and back.

"Who are you?" asked that other man's voice and this time I saw his entire face no longer moving in circles. His hand touched my cheek, his thumb sliding over my beard just once, then he took his hand away, a careless caress.

I tried to swallow, but my mouth was dry again.

The eyebrows were thick, irregular, black, his skin a light shade of birchwood. One of his eyes was larger than the other. His nose seemed to lean to one side, as if it had been broken with a punch and healed skewed. His chin was similar to Thjálfi's, as both of them were trying to grow a beard and failing. His lips... I... I had never seen... It felt as if someone had thrown the hot wine in my face.

I returned to his eyes. Deep. Brown. Huge. There was not much in the way of eyelashes, possibly because the slightly smaller eye was partly obscured by something like a fold of extra skin that did not remain where it was supposed to. The larger eye looked concerned, sad almost. The other one wasn't blind, just empty; free from any emotion. A man of two halves.

I had never seen a man's face so close, or anybody's, perhaps not even Mother's.

"I'll take him to the cave," he said before disappearing. For a blink I thought I'd only see legs again, but now I could also turn my head. A very fat, pink-skinned man smirked at me before returning to cutting something and throwing it into a black iron pot. Food, they had food. My stomach almost cried in happiness.

"He's bleeding." The woman.

With no warning, legs approached me and I felt a hand squeeze my wounded shoulder. It hurt, but just a bit, the way a bruise would. "If anybody here is bleeding," the man said with a hint of laughter, "it's you."

The woman answered with an insult, followed by someone else's unpleasant, creaky laughter. I'd never been shot before and didn't like it, but it wasn't so bad.

My thoughts seemed to drag slowly and when someone's seemingly disembodied face appeared next to me again I winced in shock. I'd seen him before, my clouded mind said, then remembered it was just a blink ago. "I'm going to free your wrists now," he said. "My friend Hillevi is standing in front of you with a bow, aiming for the heart. She'll let loose if you try something stupid. Be a good boy."

I shook my head, then nodded, unsure. When the rope fell off my wrists I sighed in relief. The shoulder had almost stopped hurting by now. I tried to reach with my other hand to touch it, but I couldn't find it, instead toppling to the side with a surprised grunt.

"I told you I know what I shot him with, Herjólf," said Hillevi. "He's not normal."

I couldn't lift myself up and I felt hands helping me. A mug appeared again, this time water, delicious, brutally cold. Freshly melted snow.

"Pig," asked the man. "When will you be ready with the food?"

"I barely started." The fat man.

"Food," I groaned.

"We'll take a hot bath," said the man with the brown eyes. Herjólf. "You'll tell me a bit about yourself, then we'll come back and eat." I was still thinking about the answer when I realised it wasn't a question. A hot bath sounded good.

A wiry man with an unpleasant, grey face appeared. When he noticed I was looking at him he spat on the ground and turned away, replaced with an extended hand. I tried to grab it, missing at first, nearly pulling him down with me – Herjólf again – then standing up. I leaned against the tree, breathing heavily, trying to take in the view that kept moving, expanding, shrinking. Seeing more than one or two things at the same time tired me. It wasn't a hideaway like mine, just a small clearing, some space among the trees. A fire. Herjólf, the man called Pig, Hillevi, the thin man. Hillevi's face appeared in front of me, even though I didn't see her approaching. She punched me in the wounded shoulder. I hissed. Didn't she know I got shot?

"If Thor now takes jobs in shitholes like Jomsborg, then cries when he gets outlawed, I'll have to find a different faith," she said coldly. "What are you?"

"I am not Thor."

"Can you walk?" asked Herjólf.

I couldn't decide whether to shake my head or nod. I tried to stand on my own and now it worked, although it still felt as if the ground was slowly rocking left, then right.

"I'm not helping," said the thin man. His voice reminded me of the sound my chisel made when I was sharpening it with a piece of rock. "He's too heavy for me. Pig can carry him."

"Nobody's going to carry him," said Herjólf. "Put your arm around my shoulders, not Thor, I'll help you. Lean against the trees. It's near."

"Unbelievable," muttered Hillevi, shaking her head.

He was much smaller than me. The top of his head reached my chin. I had problems catching my breath and we had to stop every few steps. My strength and focus were returning slowly, as if they were dripping back in.

"What was that place?" I asked.

"A camp," muttered Herjólf, then let out a grunt when I leaned over him a bit heavier than I intended. The dizziness returned.

"I need to sit—"

The woods opened to a build-up of rocks forming a cave. It looked like something a troll would have built and smelled like the troll was cooking a dish of rotten eggs inside. Steam came out of the entrance. A few more rocks, flatter, lay around. I sat on one and stared mindlessly. Things finally stopped moving.

"Take your clothes off," said Herjólf. He removed his boots.

Out of the many things that immediately flew through my mind only "why?" came out.

"You're going to take a hot bath. I assume you'd prefer not to be dressed for that?"

His cloak landed on the ground. The vest, dark brown, worn-out leather adorned with chainmail rings, tied on the sides – he grunted as he untied it, bending uncomfortably, casting glances at me. Tall boots. Loose leather breeches, a warm, lighter shade of brown. Black, maybe dark blue tunic with white stitches. I couldn't stop staring. There was nothing but Herjólf, everything else one blur, as if the stinking steam replaced the air. He was really taking his clothes off. All of them. He was going to be naked. In front of me.

"Do you need help?"

"I'm... almost ready," I said weakly.

I couldn't take my clothes off in front of him, just couldn't, I would be naked and he would...see me. I leaned back a bit too much and had to rest on my hands not to fall. Someone grabbed at my foot and I gasped. Herjólf. He removed my shoes, then the footwraps. I turned into stone. His cold hand wrapped around my foot for a moment and another shiver went through my whole body and it was not because of the cold.

"Stand up."

He couldn't see it, he would... what... what if he had already noticed?

"I'm cold. Hurry up."

With shaking hands I loosened my belt, as slowly as I could, trying to do so in such a way as to cover my crotch. When my trousers dropped, my long tunic covered... I had to take the tunic off, too, but I couldn't. My shoulder was stiff, the dull ache back. I had to bend over, so he could pull the garment off me, and now there was nothing I could hide behind.

I had never felt more embarrassed. I prayed that that Herjólf wouldn't notice my body betraying me. When he slowly, deliberately looked me up and down I thought I would die, but I didn't. "Inside this cave is a small hot tub," he said. "Three people fit inside, or four if they like each other very much. With your size, though? I hope both of us can even squeeze in." Or maybe he said something else. But he didn't laugh at me or say anything nasty or even cringe.

I had to lower my head in order to enter the narrow cave. Sharp rocks led towards steaming, bubbling water that smelled of rotten eggs. The tub was more of a hole in the ground, small, but deep. The rocks under my feet were slippery from the moss. The hot water that bubbled between my toes tickled. I was just tall enough for my head to stick out. Herjólf kept his arm on the rim to keep himself afloat, blocking my way out, not that I dared to move.

"What's your name?" he asked.

"Magni," I said, just because I didn't have enough space in my mind for thinking about anything other than his lips and his eyes and how I never really understood something until right now.

"Magni," repeated Herjólf, as if tasting the word. "Who are you, Magni?"

"A b-blacksmith." He was naked and looking straight into my eyes and I was too, unable to move without touching him and I couldn't remember...words.

"I see. Where do you come from?"

"Jötunheim."

"I've always wondered how an ice giant would feel in a hot tub," mused Herjólf. Dizzy, I couldn't have answered, from all the blood rushing both up and down, from feelings I couldn't name and thoughts that sprinted past me before I could think them. He looked down. "You're definitely a giant," he murmured. The tub became even hotter.

I wanted to run away and I also wanted to stay and I wished I could ask what was happening and that he would answer. All I knew was that I had never felt more alive. Everything was sharp, the smell, the way his hair shone, that broken nose and the shape of his lips I could barely see. The urge to touch those lips, just to see if they were as soft as I thought they probably were, was unbearable and its power over me was scary. If his arm slipped off the rim he would probably need to wrap the other one around me just for a blink. Or maybe two. Lady Freya was the Goddess of love and maybe she could help me if I knew what to ask for.

"How does a jötunn find his way to a shithole like Jomsborg?"

"I don't... don't remember. Someone brought me here."

"In a chariot pulled by goats, I bet," smirked Herjólf.

I forgot all words.

"Why and how did your shoulder heal so fast? I pulled an arrow out of it and I watched the wound close by itself. Now it just looks like an old scar." His hand extended to touch my shoulder. His thumb moved up and down just a bit. Like a caress. "Does it still hurt?"

I couldn't tell. My body and my mind seemed disconnected from each other. He took his hand away and its absence felt like a gust of cold wind. I winced so hard that I felt one of the rocks forming the tub cut through the skin on my back.

"Do all ice giants heal so fast? No wonder you're so dangerous."

"We're not dangerous! Humans are dangerous. You kill each other for Odin's pleasure."

Herjólf chuckled. "We do. How did you come here from Jötunheim?"

"I..." I began, and then felt something – I did – why, how – his hand grabbed – moved and I—

"Yes," said Herjólf politely, "continue."

This was not happening, things like that just didn't– his hand was there, its grip firm, firmer...

"Aaahhh! Stop! No! Stop...!"

His grip lightened. "You've got a choice. Either I will do this..."

"Aaahh...!"

"Or this. Mmm. How did you come here from Jötunheim?"

It was too much. I didn't want him to do it. Not this. It– it was too— *Oh, Lady Freya,* I prayed desperately, *I don't know what is going on, but I don't want it to be going on, but please, don't stop it from happening, just less—* "I was brought here," I said, I probably should be saying something else, but it was too hard to remember how to say things, "to the shore near... oh..."

"Yes, I'm listening." His hand moved back and forth just a bit.

"J-j-jomsborg. I am an outlaw now."

"Brought here how and by whom?"

"Please...!" I cried. "Don't... don't do this... you're... I can't...!"

"Oh," said Herjólf. One of his eyebrows wandered up. "I am sorry. I thought you would find this relaxing."

"Please," I gasped when he took his hand away. I was cold and hot, on the verge of fainting and more conscious than ever before, torn – I never– wanting to be kissed, but also to find out what else there was even though it felt like too much and I didn't even know how to think about how I was feeling. Nobody had ever – did other men – I thought I was – my heart was beating so hard that by now it should have broken free from my ribcage. "I don't understand," I panted. "What... why are you doing...?"

Half of Herjólf's face seemed to smile a bit more than the other half. "I'm trying to make you warm, to learn something about you. Tell me more about your shoulder." He kissed the wound. With his lips. My shoulder. His hand was still wrapped around my – it sometimes hurt and sometimes it did something I did not know how to name, but then he took it away and waited.

Stop. No, don't stop. Do that thing. Please. But not like that. Like the other way.

What was he waiting for? Ah. He asked me a question. "I heal fast," I managed.

"Are you warm?" A shiver when his lips touched my ear, a whisper nearly drowned out by the incessant bubbling of the water.

"Y-yes."

"Do you feel safe?"

I didn't know. Some of me did and some didn't and some wanted to run away and some just wanted him to kiss my shoulder again and he was so close to me and *naked*.

"You shouldn't," said Herjólf lightly. "It's the most dangerous thing that we could be doing. We are in a small cave. There is no other entrance or exit other than the one behind me. You can't reach it, I can't see it. We are naked, our clothes outside. If someone comes in here right now, we won't even notice when we die."

"Why are we here then...?"

"Because it's cold outside, unless the jarl decides to set the forest ablaze to get rid of us." I almost choked on my own breath and he laughed. "Outlaws don't die in their beds. Because we don't own any. That's why we don't fuck in beds either, Magni, son of Thor."

My mouth opened, but no sound came out. Just the storm of thoughts. Did he– how – he wrapped his arms around my neck and his lips met mine.

I had seen people kiss. I'd seen my f– Thor and my mother whether I wanted to or not before I'd gone to live with Gunnar at the forge. I'd walked into various places and then regretted having done so. I didn't know what I was supposed to do, allowed to do. I felt my body pushing away from his, even though I also wanted him closer. I was not ready. Maybe nobody was ever ready.

"So, this is how Gods kiss," whispered Herjólf and then his teeth tightened on my lower lip a bit harder and longer than I would have liked. I didn't know if I could groan in protest, but it didn't matter, because he withdrew and asked me something again. "Do you understand why you were outlawed, Magni, son of Thor?"

I wanted to answer with words, but I just shook my head, testing the lip he bit with my tongue. I didn't understand anything that happened since yesterday morning.

"You were a threat. People believed you to be your father, some of them at least, like Wojciech. He's Ludo's uncle."

"Ludo?"

"The crazy one." Herjólf chuckled. "Okay, the craziest. The thin bugger. The jarl knew you were plotting against him…"

"I wasn't!" My protest echoed inside the cave.

"Sshh. It doesn't matter. What chance would a little coward of a jarl have if a God wanted to take his seat? It never occurred to him that you didn't need his seat. Mieszko is a coward," Herjólf repeated, "who fears everything and everyone. He got rid of you at night, when others couldn't see."

That was just last night, I thought, shocked. *Yesterday I was buying food…* My stomach growled excitedly and if I blushed any more than that, blood would erupt through the skin on my face. "He should fear his daughter," I mumbled.

Herjólf laughed, then bit my ear. Light touch of his lips, then teeth that tightened until there was pain. He probably didn't know, he couldn't know, I'd have to tell him, but then he might stop altogether. It wasn't so bad, I told myself. "Mieszko knew that it would have been a bad thing for some jarl to kill a God, especially one that's loved across Midgard. I knew you were not Thor, I met your father once, a long time ago. I guess the Jomsborg vermin hadn't."

"What," I mumbled. He was saying…words.

Herjólf tilted his head. "What did you seek in a shithole like Jomsborg? Why would you let a worm like Mieszko treat you that way?"

I just shook my head helplessly.

"Why didn't you tell them who you were? They would lick the dust off your shoes. Why are you wearing shoes that are about to fall apart? And why are you here in this cave with me, Magni, son of Thor?"

"Don't call me that," I groaned. His hand rubbed against my nipple and I didn't know that my nipples could feel like that.

"No," nodded Herjólf. "The less people know, the better. One day bards will sing about you and me," he said and it felt as if a jolt of energy went through me when his hand wrapped around my... me again. *About you and me.* "I need help, if you were willing to help me, that is. You see, once you're outlawed, you can only regain your rights if they are restored either by the one who outlawed you, or the king. I was outlawed by my brothers, who also happen to be kings." His eyes changed and his grip tightened. I barely stifled a scream. "They have the coin, the army, horses, weapons. I have you, son of Thor. Would you be willing to help me?"

"Stop," I groaned. I wanted to cry. It *hurt*. I didn't want it, but he did and I wanted him and I did want the things that didn't hurt and how was supposed to tell him, to explain to him when I didn't even know what all this was *called* and then he started doing something else to me and my body was not – it felt like – I was going to –

"Will you help me?" he murmured, suddenly stopping.

"Yes," I cried, "please don't... yes...!" – and then I think I passed out or became blind or maybe the Nine just ended for a moment and I couldn't imagine that there used to be a time in my life once when I felt cold.

Herjólf was openly laughing when I came back to. "Hillevi will never let you forget that you're a screamer," he taunted. "My turn."

I was too tired to pretend. "I...don't know what to do."

He withdrew as if I were a rotting carcass. "Don't tell me this is your first time." He sounded annoyed.

It was as if I got shot again, this time in my face. I was trying not to cry inside a cave that smelled of rotten eggs, having disappointed the first person who had ever... done... I was so ashamed. *I'm sorry,* I wanted to cry, *yes, it was my first, but I will learn, I promise, just tell me what I should do and I will.*

"Don't worry, it's not your fault," said Herjólf. I clung to the sound of his voice, no longer annoyed, but thoughtful. "I knew you weren't a real man yet, even if you look like one. No harm done. What are you then? Eight?"

"No!"

He sniggered.

I was eight when mother sent me to Gunnar to learn black-smithing. Eight was a hand and a three. I stayed with Gunnar for... that was the winter after Thor massacred Trondheim, but I couldn't remember how long ago that was... so I was at least two hands old and then a bit more. With my hand under water I tried to count my fingers again.

"Three hands," I blurted out.

"Hands?"

"M-maybe one less."

"One hand less? What are you talking about?"

This was even more shameful than it being my first time. "One h-hand is one, two, three, four, five. Then two hands is five and five. Three hands are five and five and—"

"Ah, I understand. Fourteen, then?"

I couldn't tell from his voice whether that was good or bad. I just didn't want him to laugh at me again. Thoughts scrambled inside my mind. He said he thought I was eight, he must have been joking, because one hand and three was very little, but I did have a beard when I was eight and I knew that with my beard and body he couldn't guess, nobody could, even if he said he did and I was not a real man, it was my fault for not telling him, but I didn't know that I should...

"Sometimes," he whispered into my ear, as my thoughts wouldn't slow down even for a blink, "you can't afford to wait for someone to make up their mind. Sometimes you need to help them make up their mind faster. Should I teach you a few more things? Yes or no?"

I don't know, I wanted to cry, *what other things, please, can we just kiss, but don't hurt me, yes – no – maybe – later – can I think –* but he just said I had to make up my mind – did humans just *do* things, how did they know without even asking...?

"I'll take that as a yes," Herjólf murmured.

Afterwards I tried many times to remember what happened. It was like I kept falling asleep and waking up, perhaps because of Hillevi's poison? There was Herjólf telling me I was beautiful, his lips and tongue making me feel things that I didn't know were possible to feel, then his teeth pulling me back into reality, but before I had a chance to protest he was already doing something else and it *hurt* and he covered my mouth with his hand when I cried... I– I think I was crying, but I couldn't, I didn't... he told me to – I, no, I didn't want, not this, *no*, I decided now but he said it was his turn and he was *teaching* me and it wasn't his fault that it was hurting me because I didn't say, it seemed like there were two of me and one stood somewhere and just watched as a smaller, darker man did *things* to a big, clumsy, red-headed one who looked up at some point and my eyes met my eyes right before Herjólf let out a triumphant roar before sinking his teeth deep into the shoulder that he tore an arrow out of not so long ago and then there was nothing only Herjólf and me and the stink of the eggs and the pain and maybe he'd see me as a real man now.

Every tiniest bit of my skin *felt*. As if I was covered in one thick callous right until now and he'd just torn it off. There was blood where the rocks had cut into my skin, and in some other places. Herjólf gave me a peck on the cheek, like humans in Jomsborg did.

"Why are you being so nice to me?" I asked quietly.

Herjólf snorted. "Nice? You think? I wanted something, you wanted something, we both got it. It's called bartering."

Lightning struck my mind, my heart, my body, everything all at once.

"Ginger," he said, his fingers pinching the skin on my sore shoulder in brutal contrast with his soft voice. "Don't get attached."

Before I could think of something to say, anything, I saw Herjólf's naked buttocks for a moment before he stepped out and left me alone. I touched the same spot he just caressed. His teeth had left indentations, marking me. It was too dark to tell whether there was blood. I shouldn't have said he was nice, that was wrong, what should I have said?

My body was so tired and it hurt, but my mind hurt more.

"Ginger," I heard, and jerked my head up. He would tell me now that I failed. I opened my mouth to say I was sorry, but Herjólf hadn't finished. "Let's keep it all a secret, hmm? Not just your name, everything. Your age. Ludo would laugh at you. He's..." Herjólf paused. "Unusual. You'll see very soon."

"Mhm." *As long as you don't laugh at me. Please.*

"Second, get that big ass out of here. I don't know about you, but I'm hungry." He disappeared again.

All the many thoughts and voices screaming at me turned into one mess of noise, until one word emerged and overpowered the rest. *Bartering.*

I crawled out of the cave and only managed to produce a surprised grunt when something landed on my back, flattening me against the rocks, tearing skin off my knees and palms. My jaw hit the ground and a blink later a hand grabbed my hair, pulling my head up, a sharp knife pressing against my throat-apple hard enough for me to feel the skin give way.

"What...!"

Herjólf let go of my hair, but didn't take the knife away, and when my head inadvertently dropped, I nearly slit my own throat. "Never turn your back on someone you don't know well," he grunted. I'd made him angry. "Watch those you think you know, too. Sleep with one eye open. Your name is Ginger and you're nothing but a jötunn blacksmith, an ice giant, until I say otherwise." His hand grabbed my hair again, pulling my head up. The knife disappeared, but now Herjólf slammed my forehead against the rocks. "Trust no one, not even me. Especially not me. And, for Odin's sake, *never* get attached to an outlaw."

I could tell I was bleeding, my forehead, my chest, my shoulder, my throat, I didn't even know what. *Bartering.* Off my back now, squatting, he watched me, the twilight casting shadows on his two faces. The heat inside me was dissolving fast, snow falling on my naked body. *Naked. Bartering.*

"When we voted whether to keep you alive, the split was two-two, but my vote is more important than that of the others. Keep that in mind. Tie my vest for me, please." His voice was soft, kind, firm again, same as when he first asked me who I was. He saved me, I now understood, that meant he had the right to... like the King. It also meant two out of the other three wanted me dead and I didn't know which two.

I knew I would never fall asleep again, and I had only closed my eyes for a moment before my own chattering teeth woke me up and it was morning, cold and wet. Pig – the fat cook – was trying to light a fire and, as amusing as it was to watch, I took over because I was cold and hungry.

"Nothing," sighed Hillevi. She appeared behind my back as quietly as if she were a vision and I nearly fell face down into the fire. "Not even a rabbit. Unless Herjólf brings something, it's going to be porridge."

I liked porridge and said so, which caused the others to nearly collapse in laughter.

"This porridge is more of a morning surprise," she explained. "Hot water with leftovers that haven't spoiled yet."

"So today..."

"It's better not to ask," said Herjólf, appearing from among the trees. "Nothing. Porridge it is."

Porridge, I thought, my stomach perking up in excitement. Hot. I tried to catch his gaze, but Herjólf was already whispering with Hillevi, neither of them acknowledging me.

At night they slept in pairs – for warmth, Hillevi explained. Herjólf never even looked my way, just settled with Hillevi, cutting Ludo's lewd suggestions short. The ice giant – me – was left to fend for himself. I didn't understand, I couldn't, how could someone just, just kiss and do those other things and then say "bartering" and not even... In the morning, I told myself, maybe we would go somewhere and he would... he didn't want others to know. He would tell me more and explain how I should do things right, so he wouldn't be upset.

"This," I ensured, choking slightly, "is porridge?"

"For today," said Pig.

"Smells like day-old blood that he stuck in a pot and cooked," said Ludo.

I swallowed, looking at the substance I thought was pudding, trying to breathe through my mouth.

"That's because it is," he said, cheerfully. "I'll eat yours too if you don't want it."

I couldn't hand him my portion quickly enough.

"You're stupid," Ludo said, but not before he'd finished. "What do you think blood sausage is made of?"

"I'm not hungry," I muttered. I kept waiting for someone to laugh and say it was a joke. None of them did.

"Tomorrow's porridge will be today's porridge with more water, Ginger."

"Shut up, Ludo," said Herjólf. "Go and chop some wood."

"I'm making friends, your royal highness. Ginger? Want to be friends? You'll need friends now, so say yes. Did Herjólf tell you everything about us yet? I hope not, the dunderhead badmouths me all the time."

"He never shuts up," explained Herjólf to no one in particular. He picked up an axe and a stone, then started sharpening the axe. It was a good axe and he was good at what he was doing.

"I'm a fucking delight," Ludo informed me. "The nicest man you'll ever meet. Not an evil bone in my body."

Hillevi snorted.

"Wojciech thinks you're Thor, but I told him not to be daft. Thor wouldn't let some pissmouth of a jarl throw him out for sleeping with girls. Especially if they're actually boys." Ludo paused, looking as thoughtful as someone with his face could. "Or both? I've always been curious what the difference is."

"Then sit on a stick," said Hillevi. "One day someone will finally shut you up by cutting off your cock and stuffing it down your throat.

I'm not saying it will be me, but I'm not saying it won't be me either."

Sleeping with girls who are boys? Would she really cut off his cock?

"I'm hungry. We're hungry. Let's go to the farm," said Ludo. "Look at him. He needs *porridge*. Let's do the farm."

"Not on the first day," said Hillevi. "He needs a bit of rest."

"Last chance for porridge," announced Pig. I ground my teeth and took a half-full bowl, one that Ludo had licked clean a moment earlier. I closed my eyes and told myself it was just some weird pudding. A traditional human dish.

Human. No. Please. Help me, Lady Freya, stop this.

"Do you remember what I did on my first day?" asked Ludo.

"Pissed yourself?"

"That was afterwards and I was drunk! You a good fighter, Ginger?"

"Um... I don't fight." The words didn't want to pass through my throat. The taste wasn't even so bad, which made it worse. "I'm just a blacks—"

Pig took one glance at me and passed me a mug filled with water. Somewhere on the floor of the smithy I left behind sat a sack of food.

"Not anymore," Ludo said cheerfully. "You have no work, no place to stay, no bed to sleep in. You're one of us now. Want to wrestle?"

The screech of stone against the edge of the axe stopped. Herjólf's gaze drilled into me. So did Hillevi's and Pig's. There was an answer that was expected of me and I didn't know it. The human way. "I'm not really in the mood."

"But you want to wrestle, Ginger, you do."

"No, really—"

A blade flashed in Ludo's hand and in one swift motion he somehow moved from sitting cross-legged to standing over me. I gasped, trying to crawl backwards. "You'll fucking wrestle me whether you want to or not," growled Ludo, then licked his lips, still stained with the – food – and I almost threw up all over myself. "Put up a good fight, or this bad boy will land between your ribs. Or under your ribs?"

"No," I squealed. Why were the others not saying anything, not doing anything?

"Yeehaa! Stand up, coward, we're just having fun, aye? Don't you fucking dare spoil my fun!"

He was insane. Herjólf said it. An insane man was attacking me. "Please," I cried, "someone help!"

"You've got a hammer," observed Hillevi, yawning.

I stood in place, slow, heavy. My body was hurting, both nauseous and hungry. I could barely turn my head fast enough to keep up with Ludo, who kept jumping, moving, his legs bent, arms stretched, eyes burning, teeth bare. The light flickered on the surface of the knife. He let out a high-pitched *hee-heee!* and I almost wet myself.

"I don't want to hurt you," I said, more of a plea than a threat.

"We need more blood," said Ludo. "We're running out of porridge. Yours or mine, doesn't matter. Move! Three, two..."

He jumped towards me before reaching "one". I wasn't ready. His waist was probably thinner than my arm, his legs like twigs, yet he still managed to throw me to the ground. I hardly registered what had just happened when Ludo's knees landed on my chest, pushing out a surprised gasp, and he punched me in the jaw. Hard. *Fresh blood tastes better*, a ridiculous thought arrived along with the taste of warmth, iron, and salt.

"Ooooo," said Ludo, turning the knife in his hand in front of my eyes. "Won't you look at it, Ginger. I've got a—"

My hand jumped to grab his wrist. He guessed, I didn't know how, his hand shot away, the knife out of my reach. I heard the bone break, white lightning, red fire, forcing a croak out of my throat. He slammed his head right into my nose. *We need more blood*, he said, they just sat and watched. Herjólf was done with the bartering.

I wasn't.

I grabbed Ludo, rolled to be on top, let my weight rest upon him, grabbing his wrists and pinning them to the ground. His legs were sticking sideways, kicking the air. Someone chuckled. A drop of blood appeared on Ludo's face, one more, another. Mine.

"Let me go," he growled. I tightened my grip on his wrist and the knife finally fell from between his fingers. "Don't break my hand!" he cried. "Get off me! You win! You win!"

"Choke him," said Herjólf. "He likes it."

"Sick fuck! Let go, Ginger! It's over, you win!"

I couldn't stifle a sigh of relief. I'd passed their sick test.

I was already on my feet, extending my hand to help him, when Ludo's hand wrapped itself around the handle of the knife and he jumped to his feet – how – he was just lying down and now he was dancing around me again. As if he'd propped himself up with his shoulder blades. I didn't think. Ludo's body flew sideways, the knife falling on a rock with a loud *clang*. I picked it up, breathing heavily, then spat out some more blood. My nose felt like a giant hot potato stuck in the middle of my face. I was glad I couldn't see it. I looked at my hand that had slapped the side of his head and it felt as if someone else had done it.

"He lied to me," I complained to no one in particular. Pig let out a brief cackle. The insane man tried to kill me in front of them all and they just *watched* and did nothing.

"Someone finally shut him up," said Hillevi, nodding with approval. "You move like a sleeping bear and you make more noise than an avalanche, but you're strong. Why didn't you use your hammer?"

"It's a forging hammer," I mumbled.

"Ginger, you don't forge anymore, get used to it. Now it's a killing hammer."

"Don't kill me," mumbled Ludo. "By Odin, that's the worst headache..."

Pig snorted. "You say that every time you're hungover."

"Keep the knife," said Herjólf. "If Ludo's stupid enough to lose it, he can get himself another one."

I kept on waiting for someone to laugh, explain that all this was some sort of play, which was over now, and I could go back to the forge. Niedomira was just testing me, so was the jarl, Ludo was just... the "porridge" was... *bartering* was real. My nose seemed to pulsate with heat.

Herjólf wrapped a dirty cloth around Ludo's head, securing it with some sort of a pin. They were both laughing. Hillevi exchanged a few words with Pig, then sat next to me.

"How is your nose?" she asked.

"Hurts."

"It's not bleeding anymore."

I shrugged.

"Can I touch it?" She didn't wait, just gently took the tip of my nose between two fingers, then moved it left and right.

"That hurts," I said.

"Yeaaaaaah," she answered. "I bet it does. How's your shoulder? Want me to look at it?"

I blushed. I couldn't tell whether Herjólf's bite marks were still there. "It's fine."

Hillevi and Ludo swapped places. She was whispering with Herjólf and Ludo sat next to me, grinning.

"I like you, Ginger. We're going to be best of friends, eh?"

Don't touch me. Don't talk to me. Just don't. "Mhm."

"I'm finished with your axe," Herjólf announced.

"Thanks, Royal Highness."

"You're welcome," said Herjólf; then he did something strange, pulling a small, short dagger from his tall boot and examining the sharpness of the blade. I had just been staring at his boots yesterday – *bartering* – and I would have sworn I hadn't seen anything... Sun briefly peeked out from between the clouds, reflecting on the dagger, so shiny that the reflection blinded both me and Ludo, who swore aloud.

"Why do you even need those, Your Royal Highness?"

"Because they're pretty and I like pretty things," said Herjólf, not lifting his head. Screeching of metal against stone commenced.

I hated that I always blushed so easily.

"Pig's too fat to fight," said Ludo. "He can cook, though. You'll love his rat stew. Hillevi has her little bow, like a good girl that she is. You and I, Ginger? We fight like men. Your fucking slap's like a horse's kick," he sniggered. "Give me my knife, hmm? You can have the axe. Never liked it anyway."

"I'm not giving you that knife."

"But I like it!" Ludo protested. "I can look them in the eyes right before I go all in."

"I don't want your axe." All in. *All in.*

"Sword?"

"No."

"You should fight for Thor. You look alike and he's also a black-smith. Everyone fights for Odin, except Herjólf, he only worships himself. I'm Loki's." He cackled again. "If you scream 'Thooor' and wave that hammer everyone will shit themselves. Aye, scream at me!"

I moved away from him.

"Ai, Ginger! AAAHHH!!!!"

I nearly jumped out of my skin. "What's wrong with you!?"

"Me? I'm living my best life! Surrounded by friends, fighting the foes of the common folk, and by common folk I mean me. I'll take you to a very special place."

"The farm?" asked Pig.

"Where else? The food, the coin, blankets. Warm, nice blankets."

"Like you're going to even look at the blankets," said Hillevi, appearing soundlessly again and causing me to yelp. "Under, maybe. If there were any animals in this forest, you scared them off, and if there are any people nearby... aye, same."

"But, Hillevi! It's good for him. He can't fuck up at that farm."

"What is this farm about?" I asked, but nobody seemed to notice.

"Take him wherever you like, so long as you come back with food," muttered Hillevi. "Not today. Tomorrow. Ginger, what do you want, a halberd to carry with you?"

"Nothing! I don't want to kill anybody! I just want to go back to work!"

"Ginger," said Pig. "Do you like eating?"

"Eh, yes?"

"And being alive?"

I still tasted blood. Hopefully only my own. I didn't answer.

"Where do you think we get food, clothes, weapons from?"

The market.

"Adapt or die," he said. "So, you're a lover, not a fighter. No one cares. Wait 'til your innards start drying around your spine."

"Ludo," said Hillevi, "Herjólf. Let's go watch the road."

"I've got a headache," Ludo whined. "Somebody pity me."

"Watch the road or chew the bark off trees," said Herjólf, lifting himself up. "Just nowhere near me." He extended his hand and for the shortest of blinks I felt noticed, but he just wanted his cloak back.

"The farm...!"

"Tomorrow," said Hillevi. "I shot him, for Gods' sake. Go find something to eat."

"He's fine and there's everything at the farm," muttered Ludo, reluctantly lifting himself to his feet. Once I was sure he was gone, I looked at my hand again. That blow could have killed him.

"This is hard, I know," said Pig. He sounded genuinely kind and I immediately bristled with suspicion. "I'd give you more wine, Gods know you need some, but we're out. You've never killed?"

His hands kept moving as he spoke. I thought he was doing something with some sort of a vegetable, but Pig was carving a wooden figurine. With my eyes stuck to his figurine, I shook my head.

"You get used to it. If you want to keep on living, you need things, and people don't want to give us things. Sometimes we buy food, but first we have to get coin, and people also don't want to give us coin."

The tears were choking me again. "I earned good coin with my hands. You would too. You can cook, you can make those. When it's all over..."

"Ginger," snapped Pig. "Outlawry is worse than death because it's never over. You're always hungry, always on the run, hoping that you kill before you get killed and that the loot you find makes it worth it. Do you think I like this? All I want is to settle down somewhere, have a family and little Piglets running around. Nay. Can't marry a woman, can't own anything, anyone who recognises me..." He pretended to slit his throat, still holding the carving knife. "I need a king's pardon. The nearest I got to a king is Herjólf, who tried to get on the throne, failed, and now has nothing left but the clothes on his back. How close do you think you or I will ever get to a king before getting killed?"

"That's unfair," I whispered. "Like when you dangle food in front of a dog that's tied on a short..."

Without a word, Pig threw the unfinished figurine into the fire and I let out a gasp. "Life's not fair. This," he said, gesturing around, "is real. Outlaws can't enter Valhalla, we don't even get to die fair. Dogs have it better."

Only humans could call this "fair game".

The wood was wet and I couldn't work miracles, so our fire smoked. I tried to keep it burning without letting everyone around us know we were here. My heartbeat was faster than usual, beating a short phrase: this-is-real-this-is-real.

"Hey, Ginger! Pig here tells me you'd like some tips about fighting."

"Like fuck I did," muttered Pig. I looked at Ludo wearily.

"Look at their eyes. You can see it when they make a decision, their eyes change. Uh-nuh! Not with me, won't work. I don't think, don't make decisions, those take time. Hunt the fear, hunt the jugular, nah, screw all that, jump, scream, stab, kick, punch! Fuck tech-*nique* and elegance, all of them learned folks know the same things and that's is why I'm alive and they're" – a finger slid over his throat-apple, *khkhkhk*. "Don't let 'em figure out what you're going to do and don't give 'em a break. Fuck them up is what I'm saying. Hey, wanna wrestle? To keep warm?"

I shuddered. "Tomorrow."

Ludo seemed to deflate. "Maybe you're right. I still have a headache." He hit his head with a fist, as if to demonstrate, then grinned and went on talking. I didn't hear him anymore. All the voices in my head kept shouting about bartering and about Herjólf being the son of a king and having met Thor and knowing who I was and *khkhkhk*. I kept shivering and winced in surprise when someone approached me from behind and wrapped me in a cloak without saying a word. Herjólf. I lifted myself up, my mouth open. He already disappeared. If not for the cloak, I'd think I dreamt it.

I curled up, trying to wrap myself with a cloak that for me was more like a small blanket. Somewhere far away, Ludo's croaking voice kept talking about the farm in a monotone, even though he had no listeners anymore.

This-is-real-this-is-real-this-is-real-this...

When I finally fell asleep, I was woken up with a kick in the belly.

"A rider," hissed Ludo excitedly. "Fun time!"

"Bugger off," said Hillevi. "He's not starting with an ambush. Herjólf and I go, you stay here."

I was only half awake, my belly hurt, the cold shook me, and I had no idea what they were talking about.

"It's very easy," muttered Ludo, staring after them wistfully. "You grab the rider's foot, unsaddle him – if someone can do it, it's you, Ginger, just grab the foot and lift. I take care of the horse, you take care of the guy, don't get blood stains on the clothes and we're set." He chuckled and Pig joined.

"I...don't know why that's funny," I said. A rider, blood stains, an ambush.

"It's fun to watch him so excited," explained Pig. Ludo was clapping his hands. "He's crazier than a horsefly."

"Aye," nodded Ludo proudly. "I got me outlawed for fun. I'm not good with laws and rules and property. People shouldn't own things when I'm around, it unsettles me." Another cackle.

I was starting to have a sinking feeling that I was awake by now. "All of this," I gestured around, "the cold, the, uh, porridge, you think it's all fun?"

"Not everything is fun, no," said Ludo, suddenly serious. "Not my brother. He was born with all the good bones, the rule-following, property-respecting bones. A day after I got me kicked out, I came to sneak back in and make some more mess...and I saw his head on a pike." He swallowed. "One day all them good folks who watched and did nothing will wake up dead, all them fucking rule-respecting-property-owning..."

"I got it," I interrupted. Serious Ludo was even scarier. "I'm sorry."

He bared his teeth again. "They'll be sorry. Soon! So, the farm. We've been keeping it for a special occasion."

Pig snorted. Ludo was on a roll. "It's a bit of a walk from here, but it'll be worth it. Bogdan, the farmer, we used to be friends, then when I got in trouble, he forgot about me. Never forget about your friends, Ginger, it always ends badly. So, when you're taking care of him, remember, he's a nasty, nasty man. You're making Midgard a better place. I'll do the women, so you don't have to."

"Women...?" I repeated. Hot flushes and cold shivers felt as if my skin had split from my body, tortured in turns with ice and fire. I was sick. He was sick.

"Aye. Four of them, but I'm big and brave. I'll take good care of them. We'll take all they have and come back here to celebrate."

"Bring wine," said Pig. He sounded excited.

"Mead," Ludo said, then licked his lips. "I know Bogdan..."

Taking care, he said, *good care. It ends badly.* I kept scrambling for a way for that to mean something other than it did.

"Hey, Ginger," said Pig. "Don't think about it. Just do it."

"What if we get killed?" I cried.

"I don't get killed." Ludo let out another of his high-pitched cackles. "What's the point of getting killed if you can't go to Valhalla?"

This-is-real-this-is-real. Ludo was completely, through and through, utterly human. If I wanted to live, I had to become like him.

"Coin, and hardly any as well," said Hillevi, giving me a fright quickly replaced by envy. I wanted to learn that too, how to just... appear. "Nothing to eat. Ginger, I've got a present for you."

I gasped in surprise, then flinched when a pile of fabric hit me in the face.

"A cloak of your own," she said. "You're welcome and I'm hungry. You two, go to the farm, now."

"But it's better in the evening," Ludo complained.

My fingers were wrapped tight over the cloak. *Someone died for me to have it*, a part of me said. *No*, another part argued, *he was dead anyway and didn't need it anymore.*

Hillevi let out an exasperated sigh. "Don't let him set it on fire, Ginger, or Herjólf won't find us. You carry the torches and everything that burns. What he's saying is that fire looks bigger when it's dark. I've tried a hundred times to explain to him that we don't want to attract attention, but it's like his skull's made of iron."

"It is," Ludo nodded, grinning. "Good horse then, eh?"

"Good enough. Two, three days," Hillevi said.

"Why won't Herjólf find us?" I asked at the same moment. The cloak was thick. It would be warm.

"Herjólf went to sell the horse," Pig explained. "He'll ride the horse one way, but then when he sells it, he'll walk back."

Herjólf will be walking through the snow, alone, for three days. This-is-real.

I got up and let the cloak unfold. There was a hole ripped in it. The fabric was wet around the hole. Fresh blood. I cried and threw the cloak on the fire. Stinking smoke arose, then the fire died.

"Get frostbite then, ice giant," said Hillevi. She sounded like ice herself. "Ludo, make sure he kills someone whether he wants to or not. And don't dare come back without food."

"He can carry barrels," enthused Ludo. "Right? Can you carry two at once?"

"Barrels?"

"Mead barrels!"

"Your mother dropped you into a barrel of mead when you were born and you never sobered up," said Hillevi.

"Probably! Mead's like mother's milk to me. Keeps me healthy and alive. Oh boy, oh boy," he laughed, clapping his hands. I couldn't resist a half-smile. Pig was right, there was something amusing about Ludo's insanity.

A few hours later I watched Ludo stab two little girls, then their mother, then their father, because I couldn't do it, and then Ludo's cock had managed to burst from his trousers somehow and the last girl cried and screamed for help and I screamed too and Ludo turned to me and his face was not really his, as though he had a fever or as though Odin The Slayer had entered him, and there was nothing funny about this Ludo at all.

We brought food and drink. Hillevi told me I'd done well, so did Pig. Ludo loudly disagreed. I said nothing, eating something without tasting it, then drinking the wine, or maybe the mead, that I had apparently carried all the way back. I didn't even remember us returning.

Once I shut my eyes I saw Ludo's feverish face, his mouth half-open, blood smeared on his forehead, burning eyes that looked through me, then his red face was replaced by his cock sticking out through an opening in his trousers and then it was his face again and I thought I would never sleep again but I did and I dreamt about my mother and Ludo was there, too.

We ate real food for breakfast, then drank cups of hot, spicy wine. I kept thinking about Herjólf, walking through the snow for days. Then about the girls. Then about Ludo. Then I felt like I should want to vomit, but my body wouldn't let me. Ludo and Pig announced that they were taking another trek to the farm and I didn't even have to close my eyes to find myself already there.

"Come with us," said Ludo, licking his lips. Blood. Wine. "You'll bring more good stuff. You know. Blankets."

"Leave him the fuck alone," said Hillevi. "If you set that farm on fire, I will set *you* on fire when you're asleep."

"Fun-killer," muttered Ludo, but cheered up almost instantly. They were laughing as they departed, Pig's *ho-ho-ho* accompanying Ludo's *hee-hee*. I tried to hide inside a warm, woollen cape. It didn't make me feel any better that I didn't remember taking it.

Hillevi muttered something to herself, then looked at the bruised sky. It was beginning to snow. "Make us a proper fire, Ginger," she said. "They better bring those blankets, not just more mead."

"B-b-but those blankets..."

She raised her eyebrows, as if puzzled.

My hands, already shaky, dropped the flint. There were bodies under those blankets. "No," I muttered.

"I'm cold," she reminded. "What, no?"

"Ludo..." I started. I couldn't get the kindling to catch a fire. "Ludo..."

"What about him?"

"He raped a– a woman." The word "girl" wouldn't get past my throat. I looked at Hillevi pleadingly, but her face was blank. "You have to tell him... it's wrong..."

"Me, telling Ludo anything? If she didn't defend herself, it's only her fault," said Hillevi. "They raise their women weak here. Do you think nobody ever tried to rape me?"

"What happened?" I hardly dared to breathe. I once told Maya that it was the King's right to do anything he wanted. I was so stupid. I believed it when I said it.

"My parents got killed and a human family took me in. When I began to bleed, they told me it was time for me to pay for their hospitality. We were farmers, we didn't have money. Someone saw me, wanted me, he had money and liked elves. My mother perfumed me and dressed me while my father finalised the trade. I stabbed all three." She gave me a sour half-smile. "Now I'm here."

She was an elf. Now I understood why she both did and didn't look like humans or jötnar. Her hair was black, like Maya's, but different. Her face, her big eyes... like all the others, except not at all. It was hard to stop staring. I had never seen an elf and she was so beautiful, even while she was smirking. "I thought you were a princess," I said accidentally.

Hillevi took a moment before she began to laugh. "Princess...! Princesses don't get outlawed, they become queens."

"Herjólf's a son of a king, Pig said, is that not true?"

She remained silent long enough for me to feel uncomfortable and even wish that other two would hurry up. "He's got you," she finally said. "Why are you here with us, Magni, son of Thor?"

An indeterminate sound escaped my throat.

"Did you think we'd just send our leader away with a giant who shrugs off my poisons and whose wounds heal by themselves as we watch? You wouldn't heal from an arrow through your eye. I was close enough to watch and listen, Herjólf wouldn't even have to give me a sign." Hillevi sighed. "I didn't stay until the end, but I've seen and heard enough. You're a God. Why don't you go back home?"

I gawked at her.

"Build that fire already! Ludo loves this life, because he's insane. Nobody else in the Nine would have chosen it, yet you're here when you could be in Ásgard. Why? Herjólf deludes himself that he'll get his kingdom back, not that it was ever his. I'm here to cleanse Midgard of witches. Pig... it's sad, all he wants is a home and a family, but he won't get it before Herjólf sits on a throne. You?"

"Why is Pig even here? He's so nice."

Hillevi said nothing, just stared at me, making me uncomfortable. "Pig poisoned a rich family that hired him," she said finally, just as the kindling caught. "The plan was that only the father would die. He thought that saying that it wasn't his fault that his wife and daughter returned home early and joined him for dinner would set him free."

I just stared at her, trying to put a question together.

"Coin, what else? The family who hired him promised to keep him alive if he wouldn't tell the king who they were. He got outlawed. They sent someone after him..."

I couldn't hear her anymore. Hillevi's "parents" sold her to whoever was willing to pay. Once Lady Freya married King Thrymr, Mother and I wouldn't get outlawed, just killed. Perhaps get tortured to death for King Thrymr's amusement. By Maya, so she could keep her own life. They were all the same, after all, it was me that there was something wrong with.

The wind calmed down, the snow glued into thicker flakes. I added to the fire, then accepted a mug from Hillevi. "To dead witches and little Piglets," she said.

I took a sip, then another. The mead made me feel warmer and a bit dreamy. We sat in silence for a while, then I remembered something. "I met a witch once," I muttered. "She was nice. She wasn't a witch."

"Was she or wasn't she then?"

"She tried to help."

"Did she?"

I didn't answer.

"Never trust a witch," said Hillevi. "You have no idea what they know, how they can make people suffer. I met one once and it was enough."

"What did she do?"

"Nothing, because I killed her. Who knows how many lives I spared?"

I said nothing, staring at the fire, when something happened. I stood in front of Jarl Mieszko again, Dalebor's torch too close to my face, the heat on my face too intense to bear and then it was all gone. My hands shook as I took a gulp of mead, trying not to spill it all over myself. There was no Dalebor and no torch. It was the opposite, snow piling up on the side of my head, carried by wind, the frost that felt like heat.

"Why do you think Pig is so fat? He's cursed by a witch," I heard somewhere in the distance. "He hardly eats. So – why don't you go back home? Is this some sort of challenge from Odin?"

I emptied the mug and Hillevi refilled it. I took another sip, silent, searching for an answer to her question. I knew what she meant and I resented it. "I have no home," I muttered.

"They're back," she whispered, startling me. "Don't tell Ludo who you are. If you think he's obnoxious now..."

Cackling, Ludo presented me with the least bloodied blanket and a pair of boots. They were too small, but unlike mine they were not falling apart, and apparently Herjólf would know how to stretch them.

"He's a good man," said Ludo. "If you tell him I said that, I'll fucking stab you in your sleep, Ginger. He's done a lot, he's travelled... He would make a great king, if he wasn't so..."

"Vain," said Hillevi. "Cruel. Selfish."

"He's out there walking through that weather," pointed out Pig. "Hungry. I'd do anything for him to become king."

"Why," she barked.

"So that he can pardon me," Pig laughed.

More mead, a chunk of ice-cold meat, Pig asking me about pota-toes, which they didn't have here. My lips moving, words falling like snow on the blankets of dead people. The boots of a dead man waiting for my lover, son of a king, to stretch them for me, so that I could wear them together with the dead man's cloak. If I could look into my own eyes, they'd be black.

No.

Hillevi said something about Odin's challenge. Odin loved nothing more than death, so he wouldn't get any from me. If Pig didn't have to kill to be allowed to be a part of the group, then I wouldn't let them force me to do it either. I could chop wood, light a fire during a snowstorm, carry everything we had. If Herjólf could walk through snow for three days to sell a horse, I could too, even though my feet were already sore after a few hours. I would save lives, not take them. I had to hold on to that one thing, or my own life would have no value anymore.

The mead made my eyelids heavy and I was at the farm again. Ludo's feverish gaze. The girl's bulging eyes, mouth open in a sound-less scream. My body shook and I was awake again, but not for long. The not real people in the castle, Mjölnir in my hand that dripped with blood. A crash of thunder, real or imagined, bringing me back.

Sleep with one eye open, Herjólf once said. I knew this wasn't what he meant, but I tried to find a way to keep my eyes only half-closed, just enough for the blurry glow of the embers to obscure the soundless screams that replaced my sleep.

I didn't know yet that from now on every night would be like this. That I would straddle the past and the present, be constantly tired every morning and welcome it, just so that I wouldn't have to dream. I didn't know the dreams, unsatisfied, would chase me into the daylight.

~

"Not yet..." hissed Ludo. "Not yet... unsaddle the rider, take care of him, I'll do the rest."

It was just one man on a horse, going slowly, as if he felt safe. His clothes looked good, better than Herjólf's leather jerkin, which looked imposing from a distance, but up close was old, dirty, and had been mended many times. The rider wore fur. The wind messed with his long hair. I heard him whistling. I couldn't stop shivering.

"For Loki!" Ludo shouted and the rider looked up in alarm. I didn't move. I forgot how. Ludo pushed me, cursing, and I half-ran, half-fell off the steep hill where we hid between the trees. I couldn't stop, gaining speed, realising that I was going to crash straight into the horse. I put all the strength I had into a clumsy leap, and my body slammed into the rider. Both of us landed on the ground, leaving the horse frozen in place. For a moment neither I nor the rider seemed to understand what had just happened and a blink of silence stopped everything before the horse bolted away, whinnying loudly.

"Fuck! Hurry up!"

I knelt next to the rider, who groaned quietly. I knew what I was supposed to do. Herjólf didn't complain once about walking for three days or having to stretch my boots. He just instructed me to come back with a weapon on my own. I refused the axe and the knives, patting the hammer I didn't intend to use. I had a plan. I'd smash my fist against the rider's head. Not too hard.

"Ginger!"

The rider's eyes opened and met mine. She was at that age where she wasn't really a girl anymore but not a woman either. They'd want her clothes. Even if I just hit her, she would freeze to death once we took her clothes off. Ludo's cock. I couldn't breathe. I needed time to think.

"Ginger!" yelled Ludo. "The fuck you doing?"

"Thor," the rider beseeched.

I can't, I wanted to say, but my lips didn't move.

Her eyes were brown, large, filled with fear. Her skin, the same colour as Herjólf's, tight on her cheekbones. Her nose was small, straight, a bit like Hillevi's. A half-elf, something else? Her face was triangular, the chin narrow, lips shining with grease. A brown ribbon tied the fur collar of her cape. The fur was silver and black, the cape thick, blue wool, no hood. The rider wore her hair in plaits, but some strands escaped, almost black, even darker than her eyes. I had forgotten everything, how to speak, how to move. I just knelt there, committing each feature to my memory. She shouldn't be travelling alone. There were bad people around.

"What's your name?" I whispered.

"Don't," she said, her eyes narrowing, voice commanding.

"Ginger!"

In hopeless search for something that would change everything I raised my head and saw it.

A thin-limbed creature was approaching, crouching on hands and knees, pushing itself closer with jerky movements, one leg seemingly stronger than the other. It moved like an animal that had been caught in a trap at some point and had never quite recovered. It was a man, I realised, no, not really a man, a boy. He was almost naked, his back hunched, the sweet face untouched by deformation. *I can make it alright*, he seemed to promise, *you can rest.*

My eyes met the rider's again. Her lips moved, but I didn't hear her, my heart pumping blood so hard it sounded like drumming and then a hand appeared over her face and before I had a chance to understand what was happening the boy gouged the rider's eyes out with his bare fingers. A hoarse screech ripped through the air, suddenly cut short when the boy's hands grabbed her head and, with one swift motion, turned it around until the skin around the throat erupted and blood splattered all over me. *You were meant to help*, I wanted to cry, *you lied,* you – The boy's eyes were wide and very, very green, his gaze innocent as he sucked his fingers clean, one at a time.

I didn't scream. I howled, scaring the creature. It turned and escaped, faster than I would have thought possible, one leg pushing, the other one dragging behind. Tears flew down my face, my hands convulsively shaking, as I tried to turn the rider's head back into normal position, as if I could bring her back to life. Her hair was the same as before, and her nose, and the cheekbones. But not the eyes.

My stomach spasmed with convulsions and I vomited into my own bloodied hands.

"Ginger! The fuck is wrong with you?!"

I ran up the hill, ran through our camp, jumping over the fire, stumbling in search for a place to hide, tripping on ice that covered a stream. A yowl, mine, slashed through the air. I punched a hole through the ice to reach the water, the sharp shards cutting the skin on my fist. The icy water wouldn't wash the blood and vomit off. "Thor", she'd said. "Don't." I never found out what her name was. Her eyes were brown and then they were not there at all and my hands were still covered in blood and I think I was crying, but instead of sobbing or even howling my throat kept repeating the sound of the, the rider's throat being torn by the creature, the blood was still on my hands and I grabbed a handful of coarse sand and gravel, rubbing my hands with them, the blood was still on my hands—

—the boy-like creature sucking more than just blood off its fingers—

—*the blood was still on my hands* and I wanted Herjólf's thumbs to dig into my throat like last night when he'd roared in triumph as he came and I did not see anything at all for a moment, I just *wasn't*, the creature's fingers dug into the rider's eyes, but not mine. My hands hurt so bad and I could see that blood was pouring off them now, sinking into the snow, the stream now crystal clear water under the ice, but I could not stop, there was no way to scrub my hands clean no matter how long I tried, the boy's fingers would always dig into the rider's eyes and the blood was still on my hands, it was still on my hands—

"Ginger."

I wailed in alarm.

"Ginger," repeated Hillevi. "We have to leave, now."

My hands hurt so bad, not bad enough. I couldn't talk, my throat was so dry. It was not torn but I could still only make a sound like *ng-ng-ng*.

"The horse ran away. Blood's everywhere. Couldn't you just have used your hammer? Cracked the skull?"

She was angry with me. I did wrong. I didn't. I should have, but I didn't. I had blood on my hands and snow and sand bit me.

"There's too much to clean. It's not snowing. You left enough

tracks for a blind man to find us. We have to move, right now.
Ginger? Do you hear me?"

"C-c-c-couldn't. I was too af-afraid."

Hillevi let out a hiss-sigh. "Did you talk to him? Don't do that
again."

"I didn't," I groaned. So, the boy could talk. It meant he knew
what he was doing. "And I won't. Ever. Don't make me go back."

"Ginger, you're not going back, because we're leaving!"

"That rider... dead... she was a g-girl."

"By Odin, what's the fucking difference? Hurry up!"

I felt like a red stain spilling among the black, dead trees and the
indifferent snow. Walking, stumbling, failing and falling, lifting myself
up, picking up the things I'd promised to carry. My heart kept beating
this-is-real-this-is-real again, but I could no longer tell what was real.
Hillevi's eyes were brown, her hair plaited. Herjólf's and Ludo's and Pig's
faces became the boy's face sometimes and sometimes not. Back at the
forge I got used to the heat and the burns, now I had to get used to being
cold and hungry. My hands kept hurting. I had to wash the blood off.

"We have to stop."

"This is not a good spot."

"It's getting dark."

"Will you try and hunt?"

"It's getting dark, I said. Make a fire, Ginger."

I did and made it big, because it occurred to me that I could burn
the blood off my hands if I kept them in the flame long enough, but
they wouldn't let me. I fell on my back, maybe awake, maybe asleep,
her eyes were brown and her face triangular, I could draw every detail
of the plaits in her hair, what a shame the fur collar was ruined,
Hillevi would have loved the cape.

A slap in the face. Dawn. Someone pulling my arm. Funny. He
could just as well have tried to pull out a tree out of the ground. I sat
up. I knew him. Ludo.

"An old man and a full cart," he hissed. "Hurry up."

It really felt like someone grabbed my arm and pulled me back
into the place where there were always more people who had to die.

"Follow me and be quiet!"

"Don't make me," I begged. Everything felt sharp, the needles pricking my hands, each little hair on Ludo's upper lip, the grey light of dawn pushing in among the trees. A blink and I was in my hideaway in the Haunted Forest, the same light and deformed trees that cut through the sky like black lightning, another blink and Ludo's saliva landed on my face.

"I'm hungry, you dumb fuck. A cart, you hear me? He's bound to be carrying food. You kill and do it fast, understand?"

"Don't think about it," Herjólf said softly. "Don't look at the face."

"He's right," said Hillevi. "One quick blow. You can think later."

"If you don't learn now," said Herjólf, "you never will."

"Hurry!"

It was clear that I was still dreaming, or that they were making it up. We were in the middle of nowhere. There was no road, no old man. Even when Ludo slowed down, put his finger on his lips, and pointed at the horse and cart I refused to believe it. Yet the countless needles pricking my hands began to spread all over my body. I could still see my breath, sharp, short outbursts of steam, but I felt hot. I was sweating. Like it was real.

"Stop fucking thinking," spat Ludo and I stopped fucking thinking.

I leapt on the cart, grabbed the man, and the impact threw us both in the air. Something snapped in my neck. He was on top of me. Pain exploded in my eye and I howled in shock. This was no frail old man. A punch in the jaw. With my good eye I saw a fist rise again, not so much a man as a black silhouette sitting atop me. He roared. Must have thought it was the final blow. My hand just jumped, because I had stopped fucking thinking, smacking the side of his head, sending him flying. Like Ludo when we wrestled. I could only see the sky, half-see, with one eye. Like Odin.

I lifted myself to my knees, then gingerly tried to touch the eye and hissed in pain. Maybe I'd lost it. The pain in my jaw was dull, in the background. The man lay unconscious, maybe already dead. Tall, wide-shouldered. He didn't look like the rider at all and for a blink I again wasn't sure what was real.

"Move it, Ginger!" yelled Ludo, fighting the horse. The panicked neighs nearly drowned out his voice. "Breakfast time! Chop chop!"

Chop chop.

A sound: someone dragging a rock through the snow step by step, a slow *wshh, wshh.*

I shook my head. The hurt eye pounded with pain. My wet, dirty hair smacked my face. The boy was still there, kneeling next to the man. He gently pushed a strand of hair off the man's forehead, then sent me a charming smile that made me recoil with fear. Ludo struggling with the horse seemed to disperse in the air. There was only the unconscious man and me and that – that deformed boy.

No, I wanted to yell, *don't*, but I was too scared he'd answer. I just watched, paralysed, as he bent down, closed the man's nose with two fingers, and bit deep into the man's throat apple. Everything was completely silent. Blood gushed out of the man's throat when the boy shook his head like a dog would when trying to tear a chunk of meat off a larger piece. When he raised his head, his jaws were chewing. Blood dribbled down his chin. I couldn't scream, look away, I forgot how.

The boy turned towards me. The corners of his lips went up, his jaws still working. He seemed so happy. There was a question in those huge, sweet eyes, eyes that were both intensely green and burning with red fires, eyes that swallowed everything. *Did I do good?* he seemed to ask. *Did I help?*

"I wanted this jerkin, you crazy fuck!"

At the sound of Ludo's voice the boy rapidly turned and escaped, leaping like a lopsided frog. Blood was everywhere again. The horse protested loudly and Ludo shouted. My eye kept pulsating with pain with every heartbeat. I looked at the gory mess and I didn't even feel upset anymore. They were not real people like back in the City of Light, they were just humans. It was alright to kill them. They liked it.

I dipped a finger in the blood, then licked it. It tasted just like my own. Ludo gasped as I dipped two fingers in the blood and painted lines from my forehead to my chin. Hillevi appeared and grabbed the horse's reins when I burst out laughing and Ludo bolted away.

The ambush was pointless. We now had more coin we had no use for, his cart was filled with coal, and his horse, as Pig phrased it, was older than the Gods. We killed the animal, *chop chop,* cutting some chunks of meat that Pig deemed just about edible. We had to hurry again, find yet another spot, and it was my fault again. I was letting my friends and my lover down. If only I had realised earlier! They were not really people, they were humans. They didn't count. As long as I didn't kill anybody real, I was still a bit me.

We left the carcasses behind, horse and human, for the wolves and maybe for the boy.

CHAPTER 5
MAYA

"HER GRACE FREYA HAS LEFT," Thrud informed me politely.

My excitement immediately disappeared. I had forgotten. "Why? For how long?"

"She didn't say, Your Grace."

I bit my lip in frustration. Even Freya sometimes did something that wasn't buggering her brother or mourning her inability to do so.

With nothing better to do, I dragged my feet around Ásgard. I visited Granny Frigg again, but the things unsaid sat heavily between us; the hugs felt a bit stiffer. The walnut cake's slight, bitter aftertaste had nothing to do with either the dough or the walnuts. I couldn't wait to leave, so that I could stop faking a stiff grin.

Determined to tell Auntie Idunn what I really thought about her garden, which was that I loved it to death, I strode onwards. The nearer I got, the slower I moved, running out of courage. She waved from a distance, beaming. I waved back, relieved. My happy grin wavered when Bragi, her husband, emerged. I wasn't in the mood to have my ears talked off. To my surprise though, both of them just giggled, slightly incoherent, pointing at little goblets. I understood that Idunn had accidentally invented something they called "gin" and they were hard at work picking the best flavouring for it. She invited me to join and I considered it, until I noticed what they were doing with the hands that were not holding the goblets. I promised myself to never touch "gin" and ran away, followed by their giggles.

I swam naked in the lake, then dried myself in the sun. That was supposed to relieve my tension, it always had. Now I kept searching for shifters, suspecting each bird, ladybug, frog. I couldn't stop thinking of Loki's words – he liked me where he could see me. I could say the same. I hadn't managed to find Thor either, which hopefully meant that they had gone away on one of their adventures. Was there still some Jötunheim left for Thor to destroy?

I was supposed to try and solve the mystery of the man with the blue orb. I couldn't ask anything of anyone, though, without revealing that I had played a part in the hammer's theft. I got nowhere and I had nothing to show for it.

Freya kept not returning, and frustration became my constant companion. I was ready. I knew what I wanted, practised both the emotional blackmail and rational arguments. I would ignore her dramatic outbursts, remaining calm like a lake on a particularly quiet day. She would have no choice but to surrender. Once she finally came back. I'd lost all track of time, but surely it must have been winter by now?

Each year, Freyr would die on the first day of winter. Freya's wordless scream of pain would shake Ásgard. She would then mourn Freyr's death until the moon turned six times and he was reborn on the first day of summer. Mourning took the form of Freya crying her eyes out and dragging her feet around the Nine, or rather eight, in order not to accidentally grace Jötunheim with her presence. She was not in Ásgard, so the blood-curdling scream must have terrified the inhabitants of one of the other worlds...

I bit my lip, deep in thought. Where exactly did she go? I couldn't imagine her entertaining the fires of Müspelheim, the ice of Niflheim, and the tombs of Helheim. Did she travel around Midgardian towns and villages, or weep her way through the forests? Freya needed an audience as wide as possible. In order to cry her way to Álfheim she would have had to get on a ship and travel to the east of

Jötunheim first. Everyone knew that would never happen. Only the jötnar believed...

I stiffened.

The jötnar were convinced of Lady Freya's love, because Bragi had concocted a tale that spread like wildfire. Everyone knew that Freya spent each winter being dramatic all over the Nine. Nobody ever questioned it. Could it have been another of Bragi's reality-altering stories? If it weren't for my impatience and boredom, I would have never given it a thought. Who else could afford to just sit and think? Odin, with his wisdom. Frigg, who knew everything and didn't want to. And... and... I couldn't think of anybody else who had the luxury I had, of doing absolutely nothing. I felt myself blush. I was working now. Finding answers to questions no one had asked.

What would have happened if King Thrymr received the hammer in the winter? Odin would need to send the ravens on a search. From his throne he saw everything that happened in Ásgard. Heimdall reported on Midgard, when asked. Helheim, Niflheim, Müspelheim, Jötunheim were irrelevant, I muttered, counting on fingers. I didn't know how to get to Svartálfheim or Vanaheim, but she couldn't get to Álfheim without first going to Jötunheim, where she would never go. How did that go with the *knowledge* that she wept slogging all through the *Nine*? Even Freya believed, *knew* that mana couldn't be stored, Good Gods, I had seen it with my own eyes and still couldn't really believe it. How many things had I discovered just because nobody had told me they were impossible?

What if our *knowledge* that she had never set foot in Jötunheim was a lie? There was much more to it than the City of Light and its surroundings. The impenetrable mountains split the world into the west, which was Thor's playground, and the east, which was too far from Ásgard to pose any danger. There was little to the eastern part except the harbours and the constant freeze rivalling that of Niflheim. Or so we thought.

How did the goods travel between the east and the west if the mountains were impenetrable? There were no harbours in the west, not that I knew of. Was there a passage known only to traders, while everyone else still *knew* that... I poured myself some water and noticed my hands were slightly shaking. Had anybody actually taken the time to explore *all* of Jötunheim? Perhaps someone who had ostentatiously never set a foot there?

Even if she had, so what? asked a logical, harsh voice in my head. Going to Jötunheim wasn't forbidden.

I imagined Freya walking down Bifröst, dressed in rags for that extra dramatic effect, heading to the Midgardian harbours on foot. Bare feet. Sailing for Gods knew how long on a ship in the company of sailors and whatever it was that Midgard sold to the jötnar. Turnips. I chuckled at the vision, my laughter cut short when I suddenly forgot how to breathe.

My secret, my escape route in case I ever needed one. I'd spent my whole life guarding it. Did she know, did she use it? How was I supposed to find out without telling her what it was?

Once I fell asleep, which took forever, I dreamt about Freya with a blue orb under her gown, as if she were pregnant with mana. She reached under her gown and pulled out a black-haired baby girl, holding her upside down by her ankle. A scream, but not one of pain, one filled with triumph and joy pierced through me as she lifted the girl up, still holding her ankle. Her trophy. Her thing.

Mam, said the baby girl.

Come with me, Freya said, *we'll play a game...*

My own scream woke me up. "No," I panted, choking, my heart racing, throat dry, "no, no, no, not coming, no, no game...!" I jumped out of bed, tripped and fell to my knees, lifted myself with willpower more than anything, and dunked my face in a bowl with cold water. I only jerked back up, sending water all over the place, striving for air, when I couldn't take any more. I needed a mirror, so I could see a grown woman. Strands of wet hair hanging on the sides of her face. Not a girl at all. Her normally white skin had taken on a greenish hue. She looked gaunt. Perhaps Granny Frigg had a point and she should eat more.

I shook my head again, sending water everywhere, making my hair even more of a mess. I tried to smile at my own reflection. It grimaced in response. This was real, yes. Not the other thing that I was not thinking about at all anymore.

I took a few more deep breaths, then dried my face. I still felt a bit faint. Idunn's fruit would help.

Barefoot, I stepped into the garden, yawning so hard that my jaw hurt. My mind was completely occupied by an important choice I needed to make. I would eat a mango, I'd become partial to them recently. Unless, that is, I chose a pomegranate instead. No, definitely a mango. When the sound crashed into me, as if Mjölnir hit me in the face, the first, or maybe last, thought I had was "or a pomegranate".

I tried to will my ears to become deaf, my eyes to turn blind. The baby laughed again, that complete happiness that only babies knew, because they have not experienced bad things. But we had an agreement. *Wake up. Wake up wake up.*

"Who's Mam's boo boo?" Freya cooed. "Mam's boo boo must burp now! Burpy burpy!"

There was not enough warmth in Ásgard to take away the goosebumps that covered my skin. Shivers went up and down my body, as if I were sick. My throat produced a little choking sound. The triumphant shriek I thought was part of my dream was real. Freya was breastfeeding a boy. His name was Freyr, he was her twin brother, today was the first day of summer, and she'd be having sex with him the moment he figured out his hands from his feet.

"Oh, there you are," she said in a very different tone, not bothering to look up. "I've been told that you refused to wear the boots I gave you. I told you that you were a contrarian."

Where and when was I? Had I been asleep all this time? What boots? My head felt as if it had turned into my heart, expanding, then shrinking. "I'm not a contrarian," I croaked, the words pushing through teeth clenched both from fury and from sheer pain.

"Oh dear, someone's upset. Did you sleep badly?"

"Yes," I immediately spat out, "because I dreamt of you."

Bugger calm lakes on quiet days, my inside was boiling lava. She was *evil*. My gaze inadvertently moved to the naked baby and I imagined myself grabbing the giggly God of fertility, ecstasy, sexuality, rebirth, and smashing his head against the white rocks.

"How sad, honey. I truly feel for you. Isn't life a miracle?" She triumphantly lifted the baby and I didn't look away fast enough not to notice it was *definitely* a boy. "He is so happy to see you! Aren't you happy, my little sweetie boo boo? This is Auntie Maya!"

Somewhere inside me was a trap door hiding a dungeon, deep, deep down. Last night's nightmare brought me dangerously close to it. I was awake now and yet walking down the stairs, noticing that the railings grew more and more rusty as I slowly descended, until there was little left to hold on to.

"Well, say something to him," demanded Freya. "He's been reborn only today. Have you ever seen anything as beautiful as a little baby? They have their own smell..."

The dungeon smelled of mould and fungi, the white things that grew in moist darkness and fed on death. The stairs started crumbling under my feet, little more than pebbles hanging in a void. I raised the torch I was holding, its flame grey, and took a careful step over a gaping hole. I was nearing the thick iron door, half-eaten by rust. A key stuck out of the lock. I didn't touch it. With a protesting screech, it turned on its own.

"We had an agreement," I whimpered. I was both here and there. I stood on the warm rocks, in the sun, and I also tried to breathe through my mouth to avoid the stink of the dungeon. "He stays away from me. Always."

"But, petal, he's a newborn, not even a toddler. Very unlikely to make advances at you. I'm holding him in my lap. Once you stop being unreasonable and find yourself someone special, you will have your own sweet boo boo to love. There is no feeling more wonderful to a woman than to hold a newborn."

"Always," I whispered.

I couldn't tear my eyes either off Freya's exposed breast, or the door that screeched in protest as it slowly opened, its hinges never oiled. I dropped the grey-flamed torch. Its "flame" hissed under my feet when it met the dank floor.

"Oh, for my sake! You don't have to touch him, not that it would kill you!"

The door, briefly stuck, shot open, slamming against the wall, which cracked. Pieces of rock began to fall from the low ceiling above my head. I reached out to lean against a wall, but in one world there was none, and in the other it crumbled the moment I touched it. I jolted away as the first maggots emerged. "I'm going to be in my chambers," I managed, pushing the words through my closed throat. My face, my entire body was a pincushion. *Mam.*

"Fine," said Freya coldly, "if you're going to behave like a child..."

Leaving the broken wall crawling with maggots I entered the cell that had no windows, no gaps between the grey stones that formed the walls. On the ground sat a black, wooden chest with just one lock. I knelt in front of it.

We had an agreement. To protect the chest, to protect me.

"...then I'm going to send my sweet boo boo away, so you can tell me how horrible your dreams about me were. He needs to sleep too, let us hope that he doesn't dream about me. Oh, there you are, Thrud, darling. Please be careful."

"Of course, Your Grace."

The sounds, the voices came from great distance. Squirming maggots crawled between my toes, then braver ones headed towards my ankles, my calves. Further up my legs.

Dust from the ground rose into the air, forming a fuzzy shape that solidified into a key, one that wasn't made of iron, but of sticky tar. The squiggly key inserted itself into the lock. I had been successful at not releasing me for so long, but now I couldn't stop me from getting out.

The world where the sun shone was no more.

"You are safe," said a booming voice that seemed to come from nowhere and everywhere at once.

I wasn't.

"Tell me all about your dreams. Was I destroying Jötunheim again? Forcing you to look at babies? Something even worse?"

The chest opened, revealing a black-haired, crying girl. Her hair was dirty and ruffled, face a skull wrapped in grey skin. "Let me out," she cried, "please, please let me out, Mam, I am so hungry, please..."

"Maya," I whispered and bent to pick up the girl. The chest was filled with thick, black tar and I had to tug at her until I freed her – and the tar as well.

The tar erupted from the chest like vomit, drowning the maggots. It grabbed the girl and me, carrying us back up. I wasn't supposed to let her out, what had I done, she had to stay in the dungeon, I had to stay in it. "Let me out, please," the girl cried, "please, can I have some water, please Mam." I no longer held her, trying to resist, grab a railing, *something*, the girl's arms wrapped around my neck so hard that I couldn't breathe. She was suffocating me with her pain, greater than I could withstand. The tar, as dense as the lava of Müspelheim, was memories, burning me, drowning me.

Darling, you don't look well. That dream must have been truly awful. Let me help you sit. You should drink something, petal.

"Please," I cried, "can I have some water, please, Mam, please let me out!"

The tar shot out, throwing us out of the dungeon, the trap door underneath us now, but it didn't stop. Like lava, it covered everything, forcing itself into my eyes, my nostrils. The girl's arms held my neck so tight, oh, too tight, *Maya, please, please, I can't breathe.* In Freya's garden tar spilled all over the grass, greedily swallowed the daisies, climbed up to cover the white walls, the impeccable white tablecloths, everything except for Freya, who sat in front of me, and Freya, who sat in front of me.

"We had an agreement," I rasped and the worried expression disappeared from Freya's face. The other one never worried about us. She just sat there, waiting, watching as I suffocated myself with my own embrace.

"Is *that* it?" There was one Freya that was two, her lips moving and not, eyes narrowed in anger and blank. "Look at me! No baby in my hands, not even a very small one. Hands, empty! You've made it clear more than enough times that he disgusts you, but surely our agreement was about keeping him away as an adult, not as a child?"

Child—

child.

Child.

I could have built a deeper dungeon, made the stairs even steeper, put ten locks on the door and twenty on the chest, yet I could never completely seal the little girl away. An invisible strand of smoke from the black tar poisoned my dreams, an inaudible cry made me erupt in anger every time I saw the Goddess of love, who never found it in her to accept anything about me.

"Let me out," cried the girl and wrapped herself around me so tight that she began to squeeze out words.

"There was a child once, a little girl. You led the child by the hand, telling her that there was a new game you would play. The child was afraid when you placed her inside an iron cage that hung from a tree, suspended over the sand by the sea, but you smiled, you said that she could always trust you..."

"That was so long ago—"

The voice the little Maya was squeezing out of me was flat and monotone. "The child believed you. After all, you were her – you had not lied to her before. She used to play on that very beach, climb the same tree, stare at the horizon, wondering what lay beyond it. When you locked the cage and sat down, the child was in pain, uncomfortable. There was nothing to sit on, just metal rods. The child kept asking about the game, what the rules were. She began to plead, beg, cry. You wouldn't even look at her. Slowly, she understood that this game had no rules. There was nothing the child could do for you to let her out..."

"You're being childish now," said Freya, disdain dripping from her voice.

"Shut up!!!" I screamed.

A goblet fell off the table and broke into a thousand crystal shards. The sunny skies of Ásgard darkened, a distant rumble of uneasy thunder coming from afar. The echo of my voice returned, over and over, deafening, screeching, and for a moment I was overcome by the weirdest feeling that she and I had swapped places. This was the sound that came out of Freya's throat on the first day of each winter, when Freyr died. This was the pain that she felt and the pain that she had instilled in me so that I could carry it inside me forever.

"Mam," I cried, my arms wrapped around my neck.

The sky was not quite as blue as before, covered by a thin layer of the tar smoke. Freya sat stiffly composed, but a muscle twitched in her cheek, the glossy perfection scratched. Her chest wasn't moving, as if she had stopped breathing. Her face turned slightly ashen, fingernails more grey than silver. The little girl cried louder, squeezed me harder, as the tar climbed up my calves, consumed my legs, then my waist.

"I begged you to let me out, give me something to drink, to eat." My voice rose, no longer flat, words flowing faster. "I cried, I promised to be good, I screamed. Every child has its own smell? Mine was my own piss, because I wet myself, then wished I had drunk that piss! I thought I could see drops of sea water coming my way, I stuck my tongue out hoping that the wind would carry some my way. It didn't. All that time you sat on a rock, examining your fingernails, until you sighed, and I remember that sigh very well, and you drank from a skin. You smacked your lips, put the cork back in, and you went back to your fingernails. Tell me again about your little sweet boo boo, Goddess of love!"

The stink of emotions in my nostrils was unbelievable. I needed to open a window, I couldn't breathe. I paused, gasping for air, and Freya immediately jumped in. "That is not the tone—"

"I. Am. Not. Finished. Six days and five nights. Not a drop of water or a crumble of bread. The sun went up, then it went down, replaced by the moon. Not one raincloud. I watched you drink, I *beseeched* you to let me suck out the last drops. One last drop. You finally lifted your head and acknowledged me. It took my breath away. I felt so much relief, thinking the 'game' was over, you would let me out now. I would laugh, thank you even, as long as you let me out of the cage. But you just looked at me as if I were something disgusting, a stain. Do you remember what you said? I do. 'If you want water, get it yourself.' I was a little child, a little *miracle of life*, and you put me in a cage."

"Is there a point to this...performance, petal?"

My chair crashed to the ground. I grabbed the nearest object, one of the jewels that served as lamps and threw it, aiming at her face. Freya simply moved her head to the side, letting the jewel fly past her. I rested my weight on my fists, my arms shaking, legs straining under the weight of the little girl still hanging from my neck. We were completely slathered in tar dripping from my hair, squeezing itself into my nostrils, the girl's mouth. The only thing I could do not to let it fill my lungs and drown me was to keep talking. "Yes," I said quietly. "There is. I shifted at the end; I flew out of that cage. No, I didn't fly, I just dropped on the sand. You carried me back here in your arms" – the little girl with her arms wrapped around my neck sobbed "thank you Mam" – "you gave me water, fed me, washed me, praised me, gave me everything I asked for. Then more. You have never stopped giving me more than I asked for."

"I'm glad you've noticed."

"Do I look like I'm grateful?! We had an agreement," I croaked, my finger pointing between her eyes, shaking, drops of tar scattering, disappearing before they reached her. "You were going to keep him away from me, not just because he's a disgusting man, but because... he's your *child*?! How is he your – he's your brother, an abomination – what would you have done if I didn't, couldn't shift – would you just have sat there and watched me die, your little miracle – no, you'd have gone away, wouldn't you, so you wouldn't have had to watch, so ugly, the crying, the – I learned everything about love in that cage, how you – why don't you put your *real* little child, your boo boo, in a—"

"Shut up!!!" Freya screamed.

The hurricane dried the tears rolling down my face before it tore cutlery and napkins off the table, sending them through the air. Something hit me in the cheek, something else struck my shoulder. A jug of water fell, spilling its contents over the tablecloth before falling to the ground. A bowl of strawberries, shaking, slowly travelled towards the edge of the table before it too fell. Above our heads a starless night was slashed into shards with gashes of lightning bolts that struck without sound. Freya turned into a blue, cold light that pulsated more intense, then slightly darker, her veins filled with mana and her body transparent. I couldn't keep my eyes open anymore, dry from the wind. My nose, my lips, my lungs were hurting. Ice formed on my face. The way to Helheim led through the ice and snow of Niflheim. I could almost see Hel's open arms, one of them normal, one – bones with rotten meat hanging off it, crawling with maggots identical to those I carried inside. She couldn't wait to hug me. I tried to extend my hands to hug her too, but couldn't, the little girl between us protecting me, taking all the pain I couldn't handle.

And then everything stopped.

I took a while before I dared open my eyes. The sky was blue and clear, the sun shining again. Freya seemed very slightly dishevelled, breathing just a bit heavier. Only the mess around us proved that it had been more than another vision.

"You wouldn't have died," she said quietly and the tar disappeared, as if sucked back into the void it'd come from.

I picked up my chair and flopped into it. The little girl's arms let go of my neck. She placed herself in my lap, waiting, gawking. She wanted to hear more.

"I also have a story," said Freya as she stood up.

The door that looked like all the others revealed a room containing a large table with goblets and jugs of water on it, chairs... and no windows. No word said here could reach Odin's ears, or even Heimdall's. Once the door shut, so did my throat. When Freya gestured for me to sit down my body seemed to fold and drop on the chair, a wet towel thrown without much care. The little girl climbed back onto my lap. I strived to breathe. *Let me out, Mam.*

"A long, long time ago, the glorious empire of Vanaheim was at war with Ásgard," Freya began. "The war lasted until it became clear that it couldn't be won. A truce was declared, hostages were exchanged. A girl, a boy, and their father were sent here from Vanaheim. The girl was afraid... Don't you DARE open your mouth!" she shrieked and I bit my tongue, tasting blood. The little girl in my lap didn't even flinch. A stupid, naive child. "She had seen war, death, anger, and felt that she knew the solution: love. She would give them the love they desired, so they would all be happy and love her back. A stupid, naive child. She soon found out that sometimes two wanted the love of the same third, while the third desired neither. Her attempts to make things work made all three hate her. The more she tried to fix it, the worse it all got. In her fear and confusion the girl decided to turn to the most powerful of them. She asked the wise All-Father for protection, for mercy."

When her cracked voice trailed off, Odin's morose face appeared in front of my eyes. I saw him tilt his head in thought, rest it on his hand, focusing his one-eyed fierce glare on the supplicant.

"It was hatred, not love, that united the Gods and led to the first Assembly. Each of them stepped forward and voiced their accusations. Everyone but my brother and my father complained about the pain and suffering I'd brought upon them. The great Odin spoke last. He said that I'd asked him to betray them all. A judgement was passed quickly: I would be burnt at a stake. I fell on my knees in front of Týr, begging him for justice. By making their wishes come true I had harmed the Gods so badly, he said, that the punishment was *not enough*."

"Can I have some water?" asked the little girl, "please?" I shook so badly that I spilled water all over the table, then nearly bit through the crystal goblet. The water tasted like ash, smelled of wood smoke.

"They tied me to a pole, placed wood around me, made my brother and my father watch. They cried and screamed as the flames leapt up. I survived. I stood in front of them naked and unscathed. I knew it meant that I did not deserve punishment, and I said so. Týr judged that what the situation called for was a bigger stake. My brother and my father were forced to watch again, the three of us screaming as one. I survived again. Týr said that it was clear to him now that my wrongdoings were so terrible that I had to be burnt three times, three being the holy number of the Æsir. How lucky was I that the holy number was not twenty-eight?! They cut down an entire forest to build a fire that would finally kill me."

"You survived," I said.

I had never seen Freya crying like this. Her face was red and puffy, she sniffled between words, her voice was muffled. "I did. I survived more pain than I thought possible to experience. Do you know how long it takes for a forest to burn, how it feels when your body melts, you gasp for air and inhale flames? Do you know why it was a fire? So that no blood would be spilled in Ásgard."

"I don't like this story, Mam," said the little girl in my lap.

"I don't see how this is related to you putting a child in a cage," I said.

Freya wiped her tears with her sleeve and her voice turned into steel again. "The betrayal didn't end there. The Æsir hostages sent to Vanaheim united to overthrow its lawful ruler. He came here, to Ásgard, for justice, and was turned away. It was not up to the Æsir, said Odin, to resolve conflicts in Vanaheim. He wandered around the Nine, seeking solace or solution, finding none. Eventually, he decided that he wanted to die in Vanaheim, in his own world, even if he'd get executed by the rebels. What races of people are there?"

"Eh? Jötnar, humans, elves, dark elves... do Gods count?"

"Any more?"

I shook my head and so did the girl in my lap. "I don't understand what this has to do with anything."

"Nine worlds, honey. Müspelheim is fire and lava. Niflheim is ice and snow. Nobody lives there. Helheim is for the dead. Midgard – humans. Jötunheim – jötnar."

I said nothing. The sooner the lesson was over, the faster we could get out of here and breathe.

"Álfheim has the elves. Svartálfheim – the dark elves. Ásgard here has the Gods and all those that serve them. What's missing?"

"Vanaheim," I muttered.

"It turned out that all of the Vanir, Gods and mortals alike, had been wiped out by a mysterious plague. The only ones who were born in Vanaheim and are still alive are its four remaining Gods. Odin found this very sad," she hissed, "then reminded us we should be grateful, for if we had stayed in Vanaheim, we too would have been dead. Do I look like I'm grateful?"

I barely stopped myself from apathetic shrugging. I had known she'd make it all about herself.

"You were born with the sort of powers that would have had you killed in Midgard. I saw your potential. I know there's still more that you are capable of. That cage taught you that you could shift. Don't you understand? Odin sits on the throne of Ásgard, and Vanaheim is a wilderness where strange animals dwell. Odin's been perched on that throne for too long. My father deserves the honour, but he doesn't want it. I do. It is owed to me and not just to me, to everyone who died in Vanaheim. You are a weapon that has been given to me, but everything has a price, and I had to pay it."

"Hmm?"

"The prophecy," she murmured. "You know more about the future than Odin does and one day you will reveal it to him. That is the price I had to pay."

My jaw dropped. "Wasn't I the one who had to learn it, who got slapped for not speaking fast enough, the one who must die in Midgard before telling the prophecy to Odin? How's this a price *you* are paying? Don't you think you owe *me* something? We had an agreement to keep Freyr away from me at all times. You broke it. You brought him where you knew I would be."

"Honey—"

"You put me in a cage. You forced me to learn the prophecy. You sent me to Jötunheim. You call me your weapon. Where's my reward? Give me a reason why I shouldn't leave here and go straight to Odin!"

"I apologise," she said.

If I had been holding anything, I would have dropped it.

"Sending you to Jötunheim was a mistake. Both of us wasted time, and I put you in danger. The fault is mine. As for the rest..." Her voice trailed off. "Again, I apologise. Tell me what you want, and I will give it to you."

Turn back time and bring back Magni. My throat tightened with an unvoiced cry before I bristled. Freya, apologising? Twice? There was a trap waiting.

"Start with giving me less. No more gowns or boots," I said, watching her suspiciously. "I can't wear them, I never could. You can be any woman you want, I can't even grow my hair out, and whatever Thrud did to my fingernails didn't last overnight. This, here, is who I am. Leave me be."

Her nod was followed by a deep sigh. As if I had been born like this to spite her.

"You keep trying to change me to your liking, to make me find 'someone nice' at an or-org— it doesn't matter where, it will never happen. Never. That's my prophecy for you. If there ever was a chance, you destroyed it. Here's what I want. Find a way to ensure that no man will ever be able to touch me in a sexual way again."

Freya's eyes popped out as though I'd suggested tearing Sessrúmnir down and rebuilding it from black basalt. Her mouth opened, but no sound came out.

"Ever," I repeated. "No human, jötunn, elf, or whatever you called those who dwelled in Vanaheim. No Gods either."

"You are in shock," she said weakly. "It's a very emotional time for us both. Why don't we lie down and rest? I'm not feeling well."

"Me neither. Aha, when I said that I want no man to be able to touch me?"

"Darling...!"

"No woman either," I spat, already fighting with the door, then bolting out of the room. I nearly sent one of the maids to the ground, barely avoided running into a naked man statue. I ran and ran, leaving Sessrúmnir behind, panting, filling my lungs with the fresh, sweet air, until I fell to my knees, weeping.

"Don't cry, Mam," said the girl, tugging at my sleeve.

I was hugging myself, choked by sobs, rocking back and forth, the cage's rods hurting my body. I fell to my side, trying to curl into a ball so small it would disappear, my little heart beating faster and faster, racing as I hoped I could become even smaller, so small that I would fall out of the cage. And I had. A tiny, black bird that suddenly had no hands but wings it was too exhausted to flap, fell on the sand.

It wasn't Freya who lifted the bird-me up. It was the person-me, unsure whether it was safe to caress something so small and so broken with even a finger as I carried myself towards a stream. I took a little bit of water in my hand and gave it to me. Bird-me shifted back into girl-me so suddenly that I almost dropped myself, but I wrapped my arms around my neck and I held me and I whispered in my ear.

I love you.

Freya said it over and over as she carried me to Sessrúmnir and that was how I'd learned what love was.

I kept weeping at night, wetting the bed, screaming to be let out. Demanding windows be open at all times. Hiding the keys to all the locks, so nobody else could find them. Eating and drinking until I was full, then more, until I made myself sick. When I spent the whole day digging a hole in the ground so that I could hide food in there, torn apart by the thought that if I were in a cage I couldn't get to this place, so I should dig more holes, everywhere, I broke down. I couldn't live with the child, so I told her we would play a game. I didn't make the mistake of leaving space she could escape through. I put her in the chest, placed the chest deep in the dungeon, destroyed the key. Because I loved me, too.

I didn't know that I couldn't just decide not to have those memories. It worked, mostly, although I could never understand my need to sleep with windows open, and sometimes my own screams woke me up.

"I'm sorry," I whispered, kneeling to finally meet the girl's gaze. "You will never be locked anywhere again. I will carry you with me and take you wherever you want to go."

The lady who knelt in front of me was sad and I felt for her. "Thank you," I said, and her eyes filled with tears. That made me sad, too.

"You are free," I said to the girl, my voice breaking.

"You are free, too," I said to the lady. "Goodbye."

The birds sang, a bee buzzed, the stream whispered. A gentle breeze caressed my skin. Exhausted beyond belief, I flopped down on my back rather than lay down. The sun warmed my cheeks. If I had known this would happen today I would have expected to die, drown in the tar, or at least feel something... anger... peace, reconciliation maybe? There was nothing. An emotionless emptiness that made me think of the Ginnungagap, the void between the fires of Müspelheim and the ice of Niflheim, filled with steam that eventually became life.

The void inside me didn't remain empty for long.

A pinprick of blue light. Ice that could burn forests, fire that froze lava. Wrath so concentrated it outweighed the Universe. A tip of an arrow so sharp that it was no longer iron but a wound itself, forged in the fire that Surtr stoked in Müspelheim. A need.

Odin desired wisdom and paid for it with his own eye; he desired the runes and paid for them with nine days of suffering in a state that was neither life nor death. Freya took what she wanted and paid for it with *my* suffering. If I were a weapon, I was a double-edged sword. Once Odin was exiled from Ásgard, I would not allow another monster to replace him.

I wouldn't just kill her, I would destroy her. Burning her at the stake would be too fast, too merciful. I would take away everything and everyone that she had ever held dear. From her beauty, through Brisingamen, to Freyr. I had always thought of the prophecy as something that belonged to Odin. It only occurred to me now to use it.

My stomach grumbled and I felt surprised, as if I'd gone through too much for my body to have demands. Would I find Freya sitting in the garden, fiddling with a strawberry? I would join her and I would bare my teeth in a smile that never reached the eyes.

I believed her when she said that she wouldn't have allowed me to die. Dead, I would be of no use for her. A human girl could have lasted maybe one more day before simply dying of thirst. Freya was not human. Except for Idunn's fruit she didn't really eat, just played with food, like a cat would. She drank her sweet, pink wine because she liked it. Hunger, thirst, fire couldn't kill her. I wouldn't either. Death would end the suffering that hadn't started yet, torture that would make days and nights I had spent in a cage feel like freedom.

"...just one more," said Odin. "Then Bragi will ensure your fame spreads to all Nine Worlds."

"Even Múspelheim?" asked the wolf curiously.

I tried to look around but couldn't. I was dreaming.

I had to memorise as much and as fast as possible. The sharp smell and the whiteness of snow, the cool air, the hills, the presence of Odin – this must have been the north of Ásgard. Here Fenrir wolf, one of Loki's three monstrous "children", dwelled. I knew him as, well, a wolf, perhaps larger than others. Now he was towering over the hills, talking. Like the prophecy foretold. In the dream I couldn't even gasp.

"Mmm," said Bragi vaguely.

"I like the sound of that. But I don't trust you."

"I shall take an oath," said Odin. "On my own staff. You know such an oath cannot be broken."

"I don't trust that you will set me free," specified Fenrir wolf. Odin stood tiny next to him. So did Loki, whose hands were extended in a way suggesting that he was holding something so thin that it was nearly invisible, like one long, silvery hair. "I broke through chains thicker than my legs. Bragi can go and praise me already. Why would I even bother with..." Fenrir waved his paw and both Odin and Loki winced nervously.

"It is magical," piped up Loki. "Forged by the dark elves. It's the toughest of the challenges we could come up with for you."

"Twice is enough."

"Three is the holy number," Odin pointed out.

Fenrir growled. "I want to hear that oath."

"I swear on my own staff," repeated Odin. "If you can't free yourself, we will free you. It is my oath and I make it freely."

Týr cleared his throat. "I believe it to be just to give Fenrir a hostage."

Heavy silence befell the gathering. Fenrir tilted his head slightly, like a giant, curious dog.

"A hostage?" Odin finally repeated.

"A hostage. I volunteer. I will put my sword hand between Fenrir wolf's jaws."

Hush went through the crowd that I seemed to be part of, thrown into the middle of some...event. Loki had never shown any interest in his offspring and Fenrir had always been Týr's darling. I would have paled if I could. Odin was preparing some monumental swindle and Týr knew it.

"I don't want to hurt you," murmured the wolf, his voice between a growl and a purr. His pupils narrowed, Týr's face reflecting in the golden eye. I was being shown love. Was the premonition some kind of suggestion? The God of justice had only one weakness – something that wasn't an animal anymore, a beast so big it nearly obscured the giant, black wall behind it...

What wall? It seemed to stretch as far as I could see. They caged

Fenrir? Was this definitely Ásgard? Where was the shore? If only I could look around!

"You won't hurt me," said Týr, "because Odin made an oath that cannot be broken. It is only so that you have reassurance."

Not once in my life had I heard Týr say so many words in one go. He rarely uttered anything besides "it is just" or "it is unjust", thereby ending any trial or discussion. What he had just said had a hidden meaning to it, but what was it? Was it a threat? A promise? Týr was not capable of lying, but could he be concealing something?

"Wake up, darling."

"We are ready," announced Týr.

"Wake up, darling!"

"Good Gods," I gasped, sitting up in my bed. It was light outside. Freya sat on the bed next to me. The wolf, the biting cold, the wall – all were gone. I rubbed my eyes, shook my head. "This is real?"

Her eyebrows wandered up. "What is real, petal?"

"Never mind," I muttered. I had to check on Fenrir wolf right now. Whatever she wanted had to wait. "I'm a bit busy."

"You were asleep in the middle of the day, honey, you can't be all that busy. But if you changed your mind, I will not hold it against you."

She was already heading out. "Wait, changed my mind on what?"

Freya stopped, as if her feet had grown roots. Very slowly she began to turn back towards me, the black hair, unusual on her, turning into a wave of silk, like a short, shining cape. Her eyes were widened in what was probably supposed to be either fear or dread, lip slightly quivering. I observed the performance feeling both indifferent and impressed. "You know," she uttered gloomily.

"I don't," I said, my heartbeat accelerating, eyes glued to a brown pouch she clutched in her hand.

"You have forced me to bring you a..." She paused. "Magical object."

Fenrir could wait, I decided in a blink. "You have my necklace?"

"Necklace? It's not a necklace."

"Oh," I said, slightly thrown. Most magical objects allocated to women in Ásgard were various types of jewellery. "What is it then?"

"It's a bracelet, darling, but..."

I snorted. "Sit down," I said. "Water?"

"I'll have some of my pink wine, darling. Let me just tell you what it is, then I will ring for the wine and you can think about it one more time." Freya showed me what I rightly guessed to be a leather pouch, then hid it in her lap, along with her hands. I put on my dressing gown, sat opposite her and tried to stare through the table. "Was this Loki's idea?"

"Loki behaved disgustingly towards me. Talking about spreading his seed. Nowhere near me, I said. May I see?"

"He is tricking you, petal, he wants you to—"

"I want no man or woman, whether human, elf, dark elf, jötunn, or God... or whoever used to live in Vanaheim... to ever be able to touch me in a sexual way. No exceptions, no ifs, ands, or buts. Not one, not ever. Why in the Nine would he want me to be able to keep him away from me?"

"But, darling, never is a very long time. Think of all the people you have never met. Honey, I know what you said to me, but what if one day you fall in love after all?" The way she stared at me was puzzling. I smirked and her eyes narrowed, as if in sudden pain, voice becoming slightly cracked. "You would be able to marry, but not to consummate the marriage. No childr – nothing..."

I gestured dismissively. "Every spell can be undone, it's a law. There must be a way to stop this bracelet from working. Where, when did you have it made? How long have I slept?"

"It already existed, darling, Loki had it made long before you asked for it. Do you see why I am bothered?"

I tried to ask so many questions at once that they blurred into one indeterminate sound.

"The only way to remove this bracelet is either with Surtr's sword, or by cutting off your hand, petal. Loki had it made for Sif. Think about it." Freya pulled at the rope and, as always, it hardly took a blink for one of the elf twins, Gefn or Höfn, to appear.

I sat, motionless, thinking about it, as the maid served the wine and a plate with strawberries, so that Freya would have something to fiddle with. I wasn't hungry, a bit nauseous if anything. Surtr, the lord of Müspelheim, *was* lava and fire, and nothing was hotter than his sword. Approaching Surtr would turn me into a very small amount of ash. Admittedly, this would undo the spell. I could save time by having my hand chopped off... maybe I should have some wine too.

"Sif wanted to put it on Thor's wrist," explained Freya when the door finally closed. She seemed genuinely upset. "She believed that it would stop him from cheating on her. Only at the last moment she realised..."

I snorted.

"...it was pointed out to her that it would work the other way round, too. Thor would want sex, but nobody would be willing or able to give it to him, Sif included."

"No man, no woman..."

"No jötunn, no elf, no human, no God, *nobody*, honey. Just as you requested. Don't you think that's a strange coincidence?"

My stupid imagination showed me Thor approaching an unsuspecting goat. "What's the 'but' and the 'except'?"

"There is none. Unless someone cuts off your hand."

"If someone cuts my hand off, I'll have bigger problems than whether he or she desires me," I muttered, then drank some wine as well. It went straight to my head. A pink, bubbly liquid that Freya adored, its colour as fake as its sweetness. "Whose idea was this?"

"Sif's, darling."

I smiled sourly.

"I found out in time to explain it to her. She then arranged the hammer... the journey."

"Don't you think it would have been better for Thor to keep his cock inside his pants instead?"

"Darling, stop shouting at me. I have no influence on Thor's cock and Sif did not tell me what she was planning."

"It was Loki, not Sif," I muttered. "She owes him for having the bracelet made and she owes you for not having used it. I told you she was stupid. Did she just give it to you?"

"Ah," Freya said, looking slightly sheepish. "She asked for a little... But it's not important so long as you understand that you should not take it. Petal, I know it's hard for you to be rational, you are hurt, but think about children, you might want children one day!"

"I can't stand children. Give me that bracelet. I want to feel free."

"But you are free, sweetheart, you can pick any man or any woman. I would make sure they fall in love with you. I would break all the rules for you—"

"You look like me," I interrupted, and Freya fluttered her eyelashes, producing an apologetic smile.

She'd made her hair black, like mine, only long and shiny. Her many-layered gown had leather accents, some of which looked like the least useful gauntlets ever. Her lips were slightly thinner than usual, free from that red goop she usually smeared on them. Freya could become any woman, as long as that woman was beautiful. Now she was a "better" version of me, a "subtle" suggestion of how I could gain her approval. For a blink or two. Before the improvements continued. Whatever message she was trying to send, she'd failed.

Calm lake, quiet day. "You told me a thousand times that you can't just make people or Gods fall in love or stop being in love without any rules."

"Consequences, darling, not rules. This is going to have far more consequences for you than any lover could...! No, no, I made a mistake. I should have never told you about it, not yet. I need to make sure... to wait..." She nervously fiddled with the pouch and I stiffened, worried she'd break my bracelet. "Maya, pumpkin, please listen to me. Men are weak creatures. If they can't make you want them, they'll try to outsmart you, to gain more power or wealth than you. Once they fail there as well, they'll use violence, the weapon of the powerless. No, no, listen to me," she pleaded feverishly, even though I wasn't saying anything, trying to decide whether to use my powers to tear the pouch out of her hands. "A man might never be able to force you to have sex, but he will be able to—"

"Give it to me!"

"—kill you! Why are you like this? I am the Goddess of love! Freyr is the God of fertility, of sex, of ecstasy! You're throwing it all away! Don't you even want to find out how it feels?"

"I've learned enough in the cage and this is about me, not you!"

She was starting to get to me again. *Calm down*, I told myself, wiping my clammy hands in the dressing gown.

"I understand, darling, I really do, you want to hurt me, but you're only going to hurt yourself, so young, so inexperienced... This might even be Loki's attempt to separate us in some way!"

"Ah," I muttered, staring at the pouch out of the corner of my eye. "Wouldn't it be horrible if something were to separate us in some way. Oh no! He's behind you!"

My hand shot forward and tore the pouch out of hers. Freya cried out, jumping to her feet, getting her stupid gown tangled in the chair that had fallen back and nearly pulled her along. I tugged at the strings with my fingers, then with my teeth. A little *click* sounded right before Freya leapt at me and tore the empty pouch out of my hand.

I pushed her off and sat up, looking at the barely visible silver wire around my wrist. It had been open before, but now it had no lock, no beginning, no end. Only now did it occur to me that the bracelet could have proven to be another thing I wouldn't be able to wear, causing me horrible pain. No such thing happened. Nothing happened at all.

"Thank you," I said, helping Freya back to her feet. "You may keep the pouch."

The thin bracelet was not one hair, but three of them braided together. The size was just right, as if it had been made for me rather than for Thor. I tried to pull it off, tugged at it, hissed when the bracelet bit into my fingertips and wrist. It didn't break, like thin silver should. It didn't come off either. What worried me was that I didn't feel any magic in the bracelet, no mana, no power, nothing at all.

"I am very disappointed in you," said Freya sternly, then she shook her head and every single hair that had fallen out of place during the struggle returned to where it was meant to be.

I rolled my eyes. "Yes, thank you, thank you," I said. "I couldn't be more grateful. Was the time I'd spent in Jötunheim enough, or was this also for the cage and the slapping?"

"Ah," she said and that sheepish look returned. "I would like to ask you to... actually it was Sif who... she requested a little favour of you." I said nothing, but she winced. I must have made quite a face. "Darling, Thor has been missing for a long time."

"How sad."

"It's not about Sif. Thor is the protector of Ásgard and we don't know where he is. After the... you know... *that* happened in Jötunheim, he seemed very upset. Thjálfi tells us that Thor demanded to be taken to Midgard and insisted that he was never coming back."

I was caressing my bracelet absentmindedly in the same way Freya touched Brisingamen all the time. "And the little favour is?"

"Someone needs to find him."

"Ask Odin," I said without much interest, wondering how to test the bracelet's effectiveness.

Freya sighed. "Let's go to the, you know, special room—"

"No," I interrupted, my throat tightening at just the thought. "Tell me here."

She glanced around, then lowered her voice. "Loki told us that Thor is a mercenary, darling. He fights alongside humans."

"Against jötnar?"

"No, worse, against other humans. Something must have happened to him."

Freya didn't touch me, it was the memory of my horrendous trip back to Ásgard that felt like a sudden punch in the belly. Thor slumped in the chariot, hands wrapped tight around his bloodied hammer, that sound coming out from deep inside him, overpowering the goats' bleeting. *Rrrrrmmmmrrrrrrr.* He wanted to go on killing so badly that he turned against the humans who loved him the way jötnar loved Freya, only in Thor's case the feeling was mutual. Sif was human, or perhaps used to be. He killed his lover and his son, why couldn't he get rid of his wife and leave Midgard alone?

"Odin is delighted. He's collecting warriors for Valhalla," hissed Freya. "Only the biggest, strongest, stupidest would dare to take on Thor. In the meantime, we are defenceless."

"Against?"

Freya rubbed her nose, then looked gloomily at the empty pouch. "Anyone who would want to attack," she mumbled. "Even Heimdall can't stop everyone. Luckily, there is no other way to come here save for using Bifröst..."

I immediately bristled. "Or crossing Ifing."

"Sweetie pie, would you agree to go to Midgard and search for Thor? I beg you. All of Ásgard needs him back."

"Loki..."

"Don't be difficult, petal. Thor is killing his beloved humans. Do you think sending Loki to join him would make things better?"

I finished the wine, then ate a strawberry. Drops of red juice fell onto my white dressing gown, like diluted blood. "Why me? Why not Sif, or you?"

"Those are special sorts of men," Freya whispered. "Outlaws, mercenaries, soldiers... I'm sure you know what I mean. I, myself, would not go anywhere near them. You, on the other hand..."

On the other hand, I was wearing the bracelet.

"You'll be completely safe. They will *want* him gone. You can fly away from danger. You can introduce yourself as Frigg, or even me, or make up some other Goddess and let them adore you. Or simply Maya, the Goddess of... of... something."

If I were to find Ásgard's protector and talk him into returning here, all of them would owe me. I liked that idea. I just had to find the trap. "Loki will not follow me."

"He won't."

"I want to hear that from him. From a safe distance." I admired my bracelet the way she admired her fingernails, then looked at her and gulped. Freya's face was grey, her gaze glued to my wrist. I hid my sticky hands in my lap, worried that she had lied, that she'd try to take my bracelet away again.

"Darling," she said and sounded as if she'd just remembered that she was as old as the Universe. "This is not a demand, not even a request. If you don't want to go, then you don't have to. You can just stay here forever and enjoy..." She gestured around. "Just think about it. I will wait for your decision, then respect it. Now I must go."

I didn't have to ask where. Her little boo boo needed his Mam. Freya didn't joyfully skip away, though. Instead, she dragged her feet and gave me one last sorrowful look before quietly shutting the door.

"Thank you," I said, a blink too late, and nearly jumped out of my skin when a piercing shriek tore through the air. It echoed, grew, causing the goblets and jugs to shake, the sky to darken, letting the whole of Ásgard know that winter had arrived and Freyr had died... hold on, how could that be, when he'd just returned to life yesterday? I might have slept long, but surely not through the whole summer. Could she be *that* upset about the bracelet, about – for once – not getting what she wanted?

Bracelet.

I bit my lip, thinking. Loki wouldn't have given it to Sif if he had expected her to use it on his best friend. It must have been his suggestion that Sif should first discuss it with Freya, who pointed out the plan's flaw. Loki then suggested the theft of the hammer, put on a big hat, used the blue orb to deceive me so I wouldn't recognise a shifter. The wedding was his plan as well, and the fear came from knowing that he had to survive placing himself between furious Thor and King Thrymr. A very risky plan but an amusing one – to him.

I couldn't prove it, but maybe it was Bragi's tales that made us all believe that mana couldn't be stored, Ifing – crossed. What else was there? Did Odin know the truth, or truths, or was he also under Bragi's spell? When he was forced to listen to Bragi, he drank more than usual. Did that make him resistant to the newly re-forged truths? If I were to ask Bragi to spread a story, would I end up believing it? I shook my head in awe. The nondescript, mousy-haired man could reshape the Universe and his wife held the survival of the Gods in her dirty hands.

Without Idunn's fruit, Ásgard's "protector" would notice soon enough that he was getting older and weaker. It was a question of time, whether twenty or two hundred winters. Unfortunately, the Nine couldn't afford any more of Sif's plans and ideas.

Freya was right. I was the right person to do this. I could just find Thor, fly to him, tell him...something I'd come up with soon. As long as I didn't have to fly over a lake or a river that blocked mana, I was safe in Midgard and there was no Ifing to stop me from getting to the Rainbow Bridge. The bracelet kept me safe from some sorts of danger and I could escape others by shifting—

My heart stopped for a blink, then started beating twice as fast as before. This bracelet was not made for a shifter. It was supposed to stay on my wrist, not my... where would a horse even wear a bracelet? On its hoof? Leg? Did horses have ankles? I had never paid attention to horses past finding out what I should eat once I shifted into one. Even in the wine-induced haze I still vaguely remembered what happened when I decided to shift into a horse indoors, so I stepped outside. At the very last moment it occurred to me that horses' legs were probably thicker than my wrists and I shifted into a cat instead, expecting to hear a quiet *clink* of the thing dropping on the ground.

I examined my paw. Instead of falling off, the bracelet shrank, adapting the same way the crystal pendant did. I shifted into a swallow and I was almost certain the same thing happened, although I couldn't figure out a way to look at my own foot. It must have been really tiny now, I thought, then froze. What if it could only shrink, but not grow? Freya mentioned cutting off my hand. The thin "braid" wouldn't break. It would cut through my skin, gristle, bone...

Suddenly I didn't feel well at all. How would it feel to only have one hand? What about the bleeding? Did people die from losing hands? I couldn't even curse properly, just chirp. My choice was to either try and find out, or remain a small, scared bird forever.

I was so ready for the excruciating pain that for a blink I nearly felt it. I had to sit down, my knees too wobbly to keep me upright. I stared at my wrist with unseeing eyes, still half-expecting my hand to just fall off. My gaze rested on the thin, hair-like, silver chain that couldn't be broken. A blink later I was in the air, heading north.

As I approached the patch of snow that had been created especially for the wolf, or rather for Týr, I looked around anxiously. Was there something I could have mistaken for a wall? A few trees very close together, perhaps? I could only see the sun going down over the sea, hear the roar of Ifing nearby. No walls or anything else.

I landed at a safe distance, shifted into my human form, then cleared my throat to announce my arrival. Fenrir looked up. He wasn't the size of a mountain. He was, however, at least two or three times as large as the last time I saw him, and I felt slightly sick.

"Hello," I said.

He bared his teeth and let out a low growl that said "bugger off" rather than "you look tasty".

"I'm-I'm a friend," I added, attempting to grin. My dream and the "method" to remove the bracelet blended together into a very vivid vision of blood shooting out of the stump where my hand used to be. My feet were itching to retreat. "Can you talk?" I asked and for the first time in my life I saw a wolf roll his eyes, lay his head on his paws and pretend to fall asleep.

I felt the little hairs on my forearms stand up. He didn't feel like a shifter, but this wasn't animal behaviour. Loki, the best of shifters, was Fenrir's father. I couldn't tell how fast the wolf was growing and, for all I knew, he could have never changed before, then doubled in size only last night. What if he could talk, he just didn't want to talk to me?

I crushed some snow in my hand, letting the biting cold ground me. I tried to breathe deeply as the drops of water dripped between my fingers, the cold air hurting my lungs the way it used to in Jötunheim. Everything was fine as long as there was nothing that could be confused for a black wall dividing Ásgard from the sea. A construction like that was unlikely to appear overnight, or ever. Not even Odin and his dubious wisdom could come up with something so weird.

I caressed my bracelet with my finger, reminding myself that I would be safe in Midgard. I'd have to make it back here to witness the strange oath and Týr offering himself as a hostage. Despite all that safety, I felt nauseous listening to Fenrir's breathing, envisioning my hand, rather than Týr's, between his teeth.

Once I'd returned to Sessrúmnir and ate, caressing my bracelet a thousand times in the process, my imagination awoke. What if the bracelet did nothing but shrink and grow? There was no way for me to find out whether it would protect me from unwanted advances without putting myself in a situation that involved unwanted advances, say, Loki's...

I got rid of the image as quickly as I could and let out a disgusted snigger. He'd be in debt to me as well, once I brought his best friend back. All of Ásgard would be. Yes, I would accept the quest. The dream was proof that I was safe. Unless... I knew some of my dreams showed me the future, but what if this one *was* just a dream after all and I was betting my life on a non-existent wall and a giant, talking wolf?

If Thor was killing humans now, he must have gone insane. Suppose I found him in the midst of a bloodshed? What would I do? Ask him to take a break, so that I could appeal to his conscience? Should I plead with or berate him? He'd just throw his hammer at me and I'd die in Midgard as prophesied, and spend the rest of my life... the rest of my death waiting for Odin.

I swiftly refined my plan. I'd simply wait for him to finish the battling and start drinking, although I felt that would lead to bedding a woman or two before getting up and going back to work. I had never witnessed an actual war, or even a small battle, but surely they needed to rest every now and then? Or someone would win the war at some point. Then the winners would spend some time drinking and bedding, and before the next war started I'd tell Thor that he had to go home.

I imagined myself, a complete nobody, doing that. The image of Thor's bloodied face contorted with boiling fury, the sound of his guttural rumble, the red-stained remains of the wedding gown I'd never dare to joke about came back immediately. A violent shiver shook me. I would accept the quest...soon. Right after I came up with an even more refined plan. Ideally one that wouldn't require me to get near him.

The moon turned once, then twice, and I kept postponing that "soon". I only saw Freya in passing once or twice, which wasn't surprising, since Freyr was at his most...fertile this time of year. I took a lot of baths and ate a lot of cake. I combed all of Ásgard in search of Thor, in case he had fallen and broken his leg somewhere. I avoided Loki, Bragi, and Granny Frigg, in case she knew what I was or rather wasn't doing. Planning, I kept telling myself as I continued to wander around aimlessly and not plan anything, was essential. I would be ready *very* soon.

The decision eventually made itself.

I knew that every year at midsummer Freya would organise a

feast to celebrate Freyr's...middle age. I was so busy either brooding or picturing my glorious return with shamefaced Thor that the preparations passed me by. I slept at very odd hours, sometimes waking up at sunset. On a day seemingly no different from others I pulled a rope to call a maid over and ask for breakfast, as I became fond of eating in bed.

Nothing happened.

My forehead wrinkled before it dawned on me that those ropes probably wore out with time. I'd eat in the garden then before continuing to not make any decisions. I walked out, yawning aloud, smacking my lips in anticipation, then freezing mid-stretch.

For the midsummer party, this one was small. No more than a hundred or so Gods, Goddesses, and their special companions. The maids ran around, carrying trays, jugs, plates, bowls, trying to be both invisible and omnipresent. My feet seemed to have grown roots, fittingly for a garden, and I would have probably remained like that forever if someone hadn't turned and saw me.

"You there," she shouted. "More wine."

I gawked. Sif had never been my favourite, even before her jealousy destroyed the City of Light. Her biggest pride and joy, her hair that reached past her waist, was a wave of gold that could almost put Freya to shame. Apart from that she mostly stood out by being exquisitely nondescript and doing nothing.

Like me.

"Girl!" urged Sif. "I said, more wine!"

I just stood there, wondering whether she really didn't recognise me or whether she was belittling me just because she could.

"Are you stupid or deaf?" she yelled just when a sweet maid named Vanadís approached her. Surprised by the outburst, Vanadís stumbled, dropping a carafe in the grass. Sif immediately lost interest in me, having found someone else to berate.

A dark elf I didn't recognise sat next to her. His hand gently squeezed her knee. Sif stopped clamouring. He turned to whisper something in her ear and she burst out in tinkly laughter, like little glass bells falling down the marble stairs of the City of Light. He was young. Very young.

Fury, rather than my feet, carried me towards the top of the table, where Freyr and Freya presided. The twins were flanked by Heimdall, who, without his armour, was impeccably beautiful and knew it, and...Loki. The nearer to Freya and Freyr the guest was seated, the more important they were. Sif sat at the very end.

"My, my," said Loki. "Isn't that your little... what is she, dear Freya? What do you call her? Sorceress? Maid? Jester?"

"Oh," said Freya nervously, avoiding my gaze, "it's just Maya. She must be lost. Go back to your chambers, petal, I will see you later."

Freyr coughed, attracting my attention, then deliberately and slowly licked his lips.

"I have made my decision," I boomed and all four winced. "As has been requested of me, I shall..."

"Darling," Freya hissed, waving me away, "we're *busy*."

"I shall find Thor, the protector of Ásgard, the husband of Sif" – I gestured vaguely – "the one back there, and bring him back." I paused, then lowered my voice, worried, leaning towards Freya. "He's not back yet, is he?"

Loki was the first to compose himself. "How wonderful," he bellowed, "the little sorceress is going to bring Thor back from Midgard to protect Ásgard *and* his wife Sif, the one back there. Let's toast to her success!"

I caught a glimpse of Freya's face and I didn't fly so much as shoot towards Bifröst. Halfway through I changed my mind and turned towards Bilskirnir, Thor's hall, to find Thjálfi and convince him to take me to Midgard *right now*. I didn't get far before realising that I needed to go back to Sessrúmnir – quietly – to grab a few things. Then I'd... ah, I'd come up with something.

I couldn't wait to rescue poor Sif from her loneliness.

"Move, you bastards!" boomed Thjálfi, and the goats shot out in two opposite directions. I knew that would happen and my knuckles were white from holding on to the chariot's sides, but I still screamed. We hadn't even left the ground and I'd already almost lost the black bag hanging from my shoulder. "My apologies, Your Grace! They're always like…"

The chariot suddenly took flight, wobbling to the sides, both incredibly fast and dangerously low. I barely had time to blink before we were already flying over the sea, my stomach bouncing behind my ribs.

"…this!"

"I know!" I yelled back. What was wrong with me, why hadn't I just strolled down the unguarded Rainbow Bridge? "Go west! To the harbours!"

"I'm trying!"

I made the mistake of opening my eyes and immediately shut them again so hard I saw stars. If only I had a little orb of mana, just enough to shift and AAAAAAAAAAAAA!!!!! The goats hurled the chariot in a direction I completely didn't expect and, judging by the sounds Thjálfi produced, neither did he. I was too light. With Thor inside they wouldn't be able to toss the chariot around like this. For a while I couldn't really breathe as the goats briefly agreed on a direction and pulled us at a speed a flying arrow would envy. When I could think again, I felt both nauseous and sad. When I asked Thjálfi to take me to Midgard, he couldn't have agreed more enthusiastically. Someone really missed Thor after all.

I thought the worst was over when the chariot began to shake violently. It sounded like its bottom part was being whipped very fast. It rubbed against the tops of the trees now.

"Back to the shore!" I yelled and nearly bit off the tip of my tongue.

"Not the harbours?"

That was what I had planned. Sailors and traders had information—

"Here!" I croaked as loudly as I could. "Drop me here!"

The goats took that literally. The bag landed first, followed by me. I turned just in time to see Thjálfi hanging upside down, holding on to the reins, as the chariot shot back over the sea. I lay on my back and spent a while just breathing. I felt as if I had dragged the chariot here all by myself.

I slowly collected my bruised self, massaged a part or two, checked the bag. Three apples from Idunn, a chunk of cheese, bread that I knew would remain fresh for days, an empty skin to fill with water. A pouch of coin that I had gotten from Thjálfi, who just shrugged when I worried he'd get in trouble. Nothing resembling a weapon, not that I knew how to use any.

Why was I here? When I imagined the massive, gloomy pile of muscles with hair like a bonfire, bloodied clothes and a hammer in his hand, something inside me not only suggested going west, but had pointed me right here. Somehow, I knew that I would find a dust road here. I must have noticed it from the chariot. Probably. And the town I was going to. Not that I could explain how I knew there would be a town.

As I slogged down the road I tried to remember my plans that had never taken on a concrete form. I needed to find someone who would somehow know something and point me towards somewhere. I struggled to understand why I opened my mouth to tell Thjálfi to take me to the harbours and instead demanded to be dropped here out of all possible places. There better be a someone who knew something...

The small settlement reminded me of what the City of Light used to look like before, when it had been a pile of turf and wood. I clucked my tongue in disapproval. A sorceress and some marble could do wonders here. A drawbridge over a moat led inside, people seemingly freely moving in and out. I raised my head proudly and walked with what I hoped was sufficient swagger to convince the guards that I belonged here too. Nobody tried to stop me or ask any questions. So far, so good—

"Beetroots, beetroots, only here!" someone yelled right into my ear and I stumbled, startled, only to have someone else deafen my other ear with a sudden "turnips!!!" A woman bumped into me, then cursed, as I tried to apologise, mortified, only to feel someone yank at my bag. I turned abruptly, ready to send the thief flying, and faced a bunch of people staring as if they'd never seen anybody like me. Which was probably true.

Someone pulled me by my arm, and I was about to start punching everyone in the throat when the small crowd silenced and parted. I gawked as two imposing looking women on horses made their way through. Both of them sat up straight, covered in various sorts of sharp objects, paying no attention to the peasants. Shieldmaidens! I'd heard about shieldmaidens. I could pretend I was one. I just needed some weapons draped all over me and nobody would try to touch my bag again.

With my arms wrapped around the bag I found the forge, answering each baffled gawk with a glare. I didn't have time to get my hopes high. The young smith, so dirty that it was hard to identify the colour of his skin, looked absolutely nothing like Thor.

"My lady."

"I need a big knife," I hissed, leaning towards him, glancing around. "The biggest you've got."

"A sword?"

I pursed my lips and nodded stiffly. He grabbed a sharp-looking chunk of shiny metal, performed something of a dance that made me wince, then handed it to me. I grabbed the hilt with both hands and the tip of the weapon smacked to the ground. It looked lighter when he'd held it.

"Maybe something a bit smaller," I muttered, ignoring the giggles somewhere behind me.

The dirty blacksmith nodded, looking as sheepish as I felt, took the sword from me and disappeared inside. Warming my hands by the dying fire I looked at the blower, then at the roof. Placing a fire under a straw roof was exactly the sort of idea I'd expect from Thor.

"My apologies for the wait," the smith said, appearing with a few differently sized sharp objects. As he pointed with a dirty finger, explaining what I was looking at, I fought the unpleasant feeling that what really mattered about the shieldmaidens was their attitude.

I selected something that was still heavy, but only required a tiny bit of mana to help me hold it in the air. It seemed more imposing than two smaller daggers. Even I would have been afraid of myself. "It's perfect. I'll take it."

"Don't you need a sheath, my lady?"

"Ah... yes, I would like a sheath, please."

The blacksmith helped me secure it to the belt and once he let go the weight immediately pulled me down. I used mana to keep the sword and sheath afloat, stood up straight, grabbed the hilt with both hands and discovered that the weapon didn't actually become any lighter. With certain difficulties I managed to remove the sword from the sheath and keep it in the air, the blade pointing down, the hilt at the same level as my face. Under the blacksmith's perplexed gaze I muttered curses, twisting my arms and wrists, unable to turn the sword as it hovered, immobile, in the air. Defeated, yet hopeful I stopped the flow of mana for just a blink and the sword dove down, nearly tearing my arms out of their sockets. I heard the giggles again, floated the weapon back into the sheath and decided to practise somewhere else. It wasn't like I intended to use it anyway.

I paid the price he named and the dirty smith's mouth dropped, his eyes widened in shock. Bugger. I probably should have haggled. I felt myself shrink in embarrassment, then remembered I was now a shieldmaiden. Shouldn't shieldmaidens actually have shields? Attitude, I reminded myself.

"Where can I find this settlement's local tavern?" I asked in a tone as decisive as I could muster.

The poor man looked faint. I felt my face heat up, even though the day seemed rather cool for midsummer. "I, um, am a traveller," I said, "a...travelling shieldmaiden. Who's lost her weapons. Um. I do not know your customs."

"Eh," he answered.

"I need a drink," I hissed, making him wince, before he silently extended a dirty, slightly shaky finger.

Fighting the urge to run away screaming I swaggered out, somewhat inconvenienced by the weapon pulling me to one side. I used some mana to lift it up, then tried to take another step and the sword kept me from doing so. I made it float along, which looked strange even to me. It would require all my concentration to make it move in rhythm with each step I took. When I made it to the tavern an eternity and a day later, I felt I really needed a drink.

All I knew about taverns was that they tended to contain drunken men who grabbed at buxom barmaids and I nervously glanced at the near-invisible bracelet, briefly hesitating before entering. The inside housed a few benches and tables, a fire burning right in the middle, and a pot bubbling over it. No men or buxom barmaids.

An older woman emerged from the back, a ladle in her hand, stopping in her tracks when she saw me. Both of us gawked at the other.

"M-my lady," she finally said.

"Why don't you give me some ale..." My lady? Innkeeper? You there? "...good woman," I finished. I had no experience with addressing tavern-owning humans. "What are you cooking there?"

"Nothing suitable for a noble lady... my lady."

"Let me decide that."

"It's rabbit stew."

"I'll have a bowl."

The woman's face dropped.

"I'll pay double."

"Ooh," she responded. "I... I thought you were going to... I will be delighted, my lady."

"It's getting late," I observed, watching her admire the coin I handed her, bite it, then look at me in a way very similar to that of the young blacksmith. It might have been more than double. "Could I stay the night?"

"Ah, I don't know... I don't even have a barn, or a bed. No, I'm so sorry, my lady." I must have looked as perplexed as the young blacksmith when she actually handed me the coin back.

"I can pay double for that too," I offered. "Or triple. A spot by the fire?"

"I don't have a—" she started, then glanced at the fire as if she were greatly surprised at its presence. "I sleep there. I'm sorry, my lady. You should *go*."

I gave up trying to look like a regular visitor of taverns. "I'm looking for a man," I hissed.

"Then you are at the wrong establishment, my lady."

"Not like that! I need help to find someone."

Her eyes narrowed.

"A tall, strong man. Red hair, beard..."

"Our old blacksmith," she interrupted, and her dreamy sigh seemed to come all the way from her toes. "He's been gone for a while." Her features softened. "How do you know each other?"

"He's—"

The door slammed into the wall, kicked open. "Monnaaaaaa!" yelled the man. "Give me all of your mead! I'm thirsty like – what is that?!"

Two small axes hung from his belt. Not as impressive as my giant-slaying sword, but he could probably lift them without help.

"The lady is leaving," said Monna.

Good Gods, I was staring at his nether regions. "I am," I confirmed nervously, looking above his head. "Goodbye."

"Get out of my way, Jan. I insist the lady stays," said another man. Jan stepped inside, gawking at me. His friend leaned against the doorframe, blocking the exit. "My name is Dalebor. It is a pleasure to meet you." I did not like the way he accented the words "pleasure" and "meet" at all. When Monna had said this wasn't the right establishment for me she'd meant the opposite of what I thought.

"I'm a shieldmaiden," I whimpered.

"Wha'?"

"Leave her alone," demanded Monna.

I took my first step towards the door. In order to send an invisible punch into Dalebor's face I had to let the sword drop. The sudden yank made me trip over my own feet. Jan's hands grabbed the air. Dalebor moved faster, catching me with one swift motion and pulling me closer. His face was way too close to mine now and the leering smirk scared me more than Jan's axes before it changed into surprise followed by confusion.

"My... my lady," he said, then blinked, as if he couldn't figure out who I was and where I had come from. He helped me stand up straight, then released me from his embrace. The sword and sheath lifted themselves up again.

"Thank you, my lord," I said, managing to keep the shaking only on the inside. "Please let me out."

"Dalebor!" shouted Jan. "What are you doing?"

I stepped outside and hesitated just a bit too long, trying to decide how to continue with the sword either throwing me off balance or hovering next to me. I examined the cloudy sky, hoping it would get dark soon, when a brutal push sent me to the ground. The heavy man pinned me down. I barely had time to grunt in surprise. His hands held my wrists and all I could do was kick the dirt. Panic clouded my mind. Bracelet, bracelet...!

"What have you done to me? Turn!"

"I can't," I wailed. He was so heavy I could barely move.

I felt his hand squeeze between our bodies, then moving somewhere near the small of my back... when the weight lightened. Dalebor's face was perplexed again as he lifted himself to his feet, then helped me stand up as well. He looked as if he'd gotten hit with a shovel on the back of his head.

"M-my lady... I must apologise, I don't know what came over me..."

I rewarded him with a sweet smile right before he disappeared, pushed aside by Jan. I gasped. Dalebor was already lifting himself, his teeth bared, the confusion gone. I deflected Jan's axe right before it struck my face. His cries mixed with curses as blood trickled from between his fingers. I stared in mute terror. If he was lucky, he'd only lose his eye—

Dalebor leapt towards me. I sent him down and the weight of the sword nearly did the same to me. I had to run. The bloody sword kept yanking me down, then pulling me forward. I wasn't running towards the gate so much as skipping randomly.

"The witch killed Jan!"

I nearly slammed into a wall, distracted for a blink. Shit! Fire pit! I released the sword, its pull dragging me sideways, saving me. I smacked a small child with the buggered bag. I sent too much mana into the sword and when it shot up, I nearly flew over a petrified hen. An arrow whizzed past. Between the barking dogs, people's screaming and shouting, the cries of the man struck by the arrow, my own panting, one short yell cut through.

"Close the bridge!"

Shit!

I ran out of breath, I had to get rid of that sword, where did all the buggered hen come from, I could see the drawbridge going up, a bolt struck the ground next to me, *faster*! *Shift*! I'd lose the bag, but I'd live– no, if I shifted now all my things would crush me! Propelled by despair I tried to do everything at once, run faster, send the sword, sheath, and bag into the air—

—I slammed onto the ground. The ground and I both groaned in shock.

The sword was somehow still at my side, the bag on my shoulder, and I was definitely not a bird. My hip hurt. My belt had apparently tried to cut me in half. The only sounds breaking through the silence were chirping birds and the squeaking of the drawbridge still going up. They must have been as surprised as I was, even though they saw what happened and I didn't.

"Kill the witch!" someone yelled again. Another bolt hit the ground. Nowhere near me, but I still screeched. I'd almost forgotten I was escaping.

My legs refused to carry the sword until I lifted it with mana. A vague idea arrived – I drew some more mana and sent the sword flying faster than I could run. I controlled the speed so that it wouldn't drag me behind. Like it had just done over the drawbridge. If the water in the moat didn't block mana, I would probably still be flying.

The sword and I only stopped running when my lungs refused to continue breathing. Wheezing, panting, I gulped the air, my hands resting on my knees. The drawbridge was still up. I was too far away for even the best of archers.

My hands shook as I loosened my belt, slid off the sword still in its sheath, then sent both flying into the trees. If I were to list the stupidest things I'd done in my life, buying that would have ranked high. I had no idea where I was now, trees to my left, a field to my right, no way back. I scratched my chin in thought. I had little use for a field. The road would lead either towards the harbours or not.

A distant whinny, then the sound of hooves made me leap into the dense forest. By sheer luck I found myself on a thin, trodden path. I couldn't stay here. Pushing through the trees, afraid that they would hear my heart beating so hard and fast, I dropped the bag, flew up and sat on a branch. If I were lucky, they hadn't seen me.

The beat of the hooves slowed, then stopped. A neigh. The slam of boots on the road, then another. Two. I let out a little squeak, then tried not to breathe, in case they heard me. Swallows weren't smart. Or lucky.

"Wojciech! Hurry up!" I recognised Dalebor.

"I'm not going there." A voice I hadn't heard earlier, calm, deep.

"Coward!"

"I'm not going there," repeated the other voice.

"We owe it to Jan! Hurry!"

"Why aren't you hurrying?"

"She's – she's dangerous, she cast a spell on me, too!"

"What spell?"

Brief silence. "Doesn't matter. Come on!"

"Bard lives there. He'll take care of her."

Dalebor responded in a hissy whisper.

"Exactly," said the calm man. "Would you like that?"

Sssspsspsps psps.

"There's a storm coming, it's getting dark. I'm going back. Come with me and I'll drink with you, or follow the witch yourself."

"Coward," muttered Dalebor. "Fine. Let's go back. Looks bad, eh?"

"Quite." A grunt, a whinny. "What did she do to you then?"

I waited for a bit longer to make sure they were gone, shifted, found the bag. I surrounded myself with glow, just enough to see the trees and light the path. It was damp and cold in here, the smell of rotten leaves almost overpowering.

A bard lived there? Excellent. If anybody knew where to look for Thor, it would be a bard and it sounded like the path led to his dwelling. Now I'd really have a chance to find out what had happened, apart from Thor becoming a mercenary, once he was done with all the bedding—

The first thunderclap scared me so much that I screamed. I sped up, slipped on some leaves, cursed, then thanked the Gods for leading me into the right spot. I could have ended up anywhere. That was a lot of luck all at once.

A bit too much luck.

I stopped until the next thunderclap made me jump. Rain began to slap the leaves, at first here and there, a blink later hard and rapid. I sped up, noticing the path seemed to widen into a small road. A rock hit my head, no, an ice pellet that had found its way through the trees – aw! – another! Hail! Lightning and thunder struck almost simultaneously. If the people's fairy tales about Thor were true, he'd be too near for comfort right now.

The merciless blows became harder as I raced down the path that kept widening until it split the forest in two. Lightning struck, blinding me, but not before I saw that I was at the bottom of a hill, its incline long. I withdrew, hiding between the trees from the brutal punches of hail. I got rid of the glow and stared into the darkness. A flickering, orange dot. A candle. It could only be the bard's dwelling.

Something fell on my back, under my collar. I shrieked in fear, trying to slap my own back. This was not a lovely Ásgardian forest, this one crawled with... the hail wasn't so bad, I decided, then a pellet hit me so hard I cried out in surprise. I leapt back among the trees filled with wriggly life. I had to either run up the hill with my soaked, heavy bag, or stay here. A drop of icy water made me squeal again. I needed to shield myself.

I had only ever tried a fire shield once. It consumed a lot of air. Both outside and inside. Could I create a shield that would reflect objects, but not air? I wrapped my fingers around the crystal and concentrated.

I carefully emerged from between the trees and my mouth opened in awe at my ingenuity as the pellets bounced from the shield. The bubble I'd surrounded myself with used so little mana I only noticed it because I knew it was there. The water pouring down the bubble created a weird blur around me. Freya had said that I had a lot to learn about myself and my powers. It looked like she had been right. She had also been right when she'd said that if I made it impossible for men to use their cocks, they might try to kill me.

Monna had looked terrified. Was this normal? Would she be their victim instead?

"Bloody humans," I muttered, climbing up the hill. "Bloody men. Why did I ever leave Ásgard? Ah, yes. Bloody Sif! I am a calm buggered lake on a—" I slipped on the grass and slid down a bit. My knee found a rock to hit. I tried to lift myself up and immediately lost my footing again.

I dropped to all fours and crawled up towards the tiny flickering light, now blurred by the rain. The bag kept slipping off, binding my movements. Another lightning strike made me wince, but also confirmed that I was nearly there. I couldn't wait to get inside, warm up, have something to eat...

"Aw!" I cried, surprised. Rain and ice smacked me again. My shield had disappeared. There was no mana here, completely gone, as if it had been cut with a knife. Bloody Midgard! Bloody storm! I hurriedly crawled up the remaining part of the slope, then just raced, panting, towards the house. Little "aw"s escaped my lips as the hail and rain took turns whipping my body. I could almost see red marks forming on the skin in addition to the bruises I'd sustained earlier. The bard's house grew in front of me, blacker than the night, towering over the road, taller than any of the buildings I'd seen during my short stint in Jomsborg. I reached the door and leaned against it, panting, worried. I couldn't find so much as a hint of mana. I'd have nowhere to hide if the bracelet didn't work and the bard was like those two—

The door opened, I walked inside, then closed it behind me so as not to let the cold in. The strange thing was that I didn't intend to do any of those things. My body just did them without asking my permission.

"My lady," said the man holding a flickering candle. The shock when I recognised his voice felt as if lightning had struck my chest. I tried to look up in search for the blue orb. Neither my eyes nor my head would move. Only my legs.

"Don't hurt me," I pleaded as my body took its place at the table. "Please leave my bag...!" I cried as my hands handed the bag to him. He took everything out, placing two out of three of Idunn's apples to one side, returned the rest to the bag and pushed it towards me. My body remained frozen. I could do nothing but watch his thin, wiry face, his broken nose, his tongue sticking out as he licked his lips, his bony fingers wrapping around one of the apples.

"They said a bard lived here," I complained.

"Bard is my name," he said without looking at me. His hand was trembling. When he bit into the apple he groaned and his eyes closed in pleasure. The divine smell reached my nostrils. A drop of saliva slowly ran down my chin and I couldn't even wipe it away.

"Oh, sweet blood of victory, the drink of the Gods..." Bard muttered between bites. His sunken cheeks filled. The stubble turned dark. When his eyes opened, his gaze wasn't glazed and dreamy, as I would have expected, but intense and questioning. "How did you find me, little lady?"

"By accident."

"I'm letting you talk," he observed. "And breathe. Don't make me stop you from doing either." He licked the juice from his fingers, then let out a small, ecstatic groan. "Oh, Idunn, how I miss thee... the sweet embrace... Pour us mead, little girl."

"I don't want mead," I said before finding out the mead tasted like sweet fire.

"Skál," laughed Bard, raising his own cup and emptying it without taking a break to breathe. "Aaah... I can feel it in my veins, little girl. Aaah. You're so young, you just eat them because it feels nice. One day you will understand. What do you want?"

Little girl. There used to be a time when those words could have broken me.

The mead burning my lips and throat now sent a wave of heat through my body, starting in my chest, then travelling down to my stomach. My muscles relaxed. I couldn't tell whether he'd caused it or if it was the mead. "Just a place to stay for the night. I swear I had no idea..."

"You may stay." His eyes shut and a quiet groan escaped. I knew exactly how he was feeling.

"Can I have some water?" I pleaded while my hand reached for the mead again.

"Water? No pink wine?" He disappeared into the darkness, bumped into something, swore nastily, then returned with a very small cup. "Here's your water."

"Thank you, Bard."

"Bard," he repeated flatly. "Aye, that's me. Skál."

My hand put down the small cup, then reached for the bigger one again. "I don't like the mead," I groaned.

"Too bad, I want company. Drink up, little lady," he said, and my hand and mouth obeyed. "No matter what you say, you're here for a reason. What is it?"

My tongue felt a bit swollen. "Thor. I'm looking for Thor."

"He's not here."

"I noticed."

"Smart girl."

"I," I said, offended, "am a lady." Then I belched and couldn't force my hand to cover my mouth.

Bard laughed so hard he coughed. "Maybe one day, when you're even older. What do you want from him?"

I was dizzy and hot. "He has to go back. To Ásgard. How come you can control me like this?"

"Thor has a new life in Midgard now. Why don't you leave him be?"

"I was sent to find him."

"Who sent you?"

"Freya."

Bard's eyes closed and his throat moved as he swallowed. "Freya," he finally said. "Sending a little girl to do her bidding. I wish I were surprised. So, the apples are not payment for me?"

"For what, for that blue thing? Orb? How do you trap mana like that?"

"I ask it nicely and it hops into a pot, Lady Maya."

"I didn't tell you my name."

"I know a lot about you. Maybe more than you do."

"You are Odin," I whispered.

Bard laughed without joy, then brought the candle closer to his face. "Count the eyes, little girl. Left. Right. How many is that? Two. How many eyes does Odin have? One."

"You must be a God if you can do this to me. Why would a God live here?"

"I used to live in Ásgard before I was exiled," Bard said. "Skál. I visit sometimes when someone invites me over. Heimdall turns a blind eye as long as I'm useful. Odin's still on the throne, Freya's still plotting against him, Loki is still plotting against everyone. Who can blame Thor for having had enough? I can help you, little lady. He spent some time in the gord, then got too close with Jarl Mieszko's daughter..."

"A gord?"

He gestured. "Jomsborg. Down there."

"Ah," I muttered. "That gord. What happened then?"

"Why don't you just ask Odin, my lady?"

"That bastard won't tell anyone anything," the mead replied, bitterly.

Bard laughed again. Apparently, I was very amusing. "Not even a riddle? One day he'll surprise us all and actually answer a question. Yes, Lady Maya, I used to be a God. I don't know what I am now. A beggar that won't die, a servant of those who pay with just enough Idunn's fruit to keep me alive."

"I've never heard about you... *hic*... I'm sorry..."

"Odin took everything from me before he exiled me from Ásgard. My truth, my past, even my name. I am the forgotten one that nobody gives offerings to. Only I can't forget. You have it worse, little lady."

"Oh?"

"Tell me about yourself, Lady Maya."

"I'm – I'm no one, really. Just Maya. What do you want to *hic* know?"

"Everything."

"Um, I was born in Midgard—"

"No."

I tried to stare at him, but all I could see were reflections of the candle flame in his eyes – three... no, four... all of them making me nauseous. "No?"

"No. Go on."

"F-Freya took me away from m-my parents when I was six..."

"Mmm. Did she. Go on."

"Then I grew up in Ásgard and learned a lot..."

"No," he said. "Not a lot."

"Bard... Who are you? A God of what?"

He remained silent for a while. "Nothing," he said, finally. "Not anymore. Of survival, perhaps. Do you know about the war between the Gods? The one that couldn't have been won?"

"Freya told me."

"Freya," he said, then smacked his lips. "She was one of the hostages, with her brother and her father, that I sent to Odin."

"You?"

"Three were sent in return. The warrior, the wise one, the story-teller. I believed the exchange to be fair, until they challenged my authority. In order to remain Vanaheim's ruler I had to battle all three. I laughed at their audacity, then agreed. In front of all Vanir three battles took place, with a sword, with riddles, with a song." He paused. "All three ended in ties. A messenger was sent to Odin, asking him to declare a winner. The winner was not me."

"Not asking Týr? The...declarer?"

Bard's face was almost handsome now, but the grimace brought back the wrinkles that lined his face. "It was Mímir, the wise one, who asked Odin to name the winner. I did not know who Týr was. They treated me fairly, though, or so I believed. I was invited to Ásgard and named second-in-command to Odin. Always second. He knew I wouldn't be able to accept it. When I challenged him, like I had been challenged once, I was declared a traitor and exiled. All of the others agreed that it was only fair, even Freya and Freyr agreed. Didn't I know that no blood could be spilled in Ásgard? I no longer had a home, a name, Bragi's words erased me from people's memories. Don't fall asleep yet, Lady Maya."

My eyes popped open, then my body shook violently, waking me up from the mead's haze. Bard could even stop me from sleeping. He watched me curiously, as though it wasn't him doing it. The fragments of Freya's story that I remembered were different. She had never told me his name.

"I didn't give up. I wandered the Nine in search of someone who would remember me. I even found my way to Müspelheim. I still had my powers, and there are many, Lady Maya, but as the moon turned again and again I learned what my real punishment was. Eternal life is not eternal youth. Those who contributed to my exile knew that. Sometimes a visitor will come, bringing me an apple or a pear, demanding a favour. I can never say no. Have you ever lain in your own shit and piss, praying that someone would want something from you, as time passed you by?"

Needing to shiver and not being able to was extremely unsettling.

"You know what I'm talking about, little girl," said Bard slowly. "Yes, I can gather mana, travel over Ifing, take Mjölnir from Ásgard to Jötunheim. There are many more things I can do. So what? They have believers, offerings, festivals, sacrifices. None of that really matters. They have Idunn. All of them, all of us depend on her." Bard drained the last drops from his cup. "One day," he said, slurring his words, "they might lose her. Until then... Look at my face, little lady. Can you see? Don't I look better? Say I look better."

"You look better," I croaked. My body shook, as if he had grabbed my shoulders. Nausea brought the fiery taste of mead back to my throat. My thoughts seemed to slowly move in circles, just like his face lit by the flickering candle, but one of them quieted the rest. What did he mean when he said I had it worse?

"Gifts not refused must be paid for," Bard said. "Remember this." He belched, then yawned. "I talk too much, my lady. Even Gods get lonely. Go to sleep, you are safe here."

"Can I jus' ask..."

"No."

My body stiffly stood up, bumped into the table – Bard apologised – then everything turned black.

The sun woke me up. I carefully opened one eye and a headache struck like a hammer. My head and stomach protested when I moved. The jug of mead, brass cups, the candle were gone, replaced with a large, steaming clay mug. My bag lay where I, or he, had left it.

I carefully inhaled the steam. The smell forced itself in, opening my nostrils, cooling the embers inside my head. I took a sip from the mug. The drink tasted like the frosty winds of the City, hot snow on a sunny day, a glacier powdered with Frigg's sweat-inducing spices. With each sip my headache diminished. I refilled the mug with hot water, then spread the embers so as not to completely burn the pot. I felt brave enough to try and eat something, I reached inside my bag and pulled out the last of Idunn's apples. My mouth immediately watered in anticipation. It hardly lasted a blink before Bard's words broke through the haze that the mead had left behind.

He was right. The apples rejuvenated me, made me feel happy, peaceful. They slowed time down, brightened the sun. I didn't need them like he did, I only ate them because it felt good. I placed the apple on the table. Then back in the bag. Then on the table again. I sniffed it. Stopped myself from licking it.

I saw an old man, his trousers full of dried excrement, hunger and thirst ripping him to pieces as winters and summers passed. Sif bursting inside, dancing around the body of a man humiliated much more than Thor would have been even if he had actually wed King Thrymr. Sif was someone who would playfully dangle the apple in front of Bard's ashen face, taking it away at the very last moment with a giggle. Bard didn't hurt me. There was only one bed here, the one I'd slept in, fully dressed except for my boots. He'd even taken care of my headache.

I drained the last drops of my new favourite drink. The mug was half-full of green leaves that I had never seen before. I didn't know what they were, but as long as I found a way to take some with me and show them to Auntie Idunn I would never run out of them. I removed one of the leaves from the cup and waved it in the air to dry it, then looked around for a way to keep it from crumbling into dust. A piece of parchment lay on the table. If I folded it in half, I could preserve the leaf inside. There were runes on it and I absentmindedly read the short text.

Little lady,

Send your parents greetings from their fellow Vanr, who forgave, but never forgot.

Harbard.

I froze, my eyes glued to the runes, lips moving quietly as I tried to turn them into some different words.

It... it must have been meant for some other "little lady". Not for me. My parents were human, I knew, I'd been told, Freya said so. There were only three, four Vanir. Freya had never named the exiled one – Harbard, "the wanderer", a name that Odin stole from him and took for himself. Her father lived with his jötunn lover. Freya and Freyr spent a lot of time doing...

I barely made it outside before I threw up.

I was born in Midgard, I had said to Harbard last night. No, he'd responded. I was the daughter of the Goddess of love and the God of sex and fertility. Now I understood Freya's cry when I locked the bracelet on my wrist. I had rejected everything the two of them stood for. Like I'd disinherited them in reverse.

Mam, the little girl had cried. Had she known back then? "Mam" put her – me – in a cage, to see if I could be useful for something. My father used to rub his cock against my arm until I demanded that Freya keep him away from me. She'd listened. Was it to fulfil my wish or out of jealousy? I was shivering, my teeth chattering. The taste of bile mixed with the herb found its way into my nose.

Harbard had told me that I had it worse than him. At least he remembered his life, even if nobody else did. Mine had been replaced by lies. That one sentence on a piece of parchment opened another cage I didn't know existed. Freya was hardly being benevolent when she had told me there would always be a place for me in Ásgard. No wonder she had never encouraged me to search for my "real parents". I only remained her "weapon" as long as I knew nothing.

I spat on the ground, then returned inside, scowling. I refilled the mug and rinsed out my mouth with the warm water, wishing the leaves had kept their taste. My head began to spin and I had to sit down. I was a Goddess, I was immortal, and I had all the time in the Nine to find out what I had been drinking.

Every God and Goddess had a destiny. Freya, Freyr, Idunn, Týr, they all had abilities they didn't need mana for. Thor had his strength, even without the hammer. What about me? Was that what I was supposed to learn in Jötunheim? Sif learned from Idunn... did Idunn know about me, did they all know? If some human girl went to Týr to demand justice, he wouldn't even look away from his beloved wolf. I would have to demand from Odin that an Assembly be called. I would stand up and reveal that I was the daughter of the most repulsive siblings that ever existed. It would be Bragi's duty to ensure that everybody would hear about it. Only then could I demand justice. Freya would argue, point out that she had raised me, fed and tried to clothe me, and when she had put me in the cage it was for my own good. Odin would announce his sentence, forbidding her from sleeping with Freyr for, ooh, *maybe* one summer. She would cry and mourn. I would get a hall of my own that I neither wanted nor needed.

In the void I carried inside, a tiny pinprick of concentrated wrath burst with a blue, freezing flame. Týr was right. Burning Freya on a stake three times was not enough. Harbard's "visitors" periodically gave him back his strength. Freya would receive no visitors, no taste of Idunn's fruit. Instead of a hall, I would demand the keys to the white room with no windows, one where nobody could hear, see, or visit her. Except me. I might sit down and fiddle with a strawberry, looking at my dirty, bitten fingernails, as a skeletal, ancient woman tried to crawl my way, her neck adorned with gold.

The corners of my lips wandered up, something that wasn't quite a smile.

As far as I knew, there was no Goddess of vengeance. If Týr protested, I would find a way to dispose of him. It could involve his hand between Fenrir wolf's jaws. There would be no stupid, angry outbursts like the one that had cast me here completely unprepared. My headache had cleared and now I really felt as calm as a lake. A completely frozen one.

I had missed all the signs. The Goddesses didn't bleed every time the moon turned, I didn't either. My dreams showed me the future. My wounds and bruises healed much faster than any human's. When the little girl I tried to lock in a chest inside cell inside a dungeon cried "Mam", she *meant it*. It wasn't Bragi who took away my past, I did it to myself. As if I had been born the day after I closed the trap door leading to the dungeon, locking the memories away. Freya had no reason to remind me. That was why I had never worn any other clothes. I'd frozen the girl in time, her short hair, her trousers she could get dirty when she played, and the fingernails *she* had bitten. Freya had never stopped trying to tear us, or rather me, apart.

As I was leaving Harbard's dwelling, I left the last apple behind, along with the coin, bag, everything else. Gifts not refused had to be paid for. I would have paid more, but that was all I had...for now. I planned to return here.

Thor had slept with the jarl's daughter? Useful. I was a powerful sorceress, a wielder of magic, strong enough to take on the insane mercenary rapist terrorising Midgard. I'd mutter some nonsense, gesture mysteriously, cause spoons to fly. I'd make that jarl scared enough to want to get rid of both the ginger danger and the resentful witch. In the extremely unlikely case something went wrong, I'd shift and escape. A perfect plan if there'd ever been one.

I spread my wings and flew towards my purpose.

CHAPTER 6
MAGNI

"Down," Herjólf whispered. "Down. Quiet. Let them pass. Then up that path there."

We didn't question, we just followed. We had to leave that forest as far behind as we could without getting caught. I hadn't forgotten that outlaws who became too brazen burned in their sleep. I hadn't forgotten what I had done. I carried the guilt for a while. Then it became too heavy and I had to leave it behind with everything else.

I found some berries and did not share them with the others. There wasn't enough anyway. Then I threw them up. They were not good. Nobody said a thing as I shook while bitter bile pushed the poison out. None of us spoke at all. Ludo's nervous energy was gone. He moved as though his feet were chained to something heavy. All of us did. Even Hillevi was just plodding on. We ate nothing but snow. I noticed Boy – I'd never been good with naming things – following us. We kept disappointing him.

I tightened Herjólf's leather jerkin until it couldn't be tightened any more. His face became gaunt, but as our eyes emptied, his gaze turned fiercer. Even if all of us dropped dead, he would keep going. Wherever he was leading, for he was clearly leading us somewhere, I just hoped there would be food. The snow began to melt under the whipping sleet, then there was only rain. Birds, trees, bushes were bursting with life. I'd never seen spring like this in Jötunheim. But I'd survived the winter. The *first* winter.

My boots kept chafing my feet. Herjólf had sewn hidden sheaths, like his, into the boots, then gave me one of his daggers. The present kept hurting. I moved it between one boot and the other, one chafed calf at a time, wishing that I would become thinner too. I was weak, hungry, tired, but the weight I had to drag – just that of my body – never diminished, like Pig's cursed belly. His breath turned into forced wheezing. Ludo fell, then again. I picked him up and carried him. It felt like carrying a stick. We found a stream and drank and drank and drank, the water cold and clear. No fish.

Some types of mushrooms could be eaten and some couldn't, Pig warned, but maybe he was lying so he could keep them for himself. Then I remembered the berries.

My footwraps were stiff with blood and sweat. I unwrapped them and tore off the scabs. My feet bled again, just like they had when I was still alive. Then the blisters closed as I watched them. It felt disappointing. I washed the dried blood out of the footwraps, knowing that I'd have to do it again tomorrow. Strange thoughts began to appear in my mind, black and red ones. I ate blood the first morning here and I was still alive. I never asked where the blood came from, I didn't dare. Would I care now? Would I eat human meat if it was baked well and I didn't know what it was? My mouth filled with saliva.

Herjólf caught, or rather brought over, a hare, an animal that looked like it was already dead when they found it. It probably was, its body strangely deformed. Pig's hands shook as he tried to turn it into a meal. Ludo gasped loudly when a drop of fat fell into the fire, wasted. I broke each bone and sucked out the marrow. So did everyone else. There was so little it barely counted as eating, yet I felt so full it made me sick. My stomach must have shrunk.

Hillevi kept glancing at me. Every time her eyes met mine, I heard her asking "why don't you go back home?" It took me a while to remember the reason. It was pride. My belly kept groaning and growling, the unfamiliar feeling of having eaten almost torturous. If

Thor showed up, I'd have dropped on my knees and begged him to take me along.

"Ginger," said Hillevi the next day, "you're a blacksmith, forge me some arrows." This morning's porridge was water from the boiled fur and innards of the hare.

"Bring me a forge and an anvil, I will," I muttered. "You still have some left, no?"

"The greens and blacks are not your granny's arrows, they have indentations for poison. Last night I went to hunt... I missed. I don't even know where to look. I'm..." She hesitated, then looked at her feet. I had never seen Hillevi look defeated before. "I need rest too."

"Herjólf," said Ludo. "Where are we going?"

"Where we need to be."

"How much further?"

"Not much."

"A day? Two?"

"I'm working."

"Ah," said Ludo. "It's a secret. His Royal Highness does not reveal his secrets to us peasants. Look at him, on his knee with his holy knife, sharpening a stick. Why are you always sharpening something?"

"Fuck off," suggested Herjólf calmly, raising his eyes from the stick for just a moment.

"You even say that royally. That is why I go to taverns and you go to sell stuff. I wonder," said Ludo, staring at me, "what is the sickest royal secret?"

I blushed and looked away.

Just look into my eyes and don't move. Please? You'll heal before you know it, right? He gave me the dagger when he finished, as a keepsake. I thanked him.

"Big royal wanker," said Ludo.

"Shut up, lobcock."

"There they go," sighed Hillevi, "the two flapdoodlers."

"Is that all you've got, asslicker?"

"That's all you deserve, fuckmaggot."

Herjólf sounded so painfully polite that Pig snorted and not even I managed to keep a straight face.

"But you *are* one sick fuck, my prince," said Ludo, his voice suddenly dropping to a growl. "You like to see people hurt, degraded..."

"That's not true!!!"

They were all looking at me in surprise. If I could, I would have, too. "Let's not fight," I managed, my voice breaking. "Let's just go."

Ludo sighed. "This," he said, pointing at me with a stick, "is why five winters from now Herjólf will be king and I will be fodder for the wolves. How does he do it? Maybe I need a fancy leather vest too. Right, Pig?"

"Your face already looks like one," said Pig, but nobody laughed anymore.

I watched Herjólf cut the tough oak leaves, embed them in cuts he made in the stick, then hand the thing to Hillevi to examine. She just nodded. Heating the tip of his dagger, he glued them clumsily with pine gum. Hillevi tried to balance the thing on her finger and her sigh mixed defeat with an unvoiced sob.

"More?" he asked. She just shook her head. I looked away, not wanting to understand.

"We're stopping," Herjólf commanded.

I looked around, listening intently. I could only hear buzzing of insects and birdsong. It wasn't even a clearing, much less a meadow, it was just some more space between the trees than elsewhere. The air smelled different here, sweeter, making me think of honey.

"Why here?" asked Hillevi flatly, voicing my surprise.

"There's a town nearby."

"Nearby, meaning?"

"Nearby enough for us to make it there before we starve to death. There is a stream to the east as well. There might even be fish. Give me all the coin you've got, I'm going into town."

"I'm the one that goes into towns," said Ludo.

"You look like you're already dead and you're just walking out of habit. You need a shave."

"Just stop," said Hillevi. "I'm too tired for this. Ludo, he's right. You need a shave, a bath, and a gag in your mouth before people can see you."

Silence fell upon us, interrupted by Pig's wheezing. He was already sitting, his back resting against a tree, his belly, chest, chins moving rhythmically.

"He needs rest anyway," I said as I handed Herjólf the pouch that I never expected to be of use again, then knelt next to Pig. "Are you alright?"

"It's spring, hhheeehh. I can't breathe in spring, heeeehhhh."

"A witch curse," said Hillevi, squatting on the other side. "Ludo and I are going to get some water. Maybe if I threaten him with a black arrow I can force him to wash a bit."

"Is the black arrow special?"

A dreamy expression appeared on her face. "Oh yes. The black one is for witches."

When Herjólf returned, his joyful "hey!" failed to make even me wince. I just rubbed my eyes. All of us had fallen asleep. Anyone with a dislike for outlaws could have chopped us into pieces and we probably wouldn't have woken up. Once we saw cheese, greasy dried fish, flat, crispy breads I had never seen before, and a few apples, all of us livened up. There was even a skin of sour wine. It took me a while to notice that Herjólf wasn't eating, just drinking. He looked different, content. There was a gleam in his eyes and that lopsided smirk I remembered.

"I come in peace," we heard all of a sudden, a voice of someone hiding between the trees.

I nearly choked. Hillevi was already on her feet, her hand blindly searching for an arrow and emerging with Herjólf's stick. Pig's coughing fit was loud enough to wake up an entire city. Ludo froze in a pose like a frog undecided on whether or not to jump.

"You came," said Herjólf, beaming. They hugged, their hands slapping each other's backs. I managed to swallow the piece of apple that had gotten stuck in my throat and slowly lifted myself up. I didn't need to hurry. That was a long hug.

"How could I not, Your Grace? Few had faith in the return of the one true king. Now that we know... many others will come soon."

"Where are we?" asked Hillevi, her voice harsh, accusing.

"Where do you think?" asked Herjólf, laughing. "This is my friend, Thorsteinn."

I bit my lip.

Boots. Breeches. Two axes dangling from his belt, odd-sized, too large to throw, too small to use in battle. Sickly pale hands sticking out of the sleeves of a white tunic. I had to force my gaze to reach his face. His hair was even paler than his skin, completely white, even though he didn't look old. Unnatural. Some sort of disgusting creature, like Boy. He offered another, full skin to Hillevi, who crossed her arms on her chest.

"How do we know it's not poisoned?"

"I'll drink first, if you like," Thorsteinn said. "To the one true king!"

"To the one true king," we all mumbled, watching Thorsteinn's throat apple move up and down before he handed the skin to Herjólf. They sat next to each other, so close their shoulders were touching. I stayed next to Pig, added to the fire, then spread it a bit when the flames shot too high. I didn't want to watch the two of them, but I needed to.

I must have eaten too fast. The food sat inside me heavy like iron. I pretended to drink, then passed the skin further, staring at the white man out of the corner of my eye. He introduced himself as a jötunn and I almost snorted in disbelief. What jötunn parents would give their child a name starting with "Thor"? Liar. The white man came from the east, from a merchant family that had resettled "here", whatever that meant, to escape the freezing cold. Deserted his homeland to live among humans. Traitor, defector!

Pig's hand wrapped around my knee, squeezing it briefly, and I nearly jumped out of my skin, briefly terrified that I'd said it out loud. Hillevi's eyes shone in the darkness; she was staring at me as well. I knew what they meant, but I couldn't help it. Even now when

I was ostentatiously looking away I kept staring at them out of the corner of my eye, my ears catching every word said.

"There's a war brewing and it must be stopped fast," said Thorsteinn. "The enemy is at the gates. I want to live in peace."

"Ice giants don't like killing," laughed Ludo, then said something else I ignored. Could I have been wrong, could the easterners have looked like that? If I had never met a jötunn before and Thorsteinn was my first, I would have thought jötnar were "ice giants" as well. He looked as if he had been sculpted in ice and snow.

Herjólf, his arm wrapped around Thorsteinn's shoulder, whispered something into his ear and chuckled. Thorsteinn's thin lips formed a little smile and he lifted the wine skin again. If I weren't staring, I wouldn't have noticed that his throat apple didn't move. He just pretended to drink. The heavy feeling spread from my still upset stomach into my legs. He couldn't be trusted, I *had* to watch him.

Don't get attached, Herjólf once said, or was it *never get attached?* The attachment was clouding my mind. We had everything we'd been lacking. Hillevi, now relaxed, laughed out loud. Ludo was shouting about his prowess in battle. Pig fell asleep, his snores interrupted by brief coughing fits. The fire was burning higher now, Ludo adding to it, smoke billowing into the sky. I moved away from Pig, leaned slightly to my side to see better. Did Herjólf's lips touch Thorsteinn's ear? Thorsteinn glanced my way, didn't he? He could have the best of intentions and I'd hate him because I was sick with being attached.

He mentioned a war. All Herjólf had to do was wait for the two armies to bleed each other out, then arrive as the one true king. He had no army, though. Only us and the "ice giant" who'd betrayed our homeland by leaving it behind. I swallowed the bitter anger and felt it spread inside my veins. I'd left my homeland as well. I looked for the wine skins and watched Ludo squeeze the last drops before throwing an empty skin away.

Even if those two were to have sex, so what? I was tired. Tomorrow Herjólf would remember he needed Thor's son much more than *him.* The white man was definitely smirking at me. Or was it the smoke getting in my eyes, or just exhaustion? When wood cracked in the fire I winced and felt it was Thorsteinn's fault, too.

I had enough. I yawned ostentatiously, then again, succeeding in infecting the others. When Thorsteinn offered to keep watch, Hillevi let out a sigh of relief. Ludo just muttered something, then fell to his side and snored aloud. I stretched on the ground, reminding myself that I was tired, trying to stop obsessing. I couldn't even stop staring. Thorsteinn sat with his arms wrapped around his knees, staring into the fire. Herjólf looked and sounded like he'd really fallen asleep. *Help me, Lady Freya*, I pleaded. Now I understood why getting attached was bad. Getting stabbed would feel better than this. Herjólf hugged him, acted like I wasn't there, wrapped his arm around the white man's shoulders. If this hurt so bad, how would I feel if Thorsteinn stood up now, moved towards Herjólf...

Thorsteinn lifted himself up with a little sigh and, glancing around, moved towards Herjólf. My chest tightened as I waited for the inevitable. The white man, now golden when illuminated by the fire, half-squatted over Herjólf, hands resting on his knees. I lifted myself slightly, more awake than ever. What was going on? Thorsteinn seemed to be assessing Herjólf; observing. I was stiff and sweaty with deplorable anticipation that I had no right to. My innards were trying to push out the first real meal I'd had in a long time. Wood in the fire cracked and I dropped to the ground, shutting my eyes so hard I saw colours.

The next thing I saw was Thorsteinn on his knees, an axe raised in his hands, still hesitating before beheading the one true king. He glanced to his side nervously and that was how my hammer struck above his forehead, rather than the side of his head. *Plarlt* – a sound I would later hear again and again and again. The white man's head splashed around with bone and brain and blood and, and eyes and teeth and – the carcass spat out blood with each heartbeat as it slowly folded and landed on Herjólf. The axe fell to the ground. The hammer slipped out of my hand and fell too, on my foot that I'd instinctively stuck out, as always at the forge, as if hammers broke easier than toes. I felt no pain, my mind too preoccupied. I'd killed another jötunn. A real person, unnatural or not. I flew towards him rather than jumped or ran – to kill faster. Some of his brain was now on my hand.

"No," gasped Herjólf. "No."

"The fuck," mumbled Ludo.

"No," repeated Herjólf louder, his voice broken, choked, interrupted by the *unnnng* of a spear striking a tree right next to me so hard that a part of the trunk split in two. Just a bit further to the left and I wouldn't even be wounded, I wouldn't have a shoulder at all.

In the blink of stunned silence I heard Pig snore louder, then heard him smack his lips as he finally woke up, and it was as if someone released us from a spell.

Hillevi kicked sand onto the fire. I cast Thorsteinn's body aside, squatted to grab Herjólf, felt something fly *through* my hair. I threw Herjólf over my shoulder like a sack of potatoes. Yelling, left, right, many more were coming, he said, they fucking were, back off, back off, branches broke under my feet as I tried to run in the darkness, hide among the trees. Legs of the deadweight smacked onto a tree, giving me an idea. I sent a tree down with a push of my foot. Yelps of surprise. Fuck yeah! Another tree, pushing forward, then back. Push. How far... Fuck that ice giant! We must be safe, I decided, resting my hand on a tree, panting, screaming, dropping the deadweight, a fucking *bolt,* "no!", yelling, still, on the left, pain, anger, I didn't fucking – I ground my teeth, I'll fuck them all up, down the whole forest to get rid of them, fuck them! I'd lost my hammer to the white man. Fuck the white man! I put all my strength into the blind kicks, sending protesting trees down, forward, going on and on until I seemed to have run out of forest. A scream ripping through the sky, starting with "FUUUUU—" then turning into just a roar, mine, until I ran out of air and then nothing.

Silence. Almost. Wind. Screams of birds. A quiet wail coming from somewhere below.

I wiped sweat off my forehead, panting. I forgot where, what I was doing, just...fucking everything up. A blink ago or maybe a moon-turn ago we'd sat by the fire and—

Herjólf was somewhere here, unless I'd trampled him to death.

I dropped to my knees, punching the ground until I hit something soft. A grunt that was also a "no". Hate was not 'attachment' anymore, or? Broken, over. No, aye, no indeed.

I sat, resting my back against a surviving tree, feeling nothing, thinking nothing. The sun began to rise and I still sat, nothing more.

"To call him dumb would be a compliment," hissed Hillevi, squatting next to me. "He brought us to Vindland."

"Vindland," I repeated flatly. I couldn't find it in me to be surprised at her appearance. She probably had gotten here first and just waited for me to calm down.

"The 'one true king'. He never told you?"

I shook my head. Herjólf curled into a ball, barely visible in the faint light of dawn. Hillevi jumped to her feet and began pacing around him, a predator assessing its heedless prey.

"His two older brothers joined forces and they became king... both at once. Some didn't like it, said it wasn't natural. Herjólf stoked the fire, found some followers, promised them land and coin. Someone close to him went to his brothers, who actually had the land and coin rather than just the promise. He got outlawed. Now he came back to show himself to 'his people'. There are no 'your people', fucknugget!" she shouted, then kicked him, eliciting a protesting groan. "Fuck! Sees a handsome jötunn and..."

"Go back home, Magni," she said softly, her thin arm around my shoulder, hand patting my neck. Now I took a sharp intake of breath. A blink earlier she was to my left, not my right. I was going crazy. "Do you think Herjólf would have helped you? Do you think he even likes you? Ginger, just – just leave before he gets you killed or kills you himself."

"We should wait for Pig and Ludo. They might catch up."

"Don't be delusional," huffed Hillevi. "Leave him in his *kingdom* and let's go."

"No," mumbled Herjólf.

"No," I agreed. Hillevi huffed angrily when I lifted him up. Now he trudged on his own. At first repeating "no" every now and then, then silent.

I felt like a twig broken in half, then thrown into the fire. No, I didn't think he liked me. I didn't either.

~

"I miss Pig," muttered Hillevi. The meat was half-raw, half-burnt. I spat out pieces that I couldn't get myself to swallow no matter how hungry I was. Herjólf dropped on his knees, bent, then retched, but nothing came out. Pig would have turned this fawn into a feast. I missed Pig, too. He had salt.

"Sshh," Hillevi hissed right into my ear and I almost screamed. "Stomp out that fire. Quietly. There's someone there. If we can see them, they can see us. You really need to forge me some new arrowheads, Ginger. Herjólf, give me your holy knife. Be quiet and follow."

Her steps made no sound at all, as if she hovered over the ground. Herjólf or I would stand in exactly the same spot and a twig would snap so loudly it made me jump in fear. I was so busy observing her feet that when she stopped I took one step too many and both of us fell. If she weren't so fast, I'd have crushed her.

Ludo screamed.

I screamed.

A huge pile of rocks next to me trumpeted.

All of us screamed.

"Never do that again," I groaned towards nobody in particular.

"You're trying to kill me," gasped Ludo. "My best friend Ginger leaves me and takes off with the Royal Highness, then tries to scare me to death. You got something to drink?"

"Pig?" I asked.

Ludo shook his head. "Too fat, too slow."

"There goes my hope to eat anything good ever again," sighed Hillevi. "What even is this?" The monstrous pile of rocks moved and I barely kept myself from screaming and running away.

Ludo chuckled. "I don't know. I call him Troll, because, well, look at him. Had his tongue torn out, he showed me. You want to see?"

"Er, no," I said nervously, realising he was asking me. "Is he safe?"

"I'm not a halfwit who invites traitors over," said Ludo.

"I took a risk," said Herjólf. The patient voice of a father explaining something to a child was back. "And I will again."

"You got Pig killed, shitstain," spat Hillevi.

"You heard Ludo. Too fat, too slow." Hillevi's face dropped and for a blink I thought I'd see what black arrows do. "We can't stay here. Let's move on."

"I say we go back to the old camp, where Ginger joined us," said Ludo.

Hillevi frowned, but said nothing.

"It's not winter yet," I said.

"There's no law that says we can only be there in winter and if there was, I'd break it."

"I disagree," said Herjólf, calm, commanding.

We looked at each other in unspoken agreement. Now we were definitely going to Jomsborg.

The beautiful spring turned into a warm, beautiful summer. The occasional rains and storms washed dust off us rather than chilling us to the bone. There was no more waking up with chattering teeth. Troll brought us luck, we decided. He turned out to be neither deaf nor stupid, but actually quite sweet, at least from what we could tell. When Ludo joked that shaven and bald I'd look like Troll's brother, I stopped short of punching him. Good idea. When the two of us, roaring and armed with sticks, kicked in doors, few humans attempted to fight. Two died, their own fault. One tried to shoot Troll with a crossbow. One tried an axe. Others were smarter. Once we tied them to chairs, benches, or whatever else was at hand, they almost begged us to take their belongings.

We didn't raid often, since Troll and I could carry a lot. Sometimes we'd stay behind and catch up, carrying the loot, then we'd leave others behind and return. I liked it when Troll and I spent the night away from the others. He didn't want anything from me, didn't say things he didn't mean. Being quiet with him felt nice. Uncomplicated. The others' silence was different, heavy with unvoiced resentments. Ludo talked to himself a lot. We now had better clothes, Hillevi had a set of real arrows again, we ate well when Herjólf turned out to be an acceptable if quiet cook. Still, no matter how drunk we got together, each of us drank alone.

The road began to widen, the forest thicken, making our journey more difficult. "We're getting near," Hillevi warned on a day that seemed no different from most others, as she picked a stick and tried to draw in the soil that consisted mostly of dry leaves. She gave up fast. "This is Jomsborg," she said, placing a cone on the leaves. "This is the road. This is us. Down there are the harbours..."

"Are we ready for this?" asked Herjólf.

Troll and I looked at each other. Our bags, ones the villagers used to transport coal or turnips, were half-full. "We could go back one more time," I said.

"I wouldn't," said Hillevi. "We're a bit close. We'll set up camp, then you and Troll and Ludo... where's that half-wit?"

I took air into my lungs to yell and her finger on my lips startled me. "We're too close," she hissed. "There may be scouts. Look, we're here, on this...snail. This is the camp," she continued, ready to add another leaf before a gust of wind removed all of her map. Hillevi sighed. "All you really need to know is that we're getting off the road."

"Ludo," I reminded.

"We'll wait until the evening," she said, visibly displeased, "then we go."

"Afternoon," muttered Herjólf.

I nodded. Maybe Hillevi with her night vision and feet like feathers could travel at night, but I couldn't.

The random raiding, Troll's company, the constant moving deeper into the moist warmth of the woods, then back out, not giving much care to anything except not setting the forest on fire... it was almost fun. I nearly forgot where we were heading and why the camp was there. I reached for my bag in search of a wineskin, took a gulp, then handed it over. Anything not to have to talk to anyone as we sat here stiffly.

Ludo showed up, drunk, beaming, just as we were about to give up and move on.

"Where the fuck—" Hillevi started.

"I spoke with the watchmen," he said, then laughed his *tee-hee-hee* laughter, all too happy to report.

"You did what?!"

"Calm down. I'm now an elegant man and they're all younglings."

I shivered and made sure to only look at his face, nothing or nobody else. "Youngling" was one of the nicknames Herjólf had for me. Elegant Ludo was only a bit stubbly, well-fed, dressed in green and brown, but neither his laughter nor crazy eyes had changed. "We drank together. They warned me about the mountain kings that look like rocks. Fancy that, eh? Troll and you are mountain kings now!" He cackled. We didn't. "Hey, Ginger, do you go fighting on your own when we're asleep?"

"Assface," I mumbled, just in case he was trying to offend me.

"There's a mercenary that looks like you," said Ludo. "Ginger hair, beard..." He paused. I tensed under his stare. A few days since our last shave, he was beginning to grow some stubble. My hair dropped to my shoulders, my beard reached my chest. My mind went blank as I struggled to find an answer to the question he must have been about to ask. "He's...bad at it," Ludo continued, not taking his eyes off me. "Killed some king who paid for his services, because the king was too slow or not brave enough, something like that. They say he's Thor, real magical hammer, everything. You sure it's not you?"

It took me a blink or two to answer with a shrug. "Thor loves humans," I muttered. "There's no way he'd fight them. I mean, you. You call him 'father'."

Ludo continued to stare at me wordlessly, ignoring Hillevi's scolding for putting us all in danger. I could almost hear him thinking. I was thinking too. I'd killed Thorsteinn with my hammer, there were some others hunting us, the "one true king"... aye. That must have been it. A seed that started a rumour that made it here from Vindland before we did. If he were to ask, I had an answer for him now, but he just stared and I didn't know how to deal with silent Ludo.

"Come," said Hillevi shortly and I'd never been more grateful to be forced to stop resting.

She led, picking paths I would have never noticed, a route I had no idea existed. The sight of our old camp took me completely by surprise. The trees weren't bare, still covered with golden leaves. The grass I remembered peeking out from under the snow was now dried by the brilliant sunshine, covering everything but the ashes of old fires scattered by the wind. It felt wrong, like we shouldn't be here yet. The nauseous feeling returned. We should keep moving. Stopping anywhere meant death, for the "mountain kings" and everyone else. The least we could do was wait for Pig... no, he wouldn't, he wasn't... my shoulders tensed with anxiety. I couldn't explain why, I just felt that we shouldn't be here yet.

I shook my head, baffled by the gloomy thoughts. Summer was heading towards its end. The cold gusts of wind in the evenings made it clear. Soon enough I'd shiver under a thickening layer snow slowly covering my hair and face as I tried to sleep with my eyes open. Why would I want that? There would be ambushes, perhaps some other farm Ludo knew of. I'd survive my second winter, maybe. Then another one. Maybe. And then...

Ludo was saying something to me. I shook my head again to get rid of the future. "What?"

"Wanna wrestle, Ginger?"

Outlawry not only never ended. It *repeated*. I saw my hands tightening on his throat, my dagger sticking out of his chest. It would change things. And then?

"Ginger and I are going to the tub," Herjólf said. "You'll wrestle tomorrow."

So many feelings flashed inside my mind that I couldn't even identify them. A mixture of surprise, excitement, shock, sadness, anger, fear. A blink and they all disappeared, replaced by a faint hope.

I did not look at him when we undressed. My body didn't react to his presence at all. I went in first, slipping into the water, the sharp rocks scratching my back. The water level was lower than I remembered it. The drought that had made our days so pleasant reached even here. The light was different, the rotten smell the same. Our elbows touched and I nearly recoiled.

When you are unsure whether you love someone is that more of a yes, or more of a no?

Did Thor ever love Mother? Was she given a choice or did she just let him do what he wanted so that the City would be safe?

The King named her an advisor. She was being paid for having sex with Thor. Did she get extra pay when she got pregnant? How much was I worth?

The corners of Herjólf's mouth pointed down, his eyes half-shut. *What do you want?* I wanted to ask. The words that came out were different.

"When did you meet Thor?"

"Hmm? I've never met Thor. Only his son. Many times."

"The first time we came here you knew who I was. Who told you?"

Herjólf let out a little, tired chuckle. "Some jötunn, I guess. Why does it matter?"

"You're lying," I said so quietly that maybe I just thought it. He was, either then or now. I would never learn the truth. He'd tell me whatever he expected to hurt the most. *Some jötunn.* "Tell me about the white man." Herjólf's brows moved up questioningly. "Thorsteinn."

He snorted. The polite smile briefly replaced by a wolfish, teeth-baring smirk. "He's dead and you're still jealous?"

"You led us into danger. What for?"

"It was a tactical move."

"A *what?*"

"My people needed a sign that I was still there. My brothers needed a sign as well, so they would know that they shouldn't make themselves too comfortable on the throne, or thrones. Gods only know who sits in whose lap. They outlawed me..." His voice trailed off. "They outlawed me to show me that they didn't fear me enough to kill me. Like I was not important enough. Yet now they've tried their best to kill me, even sending me a beautiful man. Do you know what that means? They *do* feel I am a threat, after all. They fear me. It's a compliment."

A beautiful man.

"He talked about peace, not wanting a war. About the enemy at the gates. He meant me. I was recognised the moment I arrived in town. People crowded to welcome me. He was among them. My brothers fear me enough to keep spies around in case I show up." Herjólf seemed thoughtful for a moment. "I wonder if all of them look so good? Ah, come on, son of Thor, don't be jealous of a headless corpse."

"You risked our lives on purpose," I said coldly. "Pig died. Was that a tactical move, too?"

Herjólf shrugged. "Ludo said it, too fat, too slow. It had to happen at some point."

"I saved your life, you halfwit. I should have saved Pig instead. He was my friend. You don't even like me."

When he didn't answer I felt surprised by how much it didn't hurt.

I looked at him, *really* looked, like when I first saw him. Those sensual lips hid very sharp teeth. When his hands used to tighten around my throat there was no emotion in either of his eyes, unless blank curiosity counted. Next to Herjólf, Ludo was completely sane. At the same time, I could imagine crowds following Herjólf instead of his two brothers that were somehow one king. It took time to realise what he was and by then it was too late. I'd admired him, trusted, thanked him. Even just now I followed because he said so. I killed to save his life and I didn't get as much as a "thank you".

Herjólf noticed my stiff silence and it was as if he carefully rearranged his facial expression for me, then moved nearer, until he could wrap his hand around my cock. "Enough of this morbid talk."

"No," I said.

"You and I," he murmured, not listening. "We don't need those losers. Remember what I said once about the bards singing about you and me...?"

Losers. Memories came to me, but not the same ones I saw over and over every time I closed my eyes. I hoped no bard would ever sing of an insane monster who took pleasure in hurting a God, pushing him away, yet keeping him at arm's length in case he'd become useful.

"Stop," I said. "Right now."

"Mmm. I'll be gentle."

"I said, stop."

"I'm *sorry*. I won't hurt you again. Does that help? No more Thorsteinn, no more others. Let me—"

"Get your fucking hands off me and look outside."

Herjólf's hand still held my cock as he slowly turned his head, then laughed. "There's nobody. What's your problem?"

"What's that red glow?"

"It's sunset, son of Thor, what else?"

"And that other red glow?"

Herjólf was silent for a blink or two and so was I. One of the sunsets was becoming brighter.

"Fuck!" he spat, already propping himself up. His buttocks briefly flashed in front of my face. He stopped at the entrance of the cave, blocking it, and grunted in surprise when I pushed him away nearly sending him flying. We stood naked in the cool air of the evening, gawking at the orange, flickering glow that turned brighter as the sky above darkened. The two mountain kings had become enough of a nuisance that they had to die, even if it meant setting the forest on fire.

Dalebor had done it, my mind whispered, the heat of the torch too close to my cheek.

Herjólf shook water off his body like a dog would and started pulling up his breeches, cursing. I did the same as mine stuck to my wet thighs, forcing me to peel them from the skin before pulling them further up, then again. "Tell me one more time how bad *my* decisions are," he hissed. "How horrible it is that I wanted to go to Vindland, that we lost poor Pig. Who put us in bigger danger? Let's get out of here!"

"Where?" I cried. My hands shook, the cool gusts of wind covering my skin with goosebumps, as I fought the boots. The ground under my feet was so dry it was cracked.

"To the north, to the sea!"

"And the others?"

"If they're not blind, they'll save themselves, and if they are, then fuck them. Will you follow me or not?" Herjólf's face was contorted with anger, as if the blaze was my fault. *He doesn't even like you*, Hillevi's voice reminded me. "Fuck you," he spat and disappeared between the trees before I could think of an answer.

I just stood there, still half-naked, gawking at the red glow. If

where Herjólf went was north, then... I should hurry. Save myself.
Warn the others. I picked up the tunic that Herjólf had sewn for me
in some other life a very long time ago, still staring at the red glow,
trying to remember Hillevi's "map". If that was north, then...

The cracks of breaking branches and roaring of a bear kicked me
out of my stupor. A bear crazed with fear, running away from the
blaze, could hurt even me. I had no chance to move before a trum-
peting Troll almost fell into my arms, followed by Hillevi.

"Fire!" she yelled. "Ginger? Is Ludo here?"

I shook my head.

"Herjólf!" shouted Hillevi, sticking her head into the cave, then
coughing. "By Odin, that stink! Where is he?"

"He...left," I said flatly, wrapping my belt around my waist.

Hillevi's lips formed a white line. She gave me something of a
sympathetic glare, then glanced back at the red glow. "Oh, Ludo,"
she said flatly. "We have to get to the sea."

Had it not been for Hillevi's magical night vision and her shouted
directions we would have never made it. I walked, or rather trudged
first, pushing the trees away, the dry wood breaking with ease, as if I
were creating an oddly fortified path. Suddenly the pieces came
together and I tried to stop and look back, and Hillevi nearly got
crushed between Troll and me.

"The road," she shouted. "We're almost there!"

I almost fell off a cliff. I'd been here before. Someone had died
here at some point or other. Bloodied snow and a sweet gaze.

"Dread Gods," I groaned at the sight of crossroads. Hillevi shook
her head and pointed at the trees on the other side of the road. We
followed her now, pushing through the forest again, leaving a trail of
fallen trees in our wake. I heard the water before I saw or smelled it.
She led us straight to the shore.

The cool wind blew towards the sea. It would carry the fire
towards us.

"Herjólf!" I yelled. Troll trumpeted. Hillevi made no sound until
the dark silhouette appeared, approaching us and started saying
something. A sharp, unexpected *krlk* sounded and the silhouette
disappeared with a little yelp.

"You piece of shit!" screamed Hillevi. "How could you leave him behind?"

"He chose to stay," said Herjólf, lifting himself up. He was massaging his chin, yet his voice remained calm. Polite, Ludo would say.

"Where's Ludo?" I asked, knowing the answer.

"What do you think," barked Hillevi. "The goatfucker's getting his revenge on the good folks of Jomsborg."

I remembered her map correctly. It wasn't the forest that was set on fire, unless the dwellers of Jomsborg were so lazy that they'd just crossed the road and thrown a torch next to the gord. The hopelessly clear, starry, moonlit sky would start clouding soon, but not with the promise of rain.

"I hope you are pleased with your leadership." Herjólf sounded like ice.

"Shut your trap, or I'll please you—"

"Stop!" I shouted. "We've got to make a plan!"

The moon flickered in Herjólf's eyes. "You," he said. Disbelief dripped from the word. "You and a plan. I'm sure all of us would love to hear your thoughts."

I felt myself shrink. I... I forgot that I was stupid.

"Magni," said Hillevi so quietly the waves nearly drowned her out. "Watch. This is what a black arrow—"

Something slammed onto the sand like a rock wrapped in a rag. It rolled, spat a few times, then croaked. "Thor...!" It cleared its throat and spat again. "Thor! You must come with me to Ásgard! Please!"

"Maya?" I asked in disbelief, dropping to my knees.

"There is a fire, someone set that horrible place on fire!" There were tears and fear in her voice.

"It was Ludo," I explained.

"I can't believe I finally found you!"

"You didn't," said Herjólf. "What's this about?"

"A witch," said Hillevi coldly. "Magni, move away."

I reacted by wrapping myself around Maya. "You'll have to kill me first, Hillevi. Maya? How did you find us?"

"Oh, Thor," sobbed Maya, then stopped as abruptly as if someone had slit her throat. "Magni?"

"Give me my witch!"

"She's a sorceress," I barked, then lowered my voice. "Hug me."

"Whaaat?"

"Stop moving!" I wrapped my arms around Maya. "She's a friend of mine," I said, twisting my neck uncomfortably. "Leave her alone."

Herjólf laughed.

"I can't breathe," said Maya in a muffled voice, trying to free herself from my embrace.

"Stop moving and stand up," I muttered. "Thor is not here. It's only me. And them. Fly away before Hillevi gets you."

"Magni, I must find him, he's been gone for so long——"

"He's not here."

"I can't go back until I find him," Maya cried. "Ásgard has no protector!"

"You can have a protector," said Herjólf unexpectedly. "He's protecting you right now. We'll come with you."

Troll's heavy breathing and the waves crashing onto the shore were the only sounds. I felt Maya's fast heartbeat, or maybe it was my own. I slightly relaxed my grip, squinting, searching for Hillevi. Maya no longer tried to push me away. "Would you?" she whispered to my chest.

I ignored her. "We?"

"I am his lover," Herjólf continued. "I accompanied him on all his adventures. We were always at each other's side. On our first night he promised me that he would always help me. Or do your promises mean nothing, Magni?"

"I haven't agreed to any..." My voice trailed off as an unclear fragment of a memory appeared. I had said "yes" to something.

Was that smoke I was smelling or my imagination?

"We can't take him," whispered Maya. "I was sent to bring Thor back, but he's an outlaw now. It's bad enough..."

My arms dropped. "I am that outlaw."

"Nonsense," she said, sounding so certain she nearly convinced me. "It's not——"

Herjólf laughed. "Who do you think we all are?"

"Step away from her, Magni," said Hillevi, her voice strained like her bowstring. "Give me my witch."

"N-no... you can't be... and a mercenary, how, you don't kill? You said..."

"He does many things," said Herjólf. "You'll hear all about it when we're on our way."

"You're going nowhere," hissed Hillevi. "Let go of the witch, Magni, then go home."

"Come with me," whispered Maya into my chest. "To Ásgard."

All I could think of was Ludo, telling us about a red-bearded mercenary, a kingslayer with a magical hammer. The mercenary was real. So was the outlaw. It's just that they weren't one.

"The harbour is down there," said Herjólf. "Won't take long. Or let Hillevi have her witch and stay here with me. You know you want to."

"We're not going to the harbour," said Maya. She added something, but I didn't hear her anymore. I had said no to him earlier today and he'd just ignored me. Herjólf had me in his fist, almost, but not completely crushed, tightening the grip every time I thought I was about to be set free. He told me I made a choice, then ran away, leaving me there. I owed him nothing.

My nose wrinkled. It was definitely smoke that mixed with the cool, salty sweat of the sea.

"I love you," said Herjólf.

"Shit," whispered Hillevi somewhere very far away.

He loved me. He'd said it. He did. He just didn't want to... because... he ran away, but he said bards would sing about him and me. He promised he wouldn't hurt me anymore, he said he was sorry. It's just that I thought he didn't know he was hurting me, because I'd never said anything, but that meant he knew all the time. How could he not have known when he used his blades on me? There was Thorsteinn and there was me saving Herjólf's life and there was his quiet murmur "you and I". His tactical move that got Pig killed, then I'd killed another jötunn to save this human.

I didn't love him, I definitely didn't, not at all, but what if I would never meet anybody else like him?

"Just leave him and go already!" Hillevi yelled straight into my ear and I gasped, back to the reality where fire headed towards the sea.

"This is not your decision to make," said Herjólf. "Go for a walk. Leave us alone for a bit."

"A fucking walk," she huffed, then said something else I missed. I no longer saw or heard the sea. In my mind I heard the sound of a rock sliding down the blade of his dagger. I remembered our eyes meeting, his narrowing, mine widening. No sane bard would want to sing about what happened later. I did say "yes" to him that first time, he literally squeezed it out of me.

Alone, my heart seemed to beat, fast, hard. *Alone, alone, alone.*

"Magni," said Maya. "We must go."

I wouldn't be alone. She would be with me.

The moonlight's silver glimmer seemed to dim as the eerie, red glow gained strength. I shook my head. This, here, was real. *Wanna wrestle?* I'd have expected the crackle and hiss and protests of the trees, but I couldn't hear a thing. Only my heartbeat. The people, the animals, the forest... Ludo's feverish face, Dalebor's fire consuming everything. Maya. Ásgard that didn't have Thor in it.

"Goodbye, Herjólf," I said. "It's been fun, all the – the bartering."

"Bartering? Goodbye? Take me with you. Please? You promised. I love you. Don't leave me." Finally, a genuine emotion in his voice. Fear that came out in short gasps.

"Bugger off," said Maya. I nodded in agreement.

"Stay," snapped Herjólf. As if I were a dog.

I snorted and somehow it forced a tear out. "Let's go," I said to Maya.

"There's a road—"

A brief flash of moonlight reflecting across a blade, a thin *dink* sound, a short dagger bouncing off something invisible, flying into the darkness. The wind had changed, feeding the fire now, and for a blink I thought a gust had thrown something our way.

"He threw a knife at you... he threw a knife at you!" Maya's voice changed from disbelief into a screech.

"You're not allowed—"

Herjólf didn't get to finish. Troll calmly dropped his fist on his head. Herjólf folded, his knees giving in as he dropped onto the sand like a pile of rags.

Maya let out another short, high-pitched squeal. Even I winced in surprise. It was easy to miss Troll or just forget he was there. A silent pile of rocks that might have been the best friend I'd ever made.

When I gave him a hug Troll hooted in terror first before his arms squeezed me so tight I thought he'd break my ribs. When we both finally let go, he laughed without vowels, *h-h-h*.

"I will miss you," I said. "Thank you. Take care... Hillevi?"

"She went for a walk," said Maya, grabbing my sleeve, pulling. "Let's go." My forehead crinkled. Hillevi wasn't someone who went for "walks". Who was I to think, though? Maya pulled me again I followed, leaving behind the little chunk that his dagger had split out.

∽

"The road is there," panted Maya. "What happened to all those trees?!"

Troll and I. "What happened with that *dagger*?"

"Good Gods, we were so lucky. I put a spell into the crystal a long time ago, because the weather was awful, so the crystal would deflect rain and hail. Then I got imprisoned in a room where magic didn't work..." She stumbled and I helped her stay on her feet. "I forgot about it."

"So, it's an invisible shield for...weather?"

"Exactly."

"And knives?" I asked, stepping onto the road.

The sky above us was orange. I was used to wood cracking as it burned, now it was just a guttural growl, the fire and the wind and the trees' screams combining into a deep roar. A few animals shot out of the woods, immediately disappearing behind us. Birds cried. Outbursts of fire shot between the trees, the sky blood red rather than orange. I gawked, my mouth open, knowing that if we stayed here I'd never see anything anymore, still unable to move. My eyes were burning. Maya, clinging to my arm, made a mistake. We should have gone to the harbour—

Zing-zip-a sharp, short sound, a scream quickly muffled by someone's hand. Maya let go of me and ran down the road, already on her knees before I started moving.

"Well," said Hillevi cheerfully, "fuck me sideways if the witch didn't get me. How did you see me?"

"I didn't," said Maya.

"See, Magni? I told you about witches. I shot at her and the arrow hit me. You think that's normal?"

"Aah," I said. "She has an invisible magical shield that throws weapons back at you. And rain."

"I haven't done anything," said Maya. "You shot yourself."

Hillevi laughed, strangely jolly for someone with an arrow sticking out of her buttock. "A witch once told me... I was on the run and she took me in. An old woman. She taught me about herbs, I made various potions for her, poisons. She taught me how to hide in plain sight. It wasn't until she said that she'd teach me to read the future from fire that I realised who she was. I asked her how to never die. 'Everyone dies,' she said. How would I die then, I asked..."

A sharp intake of breath. Maya's.

"A witch would kill me," Hillevi said, almost triumphantly. "That was what she said. So, I stabbed her dead, before she had a chance. She didn't see *that* coming in her fire. I took the poisons, the herbs, everything of value. Ohhh, this feels so good."

"Good?" I asked in disbelief. The dry heat of the fire was different from that of a sun, sucking out moisture from my skin rather than making me sweat. I shot a nervous glance towards the protesting trees. "Let's get you back to the shore. Herjólf... he'll know how to take this out."

"Don't bother. This is the black arrow I made just for witches. First, it feels like nothing happened, to confuse the witch..." Hillevi groaned, as if in pleasure. "It feels good, you know? Until the muscles start to tighten. All of them. Throat closes first, before the heart stops. It's an ugly death. Magni? Where is she?"

"She left," I said quietly. Maya stood nearby, casting nervous looks at the inferno, then back at us. I needed to hurry up.

Hillevi's chuckle was short, strained. "Good. Kill me. Prove the old..." She coughed, then cleared her throat. "It's going faster... Prove the old witch wrong. Do it now, then go home." Another cough. Her breath was turning into wheezing, a bit like Pig's used to be. "My legs hurt. I'm...stiff. Help."

"You'll be okay," I mumbled. My mouth was dry and bitter, as if I had eaten ash. "I'll get you back to the beach." *Lift her*, I told myself, *run, do something*. I couldn't move.

"It's getting...bad...my moun...tain king," she rasped. "Good... friend. Smash my head...hammer. Now." Cough. Cough. Loud, enforced wheeze. All I could think of was that I had no hammer.

Something like a grin distorted Hillevi's lips. Her open eyes stared blindly into Helheim. Her head convulsed, as if her neck pulled at it. Something rubbed against my leg and I gasped. Hillevi's fingers were twisted into claws. Her arm shook as she tried to reach her own throat. I grabbed her hand, but Hillevi was surprisingly strong, pulling so hard I let go to not break her arm and watched the claws jump up, trying to reach her neck.

Help, I begged Maya wordlessly. She was looking away, waiting for me.

"Ghhhhhhhh!"

Hillevi's eyes were popping out now. Teeth clenched so hard I heard them break over the fire's growl. Her fingernails scratched at her neck until they drew blood. Her whole body twisted and I recoiled in fear, her waist shooting up as her head hit the ground, then the muscles softened again and she dropped on the road... still not dead. The arrow's shaft broke. The arrowhead, the poison, stayed inside. She had no voice anymore, just a gurgle. Hot tears ran down my face. "Please," I whispered, and a response came, but neither from Hillevi nor Maya.

The creature's leg jumped forward, the other dragging behind, frog-like, uncoordinated. Its eyes shone red. Boy was here for me and couldn't wait to help, the sweetest of vultures about to satisfy its hunger, thankful. My own throat felt like I was being choked, like a sob got stuck in it.

"I can't," I screamed at him or maybe at myself and tears blurred my vision and *the child was too weak. I've let him lead for far too long. He needed my help, protection. I grabbed the elf's hair and smashed her head on the rocky road before letting the child back in* my hand hurt and it was bloodied and I cried in fear. A blink ago there was Hillevi and now there was just a body with... with just... meat and blood and brain, my hand, wounded by pieces of her skull, still holding the hair.

The claws that drew blood from her neck wouldn't drop, stiff. I tried to bend her hands, make her body look like she had died in peace. *Don't look at the face.* My back felt so hot in the black cloud that surrounded me. A sound broke through. Boy finally spoke. No. Yelling. Maya yelling. "We're going to die!" Boy must have run away. He'd be back. I had to save Hillevi from him. "Magni, move!" Maybe he would be too stupid to understand he had to escape. Midgard would soon have two fewer monsters in it because I was leaving too. "You'll grieve later! Run!" I didn't know I'd gotten attached to Hillevi as well.

"Follow," Maya yelled, then a bird flew down the road. My eyes followed her until she disappeared in the red air that wasn't air, just heat, as I tried to breathe and Dalebor's torch was too close to my face. He'd found me, I was fair game, an outlaw. My first few steps were heavy before turning into a hurried walk, then something of a gallop. I had to outrun him, but he kept up with me easily and now he was on fire, all of him and my arm, my side, my face, my hair. So this was how meat felt when it was being baked.

Hillevi caught up with me and now the three of us ran together. Faster, faster, she shouted, as Dalebor who was only fire tried to wrap himself around me. The jarl's hall was endless, everything made of wood, I told them it could burn. I kept coughing and wheezing, stumbling, my lungs searching for air. Dalebor's roar was the same as Ifing's, but the river killed fast. He was taking his time.

I can't, I wanted to scream to Hillevi, but I'd killed her, so I couldn't. *Hhhhhhhhhhhh* my breath was red and I was wrong. It was not Dalebor, it was Ludo possessed by Odin, it was the human that gazed at me feverishly back there at the farm. He was in the jarl's bedroom, throwing the torch on his bed, laughing. *I'm a fucking delight.* Stabbing Niedomira in the throat before she had a chance to cry for help. His cock emerging from his trousers. The watchmen and their captain and Wojciech and the men and women whose names I couldn't remember, and then he came for me because he still wanted more. *Wanna wrestle?* I could have killed him, I'd had so many chances. Had Ludo not listened to what Hillevi said about setting things on fire? She would be so angry.

The wooden palisade of Jomsborg turned to ash, the marble walls of the City of Light were nothing but dust. I was crumbling into pieces too and they kept dying one by one, leaving less and less of me until there was nothing left and maybe things were just meant to end.

Rain landed on my arm and face, a lie that burned. Ash. Tiny embers. Like being poked with hot nails. No road, no air, no sky, just orange dust. A bird flew over my head, screeching, then again, a different sound than that of other birds trying to survive the night brighter than the sun. Hillevi held my hand and pulled me forward. I wasn't running anymore, only my body was. Stupid, again. Hillevi was *dead* and she was here, so that meant I was *dead* too, and we were in Helheim, the land of the *dead*. I thought it was built of ice and snow. I was wrong, always.

I didn't see anything anymore, because the heat burned out my eyes, so I stopped. Ludo and Dalebor would lead me to Helheim where I would see my mother and Gunnar, too.

"We're almost safe," shouted Hillevi. "Hold tight!"

She had forgotten I'd killed her. I was going to tell her, but instead I just screamed as my body shot forward, flying like I was an arrow now until it – I slammed onto the road but didn't stop moving, still sliding, screaming, my mouth full of dirt, sand, gravel scratching my face, my hands. Things slowing down until they stopped. Now I was dead. Please? I nearly choked on life when cool air entered my lungs. It was freezing, Ifing, no, Helheim's ice, finally, where was Hillevi? I sat up and looked for her. The blaze was consuming the forest and the road and the sky. She got lost. I had to go back and get her. She would give Ludo the bollocking of his life. Oh no. She was dead.

"Are you alright?" Maya kept asking and I was laughing and crying and coughing and wheezing. "Do you hear me? Magni? Are you alright?"

"I'm cold," I said, but the words stayed in and tears came out instead and now I just cried, rocking back and forth, until the tears ran out too and I just was.

"We can't stay here," Hillevi kept repeating. "Magni? Can you walk? Should I carry you again?"

Most of the hair and beard on the left side of my face was gone or had turned sharper and harder. My arm, the fire was still inside it. Half of me was all heat and the other half shivered from the cold. Like two people, like Herjólf. Hillevi kept nagging and she didn't look like herself at all, she looked like—

"Maya."

"Come," she said, "we need water, we're not safe yet. I'm sorry about your friend, but we have to go now, okay? Come with me? Stand up. No, this way. Good Gods, your face... come. Please. Or I'll have to carry you again."

"Hillevi," I said. Without her I'd never make it out of here.

"I know, I know. I'm so sorry. But it was the right thing to do. She died fast."

"No," I said. "Yes," I said.

"I wonder how she made herself invisible," sighed Maya, ignoring me. "I don't know anybody who can do that. Did you see her do that? Um, sorry, that's a stupid question. I wonder if witches need mana?"

A shiver went through me, the hair on my cold arm standing up. Goosebumps. The poisons in Hillevi's arrows, her ability to just disappear and appear somewhere else without making a sound... She had never realised.

"Let's just go," I said flatly. Boy, Ludo, Dalebor were following us, we were safe as long as I didn't look back, as long as I didn't see them, they were gone.

A monotonous racket. Maya talking. "I know where to go. Good Gods, Magni. I can't believe I found you after all this time. I was imprisoned for so long I thought I'd stay there forever! I'd heard from, um, somebody that Thor was in that town earlier on, so I went to that jarl, explained to him that I was a sorceress searching for Thor. I made some plates fly, or maybe knives, nothing big. I guess he was more impressed than I thought, because they put something in my food. I remember sitting there with him and the next thing I woke up in a small room, really small. There was only one window and I couldn't even reach it. Not a drop of mana, like someone had removed it. Do you know how that made me feel?" She seemed to expect an answer. I didn't know. "It was horrible. The worst thing that ever happened to me! They said I was a witch and said they would burn me at a big stake in three days. Is everyone in Midgard obsessed with witches? I panicked, so I told them I was Thor's wife, Sif. Yes, I was that desperate. I said that if they hurt me, he'd kill them all, so it would be better if they let me go. Instead, they said they would keep me around in case he came back. Back! So, I was in the right place, just too late! Do you know how long they kept me there?"

"No," I muttered.

The food was in the camp, back in the forest. We were going in the wrong direction. I glanced back and noticed that the forest was burning. I forgot. A chuckle grew inside me. Hillevi would give Ludo *such* a bollocking in Helheim. That fucking cockwomble of a delight. I glanced around again, but nobody followed us. The woods on the other side of the road caught fire, too. My right arm was still cold. Two halves, both hungry. We should go back to the camp.

If only she'd stop talking.

"I don't either! I was *so* close before they locked me there, then suddenly I couldn't do anything! Can you imagine? I had *nothing* to do, nobody to talk to, all I did was sleep and eat. Good Gods, I'm so hungry. I'll admit, they fed me well, better than I ate in Jötunheim. Not that that's hard. The breakfast would—"

"Can you stop talking about food?" I snapped.

"I can't help that I'm hungry."

"No," I said through clenched teeth. I massaged and pinched the arm that kept burning inside. There were holes burnt in the sleeve of the tunic. "You are not hungry. Hungry is when you haven't eaten for days and you catch one hare for the whole group and none of you says it, but all of you wish that there was a way to not have to share. Hungry is when you find some berries and you don't know what they are, but you know that if you ask someone they will want some, so you eat them all and get sick. Hungry is when you catch a squirrel and you eat it raw before someone notices you have one, and you wish you could eat the skull and the tail...!" I was yelling in her face, only stopping when she moved away, her face contorted by fear. *I'm sorry*, I almost said, it's just that I wasn't.

"I apologise," Maya whispered. "I didn't know. I've been so lonely in there and then all this... I don't know, I can't stop talking. I'm really – please, tell me what happened to you. I mean, if you want to."

I blinked and everything came back to me.

Everything.

No, child. There is one thing you cannot know. You've waited too long and so have I. Your elf friend was dead before I smashed her head on that road. You would suffer if you knew. I shall keep this memory from you and next time I will be faster. Because you could never take the real *everything.*

"No," I said, wiping my eyes. I had a strange feeling, as if time and space had blinked too. "You go on talking. Why do you think Thor is a mercenary?" My back, shoulders, arms hung down. Everything was crystal clear in my memory except the moment between Hillevi being alive and dead. I wished I could stop remembering all that. I escaped alive, even if my arm still burning. Would I know if I'd gone insane?

"I was told when I was locked in there. I cried, pleaded, threatened, only to find out that he was gathering an army of his own, and as his wife – bloody Sif – I was their hostage, guaranteeing their safety. Like you and your mother back in – anyway, I prayed to see Thor destroying that gord, gard, whatever that was, knowing that I would stay there forever, because why would Thor bother with a place like that at all? Last night someone just kicked the door in and told me to get the f– get out of there..."

"Ludo," I nodded. I survived, because I had made promises. I broke those promises. I had to pay for that before I could rest.

"I smelled smoke, the hall caught fire. Luckily, once I was out of that room I had mana again. I shifted, flew outside, then towards you. The moat was completely empty, which was good, because—"

"How did you know where to find me?" I needed to find a way to make up for all the hurt that I had caused.

"I didn't, I just flew towards the sea. I was in a bit of panic. Then I saw your hair... I see better in the dark when I am a bird and even better when I am a cat. You know the rest. Who was that – that *man?*"

I didn't know it was possible to use the word "man" as an insult.

"Your lover," she accused.

"I– yes."

"Why did he throw a knife at you?"

"I don't know. Because he loves me. He didn't want me to go."

"Ah, so that is love," said Maya. She sounded peculiar. "You know, Freya keeps telling me how I absolutely must fall in love, because it's the most wonderful thing there is. Tell me all about it. It's about throwing knives at someone and what else?"

"No," I said. "It's not like that at all. It's... when he says, 'you're beautiful', and you know you really are, even in your own eyes, because he said so."

"Can't you look in a mirror?"

"It's when... when you've gone hungry for days and you find one morsel of food and give it to him."

"And he takes it?"

"And he takes it."

"But he doesn't give you any?"

"There's only one," I repeated, angry with myself. Now I was talking about food.

"There is no piece of food so small that it can't be cut in halves," said Maya.

I didn't answer. Either I was too stupid to know how to say it or she was making it hard on purpose. Everyone knew what love was. It took me some time to come up with the right answer and by then it was too late and I didn't want her to answer back and make me feel stupid again. Teeth were involved each time Herjólf kissed me and he might have not said anything about love, I might not have dared to say it myself, but I knew. If it wasn't love, there would be either no biting or no kissing.

~

"Do the bird thing and eat some nice fat insects," I said.

"I can't. It wouldn't be fair on you."

I looked at her incredulously. "You're going to go hungry because I can't eat insects?"

"Listen, I'm *sorry*."

"I'll be fine once we find a farm somewhere," I said, "or maybe there will be someone passing by. Can you fly and look around? We'll rob them, I'll tell you what to do..."

"Magni...! What are you talking about?!"

I stopped. "Food. I am talking about food. I don't have any. Do you have any?"

"I don't think I know you anymore," said Maya after a long pause. "You look the same, but you've changed. I thought you died a long time ago. I'm glad that you're alive, I mean, I thought I'd never forget you and now I'm not sure if I know who you are."

We are Magni and we are Módi, and we are others, but the girl does not need to know and Magni is a child. The child is not ready.

I said nothing, just pointed ahead. What used to be a river was now a riverbed with just enough dirty water for us to drink and get rid of some of the ash. I was surprised when my arm didn't hiss as I poured water on it. It felt like it should. Baked meat that moved. One side of my tunic was darkened, spotty, covered in burnt holes, the other mostly clean. How lucky was I that my hair and beard had just melted instead of shooting up in flames? Or had they and I hadn't noticed? Would half my face be scarred now, would it be like Herjólf's, dark and light? The dagger that he gave me was still in my boot, on the right side. The other one may have been deflected by Maya's shield, but it had still hit my left side, where my heart was.

Once we sat we couldn't bring ourselves to stand up. I fell on my back, spreading my arms and legs, staring at the sky. It was either finally beginning to cloud or the smoke had reached even here. My mouth still seemed full of ash, even though I drank the dirty water, filtered through the remains of my tunic. Maya lay down next to me. Neither of us had anything to say.

The gusts of wind eventually turned from cool to chilling. I marvelled over how a small fire – like the one I'd build back at camp – could grow up to devour a town, a forest, animals, people.

Maya sat near me, her arms wrapped around her knees, staring at the flames.

"Aren't you afraid?" I asked.

"Heimdall," she answered.

"Mhm?"

"Loki is the fire that burns forests. Heimdall's fire keeps you safe and warm."

I spat on the ground, or tried to, my mouth dry again.

"They are not all evil," she said softly. "You might even like him."

The wood hissed, as if it heard her words. I looked at the darkening sky and saw a drop of water splash over me. Maya's invisible shield. She moved even nearer, her shoulder touching mine, the right one that wasn't harmed. The fire in the left side of my body left, the sore skin just itchy. The beard and hair would be back in a few days. Dreams. Which eye should I keep open as I slept?

When she lay down so did I, wrapping my arm around her for warmth, or maybe because I was feeling terribly lonely and just really wanted to touch someone who was alive.

CHAPTER 7

MAYA

WHEN WE STRETCHED out on the ground and I complained about the discomfort, but only on the inside, I felt Magni's arm wrap around me. I stiffened with fear, even knowing that he loved a man. Nobody had ever – lain with me? touched me? hugged me? – like that. It took me a while to trust it. I even snuggled into him. I felt... safe. I was grateful that the bracelet didn't push him away. I couldn't keep my mind from chattering, though, barely managing to keep the words inside.

I had spent so many days in that jarl's "guest room" that they blurred into one endless feeling of boredom. I got over my shock at Harbard's note, the fierce fury towards Freya had cooled down, then I realised something. Same as Harbard, I was immortal and had no access to Idunn's fruit anymore. They could keep me alive in here forever, if they wanted. The jarl's great-grandchildren would visit the impossibly old woman every now and then to laugh or marvel, not even remembering why I had been locked in there. None of my plans would ever amount to anything.

Even the tiniest drop of mana had been removed from this room. Possibly by Harbard. The air was stale, only coming from an opening in the door that they used to watch me through until they got bored. Smoke hung in the room and I felt as if someone had pushed my head under water and kept it there. I kept tugging at the hem around my neck, as if that would help me breathe. I paced around the small space, ate, slept, then paced, ate, slept. Telling them I was Sif, so they'd keep me alive had been my biggest mistake. As wife of Thor I was completely safe, fed well, treated kindly, and never allowed to step out of my airless cell as eternities seemed to pass.

I had prayed daily that Thor would indeed come over or that some sort of disaster would free me. When I wished for a disaster, though, I meant some sort of wood rot, perhaps a massive wind-storm. Magni and I still smelled of smoke. If not for that strange, cackling creature kicking the door open, yelling something about outlaws and in-laws...

Magni's whole body shuddered and for a blink I thought that he had heard my thoughts. His arm grabbed me tighter, pushing a small, surprised grunt out of me, before he started emitting a sound that I had never heard from a man before.

"Nnnnng. Nnnnggg. Nnggg."

"Magni," I shouted, trying to elbow him in the ribs, then slap his arm. He was pushing air out of my lungs and I began to panic. "Wake up! Magni!" I tried to free myself from his arm wrapped around me. I might just as well try to push away a tree. "Nnnggg... boy," Magni said clearly. "No. Not yours." His grip around my waist relaxed.

"It's me," I said. He neither moved nor made another sound. I couldn't even hear him breathe. I felt neither safe nor sleepy now. His nightmare could have killed me.

In the morning we acknowledged each other with curt nods before I led us towards a dusty road that I had never known about before. Still, I knew how to find it and where it would lead. I had questions nobody but perhaps Odin or Frigg could answer.

How did I know where to go? I had lied when Magni had asked me how I had found them. I hadn't seen him, or anything else. I was just flapping my wings in panic, tired from moving after many moon-turns of inactivity, carried by fear rather than anything else. I hadn't landed on the shore, I had fallen from the sky. The shore stretched far in both directions, yet I went straight for the giant red-haired, red-bearded outlaw. Who was said to kill humans.

No, that couldn't be right. It must have been a very strange coincidence. Same as all the previous ones. After all, at no point did I intend to find myself in jarl's "guest room" with no access to mana. Now I was searching for something to eat and couldn't find a thing.

"Can we stop?" I asked when the pain became worse than the shame.

"It's early."

"I can't keep walking. My feet hurt, my legs, you know, I've been sitting there and—" My voice died out.

Silent Magni's gaze was hard and heavy. The sweet man-child had grown up into a man who scared me. Wrinkles on his face suggested that he now scowled more than smiled. "Fly, then," he said and walked away.

Miserably perched on a branch with something crunchy in my beak, I watched Magni approaching me, marching like a golem. I thought him dead. He was lifeless.

I flew down and shifted back into my human self. Together with the nausea that accompanied the memory of my meal came that feeling of someone squeezing my heart. As blank-faced Magni stared through me rather than at me, I wished that I had killed that horrid "lover" of his with his own knife. No, I hoped he had burnt alive, very slowly, failing to make it to the harbour.

"I found an inn," I reported, sounding as cheerful as I felt. "It's quite far, but we should make it before the dusk."

I pointed to the right. Magni nodded, said nothing, then continued his heavy tread, leaving me behind. It took me a blink to understand our chat was over. I shifted, flew towards the next crossroads, waited, trying not to think about the first and last time I had visited an inn. No sooner did Magni appear than it occurred to me that we had nothing valuable to pay with.

I had to hold the unconscious innkeeper and his wife when he tied them to chairs, having first "taken care of them" with quick blows of his fists. The bodies would keep falling off if I didn't hold them, he explained. Once he moved the chairs and the *bodies* into the stable, he threw wood on the fire, prepared food, and poured us drinks. I just sat there, silent, numb, watching his confident moves. Freya's voice in my head scolded me again for not having learned anything. Magni had learned a lot and all of it was scary.

I only joined him in the bed that took up most of the room and let him wrap his arm around me, because otherwise he'd sleep in the stable with the *bodies*. Without the crackling of the burning wood or the gentle drumming of the raindrops I noticed he was not quiet so much as silent. I couldn't hear his breath. Once my feverish mind began to calm down, my bladder demanded relief. As I tried to free myself from under Magni's arm, his hand suddenly shot towards my throat, only to drop a blink later.

"Gods! Magni!"

"I'm sorry. I get nervous."

"You get nervous when you're asleep?!"

"Asleep," he muttered and something about the way he said it shut me up.

Once my bladder sighed in relief, I shifted into a cat. It seemed better than returning where his dreams could kill me.

"Magni," I said over breakfast, porridge seasoned with guilt. "I... look... I might have made a mistake. I thought... you are not... not who..."

"People change," he muttered, then tore off a chunk of fish and put it in his mouth. His blank stare was fixed on me.

I swallowed something that grew inside my throat. "I can't take you to Ásgard, unless you promise me that you won't hurt anybody."

"I won't hurt anybody," he said, "unless by accident."

"That's something Loki would say."

"I, Módi, swear that I will not hurt anybody, unless it's by accident. This is my oath and I make it freely. Enough?"

"Who's Módi?"

I watched, petrified, as his face changed. The wrinkles didn't disappear, but they got less deep. The narrowed eyes opened a bit wider, turned brighter. His lips became less thin, as if he'd stopped pressing them together. The eyebrows wandered a bit up, giving him a bit of that sweet look I remembered. My heart stopped beating for a blink. He'd either dropped a disguise, or put one on.

"I'm sorry that I... you know. About what happened at night," he said. My body stiffened. His voice changed too. "I don't really want to talk about it, it's just that... you were right. I cursed myself so many times. Even they told me that I should have gone to Ásgard. Please take me there." He – I wasn't sure of the name anymore – smiled softly and made me recoil. A wounded look appeared in the green eyes I once thought I knew.

"Why?" I asked after a long pause. He quickly swallowed and wiped his hands on his breeches. He was even eating differently.

"I need to go there."

"Why?"

"I've got a plan."

If my body became any more rigid, I'd turn into a statue.

"I know how to make Jötunheim safe forever," he said, lowering Magni's voice, leaning towards me, as if someone could hear us.

Instinctively, I also bent towards him, then my body shot back with realisation and I nearly fell off the wooden stool. "Surely you are not going to kill your father...!"

"He's in Midgard," Magni reminded. "Maya... I know I'm stupid, but—"

"You're not stupid."

He shrugged. "It's the best plan I've ever had. Please help me."

"Tell me what it is."

"It's better for you not to know."

His features were becoming sharper again, eyes narrowing. A thin layer of cold sweat covered me, as if I had walked into thick mist. "You're scaring me. You're so different, even your voice is not the same."

"Must be the smoke," he said, then cleared his throat. "How do we get there?"

"I... I won't tell you, unless you tell me about your plan."

"But we *are* going to Ásgard?"

"Um... yes."

"Good," he said shortly, licking his fingers, then he stood up. "I'm going to pack as much as I can, then bring those bodies back in. We can't leave them tied up in the stable, right?" I hadn't even noticed that there was a rucksack before he had already half-filled it with food. His hands moved fast. Steady, determined... practised. I did nothing, just watched him bring back the *bodies*, then cut the ropes. The innkeeper fell to the floor with a thud and a yelp escaped my lips.

"They're alive," said the red-haired stranger. "Just unconscious. They have horses, we don't. We don't need them to chase us." He took a long look at me. "I'm done with killing."

I would have been more reassured if it didn't mean that there had been a time when he hadn't been done with it.

I watched him march through the drizzle, the big rucksack on his back, as I flew above his head. My bird brain might have been small, but there was always enough space for fear. I knew I should leave him behind with "his plan". Yet, when I announced that I'd found a place to stay for the night, I saw a relieved smile that reached Magni's eyes, brightened a tired face. He blew at a strand of hair that fell on his cheek, then chuckled lightly, almost apologetically when it immediately returned. The left side of his face was nearly back to normal, but still made my heart stop for a moment. It took work not to reach out and put the unruly hair behind his ear.

His nightmares were not his fault. I must have imagined that sharpness of his voice this morning. It had to be difficult for him to hurt people and steal their food. I had no right to judge him. Once he had enough time to recover, surrounded by Ásgard's peace, things would change.

Magni's voice broke once or twice as he talked about Hillevi, the dead elf. Between words I could hear him struggling not to mention that man. We were drinking sour wine and all of it made me unbearably sad. His lover tried to kill him, then Magni had to kill his best friend. How could he not change? He sniffled, so did I, and when we snuggled to sleep I just wished that I was big enough to hold him instead of the other way round. I felt safe again and fell asleep without any nagging thoughts.

When the water slammed my face it blinded me, took my breath away. My arm, wrapped around something, hurt from my desperate attempts not to let the waves devour me. I shook my head, wet hair slapping my cheeks, spitting out the salty water, trying to inhale while I had a chance. The storm tossed the ship around like a pebble. The next big wave would take us down.

I jerked my head in pointless search for escape and saw two men, their expressions identical, blank. One was Harbard, one a stranger. Harbard's eyes met mine and he gently shook his head, as if saying "no". A scream, Magni's, as he tried to run, slipping back on the inclined, wet deck, grabbing the mast when the ship rocked again. Another ice-cold wave tried to wash me off board, the sea greedy, I screamed, wasting precious air—

"Maya," I heard through the roar of the storm. "Wake up. Maya!"

"She's drowning!" I cried. "Do something!"

"Wake up!"

It took me longer than usual to understand what happened. It was one of *those* dreams. The embers shone red in the darkness. There was no ship, no water. I was on the ground, Magni's arm around me. I gasped for breath and the clear, delicious air effortlessly filled my lungs. Like nothing had happened.

"It's just a nightmare," Magni said softly. He held me as I kept shaking, sobbing into his chest not knowing why, soaked with cold water that didn't exist. My consciousness and my body were in weird disconnect. Were his dreams like mine? I was drowning, "she" was drowning, it *hurt*. I could still taste the salty water. Harbard was shaking his head. He looked sympathetic. I had never experienced a premonition as real as this one.

I turned back towards the dying embers, tried to slow down my breath and pretend I was asleep, but shivers kept going up and down my body. I was scared to close my eyes again. What if the ship was real and this, here, a dream? Magni's fingers gently rubbed my arm when another shudder went through me. I'd witnessed my death.

~

While the sky changed from black to dark grey, Magni marched. Cold wind carried the drizzle, then rain. He marched. When rain turned to hail, I landed next to him, trying to walk as fast as he did, protect him with my shield. He waved me away and marched. Later on I watched, silently, as he smashed a rabbit's head on a rock. I looked away too late not to see him twist the head and tear it off. He then pulled a long, thin knife from his boot and skinned the animal. I felt sick, first from what I saw, then from myself. As if meat appeared on my plate from the thin air. Still, it wasn't until the rabbit's carcass was placed on an improvised spit that I dared to look at the dark-eyed, blank-faced stranger again.

The meat was bland, burnt in some spots, raw in others. The nausea came from somewhere else; the sight of the man sitting in front of me, methodically tearing off chunks, putting them in his mouth, chewing loudly. The flickering flames reflected in his eyes. He kept watching me. It wasn't late, but the leaden clouds made him look old, his fierce hair grey. With a startle I understood who his gaze reminded me of. Odin.

There was no way I could bring this...person to Ásgard. I had to find out what was going on. I'd start with small talk, I decided, then ask the real question when he expected it the least.

"Who is Módi?" I blurted out.

He swallowed, tore another piece of meat off, put it in his mouth, and chewed slowly, staring into the flames. "Just some jötunn who has an offer for the Gods," he finally said.

"But you're not. You're the son of Thor, the grandson of Odin—"

"Before we get to Ásgard, you will shave my head and beard. I am nobody's son or grandson. My name is Módi, a jötunn blacksmith who knows the way to keep Ásgard safe forever."

Out of all the things I wanted to say only one came out. "Not Jötunheim?"

"You'll see."

I don't like your tone, I thought. *I don't like your eyes, that wrinkle between your eyebrows that never goes away, the white hairs in your beard and those thin lips that made you look older than your father...* I took a sharp intake of breath. Since Magni was a God, he wouldn't die of thirst and hunger even if he wanted to. He would just age and age, become weaker with time, until he could no longer move on his own, dependent on someone who'd either give him Idunn's fruit or just kill him.

He was saying something and I composed myself quickly. "I'm sorry," I said. "I missed it."

"How will we get there?"

"Um. Let's sit down for that one."

"We're sitting down. Hmm?"

It became darker and he looked up, seeming worried. That was Magni's face, I was sure, although I couldn't tell without seeing his eyes. What about his voice? Who was sitting here next to me? Someone hurt beyond what I could imagine, that's who. Someone five times my size who knew hunger I couldn't imagine, yet divided the rabbit into equal halves. "What do you know about Yggdrasil?" I asked.

"Yggdrasil is the tree, on the branches of which lie the Nine Worlds. On its top sits the eagle, and between the eagle's eyes sits a hawk..." He paused. "Is that what you mean?"

I successfully kept the snort inside. Oh, Bragi. "A hawk," I said, trying to sound neutral. "I wonder if the eagle likes that. So, the Nine lie on branches of The Tree. Jötunheim and Ásgard are separated by Ifing. If the worlds are on branches, then where is the river?"

"Between the branches."

"Obviously," I agreed. "And the sea?"

"It's... I... I guess it's also between the branches..."

"How would it stay there?"

"By magic," Magni said, sounding offended. "Shouldn't *you* know those things?"

I sighed. "Give me some wine."

"There's no more."

"Oh? Where is it?"

"Gone."

I was almost certain that we had... oh well. "Seas don't hang between branches of trees. Neither do rivers. It's exactly the other way round. The Tree grows in the middle of the Nine, each of the world at once. It's not nine trees, it's one tree..."

"How does it do that?"

I felt my face flush. "Uh... by magic, I guess..."

Magni let out a polite sigh, like that of a parent listening to a toddler's babbling. I could laugh now, say it didn't matter, keep my secret to myself. Once he fell asleep I could leave him here and fly away. He'd proven he could fend for himself.

In my imagination Sif was dancing in front of an old, skeletal man with suffering in his eyes, dangling an apple in front of his face, her pearly laughter like a vulture's screech.

"Let me know if you see ravens," I muttered, looking around hopelessly in what was now near complete darkness. "If Huginn and Muninn hear what I am talking about, Odin will as well. I don't think I am supposed to know this, and you definitely aren't."

I moved closer to him. Heimdall could hear the quietest of whispers no matter what. I could only hope he was busy listening to something else. I took in air, readying myself to share the secret for the first time. Instead I slowly exhaled, trying to remember how exactly I discovered it.

It was before the cage. I was hiding from Freya, a giggly child that had escaped her Mam, very proud of myself, for I had found a spot where nobody could ever find me unless I wished to be found. Nobody... My forehead wrinkled when I felt that itch of *nearly* remembering. Until... I was missing something.

It didn't matter. I was so little when it happened, then I forced the little girl inside me into the dungeon with all her memories. It would have been strange if I could remember everything.

"It is possible...to travel...between the worlds...under The Tree's roots," I said, or rather pushed.

I was sweating, panting, unprepared for how difficult it would be to force the words out. You weren't meant to say it, unexpected terror whispered, you weren't meant to *know*. Decisions come with consequences.

"Then why doesn't everyone do it all the time?"

"Because everyone knows it's impossible," I said weakly. Bragi, an unassuming man who giggled with Idunn over "gin", who sang about Odin's conquests and Thor's adventures with Loki. Could Bragi have been the one who decided what was and wasn't possible, was that why Odin did his best not to listen, so that he would know the *real* truth?

"Is it?" asked Magni and I almost jumped out of my skin, so deep in thought I'd forgotten about him.

"No," I said reluctantly and that itch returned. "I found out as a child, because I didn't know it was supposed to be impossible. I can still do it. Once I get under the roots of Yggdrasil, I can just decide..." My voice died out. I bit my lip. It didn't help. "I decide which world I want to go to, then just go there."

"Then why didn't you leave Jötunheim back when... you know?"

Because we were divided from The Tree by the mountains everyone, even I, believed to be impenetrable. Beliefs were not something anybody but a very bored woman with a long face bothered to think about. Beliefs just *were*.

"What's important," I said, looking into the flames, "is that once we get to Yggdrasil I could take you to Ásgard."

"It's the smallest of all the worlds, is that true?"

"It's true."

"What they say, about Thor not being able to walk the Rainbow Bridge because he's too heavy, is that true?"

"Bifröst is neither a rainbow, nor a bridge. It's a place in Ásgard that is also a place in Midgard. Heimdall stands in that spot, guarding it. Thor can't cross it, because he's stupi – because he doesn't believe that Heimdall can be in two worlds at once."

"Nobody can," Magni informed me. "How would he do that?"

I scowled. "Um. I guess it's magic." I used to ask Freya to explain things to me and if she said "it's magic" I would accuse her of either not knowing or not wanting to tell me. I was beginning to relate. "The Tree is in nine worlds at once, why would Heimdall not be in two?"

"Because he just *can't*."

Once you believed something was impossible, so it became.

I sighed. "And that is why I can't just take you to the Rainbow Bridge." That and having to explain to Heimdall who came with me and why. "Do you believe me about Yggdrasil?"

"No," said Magni shortly. "Shall we go to sleep?"

His arm felt warm around me, even though I found it difficult to trust that he wouldn't suddenly crush me. His complete silence often turned into uneven, short breaths that sometimes became incomprehensible words or cries, and I couldn't believe there was an evil bone in Magni's body. He was suffering. I wondered whether Eir would be able to help, when it occurred to me that it didn't matter. He wanted to be "Módi, the jötunn blacksmith" and Eir was the Gods' healer. If I were to get dangerously ill, Eir would express her sympathy, but wouldn't move a finger, unless I told her who my parents were.

There was something that could render all this irrelevant. What if Magni couldn't cross under the roots of Yggdrasil any more than through Bifröst?

In the morning, when I flew up to determine the direction, I saw something new. I was already used to walking, or flying, down a completely empty road. Now I saw a cart rolling our way without much hurry. I circled it to take a closer look. A man and a woman, both of them quite old. There was no settlement of any sort nearby. If they could afford to move so slowly, they must have had enough food for a few days. We had nothing. I could eat my lovely fat insects. Magni couldn't.

I landed where nobody could see me and shifted, so that I could use my human mind.

Magni wouldn't kill the old couple. He'd render them unconscious, tie them to trees, kill the horses to avoid getting caught once they awoke. He'd make sure nobody could find them to ask what happened, where to search for the giant bandit. They would slowly die of thirst, tormented by hunger, fear, exhaustion. Those people were already old and Magni needed to eat, I thought, and the guilt nearly crushed me. I shifted and flew up again. The bird didn't feel guilt when it came to food.

Yggdrasil grew in the middle of a wide plain filled with dying grass of autumn. No wood to burn, no farms or inns, no fish, animals, even insects – all stayed away from The Tree. There would be nothing for us to eat.

The woman laughed at something the man said and pretended to punch him in the arm. He kissed her on the cheek.

"Well?" asked Módi when I returned, his eyes nearly black. I was beginning to learn, if perhaps not understand. He was the grandson of Odin, even if he didn't want to be. He was also someone who gently rubbed my arm when I shivered from my nightmare. Someone forced to kill his best friend. Someone hungry.

Did he know this was happening? Which of them told me he wouldn't hurt anyone, was the oath Módi's or Magni's? Was the other one "not done with killing"? I couldn't remember which voice said what and it was driving me crazy. I couldn't take Módi to Ásgard.

I saw a golem-like, blank-faced figure marching, marching, marching until there was someone that could be robbed, so that we would have food for another few days of marching, marching, marching. I saw the old man kissing his wife on the cheek.

"Well?!"

Cold anger, bitterness, pain, so much pain. Hunger for more than just food. A man, a boy, a bit of Odin, the God who only ever told the truth when it suited him.

To think there used to be a time when I was angry that I wasn't allowed to make my own decisions.

"Left," I said and down the empty road he marched.

"You can see The Tree from here," I said, thinking about my hot tub and Idunn's fruit. "See? There? On the horizon?"

"No."

"You're not looking in the right direction. There," I said, pointing. "Magni?"

"Let's not go there."

"Yes, that's where we're going," I confirmed, convinced that I'd misheard him. "You see, Yggdrasil is special like that. The closer we get to it, the larger it's going to become. It's much nearer than you think. We can be there..."

"No, let's go somewhere else."

That baffled me. "Magni, that is Yggdrasil. There's no 'somewhere else'. What's wrong? Don't you want to go to Ásgard? Meet Lady Freya?"

"It's – I'm afraid. Let's not go there. There must be another way. I can't go there."

I wrapped my hand around half of his arm. He was shivering. "Can you tell me what you see?"

"No. It gets worse if I look there."

"Then don't look," I suggested hopefully. "Look under your feet, or at the sky..."

"Mhm," grunted Magni, then he turned away from The Tree and sighed with relief. "Maybe we should wait until it gets dark. Make a fire. Eat something."

I was absolutely dumbfounded. It had never occurred to me to wonder why, no matter which world, there was never any life other than plants around Yggdrasil, but surely Magni had noticed that there were no other trees, no wood to burn, no animals to hunt? Not a single ant? What did he want to eat, grass? He was breathing heavily, as if the tiredness of the last days had suddenly caught up with him.

"Lady Freya..." I started, uncertain.

"Let's go somewhere else."

"There is nowhere else! What do you want me to do? Go there and ask Thjálfi to come back with the chariot?"

"Aye, good."

I was at my wits' end. "It's not – tell me what your plan is."

"No."

"You could wait here, I'd go and explain it all to them. Once they agree, I'm sure they'll be happy to send Thjálfi over," I cooed, then something struck me. "Does it help when you sit with your back towards it?"

"Mhm. I can't see it."

I bit my lip, listening to his breath. "How about we take your..." I glanced at his outer garment, which in the meantime we had used to filter dirty water and dry our bodies. "...this off and wrap it around your head, so you can't see? Then, when we're in Ásgard, I will shave you. Nobody will know."

"Odin's ravens." Suddenly there was a knife in his hand and I gasped. "Do it now."

"I'd need soap, I need water!"

"It's sharp."

Those short, barked commands again. I tensed up as doubt crept back in. I could still change my mind, make another choice. The last one I'd made saved two lives and kept Magni hungry for days. He hadn't complained once.

Or Módi.

I had to know.

"Who—" I started when he put the blade to his throat. "What are you doing!"

He shrugged. "If you can't, then you can't."

When I was finished, he looked like someone who should never be let anywhere near people, much less Ásgard. I should have worked harder on not closing my eyes for fear of hurting him. Blood trickled down his face, down his neck, the furry chest. I'd be terrified if I didn't know who he was.

I didn't.

"Um," I said. My eyes moved to the remains of his tunic, then back. More red fur covered his chest, arms, back, even his neck and his palms. I blinked nervously. I wasn't going to volunteer to shave his entire body.

"I'm ready," he said, then licked a drop of blood off his lips, without noticing. "Blindfold me."

I felt my own hairs stand up under my clothes. The prophecy... what if...

"I'm scared," said Magni and he gazed at me with those giant, green eyes. "I'd never make it without you, I'd be dead or worse. Maya? Do you... do you think it will be fine?"

It was as if the entire Nine paused for a moment, waiting for me to answer.

"Um," I said.

He looked away, then down at his feet. "Just in case something goes wrong... I just wanted to tell you..."

"What is it?"

"I got attached to you..." Magni paused. "That's not what I... I love you," he burst out, his voice choked, broken. His hand jumped up to his mouth for a blink. "I'm sorry. It's just that I think I do. Thank you for helping me out of..." He gestured, still avoiding my gaze, staring at his feet. "This. Just wanted you to know in case I don't make it. Someone once... Can I hug you? I'll be gentle."

I said nothing when my face drowned in the sweaty fur. I had no words. If he told me now that his plan was to destroy all of Ásgard, I would still take his hand and lead him there.

He sat with his eyes shut, lip quivering, as I struggled to tie the tunic around his bloodied head as tightly as I could. I didn't want to know what would happen if it fell while we were under the Tree.

The moist space underneath smelled of rotting leaves.

"I'm nervous," said Magni. His clammy hand was crushing mine. "Say something."

"They will ask me why I was sent to bring Thor and instead I brought back a strange, bloodied jötunn," I muttered. "Bugger. I will have to explain *how* I did that."

I could have probably come up with something more reassuring.

"We can tell them that I found a way to get into Ásgard," he said. "That if I made it, others might as well. If they ask how I got there, I'll remind them that Mjölnir travelled to Jötunheim, so they can think about it."

I stopped for a moment and his pull nearly dragged me to the ground. "That's not really related."

"No," said Magni, "but they don't have to know that. Or... that's stupid, is it?"

"It's absolutely not stupid. It's better than anything I could come up with."

"You're making fun of me."

"Absolutely not. I just worry they'll kill you if you refuse to tell them how you did it." *They'll kill both of us*, I thought. *Maybe even if we tell them who we are.*

"Not when I tell them about my offer."

I felt a whiff of warm air on my face. "We're getting nearer," I said, my voice shaky with excitement and nerves. "Tell me. Please."

"No. You will find out soon enough. Odin needs three days to gather the Assembly, is that right? I'd like as many of them to hear me as possible. And Lady Freya must be there."

"She would never dream of missing it," I muttered.

"What is her hall like?"

"You'll see it soon."

"No...! Me? In Lady Freya's...?"

My mouth dropped. Busy worrying about everything else, I had just been mindlessly leading him towards Sessrúmnir, because I lived there. A gloomy, furry, bloodied giant in Freya's impeccably white hall? Why didn't I find some shit to rub into my hair as well? "It's nothing special," I mumbled, trying and failing to come up with *anything* else.

"Will she be there? Will I see her?" Magni's voice was high with excitement, his sweaty grip tightened, and I had to bite my lip until it hurt not to scream. My feet felt as if I were wearing iron boots. Freya would wipe us out with one glare. *Thor's hall, Bilskirnir*, I thought hopelessly. He'd fit there... in some... dungeon...

I might have been doing the least bad thing I could think of, but that didn't mean it was right.

"It's hot," said Magni in a strained voice. "Where are we?"

In Midgard, The Tree stood in the middle of a plain covered in greying grass. Here it was surrounded by flowers, bushes, everything in ever-so-blinding bloom. Once we moved far enough away from it, there would be bumblebees, birds, butterflies... I allowed myself a blink to bathe in the familiar, sweet smell of home. It made me nauseous. "It's the sun," I said quietly. "You can take that thing off."

He let go of my hand, then froze, mid-motion. "We are in Ásgard?"

Instinctively, I nodded, then mumbled a confirmation. What had I done...

Magni pulled the rag off his bloodied head, and I shuddered. His face was already stubbly. "Ooooo," he said. When the silence became uncomfortable enough for me to worry that Yggdrasil's magic was affecting him, he spoke again, pointing. "What's that?"

I followed his finger. "Roses. Don't look too far to the left. Let's go."

"What do roses do?"

"Uhm... grow? Look pretty?"

"And there?"

"Pear trees."

"Pears grow on trees?"

"Y-yes, Magni, pears grow on trees."

"Can I see? What else grows on trees?"

"Apples, cherries, chestnuts, um... bananas..." I forced myself to slow down, realising I was nearly running. Part of me just wanted to get to Sessrúmnir, face Freya, and be done with it. Magni took over, looking around, asking questions that were both innocent and unnerving.

"Some other things grow on bushes," I said. "Strawberries, toma-toes... Gods, I forgot what else there is. Figs? I don't know what figs grow on. You'd have to ask Idunn, really, I just eat them. Peaches, um, watermelons..."

"I'm afraid," he whispered. "I think we should go back."

I stopped breathing for a moment, my feelings rapidly rearrang-ing. There was no way I was going back and he couldn't go alone. "No, no, we're going straight to Lady Freya's hall," I blabbered, grab-bing his hand again, stumbling as I attempted to pull him by the hand. "I'll introduce you to Lady Freya. We'll rest, have a long bath, eat... Those are lupins, those there are oranges, you can eat them, once we get to Sessrúmnir you can have some. Magni, come *on!*"

His response was an indeterminate sound. His feet seemed to have grown roots.

"I know," I said. Calm lake on a quiet day. "It's a lot. Quite a mess, right? I never noticed that everything just grows all over the place.

Auntie Idunn's garden is..." My voice trailed off. His huge eyes, lit by the sun, were even greener, a colour that shouldn't exist. The blood on his head, the wide, furry chest, terror on his face, the muscles moving under his skin when he nervously wrangled the remains of his tunic made Thor look well-balanced. "If you could put this back on..." I started carefully.

"It's too much," he groaned. "It's like... like a whole other world."

"Um, that's because it is another world. Maybe you could..."

"Aye, it's just that... it's so much. So... so much. Why is all this?"

"What do you mean, why? It just grows. Can you put your..."

"How do you cope with this?" He pointed at something and my eyes followed.

"With daisies?"

"With having so much all at once. Why don't you share it? Do you remember what Jötunheim was like?"

I shivered. "Vividly. Magni..."

"Módi."

He bared his teeth and the light in his eyes disappeared. My hand flew to my mouth. As if he were the opposite of a shifter, two persons in one body. I only wanted one of them here with me.

"M-m-Módi, it's is not mine to share. I just live here. Sometimes. Look, I already feel guilty, does that help? What do you want me to do?"

"Explain why none of this grows in Jötunheim. None."

"I don't know! I feel very ashamed, now just please put this on and follow me."

Winter was coming, I reminded myself. Freya would be at Freyr's side, he was an old man now and would die sometime soon. Maybe I could convince Thrud that Her Grace shouldn't be interrupted just because I'd returned, bringing a blood-covered giant along. I seemed to alternate gaits, marching decidedly, then slowing to near-crawl. Módi just followed without a word and his presence behind me felt not completely unlike being in a burning forest. I sped up again, then slowed down as I saw the familiar white walls.

"Is this where the Gods live?"

"Just Freya. It's her hall. It's called Sessrúmnir."

"So big just for one," he remarked. "Don't you think?"

"Módi," I said, my voice shaky, "you really should put your tunic..."

The entrance opened and the maid's hand flew to her mouth.

"...on," I finished meekly.

Gefn or Höfn seemed to barely notice me. Her eyes ran up and down, taking Magni in. When she finally seemed to acknowledge me, the expression on her face made it clear that she wanted to slam the door shut in our faces. The elf twins hadn't mastered Thrud's expressionless face.

"Your..." she started, then paused. "My..."

Oh no, I thought, *you* won't. "His Grace," I barked. "A close friend."

"My name is Módi. I am here to make the Gods an offer. Lady Freya—"

"We need to bathe, eat, drink, rest," I interrupted before His Grace had a chance to exude any more charm and elegance. "Is Freya here?"

"Yes, Your Grace. Does... ah... His Grace require his own chambers, or will he be staying with... I hope... My apologies if..."

"Don't worry," I interrupted. Watching Gefn or Höfn trying to wriggle her way out gave me second-hand embarrassment. Freya could tell the twins apart, but wouldn't tell me how. "His Grace Módi will take a bath first, then eat. Please prepare a meal. A large meal. Cold meats, no, roast. Both. Fresh bread... fruit and vegetables, a lot of them, every kind you can think of. Two of Idunn's peaches. Thank you."

"Idunn's...?" started His Grace.

"Shut up, Your Grace," I hissed. "We will also need Thor's clothes. Just go to Bilskirnir and bring whatever you can. Trousers, tunic, shirt, vest, boots. They will fit."

"Your Grace, I can't just...!"

"Off you go. Don't make me repeat myself. Your Grace, follow me. And let me do the talking. What is it now?"

He was pointing at a massive sculpture of a naked man, his other hand covering his mouth.

"It's a statue," I huffed. I could hear my hot tub calling my name. "It's just decoration."

"But he's n-naked."

I rolled my eyes, but only on the inside. There were many other naked statues in this hall, some combined in ways that struck me as very uncomfortable. "I'll show you around later. Follow me. My chambers are in the left wing. What is it now?"

Magni found a mirror tall enough to reflect all of him. Freya liked mirrors almost as much as she liked gold. "Is that me?"

It took me a while to find it in me to answer as I watched his mouth drop, a finger slowly extend, stopping before reaching the polished surface. "Yes," I said quietly. "It's you."

The sound between a gasp and a sob seemed to emerge from his stomach rather than throat, as if it had been punched out of him. His shoulders dropped and the remains of his tunic fell out of his hands.

I grabbed his wrist with both hands and pulled. "It's just dirt," I hissed. "Hurry up! We'll clean you up, dress you nicely for Lady Freya. You can stay with me, in my chambers, unless you'd prefer to be on your own..." The door opened silently and he yelped. "Magni? Módi? What is it now?"

"Sh– she lives in there?"

"I told you I live here. Come inside, before someone else sees – come in."

"This is all for you?"

"This is just the drawing room. Come in."

"You have a special room just so you can draw?"

"Good Gods, Magni, come on, don't just stand here!"

"I'm not... I shouldn't be here. I'll ruin it all."

"You'll stay dirty forever if you don't follow me. There's a hot tub."

"Let's go around," he begged.

"Around what? It's there, behind the door, in my bathing room. This is a *rug*, it doesn't matter, even if you get it dirty it will get cleaned! Lady Freya can't see you like this!" I grabbed his wrist again, ready to use my power to get him in, unsettled or not. He stepped inside and I was about to sigh in relief, when the door quietly shut behind him. I had no time to blink before Magni leapt and turned in the air, his arms and legs spread, fists tight, ready to fight the door. I forgot how to breathe. If it were me in front of him, I'd have wet myself.

"Let me out! I– I d-don't belong here. I'll just start working."

"Lady Freya," I repeated my spell, groaning, but only on the inside. "You must bathe first, before Lady Freya sees you, or I will... I will make you roll on this rug until you're clean and it's all dirty!"

"You wouldn't do that...!"

"Oh yes," I hissed. "With magic. Hurry up!" I was beginning to panic as well. Freya couldn't see this.

"Can't." He seemed to shrink, back hunched, head withdrawing as if to hide between the shoulders. "I'm going back."

"Good luck, because I'm not helping you. Get in there, or I'll use magic and throw you in! Good Gods, what is it now?!" Hopefully I'd scared Gefn or Höfn enough to go to Thor's hall first, or maybe Freya was too busy to be interrupted with a report, otherwise—

"It's a hot tub," croaked Magni.

"Yes, that's how you take a bath, you get in a hot tub. Get in!"

"It's inside. It's in a room."

"That's why it's called a bathing room. Get—"

"All for you?"

I nearly cried with frustration. "For me, for you, take your clothes off and get in, or else! I won't..."

Some rags landed on the floor and water splashed all over everything, including me. I yelped in surprise, then things got worse as Magni lifted himself back to his feet. When I told him to take his clothes off, I didn't think that he would be *so* naked.

"...look," I finished, covering my eyes with my hand, groaning on the inside. "Sit down or I'll look!"

"I'm so sorry. I will clean this up."

"Don't be ridiculous!" I cried, taking a quick peek between my fingers, then shutting my eyes so hard I saw colours. "That's what the maids are for. You are here with an offer for the Gods and to meet *Lady* Freya. Sit down! Are you sitting down?"

"Every time you say her name you grind your teeth," said Magni.

"Do I? Never noticed." I threw my own clothes on the ground, then climbed in and stifled an ecstatic moan, reminding myself I had work to do. "Do you need me to help you wash?"

"It's your own tub just for you and nobody else can use it?"

"You can use it as well."

"Where do others bathe?"

The interrogation was working my last nerve. "In their own bathing rooms, I guess."

"There are more? One hand? Two hands?"

"I don't know. Think of Lady Freya and turn your back towards me," I demanded.

I poured some silky oil into my hand, then started massaging his scalp, gently washing off the dried blood, trying not to open the cuts. I needn't have worried. They were gone, as if the blood had just appeared out of nowhere.

He didn't stay quiet for long. "How many rooms do you have?"

"*Magni,* I didn't get to pick these chambers. They were assigned to me. If Freya decides tomorrow that I belong in an iron cage..." My voice trembled a bit. "Then in an iron cage I will be."

He exhaled slowly. "So, it's Lady Freya's, all of this, even this tub."

"Now you're getting it. I never asked for any of this."

"This is nice," Magni sighed when I started massaging his shoulders. My fingers were aching, but I continued. "So, how many rooms do you have?"

"You've seen the drawing room. This is the bathing room. I have a bedroom, obviously. And another bedroom."

"Why do you need two?"

"In case someone were to stay with me. Like you, for instance. It will be your bedroom now, unless you want your own chambers... or unless Freya says otherwise."

"Lady Freya," he exhaled and I finally let my tense muscles soften a bit. Magni sounded as if he'd already eaten Idunn's fruit. Good Gods, I was *ready* for some. "Lady Freya... ah... do I say 'Your Grace' when I meet her? Why did that maid call me my grace? I'm just me."

My aching fingers stopped moving. I hadn't thought about that.

The way people and Gods addressed each other had to do with the hierarchy. When I made the maid address Magni as "Grace", I put him at the same level as myself. If he were to address Freya as "Grace", he would push himself down without even knowing.

"Was that a stupid question?"

"Not at all," I muttered, thinking as fast as I could. "'My lady' or just 'Lady Freya'. Let's eat in the garden, shall we?"

"What if it starts raining or snowing? It's almost winter."

"It won't," I said. Explaining Ásgard right now was keeping me from food.

"I can't sit on this," muttered Magni, pointing to the chair, which admittedly was the right size for Freya or me, but not so much for a bear squeezed into a dressing gown that I could have drowned in. It covered most of him. Except the chest fur. And hand fur. And toe fur. The knot around his waist helped with the bits that *really* had to be covered.

"It's also magic," I repeated, trying not to salivate. "It's all magic. Except the food," I added quickly, in case he'd refuse to touch it.

Magni perched on the edge of the chair, or rather squatted over it. I gulped, hoping that certain bits didn't dangle where they could be seen. I should just have used the gown as a loincloth. "I – I don't know what this is."

I followed his gaze, but I couldn't tell what he meant. The table was covered with bowls and plates. I decided to start with the safe parts. "Roast," I said, observing him carefully. "Bread. Jam, that's... boiled fruit, you put it on bread."

"I don't know how to." He was staring at his hands, hidden in his lap. The white tablecloth, the silver plates, silver cutlery neatly arranged on the sides, the crystal goblets. King Thrymr used exactly two utensils to eat with: an iron knife and an iron spoon. Magni had probably never seen a fork in his life, silver or not. I could only pray that Freya wouldn't see him eating.

"Look here." I reached for something that made everything else on the table look grey. "This is a peach," I said, sucking back the saliva that threatened to run down my chin. My hand shook slightly. "It has a big pit inside. Should I show you? You just eat them with your hands."

I didn't wait for his response, I couldn't. I sank my teeth into the peach and once I swallowed the first drops of juice everything disappeared.

It was warm. Safe. I didn't have to go anywhere anymore. No more insect hunting and... and the robbing. My worries about Freya, about Módi, about... I forgot what... I really wanted to behave lady-like... he wouldn't notice. I bit into the fruit I held with both hands, barely avoiding eating my own fingers or breaking a tooth on the pit. The gentle breeze kissed my face, its caress both tender and intense on my skin. How was it that the touch softened, yet the colours intensified, shapes sharpened? I laughed out loud, wiping my hands in the gown. "Try one," I whispered, then giggled at his face. Magni was watching me as if I'd gone insane, which wasn't completely untrue.

"It's hairy."

Another giggle came out of me, like little bubbles. "So are you. You will love it. I promise."

Magni picked up the fruit, turning it in his hands, glancing at me anxiously. He smelled it and his eyes grew wider. I laughed as he took a tiny, careful bite, then my laughter died and air got stuck in my windpipe. Magni pushed the whole peach into his mouth, along with the pit, and swallowed it like a snake would swallow a rat.

"Good Gods, you don't eat that!" I cried when I could breathe again. "Look," I demonstrated the pit to him again, "this is like a rock. Idunn's or not, you could get sick—" Magni's hand flashed before my face. The warm haze made it hard to understand what had just happened. I was holding the pit, then I wasn't. I turned my hand around, then again, then looked at him, open-mouthed.

A drop of either juice or saliva slowly wandered down his chin. He wiped it with a finger, then sucked on it. "That's so good," he mumbled. "It's – it's so good. So. Good. I want more."

The warm bubble enveloping me wobbled. Had I behaved like

that my first time? I couldn't even remember... Magni's hand shot towards the nearest thing he could find and I cried out in warning a moment too late.

"That's awful," he complained once he'd finished spitting it out on the grass.

"It's a banana, you don't eat that yellow skin, you have to take it off." I began dozing off and had to force my eyes to stay open. Magni no longer sat on the edge of the chair, instead slipping off it. "How do you feel?"

"Goooooood."

"Maybe try some meat. Or pastry." A thin strand of unease made it through my bubble. As if someone kept poking me with a blunt needle through a blanket.

"Can I have another peach?"

"That was Idunn's peach. Do you remember who she is?"

"Idunn keeps the Gods alive," he murmured. "Even the bad ones. I am eating Gods' food. It's gooood. I want to stay alive, too."

"You can't have any more."

"Why? You want it for yourself? It's been... I've never... it's so good... ah!"

He grabbed a perfectly normal peach and bit off half of it before I had a chance to blink. The pit cracked between his teeth and he let out an alarming, choking sound. "You're tricking me," he groaned, spitting again. "This is – this is something else, it's not Gods' food."

"Magni, this is Freya's hall, the Gods' world. Everything you eat here is Gods' food. Go on, try the roast, Freya's cooks—"

"I'm not really hungry," Magni said dreamily. "I'd just like a peach, but not this one, the good..." His eyes were glazed, unseeing. Saliva trickled down his chin. The wrinkles between his eyebrows disappeared, his forehead smoothed. I must have looked similar. The hunger was gone, so was the dirt and the cold. The exhaustion of the trip was replaced by the drowsiness of having sat in the sun too long. The soft grass caressed my feet. He looked so sweet. Everything was so sweet.

"All my dreams..." he said, bringing me back to consciousness. "Is this how Gods feel all the time? It's... it's so blank... like nothing..."

"Maya!" yelled Freya, bursting into the garden. "There's a jötunn in here somewh – what is that?!"

Magni opened one eye and attempted to sit up straight on the tiny chair. "My lady," he mumbled. "My Grace. Your Grace. Lady Freya..."

"Maya! Is this your lover?!"

"O lady, your beauty is truly unparalleled—"

"No," I interrupted, "he's just a...a friend. Don't forget I have my bracelet. Um, good morning, what a pleasure to be back..."

"Words fail me to describe your beautiful, eh, beauty..."

"Shut him up," demanded Freya, "or remove him, or let's go somewhere and leave him here. I can't deal with this right now. Why is he looking at me like that? Is he playing with himself?"

"Thank you for letting us stay here, this is Módi," I said. My tongue felt a bit stiff. "He is a jötunn and a smith. He came here with an offer for the Gods."

"No poems could accurately describe you, my lady..."

"A *jötunn*, here, in *my* hall?"

"Um... he's very nice." I prayed that he wouldn't start singing his song about Brisingamen being made of gold.

"He's a halfwit. How did he get here?"

"Let me sing for you," groaned Magni, then began to slide off the chair.

"He has a..." I took in a deep breath. "PLAN!!!" I screamed. His eyes didn't even open.

"You've lost your mind," Freya decided. "Is he asleep?"

"He is very tired," I said. I was briefly reminded about the strange encounter with Harbard when my body tried to tense with nerves, but couldn't. I had no idea whether my grin looked natural. Could she tell from my eyes, my voice? Had the maids told her they'd brought two peaches, not one? I glanced at quietly snoring Magni and a strange thought appeared in my mind; if he were to die right now he probably wouldn't have minded. "We've walked for a long time."

I bit my lip just a blink too late.

"Ah," said Freya and her tone sobered me up like a bucket of cold water would. "So, *you* brought the jötunn here. How? Have you crossed Ífing or has Heimdall gone deaf and blind?"

"A secret passage," I murmured. If only I could tell her to go away and come back later.

"Whose secret, yours or his? Where is it?"

"Others know that passage..."

"Then it must be closed immediately. Where is it?"

"M–Módi came here with an offer for the Gods. He wants to make Ásgard safe..."

"Do I look like I'm stupid?"

"He's a good person... please. He's been hurt, many times, but he remained g-good."

"Good, pumpkin? Good? He told you he was good, so you brought him here? Oh no, sweetie," Freya gasped, her tone changing so suddenly I blinked in surprise. "You love him. I told you this would happen eventually. But he's not one for women."

"I know."

"He is lonely and broken-hearted, but not for you."

"I *know*."

"You will suffer once he dies," she intoned, "and it will be nobody's fault but your own. What is that offer of his?"

"He will only reveal it to the Assemb-bly," I groaned. I should be in bed right now. So you know Magni's broken-hearted, that I care about him more than about anyone else, but you had already decided that he had to die, Mother?

"I'm sure Odin will be delighted to call the Assembly to please a strange jötunn, honey. Do tell, how did your mission go? Will Thor be joining? Is he at Bilskirnir now, resting after his journey through the secret passage?"

"He... I think... Odin would have to send a raven. Or tell Thjálfi where..."

Fake shock appeared on her face. She even managed to pale. "Oh *no*, sweetie, how can that be? Did that brute Thor refuse to return? What did you say to him?"

"Um... not... I mean..."

"Can you try and speak in actual sentences, honey?"

Her hand rose and I flinched, but she just reached for a strand of my hair, rubbed it between her fingers, then, seeming satisfied, let go. I was right to start with a bath. "I haven't found him," I muttered.

"Really, pumpkin? Really? Perhaps I should try and be more clear, since you are so tired." Freya picked a grape and started fiddling with it. "You volunteered to bring Thor to Ásgard. You were away for – how long? So, after you did not achieve what you promised, you decided to bring this jötunn here instead. Through a secret passage."

"Lady Freya," sighed Magni dreamily. He tried to lift himself with his hand, which slipped off the chair and he nearly fell under the table. "If only Gunnar could see me now..."

"Get rid of him," Freya hissed. "Right now. Or I will."

"Módi," I said. "Módi! Can you go back to our chambers? Lie down and rest! Do you hear me?" I waved my hand in front of his face. "Chambers! Bed! There! Have a nap or something."

"Your...Highness, your beauty and goodness are unparalleled. The stories have not done you justice..."

"Get out," Freya spat. He slowly withdrew, backwards, not taking his eyes off her. She stared at me without blinking until he disappeared inside, her lips a white line, her immaculate fingernails drumming on the white tablecloth. "Where. Is. Thor?"

"I don't know. In Midgard."

"And where are you?"

"Um, here?"

Her eyes closed in faked exhaustion. "Do I need to make this even clearer?"

"Thor is a mercenary. He fights alongside humans against other humans. To please Odin. Why would he ever listen to me over Odin's orders?"

"I don't know, honey, but don't you think it would help if you actually tried?"

"I did! I was held captive for I don't even know how long for just asking whether Thor was around!"

"Lower your voice when you speak to me."

Yes, Mam.

The knowledge was too important to waste in one frustrated shriek, but the words kept trying to come out. *I am your daughter that you put in a cage. You sent me away, twice, to places where I could have died. You see me as a "weapon". You had a child with your brother and that child is me...* I tasted something strange, sweet and salty and metallic. I'd bitten through my lip again.

"I was imprisoned in some jarl's hall, which then caught on fire. I escaped, bumped into a group of outlaws... by accident..."

One of her eyebrows wandered so high that her eyes became asymmetrical.

"Módi here was one of them," I plodded on. My stomach growled, its hunger no longer tamed by Idunn's fruit. "He is special..."

"I can see *that*."

"He is here to—"

She raised her finger towards her lips to silence me, then leaned closer. "The jötnar are gathering on the other side of Ifing and their numbers keep growing by the day. We need Thor to go and clean it up. Instead you brought us a jötunn boasting about a secret plan and you won't tell me how you came here."

"I... I brought him. It was my decision."

"And who gave you the right to make decisions?"

"You," I said.

The grape between her fingers exploded, sending drops of juice flying. I stopped breathing. It felt as though even the wind had stopped and the birds had fallen silent.

"It appears that I'm still not being clear enough," Freya said quietly. "There is a war brewing. Ásgard's protector is missing. Jötnar can arrive here through a passage—"

"No, they can't!"

"You told me that others know about it. Have you lied to me, darling?"

I said nothing, staring at the roast, then moving my eyes to the steaming broccoli. I'd never even liked broccoli.

"I will ask Odin to announce an Assembly, as you and the jötunn wish. I will miss you when you're dead, but not too much. You two don't even have sex? What did he offer you that Ásgard doesn't have?"

"Ásgard has everything," I muttered.

"You sound like that upsets you. Have you chosen a side already? No matter how big that army, do not underestimate the power of the Gods."

"I swear I had no idea there was any army. Who's their leader?"

Freya pursed her lips, then reached for another grape. "We do not know. He seems to be a very powerful mage of some sort, but the ravens failed to spot him. He had a great tent built, one that he never leaves, but the effects of his magic are..."

I raised my finger and her voice died out. "A very powerful mage went to Jötunheim once, with a blue orb of mana. He has reasons to resent Ásgard and all its residents. His name is Hhhh... Bard."

Why did I always stop one sentence too late?

Freya gawked at me, her lips forming a perfect "O", before she hid her face in her hands. "That's just wonderful. Bard uniting the jötnar against Ásgard. Maybe now Odin will finally bother to send a raven to Thor. You must tell me..."

"We came from Midgard," I interrupted. "Not from Jötunheim. Without my magical powers Módi wouldn't even have found the passage."

"Your magical powers," repeated Freya flatly. "Bard, if that's him, can contain mana. He can control weather. All of it, clouds, winds, heat, cold. You? Powers? The ravens are in Jötunheim, Odin might not know yet what you have done. Reveal the passage to me and I shall forgive you for failing me again. The jötunn will die quietly before he is noticed. His suffering will be over. You will go back and find Thor."

I couldn't resist anymore. Holding Freya's gaze, I tore off some meat with my fingers, stuck it in my mouth, then wiped my fingers on the white dressing gown. Like Módi had, back in the inn. Freya scowled, but didn't comment. I had the upper hand for as long as I stayed calm. So, not for very long.

"Módi's heart is not so much broken, as destroyed," I said. "He feels he's got nothing to lose."

"Wonderful. Now my trust in him is complete." Her look was so cold I felt goosebumps under the gown. "You will be accused of great treachery. You know the punishment for that. Unless..." Her features softened a bit. "Unless..."

I stopped chewing.

Tell me, I thought. My lip hurt, but I bit it anyway to stop it from trembling. *Please tell me. You don't have to apologise, just...acknowledge me. Please.*

"Unless you convince Týr that you are worthy of being listened to," she said, examining her grape. "You may be just a human, but you are...known here. Plead with Idunn, Frigg, Sif. Reveal the passage to Odin. Lick the dirt off his boots."

"And you?" I blurted out.

"I must remain neutral in this," she said. I could almost hear her not looking at me. "You are my—"

Please, Mam...

"You serve me." A deep sigh. "Not that I see results."

I closed my eyes and saw the tiny, blue, icy flame grow again. I was so tired. "Take Thor's chariot," I said. "Go to Jötunheim. Speak to the jötnar. They love you. Módi does not fancy women and you reduced him to a blubbering wreck. Tell that army to bugger off and go home. Let Odin figure out what to do with Harbard."

Her fingernails stopped tapping on the table.

Why? Why did I always have to say the wrong thing? Three runes that made all the difference between the name I was and wasn't supposed to know. There went my upper hand.

Without looking at her, I took a plate, and loaded it with food. "I'm going to my chambers. I need rest. We both do. Módi will be staying with me, in my guest bedroom. I will prepare him for the Assembly."

"Maya," she said. "Just one more thing before you go."

I looked up. A little smile was playing on her lips, a real one that reached her eyes. She steepled her fingers and leaned towards me. "If I see or hear that jötunn before the Assembly," she said, her voice warm, dripping with honey, "blood *will* be spilled in Ásgard. You are forbidden to leave your chambers. Leave my garden right now."

~

The plate I held landed on the rug.

"Magni...!" I cried. "Why are you on the floor? Good Gods, cover yourself! I– I'm not looking! Are you covered? Wake up! Say you're covered!"

"I envy the Gods."

I dared to glance. Luckily, Magni turned, now lying on his belly. His voice was flat, face blank, eyes empty.

"Every night I dream about the bad things I have seen and done. The day I threw Mjölnir to Thor and got the City destroyed, the day Hillevi died... I killed her. No two nights are the same. There are so many things, many dreams to choose from. Ludo, the rider, the girls, Boy's eyes, the white man, blood all over me. Sometimes I don't even need to be asleep, I'm talking to you or I'm building a fire and suddenly that's what I see." He paused. "I once had blood for break‑ fast. I still don't know whose blood it was, maybe a horse's, maybe a man's. I think it was boiled."

The meat I just ate demanded to be let out.

"Herjólf... that man... you don't understand, I know, but it helped. I don't know why. The drink helps, sometimes, when there's a lot. But always just for a bit, like all this just takes a step away and just waits to... Maya... give me more of those peaches and let me sleep."

I shook my head wordlessly.

"Just one more. Please. I won't tell anybody. Do they count them?" His lip trembled and I thought my heart would explode.

I dropped to my knees next to him. "It's not that." My eyes were welling up. "Idunn's fruit is extremely powerful, the strongest drink is nothing in comparison. You can only eat it once every turn of the moon. You would get sick, very sick, you might die."

"They say Odin drinks Idunn's wine all the time. Is that a lie?"

I shook my head again and the movement seemed to push a massive sigh out of me. "There is only one Odin. The wine is made of grapes... grapes are, um, what wine is made of... that are only grown for him. He spends his life inside his head, in his wisdom. Once we stand in front of the Assembly, he will use that wisdom to cheat you. If they even let you speak. Be wary that no oath made on his staff, his or yours, can be broken. It's one of the laws governing the Universe... oh wait, I was talking about the wine. No, I don't think you can drink it without becoming, um, like Odin is. And you don't want that."

Silence.

Carefully, I looked with a corner of my eye. Magni lay down on the rug, completely silent, without a cry or a gasp. I covered him with a fluffy blanket and let tears flow down my face. I remembered the little girl I'd hid in a dungeon. We were one now; the only reminder of her existence was the icy flame. Magni mentioned a boy who followed him everywhere. Freya could cure his heartbreak, Bragi could rewrite his history, but I knew the boy, Módi, would never go away.

I prodded my swollen lip with my tongue. Once I found out what Magni's plan was, I would stand in front of the Assembly, reveal who I was and who my parents were, then ask only for one thing. Someone had to force Módi to leave and never return.

CHAPTER 8

MAGNI

"Tell me," Maya begged as we headed towards the Great Hall. "A hint. Something."

I didn't even look her way. Maya had spent the few last days trying to scare me with stories of how terrifying the Great Hall would be, then refusing even a tiny bit of fruit to help me find courage to enter. She showed me daisies and lupins and roses and pears and berries and I pretended to listen, nodding. I only cared about the fruit that I couldn't get. Sometimes a maid would appear and her head would just be hair and pieces of bone, brain, blood. Then the pulp would move, chunks smacking against each other, and *your grace* would come out instead of *khhkhhhhkhhh*. I'd ask for just a tiny bit of the good fruit again, and Maya would say no.

Sometimes I was glad I couldn't recall Hillevi's death and sometimes I wished I would, so that I would know what it was that I so badly wanted to forget.

Lady Freya refused to see me. I told myself I didn't mind. I saw her for a blink, although I couldn't remember it very well. I slept in her hall. Maya explained to me that Lady Freya was staying with her brother, Freyr, because he would die soon. It had nothing to do with me, she said, then poured me more wine and asked about my plan again.

The plan was short and simple. At first I was going to say it was a gift, then realised that would be too suspicious. I had to ask for a reward. Picking it couldn't have been easier, except for the nagging temptation. I could ask for Odin's wine instead.

We took a turn and my feet grew roots. My eyes travelled up, up, up...

"I told you," Maya sighed.

The Great Hall looked as if a real giant had taken a black, shiny rock, nay, mountain. He then cracked it into sharp shards, piling them next to each other as though building a bonfire so tall that it could scrape clouds from the sky. Magic was poured all over that pile, wrong, unnatural. I wanted nothing more than to run away. I couldn't even ask for a blindfold if I were to speak to Odin and act like we were equals. Before I saw the Hall it was easy to tell myself that the only thing I had to worry about were his slippery words. I didn't expect to feel like an ant about to be crushed by someone's boot.

"I'm going to be sick," I grunted.

"It's worse inside," muttered Maya. "Magni, I'll help if you tell me, take me hostage!"

The statues guarding the entrance were hardly elaborate, just piles of large boulders placed on top of each other, making Troll look beautiful. I squealed when they began to move. It was all I could do not to soil myself. Golems only listened to those who knew their names, so not to me. They bent – each of the boulders moving separately, unconnected to each other, forcing me to close my eyes and bite my tongue not to scream, until a crack like thunder caused me to jump. They made parts of the construction move, *wrong* parts, as if the shards split in half where there was no split before, creating a gate that could fit someone like me a hand of times and even more than that—

—some force sent me flying into the hall, flapping my hands, yelling something, until my body slammed onto the ground, then slid as if on ice, forward, forward. A deafening *whoomp* behind me sent a wave of sound that landed on my back and kept jumping on it. My hands shot to cover my ears, the *whoomp-whoomp-whoomp* went on and on, now joined by endless laughter coming from above, men, women... Gods laughing at me. The floor vibrated from the din, kicking me in the ribs, legs, back, turning me into a speck of dust with one whimper of a thought, *please stop please stop please stop please—*

The silence that fell over the Hall felt as if someone had thrown a bucket of void at me. I couldn't move. Who was I to come here, to think I had the right? Maya had brought me here, Maya had said "take me hostage" right before this happened. What did that mean? Could I have misheard her? If I were to take my hands off my ears, would they laugh again until my head exploded? *Take me hostage*, her voice repeated, then again, quieter, and then there was nothing left but the urge to escape. I couldn't. I had to face Odin.

Every part of my body was shivering, knees, elbows, ankles threatening to fold at any moment. I felt drowsy, everything doubling and blurring in front of my eyes, as the colossus watched me lift myself up. I knew my eyes were lying, that Odin was the size of a normal man, much smaller than me or Thor. Not here, though, not right now.

Two black ravens were perched on the sides of the throne's high back. Odin's right hand held a wooden staff. The only light seemed to be somewhere on top of me, casting a bright circle with me in the center, obscuring everything else in darkness. The throne was just on the edge between being and not being visible. His remaining eye was a fierce, red pinprick, reflecting blood and flames that weren't there.

"Come closer."

The low voice reverberated from the invisible walls, coming back quieter, then louder. I would have turned away and run if the golems hadn't closed the only exit I knew of. My hands hurt from all the effort I had to put into not allowing my fingers to block my ears. The last thing I wanted was to come any closer to Odin the Murderer, the Slayer, the Hateful. My grandfather. *Cry*, my mind whispered, *plead for mercy, maybe you will be allowed to escape with your life, even if they laugh at you again.*

I took the most difficult step of my life, then another. I couldn't manage a third. My feet wouldn't listen.

"Tell us whatever it is you've got to tell, so we can kill you," Odin said. He sounded slightly bored.

I forgot what I was going... Gunnar, Mother... who else... not for me... Jötunheim. "My name...is Módi," I croaked. "I am, a, I am a smith... and..."

"A jötunn spy in Ásgard during wartime," said a voice somewhere above me. I jerked my head in alarm, trying to tell which direction the voice came from as it bounced from the walls. The light that shone from somewhere above blinded me. "Let's kill him and move on."

"Not yet," said Odin. "Go on, jötunn."

I couldn't remember any words anymore. My knees began to bend. There was nothing I could do but plead for my life. I had failed.

Move away, child, go to sleep. Yes, you have failed. You will return when I permit you.

Ahhh. Much better.

"I have an offer for you, Gods," I said, my back straight, legs no longer soft. "For Ásgard."

The corners of Odin's mouth formed something that wasn't quite a smile. "What can you possibly offer us that we don't have?"

"Safety. Protection. Ending the war before it begins."

I heard hushing and grunts above me. A smirk appeared on my face. If they needed to resort to tricks like loud echoes and darkness and lights, the unnatural magic holding all this together, they were afraid. *The child could never understand. He is a danger to all of us. He shall never come out again.*

"How are you going to do that?"

"I will build a wall around Ásgard," I said.

I recognised Loki's laughter. "No roof?"

"Silence," said Odin. "Why would we need a wall? We are safe thanks to Ifing."

"I've heard that you are upset because an army of jötnar is gathering on the shores of Ifing," I said. "If you're safe, why do you fear?"

"We would like to know how you got here."

I smiled. "I've heard a man stole Mjölnir, then crossed Ifing using magic, bringing the hammer to a jötunn king."

"That king is dead now," answered Odin. He didn't sound so bored anymore.

"Thor took care of that. Where is he now?"

"How did you come here?" Freya. "Where is that secret passage...?"

"How would a wall stop anybody?" interrupted Loki's disembodied, screechy voice. "They can climb it."

"I will build a wall that cannot be climbed."

"They'll get on the shore, then destroy it."

"No," I said. "It won't be built on the shore but in the water. No ship will be able to land, no one will be able to climb the wall."

"What a lovely fairy tale," said Odin. "You should be a bard. You've got almost as much talent as Bragi."

"Ex-*cuse* me," said an offended voice followed by Loki's chuckle, multiplied and reflected by the invisible walls of the Hall. I failed not to shiver, scowling. I could just about withstand everything else, but Loki's cackling sounded like someone repeatedly scratching a rock with a rusty nail. Not unlike Ludo's.

"Unfortunately, if someone can cross Ifing, they will also be able to go around your wall," continued Odin.

"Not if I surround all of Ásgard with it."

"How amusing. You seem to believe you can do that."

"If anybody can, it's me," I said, puffing my chest up, crossing my arms.

"Are you a mage? A sorcerer?"

"No and no."

"What will you need?"

"Tools, materials, time."

"We don't have time," said Odin. "As for the rest, anything you want is yours."

I smiled. This was going well.

"Name your price, jötunn, as surely you are not just making this offer out of your good heart."

"I want Freya," I said, my fingers already on their way to my ears.

The angry voices, their echoes, Loki's piercing laugh penetrated my skull anyway, but it was Odin's booming "silence!" that shook the ground. I barely remained standing. *Would you have really dared to say it out loud, child? That is why I had to send you to sleep.*

"What do you mean by that?" Freya's icy voice demanded.

I ignored her. "I want her to be mine," I said to Odin. "Not so much as a wife, but as a possession."

"I see," he answered in the tone of an adult patiently explaining to a kid that stars were a giant's teeth. "What else would you like? Perhaps the sun and the moon?"

"If you're offering..."

"The sun and moon are not mine to give," Odin answered, completely seriously.

"Neither am I!"

I smirked.

"Silence! Assuming that you can execute your idea, jötunn, what is it that you would use Freya for?"

"I'm going to sell her to the highest bidder," I answered, and even Odin couldn't stop himself from producing a muffled sound of surprise.

"All-Father! Surely...! I– Kill this jötunn now!"

"I preside over this Assembly," said Odin. His voice was quiet, yet it drowned out Freya's shrieks. "I am the ruler of Ásgard. If there is a challenger, may he or she announce it openly."

"I challenge him!"

"Not him," murmured Odin. "Me."

The echoes died out, as if the walls had finally sucked all of them in. The complete silence was more unsettling than the endless noise.

"I think it's a very interesting idea. Of course, you would start from the side of Ifing, to protect us as much as possible, and continue from there."

"That is my plan."

Odin shifted on the throne, leaning towards me with the help of his staff. I took another step forward and he backed off so subtly the child would have missed it, busy shitting his breeches. "How many jötnar do you intend to bring over here to Ásgard to help you protect us? A hundred, a thousand? Do I look like a fool to you? Reveal your secret passage, or you shall die now."

"I will," I said immediately, "for a lifetime supply of your wine."

"This is not possible," said a strained female voice. Probably Idunn.

"Lifetime," mused Odin, "is a relative term."

I forced a smirk, my mind working as fast as it could. I was not any wiser than the child. A...hand of... a hundred, a thousand, Odin just said, that must have been a lot then? "Do you accept my offer or not?"

"Under certain conditions," Odin said. I tensed up. The dangerous part was coming now. The girl should be here with me, helping. I couldn't stop myself from looking around, as if she were going to appear out of thin air. Everything was possible in this place that dripped with sick magic.

"I have an idea," squealed Loki. "He looks so very certain, and such a big and strong man as well. A true giant. I'm sure he can do it by himself."

I never planned otherwise.

"You will get your prize..." Odin started slowly.

"He will not!"

The tiny, red light of Odin's eye flickered. "You *will* get your prize, if you can meet three conditions. First, you will not have any outside help, not just jötnar, none whatsoever, whether a giant or a field mouse. Whatever you need, you must find here in Ásgard. Second, if the wall is not finished, if it is possible for even the smallest child to pass through once your time ends—"

"Bifröst," someone said.

"You will leave an opening for Bifröst."

I didn't mind. Thor couldn't cross Bifröst. "My time ends? What does that mean?"

"Third, you must finish within one winter. I don't know what your kinsmen are planning, whether you are part of it, I don't know how you even got here at all. You will show us that passage, then build a wall around it as well."

"Wine," I said shortly. "And no attempts on my life. I want to be immortal, like you."

"That's a very long time to spend suffering," said Loki, "and some of us are inventive with torture..."

"Silence!" yelled Odin, a blink too late. "No immortality and no wine."

"No me!" shrieked Freya.

Once, in another life, on our way to Jomsborg, we had taken care of a whole family. Once Troll and I had put the bodies in the stable we had stayed in their house all night, drinking, singing. Ludo and Herjólf had decided to arm-wrestle. Ludo had come up with an interesting addition to the game – candles, lit and placed so that the loser would have to slam his hand onto the hot wax. He'd soon regretted it. His brisk, nonsensical moves of a man possessed were of no help against someone stronger and smarter. Herjólf had bent Ludo's arm slowly, until the flame had licked Ludo's hand, then he held it over the burning candle, smirking at the cries for mercy. Ludo wasn't me and the resulting burn took a long time to heal.

I wondered how long Odin could withstand the flame.

"No wall, then," I sighed. "I wish you would have agreed, but—"

"Ifing," said someone, and I heard fear, "can it be crossed then, have you done it?"

"Yes," I answered, my fingers already in my ears. I had been in Thor's chariot, on my way to Midgard, but that was not what they asked. I waited until Odin's "silence!" shook the ground again before taking my fingers out of my ears and wondering how much magic they poured into keeping this pile of rock in one piece.

"So, it is possible," mumbled Odin. He seemed even older now, nearly hanging off his staff, as if he would fall off his throne without it. My grandfather. "Do you really believe you can build your wall within one winter?"

The winters in Jötunheim and Midgard seemed to last forever. That was many, many hands of days and Ásgard was small. Maya confirmed that every time I asked. Odin was wise, though, where I was stupid. There must have been a catch, perhaps more than one, and I couldn't see it. Whose hand was now held over the flame? Both?

I felt the child, awake, trying to push back to the surface, his attempts sucking out strength I was already running out of. *It's not about my life*, he squealed, *it's for Jötunheim, the chariot can never fly over Ifing again.*

I silenced his nonsense, but he was right. I had no need to worry, what he and I decided to do would only take a hand of...hands of days. Once I was done, the girl would take me back through her passage. So simple – hide our face, push the child under for just a blink, tell her I loved her, ensure her loyalty, let the child back in.

I puffed up my chest and crossed my arms. "Yes," I said calmly.

In the complete silence I couldn't hear their fear. Only smell it.

"You will leave now," said Odin. "Wait outside. We must discuss your offer. I suggest you don't attempt escape or treachery, for my ravens will find you..."

I laughed in his face. "I'm not going anywhere until I get what I want."

My grandfather shifted uncomfortably on his throne.

"I see a problem," Loki piped.

"So do I," said Odin, "and we shall discuss it once the jötunn is removed from here."

The "door" opened and I emerged outside, blinking, blinded by the sun. Before I could see again, look for the girl, the entrance slammed shut again and the golems returned to their previous positions. The girl was taken inside.

Not even the smallest child could crawl through the wall, he'd said. That was the trick. Dwarf children were probably tiny. The wall had to be both impenetrable and as tall as the trees in Jötunheim, the chariot couldn't fly high enough not to rub against their tips.

The golems, immobile again, were unsettling. I tapped one on the "ankle" to see if anything happened, then took a few steps back, trying to assess how tall they were. Unlike the Great Hall, they didn't radiate unnatural magic, they just stood there until they didn't. If I placed them next to each other... nay, they would leave enough space for even me to pass between. Maybe if they were wrestling, or one stood on its head... Let's say I had a hand of golems. They could lie on top of each other then. Holding hands. Wrap their "feet" around their "heads". How did one make golems? All I knew was that I would have to come up with names for each of them.

I had never been good with names. I could call one...Ludo. One – Troll. Mieszko, Wojciech. How would I know which one was which? I could neither place numbers on them, because I couldn't count, nor runes, because they were unnatural and I didn't want anything to do with them. I grabbed a short stick and began drawing golems inter-twined in various ways, chuckling at some of them, when my hand stopped moving.

I intended to only build enough of the wall to protect the shores of Ifing. That wouldn't do. The chariot could simply fly around, taking perhaps a few blinks longer to get where it needed to be. The wall needed to be much longer. It really had to encircle the whole of Ásgard. Odin had already demanded that I leave Bifröst open. Thor couldn't walk through the Rainbow Bridge, but if the opening was wider than the chariot, there was no point in me even starting. Thjálfi took me from Jötunheim to Midgard, proving it possible. I had to trap the chariot here.

I dropped my stick. The last time my stomach felt like it did now was when I had eaten those berries in my old life.

I had to run, but where? The ravens would always find me. The girl was inside and I couldn't get to Yggdrasil on my own. Panic. The child kept trying to take over again, exhausting me. Why couldn't he understand it was for his own good?!

All of us had made a stupid mistake. The plan's seed was his, but we'd planted it together, him, me, the others. It was the best we all could come up with, carefully adding to it, whispering, so that the child would think it was all his idea.

When the golems moved to open the entrance to the Hall I still had nothing. Could I destroy the chariot, could they build another, narrower one? The goats were said to be immortal, was that just another tale the girl would have laughed at? I needed her. *I forgot I was stupid*, the weak voice piped up, and it was all I could do to push him back down before he took over. I paraded inside as slowly as I could, trying to puff up my chest, then failed to contain a surprised gasp.

A naked woman knelt in the middle of the light circle. Her head hung down and long, flowing locks of golden hair covered her face. Freya...? Next to the woman, the girl, her face white with terror, stood with enormous shears in her hands. She was visibly shaking from the effort. The shears looked rusty, probably blunt. My nose wrinkled. That was the best they could do?

"Do me a favour, jötunn," said Odin. "Hold this woman still."

"This woman!" she cried, her face, red and puffy with tears. "This woman! Is that my name now? I am your daughter-in-law!"

Odin's son was Thor, his wife was Sif. My stepmother.

"What's going on?" I asked.

Odin ignored the question. "Make sure she can't move her head, jötunn. Maya, do what you've been told to do."

"I will not—" started Sif, lifting herself up. I didn't even need to push hard to send her back to her knees. Maya let out a little cry. Sif kept shaking her head, screaming, leaving me with no choice. One well-aimed blow of my fist and she dropped to the ground, unconscious. Collective gasps, then growls echoed from the walls.

"Now she won't hurt herself," I explained. I was beside myself with curiosity.

"Start," said Freya, her voice reverberating across the walls like a slap that came once, twice, a hand, a hand of hands of times.

The girl was too weak to use the rusty shears. The Gods were really badly in need of a blacksmith, I thought. Or was this a part of the punishment? For Sif and possibly the girl as well? She fought with the shears until they opened, nearly dropping them as she tried to get some hair in between. Her face was distorted with effort. The shears wouldn't close.

"This won't work," I informed Odin. "Let me do it. I can tear it out."

The girl's eyes, giant now, filled with tears and fear, met mine. "It's you," she whispered. "Módi."

I smiled reassuringly. She had no reason to fear me until I decided her company was no longer required.

"It will bleed," squealed Loki when my fingers were already entangled in the blond locks. "No blood can be spilled in Ásgard."

I let Sif's body fall, knelt next to her, pulled the dagger out of my boot. Lock after lock landed on the ground as I half-listened to the voices, half-ignored them.

"Who let him in with a weapon?"

"This is sharp! He's got a sharp knife!"

"He could have attacked...!"

They were interrupting my work. "Silence!" I roared.

My voice didn't reflect from the walls the way Odin's – or theirs – had. Disappointing. Still, they quieted a bit. "I'm here to build a wall," I continued. "I'm doing you a favour, as requested. I hope you don't forget that."

"Oh," said Loki, "Sif definitely won't."

"Does it all have to be gone?" I asked, inadvertently sliding my hand over my own, already stubbly head. Sif began to move and moan again, so I pressed her to the ground with my knee. Gently, because the girl was watching and she'd already judged me to be evil.

"It looks good to me," assessed Freya. Some patches were bald, some had tufts of hair sticking out. Not a drop of blood had fallen. I knew that would have resulted in me getting in trouble for breaking a rule.

The girl just stood there, her shoulders drooping, the shears on the ground.

"Step aside, both of you," said Odin. Water fell from somewhere above, as if an invisible servant had turned a bucket upside down, wetting Sif, splashing towards the girl and me. The girl let out a little cry. I didn't, but recoiled slightly as I watched Sif kneel, then touch her head before a shriek began and continued, without breaks for breathing. The sound was painful, high-pitched, piercing, as her hands moved up and down her head, then grabbed the golden locks that were now little more than a puddle of straw. One of the hairs got stuck to my finger and wouldn't come off. Not taking my eyes off Sif, I put the dagger back in its place. I'd have to sharpen it again soon in Thor's forge.

Or maybe, since he wasn't here, it could be *my* forge.

"It hurts!" Sif cried, grabbing on to her head. "It hurts! It hurts!"

"It doesn't," I sniggered, proud that I had stopped myself from using words I'd learnt from Ludo.

"It hurts! You will die! And you, and you, but you will be first, you little bitch, and...gmff!"

"Should I let go?" I asked politely, my hand covering Sif's mouth, two fingers shutting her nose, a useful trick the child had been taught once.

"Let go, jötunn," nodded Odin. "Sif, I suggest you stop making noise, or I will change my mind."

Sif hid her face in her hands, her scalp a sorry sight. She kept sobbing, shaking, muttering curses, but no longer screaming. My whole body relaxed, free from the pain her screeching had caused me.

"Take your linen sack and leave." The thunder of Odin's voice made me stumble. "You will cross Bifröst and not attempt to return unless you can complete your task within one year and one day. If you don't..."

"I take bets," sniggered Loki.

Sif's gaze shot up, then she looked around, unsure. It wasn't just me who couldn't tell where the voices came from. Someone laughed, then another one, then another. The echoes hurt even when I put my fingers in my ears. Sif ignored the laughter, taking a step towards us. Her face was contorted, teeth bared, nose like a sharp beak, fingers bent into claws. When her mouth opened, the sound that came out was that of metal being sharpened.

Sudden silence befell the Hall, even though Sif's mouth remained open. I carefully lowered my hands, prepared to defend myself if she were to leap towards us. The scraping sound of the entrance opening made all of us wince.

"Thor left because of your scheming, now you will bring him back. A year and a day. Now get out," said Odin.

Sif's transformation was nothing like the girl's. Her nose elongated, lower jaw grew to meet it, eyes relocated to the sides of her head, making me gasp. She squatted, spread what used to be her fingers, her naked arms changing into wings that were little more than broken feathers. Legs shortened, toes changed into claws that made me inhale sharply. I couldn't breathe even after the bald vulture ran rather than flew outside, croaking loudly, flapping its wings, trying to jump in the air.

Dread Gods, I could only think, dread Gods, dread Gods. Nothing that I had seen or experienced so far had terrified me more. The child could never find out about this.

"Did anybody know..." started a man's voice I didn't recognise.

"No," said Odin shortly and waited for the golems to shut the entrance as if nothing had happened.

A question broke through the mess inside my head. How did the golems know what to do? Was there someone whispering their names very quietly? Did they hear it outside? "Come closer, jötunn," Odin said, interrupting me. "Do you know what makes this staff special?"

The child would have never dared to march towards Odin, causing the elderly God to involuntarily withdraw into his seat. *You might have been born first, child, but it's not you that Odin is afraid of.* "I know," I said. "An oath made on your staff may not be broken."

"We accept your conditions," Odin said shortly. "We will now..."

"I don't accept! You don't get to, to – to sell me...!"

"Would you like to join Sif?" asked Odin quietly.

There were no more protests from Freya.

"We will now swear our oaths," he said. "I, Odin, the All-Father, will give you Freya to be yours to do whatever you want with her once you build a wall around all of Ásgard..."

I heard the girl's sharp intake of breath. I forgot she didn't know my plan until now.

"...with the exception of Bifröst, a wall tall and strong enough to make jötnar unable to attack forever..."

"No," I interrupted. "You're trying to trick me. 'Forever' is a very long time and I will not wait for my reward until 'forever' comes to pass."

"I, Odin, the All-Father," he repeated without acknowledging my words or berating me, "will give you Freya to be yours to do whatever you want with her once you finish building a wall around all of

Ásgard with the exception of Bifröst, a wall tall and strong enough to make jötnar unable to attack. You will complete the task within one winter, starting with the death of Freyr and ending with his rebirth. You will be provided all that you need to complete this task. You may neither accept nor demand any help that would come from outside Ásgard. Is that agreeable to you?"

I nodded.

"This is my oath, and I make it freely," finished Odin. A smirk appeared on his face. He'd said nothing about small children not getting through. He didn't have to. I couldn't imagine fulfilling those conditions. The only trick was the one I had played on myself, imagining I only had to build a small piece of the wall. If there was a wise one among us all, inside this body, he or she was in hiding.

"Your turn," said a man's voice in the darkness.

"All that I need?" I ensured. "I need a hostage, a place to stay, tools, materials, food—"

"All, I said," interrupted Odin. "Go on."

"I will build a wall around all of Ásgard except Bifröst, a wall tall enough to make jötnar unable to attack. I will do so within one winter, starting after the death of Freyr and ending with his rebirth. I will neither accept nor demand any help that would come from outside Ásgard. Is that agreeable to you?"

"Reveal the passage," Odin said shortly.

"Wine," I answered. "I tell the truth when I say that no jötnar can use that passage the way I did."

I said too much, I realised, when he made himself comfortable on the throne, no longer an old man leaning on his staff. He was supposed to remain afraid.

"I gather that's it," I said. "This is my oath, and I make it freely." My hands, curled into fists, opened, and I took in a deep breath. I hadn't realised how tense I was. "When will Freyr die?"

Freya's wordless cry reverberated through the hall.

"Soon," said Odin. "Very soon. It is a matter of days, maybe four, maybe seven. I believe winter is very, very close now."

"I will take Thor's hall as my dwelling," I said.

Fire shone in his eye and an angry huff burst out. "You have no right to enter Thor's hall without his permission."

"You just said I can have all I need. I need his dwelling."

"Why?" asked a disembodied voice that came from somewhere in the darkness.

I shrugged, staring into Odin's face. "Because I decided I need it. He isn't here, neither is Sif. The hall stands empty, there are tools, forges, servants. Either that, or I need a new hall built before the winter starts."

"It is just," announced the same voice, and Odin jerked his head up.

"Are you sure?"

"It is just."

"Týr says it is just," sighed my grandfather. "Very well. Bilskirnir is yours to use however you want..."

"Hostage," I reminded.

"I am not coming with you!"

"Keep some dignity, Freya," sighed Odin. "Why do you need a hostage, jötunn?"

I blanked. Because the girl said that I should take her hostage. "I don't trust you," I said as slowly as I could before the revelation came. "I want this girl here, Maya, with me. She knows the passage, too. She will wait in Bilskirnir until..."

She hissed sharply, but if it was supposed to mean something, I didn't know what.

"...I am done with my work."

"It is just."

"I need her," snapped Freya.

"Too bad," muttered the girl.

"Darling!"

"If you need anything else, jötunn," Odin interrupted, "please talk to any of us. Later. Now take your hostage and leave. Maya, you will do as he tells you."

The instant the "door" shut, the girl slapped me in the face. That must have hurt her hand. She might need a reminder that I loved her.

"Get out of him!" she shrieked.

"They can hear us," I answered.

"Nobody can hear us, same as we can't hear them." Nevertheless, she started marching away so briskly she was almost running, forcing me to chase her, before she suddenly stopped to wave her finger in my face. "Leave Magni alone. You're some sort of monster."

I laughed. "Can you imagine him going through with this? He'd just cry and cry."

"I'm going to do everything in my power to help."

"Good."

"To help *Magni*. Not you. I can tell which one I'm talking to, you can do many things, but not change your eyes. What are you, some sort of... I don't even know what! Leave right now!"

"Make me."

The girl quieted, then stared at me. Her eyes narrowed. "I know your secrets," she finally said, then nodded towards the Hall.

"If I die, he dies."

"On the other side," she immediately answered, "if he dies, you die. I love Magni, he is my brother. You're something evil, you enjoyed what you did to Sif! What even are you? Answer me! We don't have much time, they're still debating, then there will be drinks and snacks..."

"Snacks?"

The girl took an inadvertent glance back. "Small pieces of cheese, that kind of thing. Granny Frigg came up with... Stop distracting me! What are you doing to Magni?"

"I am protecting him, foolish girl. Haven't you laughed at him once for thinking that he could get away with not killing anybody?"

"I was stupid."

I shrugged. "He still is."

"Were you always..." She gestured, searching for words.

"No. The child has occupied this body for longer, but I am older than he. I know all that he knows, he only knows what I tell him, or he'd break. I can tell him whatever I choose to about the Assembly. I can leave him not knowing that he has offered to build a wall."

"I will help Magni and Magni alone. Leave and do not come back."

"And what if I do? Hasn't Odin told you to do as I please?"

The girl pursed her lips and crossed her arms on her chest. I waited, watching the Great Hall out of the corner of my eye, an idea slowly forming. "I am human," she finally said. "I may have been raised here, but Odin would argue that I come from the outside. I am going to shift into a mare. I doubt that even Odin bothered to memorise every single horse in Ásgard. I'll pretend to pull a cart, help you load it..." The girl paused. "I assume you have a plan for this."

"What is the Great Hall made of?"

"Magic," she said. "And basalt."

"This basalt, can I get more of it?"

She slowly turned to stare at the Great Hall with me. "Yes," she slowly said. "I see. The wall behind Fenrir wolf will be black, like the Great Hall. Oh, Granny, I wish I'd listened to you back then. That I understood."

"Are you drunk?"

The girl turned on her heel. "I want Magni here. Right now, when the ravens and Loki can't see or hear us. If I see you emerge even for one blink, I shift back into my human form and you can finish the job by yourself."

"I love you," I tried.

"Bugger off, Módi! Oh, and I want an oath on Odin's staff. Hurry up."

"How wide is Bifröst?"

"I said hurry up!"

I lost. For now. I needed her magic. A normal horse couldn't transport those shards, not even a hand of normal horses, or two hands. "The child – Magni will return and remain in this body until the wall is complete. I mean, until the end of winter..."

"No, no, I like that better. Until the wall is complete. Go on."

You'll suffer for this. "This is my oath and I make it freely. But why do you offer to help? I thought I'd need to..."

"I want you to get the prize you asked for," she said with a strangely smug smile. "Even if you never do anything with her, she will know that you can. I would very much like that. Now get out of here, because I have to explain to Magni what just happened before they come out. Nobody can know the horse and I have anything in common."

Here are the memories you need, child. I'll give you more later. We will watch, we will step in if you need protection. We'll always be here for you.

I bent and vomited on the ground.

"That was horrible," I cried. "This place is sick, it's unnatural! Why are you looking at me like that?"

"Do you remember what you promised to do? Hurry up, I have to shift into a horse."

"It's not going to work," I groaned. "I made a mistake."

"It will—" started Maya, looking strangely sad, then turning her head with a gasp. I looked too. The golems moved, their "bodies" rearranging to open the entrance. "You hid me somewhere," she blurted out, "doesn't matter where, I'm your hostage. The horse has nothing to do with me. I'll help you. It's a great plan. Almost forgot! Remember, if you want something in Ásgard, just wish for it and you will find it!"

"What great plan, what do I wish for...?"

The black mare didn't answer. I touched her gently, half-expecting her to disappear, then caressed her mane. She felt, looked, even smelled like a real horse. There was something on her neck. A leather strap with a small crystal hanging off it.

The horse looked towards the Great Hall, whinnied sharply and bolted away. One quick glance at the open entrance was enough to send me running after her. Fragments of thoughts and memories bounced inside my head. The Hall's magic must have obscured most of what had happened. Maya was my hostage and I'd hidden her. Somewhere. The horse was not Maya at all. No help from the outside. I was going to stay in Thor's hall... Who came up with that? I'd rather sleep on the grass outside than stay in Bilskirnir! *No, fool,* a voice in my head whispered, *you need the forge, the tools, everything.*

Maya whinnied, irritated. I hadn't even realised that I'd stopped moving. I needed someone else to talk to. Did people talk to their horses? Even if, she wouldn't answer. I was on my own.

I tried to leave the gloomy thoughts behind as I followed her again, slower now. My hands folded into fists. I would either change the Nine, or die trying. I meant that. It's just that Bilskirnir seemed to be quite far away from the Great Hall. True, she probably took a longer route to avoid approaching Yggdrasil, but when she said Ásgard was small I thought it was... smaller small. Dread Gods! I forgot about Bifröst, I had promised that I would leave an opening for it. It must have been Odin's trick to slice my memories like this, so that I would forget! Well, I wouldn't, I thought, turning back to glare at the magical Great Hall that had stolen my memories. As tall as it was, though, I couldn't see it from here anymore and we were still not at Thor's hall.

Ásgard really wasn't small the way I'd imagined it.

Had Maya said I could just wish for things? Could I wish for a wall? That would be great. Basalt, a word floated by, confusing me until I recalled what that was. I needed basalt and Maya's magic. I also needed Idunn's fruit, so that I could sleep—

I blinked, then rubbed my eyes. Was I dreaming already? Maya was leading me towards something that looked like two buildings crashed into each other. One path led towards them, then split into left and right. To the left stood something that was white and pink and had a lot of thin, yet tall towers sticking up, little green and golden flags, roofs in so many colours it made my eyes hurt. It was fascinating in its monstrosity and I couldn't tear my eyes away until Maya whinnied, bringing me back. My attention moved to the other half of that...creation.

It was inconceivable that those two buildings were even near each other. I was gawking at a fortress that could withstand anything. Red brick, black iron, thick wood. Instantly, I knew that it wouldn't be white inside. I could be as dirty as I wanted here after a day of forging and I would not need to worry about stains. This was Thor's hall and if I could have a hall of my own and they told me it could be anything I wanted, anything at all, I could only hope that I would have enough imagination to come up with something like this. Just without that other attached thing.

Another memory floated by – Sif, Thor's wife, wouldn't be here. Odin sent her somewhere. With it came a brief vision of a hand closing someone's mouth and nose, a cold, observing gaze. Herjólf. I shivered. The dreams followed me even here, no longer waiting for me to fall asleep. I needed the fruit, Maya didn't understand, but I *had* to get more of it if I couldn't have Odin's wine. I shook my head and my gaze fell upon something that made everything else irrelevant.

I was almost salivating as I slid my fingers over the perfectly round, smooth shape. The only hammer marks could be seen where the artists wanted to add texture. Both the gate and the fence surrounding everything were airy and impenetrable, flowery forms wrapped around branches. I slowly walked away from Maya, touching the wax-finished black iron. I took a sharp intake of breath when I noticed that each section presented different plants. No fence in the history of Nine ever *needed* to look like this. It was done just for fun. I hadn't been a bad blacksmith when I still worked at the forge. Still, even the simplest of those leaves and flowers would take me a hand of hands of winters of practice. The fence stretched as far as I could see.

I felt pinpricks of sweat all over my skin and had to hold on to the fence not to drop to my knees. How long was this whole thing? A mile? I expected all of Ásgard to be about this long and I still thought I'd undertaken a job that was near impossible to complete. It felt as if I had eaten a rock, heavy inside my belly. I tried to tell myself that the sickly feeling came from Yggdrasil being somewhere very near, hidden by magic. The nausea only intensified. On my way here I hadn't seen Yggdrasil or Sessrúmnir, or...wherever the other Gods lived.

I returned to the gate, holding on to the fence, feeling faint. All I could think of was that crafting this masterpiece must have taken many men many winters. I only had one. Ásgard was meant to be small, I thought, my mouth filled with bitter taste of having somehow been cheated.

"His Grace Thor——" someone started and my hands were immediately on the attacker's throat. Both of us let out horrified gasps. It was Thjálfi.

Thoughts ran through my head like Thor's goats. Thjálfi had only seen me up close once, when he took me to Midgard. He probably wasn't really looking, busy with the chariot and all. Maybe he didn't even know Thor had a son at all. I was still choking him.

I lowered my hands and my eyes, then grimaced in a fake, lopsided smile. He most probably wouldn't recognise me, almost definitely. Possibly.

"His Grace Thor and Her Grace Sif are away, my lord," said Thjálfi. He sounded offended more than throttled, less shaken than I expected, even though I could see the traces my fingers left on his throat. They reminded me of... I was about to apologise when I remembered something. A servant calling me "my lord" meant that he was aware of his lower position, but didn't feel like I commanded respect. As wrong as it felt, I couldn't afford to apologise. I needed him to respect me.

I straightened my back and now towered above him, my arms crossed. "This is my hall now," I rumbled, "given to me by Odin."

Thjálfi's eyes widened. "G-g-given?"

"Thor and Sif will not be using it for a while."

"Ah," he said weakly. "Your Grace, I don't want to sound impolite..."

"Then be quiet," I said, patted Maya's neck reassuringly in case she was anxious, even though I wasn't at all. I let myself in, keeping my back so straight and chest so puffed up that it hurt. It sounded like Maya followed. Only now it dawned on me that since I'd never been able to ride a horse, I knew nothing about them. I could just about shoe them and I didn't like doing that either.

"You there!" I heard. A girl was running towards us. She looked so much like Thjálfi, only being a girl and without the few hairs that stuck out of his chin, that I did a double take. There was one more difference. The way her hair was cut suggested that she enjoyed being constantly poked in the eyes. "You can't come in here. His Grace and Her Grace..."

"Röskva," said Thjálfi, catching up, "apologise immediately. This is His Grace... uh..."

"Módi," I said, biting myself in the tongue just in time. "He will be staying here for the time being."

"For as long as I want," I said.

"It's that jötunn," Röskva said in disbelief. She glared at me, then back at Thjálfi's white face. "Oh," she said. "My sincere apologies, Your Grace. I *guess*." Her hands were folded into fists and I had a feeling that she wasn't really sorry.

"Röskva! You will take care of His Grace's horse."

"No, I'd like someone I can trust—" I started. The words died on my lips when Röskva's face changed, her jaw dropped.

"Oooo..." she said, then paused. "Is it true? Can I? She is so beautiful."

"His Grace doesn't ride horses," said Thjálfi, "he's too tall and heavy. We rarely—"

"May I ask what her name is, Your Grace?" Röskva's eyes shone like stars. She wasn't even looking at me, just at... eh... The entire language and every single name disappeared from my mind. Both siblings aimed their questioning gazes at me now and I tried to stop the blood from gathering in my cheeks. Names, what names were there...

"Horse...y," I said, feeling a bit faint again. "That's right. My horse, Horsey. She needs good care."

Thjálfi looked me up and down before answering. "No offence meant, Your Grace, but you are almost as large as His Grace Thor, who cannot ride a horse, especially not one as small as yours."

"She has no reins," said Röskva, amused.

"She doesn't need reins," I said weakly. "Horsey is, ah, very well behaved. She is going to pull the chariot," I remembered.

"Off you go, Röskva," said Thjálfi. "She loves horses." Röskva's eyes were stars, her touch on Maya's... Horsey's mane was light as if she were afraid to touch her. "I promise that Horsey will be taken very good care of. However, I'm afraid you can't use the chariot, Your Grace, not without His Grace Thor's permission."

The chariot. By Freya. I just meant *a* chariot, something that

Horsey could pretend to be pulling. If I could get my hands on Thor's chariot, I'd just destroy it with one blow of my fist. It was hard to keep myself from grinning. "Odin has given me permission to take anything I want, Thor's chariot included. Neither Thor nor Sif are here and they're not coming back anytime soon. And I only like goats on my plate."

"Your Grace...!" gasped Thjálfi.

I grimaced. Being yourgraced at all the time made me feel uncomfortable. "Just call me Módi," I said.

"That wouldn't be appropriate, Your *Grace*."

I ground my teeth. The bastard was making fun of me by addressing me the way I'd forced him to. "Say, where do I find my new chariot?"

The badly hidden grin immediately turned into a badly hidden scowl. "Near the s-stables, Your Grace." He gestured in the direction where Röskva had taken Horsey.

"And the forge?"

"I'm afraid that His Grace Thor's forge—"

I cleared my throat.

"Behind the stables, Your Grace," sighed Thjálfi.

Trying to take in as much as I could, I plodded towards the main entrance. The door was made of oiled wood reinforced with iron beams. I couldn't stop myself from sliding my finger over the smooth shapes of the hinges before letting myself in. The staircase in front of me was made of the same golden wood as the door, the rails forged. A light shone above me. A candelabra that nobody could possibly reach, yet many, many candles burnt in it, all looking like they'd been lit just a blink before I entered.

"This is so beautiful," I whispered, touching the rail.

"His Grace's work is unparalleled," said Thjálfi. His voice, which had a rather unpleasant tint to it when he addressed me, now rang with pride.

I swallowed something that unexpectedly grew inside my throat. "Thor made all this?"

"That's right, *Your Grace*."

"All of it," I said flatly.

"All of it, *Your Grace*."

"If you don't start calling me Módi I will have you whipped."

"B-b-but, Your Grace, I can't – it wouldn't be appropriate."

"I am now the grace in here and my grace wants to be called Módi."

"Can I at least call you my lord, Your G – I beg, Your – my..."

"I will think about it," I said, scowling. All this being important and not being important because of being a lord or a grace or something else. If I were so important, why couldn't I tell a servant what to call me? The rail, the fence, the hinges kept distracting me. I didn't need to ask to know that Thor would never use magic at the forge. How long could it have taken to create all those wonders? Was that what he was doing when he wasn't busy killing us? By Freya, what would his forge look like?!

"If you follow me, my lord, I will show you around."

His lord just wanted him to go away so that he could drop on his knees and admire every rivet, forge weld, wish he had a father who would teach him how to produce such art. I couldn't tear my fingers away from the metal as we walked up the stairs. Just as I was about to remark on the darkness of the corridors, torches in the walls lit up by themselves. I screamed out in surprise.

Thjálfi turned back with a grin on his face. "It's just crystal magic, my lord."

"I just didn't...expect it... of course it is. Go on."

The torches would shoot up in flames, then go out as we passed. That magic was so much nicer than Sessrúmnir's transparent doors that were also windows, jewels that I had to touch for them to glow a light over the white everything, and that Great Hall. Would the forge fire also light by itself, or would I need helpers to work the bellows?

"To your left is the dining room, my lord..."

The dining room looked like a gloomy inn, but when we entered candles and torches lit themselves and the hearth spat out a ball of flames before settling down to a roaring fire. I knew he expected me to yelp and I was proud that I stopped breathing instead. There were two tables that stretched long enough for a hand of hands of eaters, long benches along them. Thick wood, brass plates, tankards set up as if guests were expected any moment. To my right I saw barrels, all wood and metal, placed on thick iron stands. The barrels all had taps, something I'd seen in the Jomsborg tavern, except they only had one barrel like that. Here I could see a hand of hands and maybe even toes of barrels.

Nothing white.

Too much. Too big. But oh, so beautiful. If I had any friends, I would love to invite them here.

"Show me the bedroom."

"A guest bedroom, my lord?"

I made sure he could see my smirk. "His Grace's bedroom is mine from now on. I am not a guest here. I am... I am Odin's special... builder. Of walls. Never mind. Does Thor have a drawing room?"

"A what – no, Her Grace has a drawing room."

"Are you the only servant here?"

Thjálfi let out a snort, then pretended to cough very badly. "Please forgive me, I have a bit of a cold, my lord. No, I am not the only servant. Just His Grace's steward. You don't have to see me at all if you don't want to."

He shouldn't have put a challenge in his tone.

"I decided that you are going to be my favourite, Thjálfi. I would like you to attend to me every time I need something. Make sure that cold is gone fast. My bedroom, now."

The torches lighting up then dying down behind us weren't as exciting now as we passed by what seemed to be hands and hands of doors. Unsure why anybody would need so many rooms, I became concerned about having to count them all, but I needn't have worried. We reached the end of the hallway, where there was only one thick door, made of wood darker than I had ever seen before.

"This is the master bedroom," Thjálfi announced as he let me in, then mylorded something more, which I barely heard.

I wanted to cry.

The bedroom walls were made of wooden logs, painted with the same golden oil, beautifully complementing the rich, dark brown wood the door was made of. The red brick inglenook fire made the one in the dining room look tiny – there were benches covered with furs inside, in case I wanted to remind myself how being baked alive felt. The flames were low, the room just warm enough. The bed was the size of Jomsborg, covered in so many furs and skins of various sorts that it was difficult to say whether there was anything underneath, or it was just one huge pile of furs. The flooring was made of real, proper rocks, not shiny white or black marble, all of them carefully rounded. Cow skins, sheep skins, wood, iron, rocks, bricks, fire. Only now did I realise how uncomfortable I'd felt in Sessrúmnir, Lady Freya or not. Everything here was...real.

Unexpected anger burst inside me. Sleeping on the ground, my stomach empty and my teeth chattering, the rain too thick to keep a fire going, the blanket I was wrapped in just as soaked as everything else. The pile of straw in Jomsborg, the walls that stank of Kowal's "drink", Wojciech's half-afraid, half-hopeful bows. Dalebor's torch. This bed alone was larger than Gunnar's living space and work space, together.

More memories. Niedomira's triumphant grin. Pig, shivering with fever, covered with Herjólf's vest and with leaves, since we had nothing else. Ludo, too hungry and tired to even talk to himself. Thorsteinn's raised axe, my hammer smashing his skull. My hands dripping with magical blood that soon became real when Mjölnir smashed into the walls of the City's castle. Thor's never-ending roar of triumph, punctuated by thunder. Hillevi—

"My lord... is everything alright?"

"I need some fresh air," I said. I couldn't look at Thjálfi, his throat apple bitten off by Boy, blood gushing out. "Food."

"His Grace's favourite place to eat is outside, on the balcony. I will make sure that... I will alert the cooks."

I approached the tall barrier, looked down, then stumbled and almost fell on a fur-covered bench behind me. This was not Freya's garden with flowers and... and with more flowers. The sharp cliff faced a dark forest, so far below that the tips of the trees were at the same level as my feet. A table with a big brass tankard, a barrel on a stand stood next to the bench, just waiting for Thor. Or me. I was alone now and fought the temptation to just stretch out on the bench and fall asleep.

I examined the rest. Another thick oak table, next to it two more benches, at its head a chair just the right size to fit Thor. Or me. Everything was so *tangible*. Through the middle of the massive table ran an opening with blackened, iron edges. I didn't have to ask Thjálfi. Freya had pretty jewels that needed to be touched to emit an unnatural glow. At my hall, once it either grew dark or colder, fire would burst right from the middle of this table. Or maybe once I sat down. I would find out soon.

My hall? I felt the hairs on my skin stand up, but not out of fear. I hoped he would never come back and that Sif wouldn't either.

I spilled some of the stout from the barrel before I figured out how to use the tap. Why is all this? I had asked Maya once, and she hadn't understood. What had the Gods done to have it all here, gathered in one place, when Jötunheim survived on sausage, fish, and onions? I had never seen fruit other than bruised apples before coming here. My breathless admiration changed into anger. How many skins and furs were piled in that bedroom? How many were in the guest bedrooms? Again, I saw Pig, shivering, sick. Herjólf shivered next to him, having given Pig his vest. We tried to share the warmth. Maya had a hot tub for herself.

"I will build that wall," I whispered to the forest. "Then I'll sell Freya back to them and take all this to Jötunheim. This is my oath..."

If you manage to build that wall, a harsh voice inside me said, *you'll never see Jötunheim again.*

Each bite of roast I was served made me think of hunger. A sip of stout – of drinking dirty water filtered through my tunic. When Thjálfi waved a hand in front of my eyes I felt as if someone had yanked me from one life back into another, one of them real, one a nightmare. Which was which?

"My lord," he said, his voice shaky, "please forgive me, but you were not responding. There is a guest for you; it is Her Grace Freya. I don't know how she knew you would be here. She is angry, I..."

"Get out of my way!" yelled Freya. "Get out of here!"

"I don't have strength for this," I said flatly to the air.

"See yourself out, servant, and don't return until I ring for you!"

This felt like being poked with the tip of a blade. "Don't go too far, Thjálfi," I said. "Her Grace won't be staying."

"How dare you!" shrieked Freya. I closed my eyes. I had to make sure they would never let her in again. I'd complain to Odin. "I think he's gone," she said in a normal voice, then exhaled in relief. "Now we can talk. I brought you something."

That brought me back.

"You're not angry?"

"Why would I be? I came here to offer my help. I want this wall built."

I flinched. "Why? I'll be able to do anything I want with you then."

"I'm sure we'll be able to..." Lady Freya, for she felt like a lady again, smiled sweetly. "Come to an understanding. I know you have made an oath not to accept outside help. I am not outside help. I live here in Ásgard. And those," she said, pointing at a basket I hadn't even noticed, "also come from Ásgard." She lifted a white cloth that covered the basket and pushed it towards me.

I saw apples, peaches, and a lot of things I didn't even know the names of. I caught a whiff and before I knew it my hand was already moving by itself to dig into the basket. I forced myself to withdraw it. "Why? What do you want?"

"They will give you the strength and rest that you will need. Leave the basket here, on this bench, so I can visit, dressed in my magical falcon cloak. The basket will always be full. Eat as much as you want, my dear boy."

"But Maya said..."

"Maya is just a maid. How very smart of you to take her as your hostage! Could I see her? Just to ask a few questions, nothing more."

I bristled.

"Oh, my dear boy, surely you have noticed that I am on your side! I love my friends more than anything and anybody in the world, and we are friends. Here is the proof," said Lady Freya, patting the handle of the basket. "We will have your wall ready in no time. You can tell me everything. Is she here then?"

"No," I said, relaxing, my attention focused on the basket. Lady Freya would know better than Maya what to do with Idunn's fruit and I needed so badly to talk to someone I could trust. "I mean, yes. She's in the stable."

"Goodness me, what would she be doing in the stable? Don't tell me you sent her to clean it."

"No, she is going to be my horse. Her name is Horsey now," I said, lowering my voice.

"Horsey?" Freya laughed. "That's incredible. I love it. Keep it a secret, my dear boy, even if those awful ravens seem to be away. Loki is wise, witty, dangerous. He is the best of shifters, my dear boy, he could even turn into a fly and watch you from afar. You should never feel safe, for Loki's wit is second to none. Hmm, possibly second to Odin's, but with an emphasis on 'possibly' if you know what I'm saying."

I blinked a few times. I didn't know what she was saying. I must have already drunk too much. "What if I demand to marry you, like King Thrymr did?"

She waved her hand dismissively. "I know what you want and it isn't me. Anybody I know?"

Despite the sun, the view of the forest made me feel cold. I would leave this fortress and sleep on rocks again if it helped me forget about him.

"I understand," said Lady Freya. "You don't want to tell, not yet. It's completely fine with me. You will tell me when you feel like it. Once you are done with your wall, we can search for your lover, you can be together again." She playfully petted my hair, making me wince in shock. I already had hair again, more than just stubble. Lady Freya didn't seem to notice. "How is Maya going to help you?"

I explained everything and she seemed impressed. "That's wise," she said. "I underestimated her and you. Few could come up with a plan as wise as that, probably only me. Ah, and Loki, obviously. Perhaps Odin, if he used his famous wisdom, which, let me tell you, is not as great as you might have been led to believe. Anyway, gotta go, I have a lot of duties, being a Goddess and all. Have you thought of what you'd say if someone were to ask you where Maya disappeared to?"

"I don't know."

"That is an answer," Freya nodded, "but not the best one. Even I might need to ask you in public if I notice Odin's ravens are listening. As if this conversation never took place. Just come up with a place in Ásgard that none of them will be able to check!" she trilled. "I love solving problems! My dear boy, don't take it personally, but I'm going to ring for Thjálfi now and scream at you."

"Scream at me?"

"Yes, all the servants must remember very clearly how much I hate you. If you ever see me somewhere, I will probably scream at you again, curse you and everything, since... see? I almost forgot. Loki can shift into absolutely anyone. Thjálfi, Röskva, Thor, even me, Freya. Imagine!" She chuckled lightly. "I'm sure he would never dare do that, but still, never trust anybody. Don't tell anyone about me. Even our Horsey could be Loki. Sleep with one eye open..."

"I know how to do that."

"Ah, that's great. Can you open this door for me? It's very heavy, and I am but a weak woman, my dear boy."

Lady Freya dutifully screeched at me, which was so comical I couldn't stop laughing in her face, until she seemed to get bored and marched away, huffing. I sent Thjálfi after her, asking him not to come back unless I rang for him, locked the door and returned to the balcony. I hung off the railing and almost fell. I wouldn't have survived that, as the cliff was practically vertical. Above me was just stone. The forest was too far for any creature, whether a raven or a falcon, to listen or see me without being noticed. There was nothing I could do about a fly, so I would just... I had no duty to answer questions asked by flies. I was safe.

I sat next to the basket. I turned it so that the handle was exactly perpendicular to the back of the bench. I moved it a bit further from myself, then pulled it a bit closer, then turned it so that the handle was diagonal. I was afraid. Lady Freya had explained to me why she was helping me, I was sure she had, but then she mentioned "a man" and the rest of the conversation seemed to blur.

I drank from the tankard and the stout tasted of his lips. The pain of his teeth biting through my lip, warm metal of my own blood, my eyes opening to see him staring at me as if he wanted to see how far he could go before I protested. I never had. The only one I had to blame was myself.

I tore off the cloth, grabbed an apple so perfectly red and round that other apples would look at it the way I looked at Thor's craftsmanship, and ate it in two bites.

...my neck was sore and stiff, my stubbly chin wet from the juice. I lifted myself from the ground, rubbing my eyes with a sticky hand. I must have dozed off. The stars in front of me, the moon, the silverlit tips of the trees were more precious than... I forgot to ask Lady Freya if I could see the Brisingamen. I stood by the barrier and realised I was dreaming, that if I jumped now I would fly. I was a God, like Odin was a God, I was his fellow God. Odin and I, I and Odin. I didn't need his wine, I had Lady Freya on my side, bringing me Idunn's fruit.

In sudden terror my body lurched rather than turned, in two parts, first the legs, then the rest. The basket was half-empty. I found the white cloth – I must have spilled mead on it at some point, it was sticky – no, my hands were sticky, so was my stubble, or rather short beard. I delicately covered the remaining fruit. "Sleep well," I whispered, then laughed.

I was free. I was a God. All I had to do was wait a week for my hair to grow out, then go to Odin and tell him I was his grandson and that I wanted a hall. Same as Thor's, but bigger. And without that pink part with little towers and spires. I stood by the barrier and realised I was dreaming, that if I jumped now I would fly. I was a God.

"How funny," I said to the basket, "it's like that already happened."

I wanted to pour myself mead, but couldn't find the tankard. It must have fallen off the cliff. *I better go to sleep*, I thought. I caressed the flames bursting out of the metal opening in the middle of the empty table with my fingers. I could do anything, fire had no power over me. It hurt, though, my fingers hurt, and I didn't know why.

I better go to sleep.

The door stood ajar. I must have opened it. I couldn't remember doing it. Was it Thjálfi? Did he take my basket away? I told him not to touch the basket, *not* to touch the basket. I returned to the bench and sighed in relief. It was still there. I better go to sleep. I was Odin's fellow God.

I spread on the furs, growling quietly in pleasure when something tickled my neck, then lifted myself slowly to take off all my clothes. It was so much nicer naked, with the soft furs caressing my skin. So wonderful. So perfect. It's just that my fingers hurt and I didn't know why, like a pinch of salt in something that didn't need salt. I was dreaming, I realised, and in my dream I was a big, naked, hairy man stretched on a massive pile of furs inside a room made of wood and brick and stone, illuminated by golden flames and silver moonlight. I wondered who I was, then I remembered. I was Odin's fellow God, I could fly, I could do anything.

Someone was gently scratching my back and it felt so wonderful. I hadn't been touched like that... ever. I wanted to thank that some-one, only to realise that it was me who was gently moving, rubbing my back against the furs. Was this really my body, was I like that? I raised my hand – why did my fingers hurt – and ran it through the fur that covered the wide chest. It was like someone took me, a black-smith's boy, and put me inside this big body that I had to grow up to fill. Maybe it was just borrowed. I was Odin's fellow God, I could probably do that. I was dreaming, but if I jumped off the balcony now I would fly over the trees, they would tickle me the way the furs tickled that big body that I borrowed. I laughed and winced at how unpleasant the sound was, the man's laughter was not nice. I told him to go to sleep and I shut his eyes and it got dark.

I was neither awake nor asleep, like I was having a dream in which I was awake. My arm started tingling, so I turned to the other side. I was too warm, I decided, I would take some clothes off. The man's body was already naked and at first it felt disappointing, then made me emotional. This poor body used to sleep on the ground, it had walked around hungry, cold... forest fire. The body was so scared and hurt, mistreated. The man still trusted me enough to let me use it. I wouldn't fail him. I would keep it fed and warm, feed it the fruit to keep it rested and young. I had a feeling that this was how being young felt, only not so large and not so furry. So this was what my fellow Gods felt like all the time. Maya was not permitted to eat the fruit more often, because she was not a Goddess. Only the true Gods like Odin and I deserved all this. I winced, hearing a strange voice, the boast coming from the man's mouth as he spoke my thoughts aloud. Or perhaps his thoughts? My hand was illuminated by the orange flames and the silver moonlight. Was the body not in bed just now? The hand had one, two, three, four, a hand of fingers and it was just so *fascinating* that I could move them, like they were mine. I just wished they wouldn't hurt. That was not nice.

The wall, I suddenly remembered, and the body let out another spurt of laughter, but this one was nice, it sounded happy. It made me smile. I would soon be known as the saviour of Ásgard and Jötunheim. All the deaths the body's owner contributed to, all the hurt... I saw a brief flash of Hillevi's face, laughing freely, a sweet sound I'd never actually heard. I couldn't stop grinning, my face fixed in a smile that almost hurt, it was making me *so* happy to see her like this. She was so beautiful and so special. She might have not been a princess, but she deserved to be one. The past was gone. Now I was finally the real me, even though I was only borrowing the big man's body. Would he let me keep it if I promised to protect it? I could do so much good with it. Someone hurt it, I remembered, and scowled. That was not a nice thought. Outlaws. I would outlaw making people outlaws, I decided. I could, as a God. The body giggled, but it sounded a bit like a screech. It reminded me of something... someone. Beautiful, worried, sympathetic eyes. *What's wrong?* Boy. He was here with me, in a corner. He followed me inside, unnoticed. To help.

I couldn't breathe for a moment, then the big, clumsy body shot up, slipping, falling – *AHH* – but I just wanted a little piece of fruit. I couldn't tell anything from each other in the faint light, so I just picked something at random and bit off a small chunk. It was hairy and the skin was thick, but it wasn't about taste. I spat out the pieces

293

of skin, down the cliff, before it dawned on me that I didn't have to chew them, I could just swallow the whole thing. Soon I could fly again, like Lady Freya in her falcon cloak. We could even fly together. She was so kind and good to bring me all this fruit. It was so different to just be with her. I remembered when I first saw her and she seemed angry, radiating this... God-ness. Now she came here and promised to help me and it was like just having someone nice who was also beautiful and brought me fruit. Lady Freya told me that we were friends.

A sudden worry. Did Thjálfi steal my basket? No, he didn't, I was sitting here, naked, next to the basket. I should probably go to sleep. I admired the flames bursting out of the metal opening in the middle of the empty table and reached to caress them. The body's hand recoiled, not listening to me. I remembered. This body was threatened with fire before, many times, with a torch and with a forest set ablaze. But fire was my friend, a work tool and a lifesaver. I loved it back. I could stick my whole head in the fire if I wanted to, breathe it, bathe in it. Just not now, because I was tired. Or was the borrowed man tired? I would ask him if I could. He should really go to sleep now. I wondered if Odin was now in Valhalla, drinking wine and watching the warriors fight, or did they go to sleep at night, too? I had to ask Thjálfi. I had to tell him not to touch my basket.

I was standing naked again, resting against the railing – such beautiful work, Father, so well done. My neck was no longer sore, but my arm was still tingling, I stretched my fingers, then again, then moved the arm. I must have slept wrongly. But it was still night, although it seemed to be getting lighter. I should probably go to sleep. This forest was so beautiful, everything was. My father had provided me with such a perfect place for me to stay. I loved him so much more than I could ever say either to him or even to myself. He had never spoken to me, but I knew he loved me, he had to. Fathers loved their sons. Like Gunnar had. I lost Gunnar, but it would be alright, he would catch up with me. Past always did. I would introduce Gunnar to Lady Freya, share a drink, then some fruit... I felt Gunnar's clumsy embrace and this time I reciprocated and said, "I—"

Suddenly, with a loud yelp, I backed off right before I fell off the balcony. The body started falling asleep by itself, leaning further and further over the railing. How did that happen? It was getting light. Jomsborg was on fire. Somebody set the forest on fire to get rid of the outlaws... was my basket here? I had to tell Thjálfi not to touch it. I had to go to sleep, because as long as I stood here naked Lady Freya couldn't come here, in her falcon cloak, and refill it. Or take the basket and bring another one, yes, that would be so much easier. She was so wise, she would find the best way. I would not look. I would go to bed, I really should go to sleep now. Someone's clothes were on the floor! With a gasp I looked at the bed, but it was empty. Someone just left their clothes here and went away. That was nice, they would be useful, because I was naked. Lady Freya would bring another basket, then take this one, that made sense. Lady Freya was going to help me build the wall. Ooo... I was a God and she was a Goddess. We were equals, too. Although she didn't know that.

I was feeling a bit sick now, because of all the... all the everything... I should probably go to sleep. Yes. It was time. I thanked the man who let me use his body. I would not allow it to be mistreated again, I promised, the thought turning into something of a slur. The body crawled on the pile of furs that tickled and caressed, every single muscle relaxed and rested, the skin on the body's face smoother. The sweet darkness took me in his arms again, safe, warm, coddling me in a way I had never known to wish for before.

I woke up with an unpleasant taste in my mouth, my head feeling as if someone had wrapped a scarf around it too tight. It took me too long to recognise the place where I was. My mouth was dry and I couldn't even spit. I would find a peach and it would taste nice again.

The floor of the balcony was a mess. Someone spilled mead on it and my bare feet stuck to it. Disgusting. There was a basket on the bench, though, and I stopped breathing for a moment before daring to lift the white cloth. I saw peaches and apples and yellow things and small red things with green dots on them and things that I didn't know what they were, but they were all mine. I picked up a red thing with green dots and looked at it closely, wondering if the dots were eggs or some sort of maggots. They were not moving. The thing smelled wonderful, sweet, but I didn't know... I tried to pick out one green maggot egg with my fingernail, but it was holding on. Idunn grew very strange things.

I carefully arranged the cloth again, then rang for Thjálfi. I was ready to break my fast and start the day.

"My lord," gasped Thjálfi, appearing in the door, looking me up and down, then immediately disappearing.

I looked down as well, surprised, only to discover that I was naked. I... I didn't feel naked... I dressed, noticing I now had a beard Thjálfi would probably kill for and that awkward hair that was just too long to be short. I needed a shave and a bath, and the balcony needed a thorough cleaning. I was starting to have an unpleasant feeling that the person who made all this mess might have been me. I took a close look at my hand, which was red and itchy. Something happened to it during the night.

"I'm hungry," I announced upon Thjálfi's careful return. His face was even paler than usual. "I need lots of fruit, all sorts."

"Just fruit, my lord?"

"Eh, no, some eggs. Aye. And bread. And meat. But mostly fruit. You will eat with me."

Thjálfi sat stiffly as two men brought a cart filled with plates and bowls. He looked as though he were waiting for his own funeral. One of the men dropped to his knees to clean my mess, saying nothing. My face must have been puce. Should I apologise? Give them...something? *Never again*, I silently promised myself. This would never happen again, although I still couldn't remember what I'd done. I remembered that I had eaten an apple, had fallen asleep on the bench, then woke up in bed naked.

When Thjálfi and I were left alone I forgot what it was that I wanted from him, tormented by the worries that more servants had just seen my hair and beard. "I need a shave," I muttered, avoiding Thjálfi's gaze. "Every morning."

"My lord."

"I don't like having hair. It's so... you know. Hairy."

"My lord."

I could have probably told him to pour me a drink, maybe I should have, but I was too ashamed. I emptied a mug of water, then another, as even thinking about stout or ale made me feel sick. I glanced around, searching for something to say, then remembered why I'd asked him here in the first place. I pointed at a red thing with the green insects. It was smaller than the ones in the basket, but almost definitely the same. "Do you like those?" I asked.

"Strawberries? Very much, my lord."

Straw? Hmm. "Eat it."

Thjálfi looked at me in a very unsettling way. I watched him stick the thing in his mouth, holding on to a little, green, leafy top part. He took that part out, but swallowed the green maggots. Strawberries. "What about those, do you like them?"

"Grapes? They're wonderful."

"Eat one." He was picking things out of his mouth, little things, looking at me a bit sheepishly. Eggs? Pits?

"My lord, why—"

"I like watching you eat. It's a, eh, my thing." I dug out the yellow thing that I once bit into. I couldn't remember what Maya called it. "This?"

"My lord," said Thjálfi quietly, "please forgive me if the question is inappropriate, but... perhaps you would like me to name them all for you and explain? I know they don't have them in Jötunheim."

I only didn't drop the suggestively shaped yellow thing because I had turned to stone. Thjálfi's strange expression took me a moment to identify. Warm, serious, with a note of concern. Gunnar. Gunnar used to look at me like that. I felt my eyes get sort of itchy and just nodded.

"This is a banana," said Thjálfi, then he demonstrated how to peel it and explained, as Maya had said, that the yellow, very thick skin was not edible. I peeled one myself, then put it aside, more curious than hungry. The next one was a kiwi, a potato-like, hairy thing that looked like an egg of a particularly nasty creature. Once removed with a sharp knife, the hairy skin was discarded. I promised myself to never touch that one, then a faint memory of last night returned and I grimaced.

An orange was, well, orange-coloured, a ball that had a thick skin he tore off bit by bit with his fingers. It shouldn't be eaten. The flesh inside was covered with ugly-looking white bits, but those were fine to eat, as opposed to the pits which should not be bitten into and instead spat out. There seemed to be a lot of parts to oranges. I already forgot if kiwis had pits to spit out and we'd only just began.

"I think that's enough for now," I muttered. I wanted to sound lordly, but I could barely force myself to look up at Thjálfi. A heavy feeling of constipation, my stomach full of rocks, accompanied me since I'd woken up and so far I'd eaten nothing.

"My lord, when Thor took us from my parents' house... We were a very poor family, my parents and us, I mean me and Röskva. Thor and Loki came over and we offered them a place to sleep, but we had no food to give them." He paused to fill our mugs. Water seemed to be the only thing that didn't make me gag. "Thor killed his goats and he told us they would come back to life as long as we didn't break the bones for the bone marrow. I was still hungry when we finished eating, and I loved bone marrow, I don't anymore, because... because of what happened. I just took one bone, not even the largest. I was too young to know better."

You are still young, I almost said. He was a kid, in that awkward stage I seemed to have skipped, between a child and a grown-up, three hairs sprouting from his chin. The same age as the rider that Boy—

"When Thor found out, he threatened to kill us all and burn the house to the ground," continued Thjálfi. "I was so scared, not for myself, but I didn't want my parents and my sister to be hurt. I admitted my fault. Loki stopped Thor from breaking my neck, he saved my life. He suggested that Thor could do with someone to clean after the goats, feed them. They took Röskva and me, leaving my parents behind. We cried, they cried..."

"The goats came back to life?" I interrupted. "That's not just a legend?"

"They did, my lord. But because of what I had done, one of them will remain lame forever."

"Will it," I muttered. What if someone were to cut the skin into very tiny parts, ground the bones into powder, eat all of the meat... Hunger and nausea overwhelmed me, cold sweat on my skin. For a blink I was concerned that I was getting ill, then half-smiled. A piece or two of the real fruit and I would feel much better. "Can't you take some other goats?"

"No, my lord. There are only two goats like those in the Nine. Röskva and I swore to guard them with our lives."

I said nothing.

"It didn't end there, my lord. We would visit our parents, bring them food. I had to explain to them what a banana or an orange was too, show them how to eat it, but first somebody had to explain it to me. I had never seen an orange or a banana, I'd hardly seen an egg. My parents are dead now, but my sister and I are still alive and young. His Grace Thor takes very good care of us, still. I don't mind cleaning goat dung for the rest of my life, my lord, I would wipe his ass if he asked me to." His voice broke slightly. "He loves you too," Thjálfi finished in near-whisper. "I'll be there whenever you need me, my lord."

I barely noticed him leaving.

I lifted my feet to the bench, wrapped my arms around my knees, weeping as quietly as I could. My stomach kept aching, but my head felt lighter once I let the tears out. I could eat a straw-berry now and stop thinking for a bit. Yet something wanted me to hold on to Thjálfi's words. "He loves you too." I felt silly now, having thought that it was enough to shave my head to mislead all the Gods when even Thjálfi knew who I was.

I reached to scratch my bearded chin, then raked my hand through my hair. It was already long enough that I could tell it was curly. All that within one day. I would need a shave three times a day to keep my face and head smooth, wasting time I needed to build the wall. I was sleeping in my father's bed, wearing his clothes, watching his sunset in Ásgard. His servants brought me his food and I washed it down with his stout. He wasn't here and once I was finished, he would never return. It didn't matter what they would call me, whether they knew who I was or not. I would be Ásgard's protector. Thor could stay in Midgard forever, a mercenary killing his beloved humans because he ran out of jötnar. Soon everyone would hate him as much as I did.

I had to bite my lip, surprised at the sudden sting of pain the thought caused me. I forced some cold meat in, wiped my hands on my breeches – his – then decided to go out. I couldn't start working until Freyr's death, but that didn't mean I had to continue moping in Thor's bedroom.

The stable looked impeccable and so did Horsey. I stopped myself from telling her about the fruit. Lady Freya said that Loki could turn into anything and anyone, even into Horsey or Thjálfi. Or a fly. I shouldn't trust anyone, just keep everything to myself. So I just petted Horsey's mane, assured her she was beautiful, told her the day seemed nice. She rolled her eyes, making me feel stupid at first, then irritated. I didn't know how to keep magical horses entertained. I didn't even really know what horses ate. I was already too heavy for the largest horse in the City before my beard started growing properly. All I'd needed to know was that if you weren't careful when shoeing a horse you ended up with a broken nose.

I felt a strange tug at my heart when I entered the forge. Blackened brick walls. Solid floor made of stone. A row of hammers of various sizes, anvils, tools I couldn't even name. A massive fire right in the middle, elevated, so he wouldn't need to bend to use it. I picked up a pair of tongs, then a hammer, let it bounce on the anvil, listened to the *tinnngggggggg*, fascinated. I had never seen an iron anvil before. How had he forged an anvil? Everything was perfectly adapted to my height, Thor's height. His Grace's forge. Nobody else worked here, nobody would be tall enough. The smithy would have fit Gunnar's a hand of hands of times and there would still be space left.

I picked a large hammer, threw it in the air, grabbed the handle. A vision of another hammer appeared in front of me, as real as if the forge had been swept away and replaced by the crumbling City. I put the hammer away.

I pulled at the blower and the fire came to life. The blower continued moving at the same speed until I stopped it and the fire immediately died. The memory of my first day with Gunnar came back, the day he had told me to just pull as hard as I could, so I had. It had taken many days until a new blower had been delivered, the old one torn in half.

I picked up an unfinished, slightly rusty flowery ornament from the floor, traced the edges with my fingertip. I saw faces of those I wouldn't be able to share it with. Gunnar, Járnsaxa, Maya, Hillevi... Herjólf. I closed my eyes, my hand folded into a fist, crushing the ornament, so the physical pain would make my heart hurt less. Instead of relief I saw more faces, heard more voices, screams. They left me alone last night. Now I was just lonely.

I couldn't be in this forge.

Röskva, who looked like she carried a knife behind her back, pointed me towards the shore. It turned out to be quite near and I felt slightly encouraged. Maybe Ásgard wasn't *small* small, but *not very big* small. That could do. I passed by shores, cliffs, beaches, two small forests, grain fields men and women worked on, one hall. One out of how many? The heavy rock inside my stomach seemed to grow heavier with each step. Bays and peninsulas turned the shore left and right. The wall would have to turn accordingly, growing longer and longer.

I heard Ifing before I saw it. The water, peaceful until now, was becoming restless as the current pushed it faster and faster. The air got colder. I had to go around some thick bushes before emerging on a beach, its sands golden in the sunlight. Over my head the sky was clear. On the other side of the river it was dark, the clouds briefly flashing with lightning. The Gods even kept the sun to themselves. If there was a camp there, the fog from the rain made it impossible for me to see it. My home was hidden from me and for a blink I felt like a traitor before remembering what I was doing here.

"I need basalt," I muttered under my breath, walking down the beach. The sand under my feet turned from golden to black. The roaring Ifing made it hard for me to hear my thoughts. That odd, black beach was narrowing and the cliff to my side grew taller and taller. I squatted, rubbing black sand between my fingers. It wasn't sand so much as tiny black pebbles and I felt the hairs stand up on my skin. I was walking past a basalt cliff, staring under my feet and muttering about how I couldn't find any.

The cliff looked like angular columns that somehow became one. Like the wall I had in mind. A tall palisade like the one in Jomsborg, but made of stone like the walls of the City, impossible to burn or climb. How lucky was I that this vertical cliff already formed part of the wall? Otherwise, once I split it into separate columns or shards, I'd have to come up with a way to place them in the river that roared at me from behind.

Somewhat reassured, I continued my trek. I found an incline leading from the beach up the cliff, almost a path, about as wide as a horse with a chariot would be. It would be very handy if I were to transport, say, basalt columns up the cliff—

That gave me a pause. I wanted basalt and I'd found it. Not just some chunk of it, but those black, majestic columns. Now a path... Maya said I could wish for things in Ásgard, or something like that.

"I want Ásgard to be surrounded by a basalt wall," I said to the columns hopefully, quickly adding "...with me inside." When nothing happened I shut my eyes, in case the wall didn't want to be seen as it appeared, and repeated my request. The wall continued to not be there. There must have been some sort of rule to it that Maya didn't have time to explain to me. I couldn't ask the other Gods about it unless Lady Freya paid me an official shouting visit again.

Suppose, I pondered, dragging my feet back "home", that I wanted a particularly shaped chisel. I wouldn't find it in the part of the forge that I had looked at already, because I knew it wasn't there, but perhaps if I checked in a dark corner I'd overlooked... Was it possible that the cliff turned out to be made of basalt *because* I wasn't looking? It *could* have been basalt, therefore it was?

My feverish mind continued coming up with ideas, both plausible and ridiculous, until I sat next to the basket and carefully lifted the cloth. It seemed so dangerous to just leave it here on the bench. I'd have preferred to hide it. What if someone came and stole my fruit? My heart sped up and I ate a straw-berry to calm myself down, then a few more. They were delicious and so small that nobody would notice... what was I thinking? They were all mine. It didn't matter who noticed or didn't. I continued eating, delighted to find something my stomach accepted. Gradually the tension and nausea disappeared, turning into something like blissful absence, a half-sleep that was the opposite of my regular nights, the visions from the past replaced by hazy images of possible futures.

$\sim$

"I'd like you to take me for a flight," I said to Thjálfi in the morning, once I'd made sure that Freyr hadn't died yet. "First, towards Ífing."

"My lord! I can't take you to—"

"To what? Ah, no, not to Jötunheim! I just want to, ah, see, I mean, yes, just... check something."

Thjálfi seemed relaxed, the goats agreed on a direction for once, and another sensation came from my stomach, one that wasn't the dull ache of constipation. He was supposed to protest.

"That's where we usually depart from," he said, pointing towards my basalt cliff.

"But that's a wall," I said, baffled.

"That's why we have to take a different route to come back..." The chariot began to shake, the goats visibly upset. "May we turn away, my lord?"

I nodded, forgetting he couldn't see me, then yelled my permission. Once we were no longer heading towards the river, the goats calmed down. I didn't.

"There are no trees here, only grass and a few bushes," Thjálfi explained. The goats seemed relieved, pulling the chariot just high enough for it to never touch the ground, our flight fast and smooth. "They don't have to pull up. It's only when we're over the river that they get scared and head straight down. It makes them more comfortable." He let out a deep sigh. "Not me, though, or His Grace."

"It's Ífing," I groaned. "How can they feel more comfortable?"

"They're scared of heights, my lord. That's why we can't come back the same way or fly over high trees, they will never go that far up. They may be magical, but they're still just goats. You can't reason with them or explain what Ifing is, my lord."

The rock inside my stomach seemed to turn into a boulder. My goal was to surround Ásgard with a wall that would trap the chariot and the goats *inside*, while Thor would be kept *outside*. I couldn't place the basalt shards in the middle of Ifing any more than fly over it myself. I had to put a wall on top of this wall.

"Bifröst," I said weakly. "Take me to Bifröst."

"Of course, my lord."

"Just not near that tree."

"Yggdrasil, my lord? The goats wouldn't want to go there either. And, uh, neither would I. It's a very peculiar place."

I didn't speak and barely saw my surroundings. A wall on top of a wall solved the problem of having to place the columns on the bottom of Ifing and ensure they would stay there. It's just that if I were also using that cliff as material, I didn't know where to build until I was finished, so I would have to keep that spot for the very end. The opposite of what I wanted. Maya would have known.

"My lord?"

It took me a blink or two to remember the lord was me. "Uh?"

"Please hold on—"

The chariot slammed into the ground, bounced, hit the ground again as both the goats and I cried in protest. When Thjálfi managed to calm the animals down enough for us to stop moving, both he and I needed a few deep breaths. "That's Bifröst in front of us, my lord. I'm afraid you will have to walk from here."

I counted my arms and legs. All of them seemed to still be there, despite the way our trip had ended. I was already stepping out of the chariot, when I stiffened at a wrong moment and nearly fell on my face. "Why is that? Is it forbidden to go there?"

"The goats," muttered Thjálfi. "They really don't like Bifröst. We could travel to Midgard any other route, but not this one. The Rainbow Bridge is also a very peculiar place."

"I think I will walk back from here," I said, trying to hide my excitement. We weren't even near. It didn't matter how wide the opening I promised to leave had to be. "Why don't you go have, ah, a nice flight for the rest of the day?"

"My lord! What have I done?!"

Even the goats seemed alarmed until I quickly clarified that all I had meant was that I wouldn't be needing his services any more today. Before I took a step it dawned on me that on top of the goats being immortal a chariot that survived repeatedly hitting the ground like this was indestructible. A wall it had to be. At least now I knew for sure that the columns split from the cliff would be tall enough. I only had to figure out how to do it.

As I neared the Rainbow Bridge fear engulfed me, fear and disgust and the conviction that it was *wrong*. The feeling I experienced when approaching Yggdrasil. To my left was a sandy beach, sunlit shore of the sea. The more I tried to look to the right, the more everything seemed to blur and the sicker I felt. It wasn't just the goats that couldn't stand the place.

I gulped. Alternating between bad and good news like this was exhausting. I needed to go back, drop on the bed, eat some fruit, stop thinking about all this for a while.

"Sire."

I almost leapt out of my skin.

The first thing I noticed was the knight's armour. Silver and gold were very soft metals. No sane smith would forge armour out of them. My eyes dropped down to the sword and my mouth opened in awe. It was difficult to stop myself from either dropping to my knees or begging him to allow me to examine his weapon. Even like this I could see how immensely beautiful it was – thick, long, heavy, silver and gold again, and very sharp. A sword that would cut through a hair floating in the air. This was not the metalwork of Thor or any jötunn blacksmith, it must have been made by the dwarves in the Svartálfheim's forges. So, this was Heimdall.

The visor of his helmet was open. Our eyes met and all of my thoughts dispersed into something resembling very warm fog.

By Freya.

There were no mirrors in my hall. Thor's. I'd had enough chances to find out what I looked like at Sessrúmnir, where mirrors hung everywhere. My skin was pink and red where the sun touched it, now it must have been the colour of straw-berries. My hair was orange. I hardly even had any lips under the moustache that I had to cut every day. With it came the beard that collected crumbs and worse. I was as hairy as an orange bear could be and under all that fur my skin looked like plucked chicken. I didn't need a mirror to know that. Still, seeing all of me at once made everything so much worse. I knew Herjólf had only ever said I was beautiful when he wanted things from me, but I didn't know I was like *that*. I had never thought about how I would have liked to look instead. Until now.

I wanted perfectly sharp, black eyebrows that looked painted, ones that didn't have hairs sticking out in every direction; skin the colour of bronze on a light, but not too sunny day; eyes big enough to get lost in, so dark I could barely distinguish the pupils. Eyelashes longer than I have ever seen on a man. Or a woman. His gaze seemed both friendly and very focused, safe and dangerous. A friend who would only need a blink to either save my life or kill me. He was even taller than me, I realised, shocked. With his helmet still on I could just about see a part of his nose, but not his lips. I *needed* to see his lips, so that I would know what I wanted mine to be like.

I needed him to be a monster, because I had to hate him.

"Sire," he repeated. "How can I help you?"

"Yes," I accidentally said, then bit my tongue so as not to continue. None of the thoughts in my head were suitable to be voiced. *Could you take your helmet off, so I could see more of you? Who made this armour? Can I touch it? What about your sword?* I felt my cheeks become even hotter as he waited patiently. My own silence made me so uncomfortable I felt a stream of sweat going down my spine and shuddered. One of his perfect eyebrows moved up slightly. I wished I could hide my puce face under a helmet. Or just disappear.

"You are Heimdall," I finally managed, instantly drowning in shame.

He nodded and said nothing, but crinkles appeared around his eyes. He was smiling. I couldn't tell whether that made things better or worse.

"I just came to look," I said, my voice little, "I mean, at Bifröst, yes, just that."

"It's right there, sire." Another little nod.

Why was he calling me "sire"? What did that mean? Maya explained the mylording and the yourgracing, but said nothing about siring. I was about to ask and make myself look even more like a fool when Heimdall took off his helmet and then I didn't really remember any sentences for a while.

"I can't," I said, which was true in more ways than one.

"It might be the magic. Thor can't look at it either, or cross it. I would assume that you would find it difficult to approach Yggdrasil as well, sire." One corner of his lips went up and he nodded, as if answering his own question.

"A wall," I groaned, trying to remember more words. "That will leave space... I have to build..." He licked just the corner of his lip, his tongue appearing and disappearing so fast that I could have imagined it, except I didn't, and I forgot about walls and Rainbow Bridges, even the sword. Heimdall himself was a weapon.

"I might be able to help," he said. "From my experience with His Grace Thor I know how far you should be able to go before you have to stop. I could try and place something between you and Bifröst, sire, so you don't need to look at it."

"Why...?"

Heimdall's eyes narrowed slightly. He said nothing. Even if he had, I wouldn't have understood a word. Heimdall knew about everything that happened in Midgard, heard the grass grow, worms digging in the soil, each drop of rain that fell anywhere in the world. He could hear it when people had sex. I felt weak in a way that had nothing to do with magic or basalt. My mind only left space for one thought.

He would know where I should look for Herjólf.

I would have sworn that I had only just closed my eyes when something began to drill into my head and wouldn't stop. A sound so piercing it caused me pain, worse than anything I had heard in the Great Hall, not ceasing even when I forced my fingers into my ears and screamed as well. The skies outside were black and lightning struck, once, then again, but the thunderclap never arrived, unless the sharp-edged howl had drowned that out as well.

Nobody had to tell me that Freyr had died.

"*The* chariot," I spat, ignoring Thjálfi's half-hearted protests. "Horsey. Horseeeyyy!!! He died!!! Oh. You know. Okay, okay, I'll – what?" She kept shaking her head and producing neighs that sounded like growls. "That's right!" I exclaimed, then lowered my voice. "Oh, ha ha, I'm talking to my horse as if she were a person! Look at how nervous—"

Horsey tried to kick me and I stopped.

I had everything at the ready and just needed to load it on the chariot. I believed myself to be prepared, yet there I was, shaking, unable to think. I started throwing things, too nervous to carry them properly. I only slowed down when one of the men yelped, barely avoiding getting flattened by my small sledgehammer. I sent a huge, sharp chisel flying over the chariot, ramming into the ground. *Breathe*, I told myself, panting. *Freyr only just died. He's not coming back anytime soon. Lots of time.*

"I don't think a horse can pull this," braved Thjálfi. Horsey snorted. He looked baffled and I scowled at how well my completely normal horse seemed to understand what was being said. I thanked Röskva, who brought me food for the day, or, judging by her face, a collection of strongest poisons in all of the Nine. We were ready to begin.

My mind was blank.

Horsey was a horse. I was her master and had to tell her what to do. I looked for the reins she didn't have, then pointed towards the shores of Ifing. She shook her head and neighed.

What was that supposed to mean?

"There," I said, pointing into another direction. Horsey rolled her eyes, then produced a sound like "*pftftft*". Röskva and Thjálfi observed us with great interest.

"I think I will just sit in the chariot," I tried and Horsey let out what sounded a lot like a sigh of relief. When the chariot began to move, I shifted myself a bit, so as not to sit on a chisel. The wood creaked, becoming completely silent a blink later. I tried to inconspicuously glance at the wheels. They were not turning. The chariot hovered just above the ground.

Half of me felt calmer. Half more tense, repeating random parts of my plan and confusing me. Half insisted I should stop eating rocks.

The calmness disappeared once I jumped out of the chariot and Ifing's endless roar drowned out my thoughts. I intended to clear off the grass and soil, then use hammers and chisels to split the basalt columns. It had sounded simpler until right now when I actually had to start. I gawked at nothing until Horsey's impatient whinny brought me back.

With a spade, I dug, finding roots, stones, more roots. The sun was all the way up before I hit the rock. I wiped sweat off my forehead and tried not to think about how long it would take me to reveal the rest of the basalt. I kept pushing away the variations on "what have I done" that clouded my mind.

It turned out the digging was the easy part. I tried various combinations of tools and chopped off small shards that fell down onto the beach, sometimes swallowed by the river. None of them was longer than my forearm. How did they build the Great Hall? By magic, I'd bet, and probably not "simple crystal magic". I went down to the beach, crossed my arms, and stared gloomily at the black cliff. It really looked as if someone had taken perfect basalt columns, then put them together. This was exactly what the wall looked like in my imagination. Clear shapes, angular columns, all crowded into one mass that looked as if someone had forge-welded them together.

Sometimes forge welds didn't go right, when the metal was either dirty or heated unevenly. The axes or swords would break, often hurting their owner rather than the target. Poorly welded metal, when dropped on a hard surface, didn't produce a long, clear *dinggggg*, just a short, cracked *unk*. I couldn't lift a cliff and drop it, but it felt like an idea was forming itself inside my head. Even a good forge weld would show edges if you knew how to look for it.

Just getting rid of most of the dirt with the spade was not enough. I needed to see the top of the cliff free of any remaining soil or grass. I dug with my fingers until the sharp edges I was searching for began to draw blood, but I had gotten what I wanted. Next I wanted to see myself placing that huge chisel, taking the sledge-hammer I'd nearly killed a man with...

I expected a loud noise, but I didn't think it would make the ground shake. Horsey, torn out of her bored trance, kicked her front legs in the air, scream-neighing. I landed on my butt, sent back by the impact. The echoes of the blow were replaced with another sound, one I didn't expect, a long *nnnwwwwaaaaaahhhh* going from surprise to resignation, one that seemed to last forever. I lay on my belly, crawling towards the shore, both afraid of what I was going to see and nearly unconscious with excitement. A thick, long, angular, beautiful column of basalt leaned lazily towards the river, bending more and more as the crack ran down, still chased by my blow. The groan of the stone was suddenly cut by a deafening *krak*. With my mouth open I watched Ifing greedily grab the black column, break it into shards, larger, then smaller, then rip all of them away from me.

"Horsey," I growled. "We've got it. Almost. The next one... ah, how wonderful would it be if it just placed itself on the beach instead of falling in the river? You know, as if by magic?"

Horsey let out that "*pftftft*" sound again. Nevertheless, when my blow made the ground shake again, sending some small and not so small rocks down first, she approached carefully, as if to watch. In near ecstasy I stared at the column breaking off, then slowly rotating and gingerly placing itself on the black sand. If I were not already lying down, I'd drop on my knees from sheer relief.

Before I declared the day to be over we had three columns ready and waiting to be placed. I tried to ignore the nagging reminders that I hadn't figured out how to do it, that with three columns a day I would need more winters than I had fingers and toes. It was time to go home, eat dinner, drink some stout, watch the sunset, then go to sleep without even touching the fruit.

It must have been nerves, I told myself, tearfully staring at the food that smelled divine, looked even better, yet I couldn't force it in. My gaze kept escaping towards the basket. I was nervous, some fruit would calm me down. I had to eat something, and since "normal" food wasn't really working, maybe a peach or a hairy kiwi thing, once I peeled it... it would be good for me. It would help me relax, help me sleep...

No, I repeated to myself, resisting the silent song of temptation. *Not tonight.*

On legs stiff from exhaustion and anxiety I made it to bed. It took me a while to fall asleep and once I had, I slipped into a dream. A tall knight took his helmet off and the remains of Hillevi's head appeared. My own scream woke me up. I needed a drink, something strong, not the stout that would make me spend the whole night pissing.

"Gin, my lord," suggested Thjálfi. "Her Grace Idunn invented it a while ago. Please be careful with it, my lord, it's very strong—"

"A barrel."

He didn't shake his head or mutter anything under his breath, but his disapproval was palpable.

In the morning I couldn't recall any dreams, or whether I had even slept at all. My head was full of ache that felt as if I had used the chisel to split my own skull. The mere suggestion of breakfast was enough to nearly send me back to bed, clearly ill. I refused myself the luxury. I also promised myself never to touch gin again.

I suffered in grumpy silence until we reached the cliff. Just the sight of the tools I left there yesterday made my head pulsate with heat. I had a feeling that the icy gusts of wind Ifing brought along might clear my mind a bit, so I half-walked, half-slid down the path to the shore.

I rubbed my eyes. How strong was gin exactly? The sight took both my breath and headache away.

I counted the columns, poking them with my finger to make sure they really existed. Two. Hands. No fewer than two hands of perfect black slabs lay on the beach. I stared at my fingers for a while, wondering whether I'd always had that many. How would Lady Freya possibly have managed that...? She didn't look like someone who could so much as lift my hammers. I prayed to her all my life, made my little offerings, but I never knew she was that powerful.

Magic was unnatural, sickening, wonderful, helpful, it was something I might never understand, but right now I could only whisper "thank you".

I planned to use this cliff both as building site and material. Now, though, with two hands of columns down, I could see the cliff's shape was already altered. As if we were building a new, small bay, its bottom made of sharp, irregular shards where the columns broke off. I would block it once I was done with the whole world that wasn't really *small* small... with all its other cliffs and mountains and forests and everything else. The headache from the gin was nearly gone, but it felt as if a new one was beginning.

Once Horsey reached the shore, not so much pulling the chariot as keeping it from rolling down and hitting her, I took in as much air as I could and lifted a column with my hands. For a blink I was shocked by my strength, as it was so light that it seemed to float in the air. It didn't break or bend when I moved it to the chariot. Only when I looked very closely could I see that it wasn't really touching the chariot's sides. Once we were at an incline the columns could fall to the ground and break... yet something told me they wouldn't.

I couldn't resist kissing Horsey between the eyes. She tried to bite me. I laughed. She rolled her eyes, then snorted.

I had to pick a spot to start, one where we could bring the unwieldy baggage. At a sandy, golden beach, quite a bit from Ifing, I took off my boots and stepped into the sea. The water reached my knees, then waist. Was this enough? I couldn't allow the enemy to land—

I laughed nervously. "The enemy." For a blink I had forgotten why I was building this wall. It could be a foot away from the shore, so long as the goats couldn't jump over it. There was only one thing left to figure out. How would I stop the slabs from moving or breaking, once I embedded them in the bottom of the sea? Which really meant two things, because I didn't know how to do that either.

I brought one column over, or rather allowed it to float just above my hands, then put it upright. It kept bending even in the gentle breeze and I had to hold it to stop it from falling. I couldn't fly above it and use my sledgehammer to drive it into the bottom of the sea. Horsey could probably keep it upright, but no matter how strong her magic could be, Horsey needed to sleep. So did Maya.

I twisted the slab, pushed it down, grunted. Once I felt it was secure I let go. The column fell, breaking in two before it even splashed into the water.

The rest of the day was a failure. Attempts to sharpen the basalt with my tools broke it into shards, one of which wounded my finger just deep enough to make it irritating, no matter how fast it would heal. I needed one more idea and I had nobody to ask, because nobody had done it before. How did they build the wooden palisade in Jomsborg? I wondered, before remembering that the palisade was barely taller than me.

As the chariot soundlessly hovered over the road, I stared at Horsey's rump. Without her I might as well give up and really jump into the river. If something were to happen to her, Odin could offer me all the horses in Ásgard and I still wouldn't get anywhere.

~

"Röskva, I need you to do me a favour."

"Your Grace." If looks could kill, I'd be minced meat right now.

"Would you be willing and able to take full responsibility for Horsey? I need to know that she is as safe as possible. Well guarded, well fed, anything that she needs. I feel like you would be—"

"Oh...! Your Grace...! Please! Thank you!"

Her eyes became shining stars, her voice filled with joy. She loved Horsey as much as she hated me. "Er," I said, "what is it that you actually do? Because we'll need to find someone else to do that."

The smile disappeared, her gaze gloomy again. "I am the house-keeper of Her Grace Sif," she uttered. "She has been forcibly sent away. She will come back, though." The last sentence was clearly supposed to be a threat.

"Of course she will, of course," I immediately agreed, already retreating. She was acting as if this were somehow my fault.

Using a sharp, long piece of metal that was somewhere between a small poker and a dagger I picked up pieces of meat, dipped them in spices, and roasted them over the fire bursting from the table. Some were still a bit raw when I ate them, but at least I was eating. And thinking. The dagger I was holding was thin and sharp, like the basalt slabs, just much smaller. I could smash it into the table so hard that it would remain there either forever or until the table was cut into pieces to get it out. It would never break either, at most bend.

All of a sudden I felt the hairs on my back stand up. If the slabs of basalt broke from just bending under their own weight, stronger wind or waves would send my entire wall down. I could ask a lot of Ásgard, but there was no way my columns would become tougher without using—

Magic.

I decided to check what a baked Idunn's apple would taste like, still thinking. Maya had a simple crystal that could throw things away with an invisible shield... ohhhh... I should have waited to partake in the apple's sweet haze... it was difficult to recall Maya's words. You could put one spell in a crystal and it would just do that thing. If the thing was to hold the slab up and keep it from breaking down – I dried my mouth with a cloth, the warmth of the apple like a gentle hug that enveloped my entire body. Breaking down... no, *not* breaking down. I'd place a crystal under each column and it would hold up. In order to remove the crystal it would be necessary to lift the column, which couldn't be done, because the crystal would hold it in place.

Hopefully.

I grabbed at the rope without thinking, then stiffened. I should have waited on eating the apple. Would Thjálfi notice? He wouldn't, or would he? Should I hide the basket before he stole it? No, it had to remain there. He hadn't asked about it, why hadn't he asked, or had he and I had forgotten—

"My lord."

I held the cloth to my mouth again, worried that I might have been salivating, then I felt that the cloth made it look more suspicious, so I put it down and started licking the corners of my mouth over and over again, then chewing on my lips. Thjálfi stared in a way

I'd describe as politely questioning and I began to sweat. I wanted him to go away. No, I had to ask him first. I looked away, then back at him.

"Where do you get crystals from?" I asked. Was my voice strange? I licked the corners of my lips again. I should be relaxed, why was I not relaxed? "You know, the ones for fire and all."

"I don't know, my lord. It's not something I do. You might need to ask Her Grace Maya."

I almost bit my tongue off.

"Your hostage, my lord. She understands magic."

"Ah, yes, that Maya," I said, feeling a drop of sweat run down my spine. I forgot to come up with some place where I was keeping her hostage. "I don't think she likes me a lot. Anybody else?"

"Her Grace Freya... no, probably not," mused Thjálfi. "His Grace Odin... Loki..."

"Loki?!"

"His Grace Loki," said Thjálfi, both his tone and facial expression indicating that we shared opinions on His Grace Loki, "is aware of some magical...things." His grimace was apologetic. "Her Grace Freya and the All-Father know the most, my lord. I fear they might not be willing to help, though."

"I don't need them to actually do the magic," I said. "I just need to find the crystals... wait... we are in Ásgard..."

"My lord?"

"That will be all," I said, waving him away absentmindedly, only realising how rude I acted when he mylorded and left. I nearly grabbed at the rope to bring him back, so that I could apologise. No, no, I was simply a bit nervous. I just needed some more fruit, some peace. Tomorrow I would wish for crystals and find them. One thing for sure was that Thor wouldn't have a chest filled with magical crystals, which I knew, because I wouldn't either.

I needed many columns, so I also needed many crystals. It made me nauseous, all those nerves, too much gin, not enough fruit. It was odd that my mind felt like it was floating, yet my body felt heavy, my bowels filled with gravel. Maybe some mead would calm me down. I had never felt like that, but I had never offered to build a wall around the Gods' world either. Why couldn't I stop thinking about it? Just a bit more fruit and I was sure I'd feel just as good as that first time.

It was known I had no magic. Or wasn't it? Had I promised not to use magic?

I, Odin, the All-Father, will give you Freya to be yours to do whatever you want with her once you finish building a wall around all of Ásgard with the exception of Bifröst, a wall tall and strong enough to make jötnar unable to attack. You will complete the task within one winter, starting after the death of Freyr and ending with his rebirth. You will be provided all that you need to complete this task. You may neither accept nor demand any help that would come from outside Ásgard. Is that agreeable to you?

I blinked.

I didn't just hear the words. I was there. That light, the nauseating energy of the place, the echoes of Odin's voice, the fire in his eye. It wasn't like my visions; it was real. Why wasn't the fruit putting me to sleep? I needed sleep. Just a bit more and I would definitely... I could demand any help that came from inside Ásgard. I could go and make Lady Freya put the spells into the crystals. Oh, my stomach *hurt*. I had to lie down. There was a red light outside. The forest was on fire, my thoughts remarked lazily. No, it was morning. How was it morning? I couldn't remember sleeping at all. A straw-berry, the one with the seeds that were not maggots at all. Or two straw-berries. They were not big. Ahhh... that felt so... so right. Yes, now I could... I could think... no, actually I was a bit woozy now... confused. I... why did I do this? I didn't plan to do it, not in the morning. I planned to go to Lady Freya—

Lady Freya didn't come from Ásgard, she came from Vanaheim. Every jötunn knew that. Odin could say she was outside help. She was already breaking the oath by bringing me the fruit. I returned to bed, to give Lady Freya time to replace the basket. How odd, I thought I was in bed.

It was winter now. That meant Lady Freya was away, mourning Freyr's passing. I could just go to Sessrúmnir, demand crystals, remind them that Odin had permitted me to do and take anything I wanted. Nobody could stop me.

It wasn't until I was on my way back to Bilskirnir, whistling a song I had penned about Lady Freya's golden hair, that something gave me a pause. If she was now wandering around the Nine, mourning the passing of Freyr, she was taking a great risk coming back every morning to bring me the fruit. Which I wouldn't eat so early in the day anymore. I now held a bag full of small crystals, but I couldn't recall arriving at Lady Freya's hall or asking for them. The fruit cleared my mind until there was nothing left. No wonder I had no idea how much time had passed.

Horsey was very smart. I just had to tap a new crystal against her old one, musing quietly about how great it would be if the columns would just drop into the bottom of the sea because they were so heavy and how they would never break because they were so... unbreakable. We ran out of basalt long before sunset arrived and I stared at the result in awe before the realisation struck like a punch in my already aching belly. I broke three columns when I tried to sharpen them. So those were one hand and two more. It took us three days. Or four. Time was already becoming a blur and we'd only just begun.

I was counting my fingers, attempting to figure out which day it was and how many columns per day we'd have to put up, which was a lot of counting, when Horsey whinnied behind me. A sharp, urging sound.

"Coming," I said, frowning. I lost count of my own fingers. The only result I came up with was "lots".

"It's fine," said a man's voice. "I'll wait."

My feet grew roots as thoughts ran through my head. I didn't bother shaving my head. He'd figured out I had help from Maya and Lady Freya. He came to kill me. "All-Father," I said weakly.

"I notice you talk to your horse a lot," Odin said after a silence that lasted long enough for an itchy drop of sweat to appear on the tip of my nose. "Where did you find her? I don't remember seeing her around here."

"Oh... I wouldn't know. She was just walking around and you said I could just take anything I wanted."

"Yet nobody complained about a missing mare."

"That's not my fault." He couldn't prove anything, I told myself.

"Are you sure she is just a horse?" he murmured.

I risked a quick glance at Horsey, who looked more like a horse statue right now. "Who knows," I said, trying to sound wise, "in this drea – in this... Gods'... place... world..." The longer Odin stared at me silently, the more words I kept forgetting until I ran out of them completely.

"I seem to recall that you promised to take me to the secret passage." He scowled. "Is your horse coughing?"

I started coughing as well, searching for answers and finding none, slightly choking on my saliva and nearly drowning instead. "It must be the dust," I finally croaked.

"It must be. You were telling me about the secret passage."

"I wasn't," I answered, trying not to grind my teeth aloud. "All-Father, I don't want to sound impolite, but I don't have much time and you're interrupting me."

For just a blink Odin looked like the God of War that he was, and my bowels nearly unblocked. Unexpectedly he smiled, the warrior replaced by a polite old man with a hunch. "You are completely right," he said. "I apologise. Please continue."

I had to sit down, my heart beating way too fast, air refusing to reach my lungs as I tried to fill them with small, sharp pants. My gaze met Horsey's. She looked shaken as well. I needed to calm down, to rest. Just some fruit. I should carry it with me all the time, just something small to... in case Odin... just nerves... yes, it made sense. Did he know about Horsey? I had to talk to her less. Be more careful. After I got some rest.

In the evening I used an axe to get inside a massive, green, round thing that took up half the basket. I would have never known it was fruit. One blow and it split in halves, both of them smelling divine, red with black pits. I ate, carving chunks out with a knife, spitting out the pits. As they flew towards the trees they were first just black pits, then, as the soft warmth took me in its arms, they began to glow softly. I was mesmerised by their beauty. Everything was beautiful. I shut my eyes, my eyelids heavy, and more beauty appeared. Heimdall's eyes, his nose, his lips. I couldn't remember his whole face at once. I needed to stare at him longer, up close, without him noticing.

He heard everything in Ásgard... in Midgard... was it both, if he stood in both worlds at once? "I want you," I whispered, surprising even myself. Heimdall's face seemed to change, his features sharpening, skin lightening, until Herjólf's narrowed eyes stared into mine. A dream with one eye open. If he were to hear me, I'd have to pay for this.

The thought made me want to just stick my face inside the red flesh of the big fruit and slurp it all out. So I did.

It took Thjálfi a while to wake me up in the morning. He cast a dark look at both the messes, the one on the table and me. My beard was like a sticky plank, stiff with the dried juice. Two men whose names I didn't want to know, because then I'd feel more guilty, cleaned everything up. I was wearing breeches so as not to shock Thjálfi by being naked, but I couldn't remember taking off the rest of my clothes and I didn't know what happened to them. Had I rung for Thjálfi in the middle of the night? To talk? Had I cried? I glanced at his face and my throat seemed to swell with something. He was sad. For me.

"Breakfast..." Thjálfi started when he noticed I was looking at him.

"Small," I just said. Had he, had they noticed that I had not been served the big green fruit for dinner last night, yet it had appeared as if out of nowhere? Had Thjálfi asked, had I answered? I would take some smaller things with me today in case Odin... When was that? Was it yesterday or longer? Everything was becoming a blurry mess. I shouldn't. I was so tired now. Had I slept at all? I had flashes of myself standing on the table and screaming something, I... I pissed off the balcony, *why*? Did that happen, did I dream it? Dread Gods! Heimdall would know everything and tell Odin about it. What was going on, was magic driving me insane? I grabbed at my head and squeezed it, wondering whether I could make my own skull explode.

"Your food, my lord." Röskva was handing me a bag again and this time she looked so sweet that now I was really worried about poison.

"Ah," I mumbled. My hand inadvertently patted a small bag of my own. "Thank you."

At the cliff I split off one hand and two columns, watching them gently place themselves on the black sand. As before, we took them to the place where we were working yesterday. I gasped. The chariot let out a warning creak, as if Horsey forgot about her magic for a moment. There were more basalt slabs standing up. Yesterday I had enough fingers to count them and now I didn't. I looked at my hands, then up again. Did more time pass? Could I have forgotten that I had worked all day? Was this, too, caused by the fruit?

I was about to ask Horsey when I remembered Lady Freya's warnings, Odin's odd visit yesterday. Unless it wasn't yesterday. It didn't matter. The work was progressing somehow and all I had to do was be quiet.

Who knew it was so difficult not to share anything with anyone? I really, really wanted to tell Horsey at least about Lady Freya hiding somewhere in Ásgard, risking it all to help me, to bring me all the fruit. But no. Maya told me not to eat it. She wouldn't understand. She'd be angry, even.

The day was both uneventful and exciting as the wall grew and I wondered what I would see in the morning. Then the worries caught up. What would I do if I were to run out of basalt? How large was Ásgard, really? I tried and tried and couldn't count the looming slabs anymore. I needed more numbers.

I asked Thjálfi to join me for dinner and plied him with mead until he relaxed enough to forget about mylording me at least sometimes. I frowned. I was completely sober and he wasn't. Still, even though we both used the same utensils, his clothes stayed clean and mine were dripping with grease. Without thinking I wiped my mouth with my sleeve, then quietly cursed. Even Thor had a cloth for that.

I emptied the tankard with one gulp, yet cowardice still stopped me short of what I really wanted to ask. "Why is it always you who steers the chariot?"

"I've been taking care of His Grace Thor's goats ever since I arrived here."

"How long ago was that?"

Thjálfi looked up, thinking. "I am not sure, to be honest. Two hundred winters, three? I'm... he keeps us immortal as long as he wants to. I lose track of time."

So do I, I almost said. "But we have more winter left, a lot more...?"

"Oh, absolutely. The moon has not turned once yet."

"And... say... a winter is how many moon-turns?"

"Six, my lord."

"Six," I repeated, staring at my hands. Six was more than a hand. He was looking, he'd know... I quickly wiped my hands in my breeches. "And one moon-turn is...?"

"Twenty-eight nights, I believe."

"Ah," I said, somewhat nervously. "Of course, twenty-eight, I can't imagine I forgot..." I ran out of fingers, tried to add the toes. Eight... twenty... I had to ask, but my mouth wouldn't open. I'd need to drink a lot more. Maybe eat some fruit, no, later, when he couldn't see. He was a servant. I could ask anything of him. It's just that I *couldn't.*

"That... that would be four hands..." started Thjálfi carefully, then looked at me questioningly. I nodded, wishing I could refill the tankard without him noticing. "One hand is five," he said. "Two hands are ten. Twenty is two times ten, which would make it four hands. Then we have eight, which is one hand plus three."

I couldn't go on without more mead. "Of course, twenty-eight," I repeated, my hands shaky as I refilled the tankard. Shame, excitement, terror, gratitude. That was a lot to feel all at once. Feeling things was so difficult. The basket... As if he could hear my thoughts, Thjálfi reached for a bowl filled with straw-berries, normal ones, not Idunn's. It still made me wince. As if he were stealing my fruit.

He was saying something.

"I'm sorry," I said, shaking my head. "Can you start again?"

"One, two, three, four, five," said Thjálfi, moving some straw-berries aside one by one. "Five is one hand." He lowered his voice and I felt so incredibly grateful it hurt. "Six," he said, "that's one hand and one, five and one. Or – three and three." He kept moving the straw-berries and I kept swallowing saliva, trying my best to understand and memorise his words. "Seven – that's five and two..."

I sent him away, exhausted, once I had learned all the numbers between five and ten, which was two hands. Twenty was two tens, so four hands. So one moon-turn was four hands and eight. Which made it five hands and three. Five hands! A hand of hands was five hands! So five fives! And then three, so almost six hands. Six fives. Only a bit less.

I could stare at my fingers openly now, move the straw-berries around, but I was already forgetting the tens and twenties. How did people just remember all this? It was making me dizzy. Or maybe it was the mead. So many straw-berries. Why would anybody call them that? There was no straw to them anywhere and they didn't look like other berries either.

I added some real ones from the basket. Even when I moved them around and pretended not to know which were which, Idunn's ones made the others look grey.

There was a certain proportion of mead and fruit that was just right and tonight I found it, and I really wanted to share it with someone but there was nobody and anyway they would want to take my fruit and then I could run out.

When we arrived at the shore, the beginning of the wall had grown again. The new columns, from what I could tell, were as solid as mine. Ours. I'd hide a crystal in my hand, touch Horsey's one with it, go into the sea, stick the crystal into the sand, then put the basalt column on top of it, not even bothering to stick it too deep. It seemed like the sea bottom sucked it in. The sudden memory of the slabs breaking returned. Was it really working?

With all my might, I slammed one with a sledgehammer. All of a sudden I couldn't see, thrown into the water by some unnatural magic, my forehead hurting. It took me a while before my thoughts cleared enough for me to understand. The hammer bounced from the basalt without breaking it and struck me in the face. And Horsey was laughing at me.

The stomach ache and the blocked bowels continued. Too much magic. How could Thor live in this place? Sometimes it would feel like my bowels decided to empty themselves without any prior warning and I'd run into the nearest bushes, holding on to my backside, baffled and scared in equal amounts. I noticed that Röskva seemed concerned – for me! – when I returned the still full bag of food she had prepared for me, so I started throwing it away.

Thjálfi's worried looks as he came to eat with me caused me to request dinner early, then throw some it away off the cliff to make it seem as if I had eaten before inviting him to join me. Lady Freya was taking such a big risk for me, yes, I owed it to her to keep it a secret. I wasn't hungry anyway, thanks to the fruit magic. The wall kept growing and I kept sleeping well. Even if sometimes there was mess suggesting I got up at night and did...strange things.

Our trips from the basalt cliff were becoming long and inconvenient, and I started wishing that we could find another one. The sun barely moved before my wish came true. I took Horsey back, we shut the gap that we left, and the entire shore of Ifing was finally blocked.

The water I had to step in turned colder and colder. Sometimes there was ice. The real winter had arrived. Hills appeared, for the first time, turning taller, becoming snowy mountains. Getting to the shore was already becoming a problem before we encountered a wolf so huge it could eat Horsey in a few bites. Horsey let out a scared little sound, more of a squeal than neigh. I was just as nervous. I didn't expect a wolf, giant or not. I thought we were safe here.

"We're friends," I said, trying to keep the shakiness out of my voice. "Just...passing."

The wolf sighed. "Be quiet," he murmured.

The shrieks that Horsey produced, sounds that had no right to come out of a horse's throat, made both me and the wolf flinch. She bolted away together with the chariot, scattering basalt slabs, their broken chunks flying around. "Horsey!" I yelled, then froze, almost literally. "I'm so sorry," I whispered to the talking wolf. "I really didn't... it wasn't..."

"Just stop talking already," muttered the wolf, then pretended to fall asleep.

I was so upset by this that I needed a grape. Perhaps two, but no more. Maybe if Horsey were to have some... no, horses didn't eat grapes, also I could run out. I would remind her that no blood could be spilled in Ásgard. I just hoped that it also applied to horses and that the talking wolf knew that.

I managed to talk Horsey into returning. It looked like it wasn't the wolf she was afraid of, just the talking and, oddly, the wall growing behind the animal. Was it still an animal if it could speak? Maybe it was Loki. Just in case, I also didn't talk to Horsey until the wolf was behind us.

A feeling both unpleasant and familiar began to affect me. A lonely, tall rock stood on the shore. As we approached it I felt as if a giant, invisible hand pressed on my already sore stomach, pushing me away. When I attempted to look around, my gaze would glue itself to the rock. Like my eyes refused to see what was further... unnatural, something inside me whispered, and I guessed. The Rainbow Bridge! Heimdall placed the rock here.

If I couldn't pass this spot, the goats and Thor couldn't either. But they didn't have to even get near it. I did. I tried to move sideways, then with my eyes closed. Sweat was dripping off my forehead, my teeth clenched so hard they hurt, even though I was barely touching the column hovering over my shoulder.

Without warning the basalt slab slipped off my arm, as if it had gotten stuck in the air. It slammed onto the ground with its entire weight and broke in two uneven parts, one jumping back up and nearly crushing me, the other flying in a direction I couldn't even look towards. I turned to berate Horsey and the sight made my hand instinctively try to dig into the small bag I carried.

"It seems to be going very well," said Odin. The smile on his face was curious. As if he knew something I didn't.

"All-Father," I said weakly.

"I must admit that your horse is a beauty the like of which I have never seen before. She almost feels like magic itself."

"Ah," I answered, glancing towards Horsey. She was staring intently away from us and towards Bifröst.

"Most animals are afraid to be here," Odin remarked. "Horses have to be led towards the Rainbow Bridge carefully, their eyes covered—"

Horsey performed something of a dance, turning away in place, twisting her neck away. I was about to explain to Odin that she forgot she was afraid when I remembered something she had said. Shifters could sniff out shifters, or something like that. He knew she wasn't a horse.

"She is very special," I said. The droplets of sweat going down my forehead rushed to meet on the tip of my nose.

"You have asked for a supply of my wine," he mused. "I could offer you that if you'd be willing to sell your horse to me."

I gasped at the audacity. She wasn't a horse, I wanted to say, she was a friend – ah. That was what he was playing. Such a cheap trick! How stupid did he think I was? "No" was all I had to say.

My mouth opened and no sound came out.

How much wine? No, *no*, but could I try some first? *All-Father, did your stomach ache too? Come on*, I begged my own throat that seemed blocked, tongue that wouldn't move, *just* say *it, there's only one answer to this, a word so short that a shorter one barely exists.*

"Maybe later," I mumbled. "I need her very much, as you can see. It's a lonely job," I continued, unsure why I was talking, "I talk to her a lot, yes, who am I supposed to talk to that won't interrupt me, like, hmm, now?"

How come I could say so much, just not the only word that needed to be said?

Fire and war flashed in the red light of Odin's eye before the shadow hid it and the polite old man returned. "Your hair and beard have grown out fast," he said. "They suit you."

Every word of his felt like a trap. I stiffly nodded and said nothing, feeling goosebumps all over my body, all the little hairs standing up to attention. *Go away.* Unexpectedly, I sneezed and wiped my nose with my sleeve. The sneezing was becoming more frequent. I never got sick, so it must have been dust.

"Go on," said Odin. "I apologise for interrupting you. You could consider that cheating as well, but the truth is, I'm just very curious how you're managing to do it so fast."

"Your Grace," I said. When he finally took the hint, I needed some fruit. I needed to take a shit. I needed to lie down and rest.

The cold, sticky sweat covering me, the sneezing, the shivers, the blurring of the days... I had to lie down on my side, facing away from Bifröst, trying to breathe deeply and slowly. I fished out a grape, almost certain Horsey couldn't see. Why was saying "no" so difficult?

~

A beef roast the size of my leg awaited me when I returned. I couldn't even grasp the idea of eating it, although it smelled wonderful. There was a smell much more divine awaiting me, truly divine, straight from the hands of the Gods. Without giving the roast another look I dropped on the bench, lifted the white cloth and looked at my fruit.

I put the cloth back.

I lifted it again. Everything inside the basket was perfect. I was given another huge green ball that was red inside, exactly what I needed after this day. It was really big. It was too much. I wouldn't eat all of it, maybe just half, or even half of a half. No, really, a half seemed just right. Yes. No. It was such a difficult day. I deserved more than... I should eat the roast first. Some, at least. The cold sweat, the goosebumps, the *need* that pulled my hand towards the basket. I could already taste the red sweetness that hid inside the green shell. I could already see it. I shook my head, blinked. The cloth was up, my hand already touching the green shell. I needed it more than the roast, more than anything—

The stomach ache, the constipation followed by diarrhoea. I barely ate anything but the fruit. The sneezing, the itching, the *need*.

My hand jumped away as if the green ball was white-hot iron, but I couldn't get myself to put the cloth back.

Absolutely no more. I would take a break. Just for one day. Or one evening, really, because I'd had some earlier. I could stand one evening. I'd eat some of the roast. Even though the fruit was a necessity, helping me sleep and work... without warning my bowels had unclogged and I sprung up, holding on to my backside, barely managing to drop my trousers in time and grab the chamber pot from under the bed. The sound and the smell were sickening. I brought the chamber pot outside and emptied it, but the stink lingered, the greenish substance that erupted from me smeared all over the pot. I couldn't bring that back into my bedroom and I couldn't imagine asking anyone to clean it. I threw the chamber pot down the cliff. I'd ask for a new one, because... because this one had gotten...lost.

I was falling apart. I had to eat the roast, not the fruit that was making me ill. Would Odin's wine help? The wine wouldn't give me this pain. Odin didn't eat, he just drank the wine, or so they said. *Lady Freya, help me understand... Just some small...*

I returned to the table and cut off a small slice of the roast. It was wonderful, as expected, dripping with a thick sauce that was taste itself. I owed it to the cooks to eat it. I put the slice on the plate, then cut it in halves, then again. I tried to swallow a piece the size of my fingernail.

My stomach protested, the rock inside it growing, as if there was some sort of passage the meat had to travel through and it had gotten stuck. The food seemed to be intruding. All I really wanted, no, *needed* was in the basket. Thjálfi would come here and notice, we were going to work on numbers again. He would look at me with that worried disapproval, saying nothing, like when I demanded a new barrel of mead every evening. Anger overwhelmed me for a moment, coming out of nowhere. A servant had no right to judge me! I was a God. I could do what I wanted.

Just one very small piece of fruit, a peach. Yes, not the green large thing. A peach was reasonable. I didn't want it, a thought flew by, quickly erased by the relief.

Ahhhh...

So clear. I had to throw the roast off the cliff. Only keep the bones, as if I had actually eaten it. He wouldn't believe I was hungry enough to eat the bones too.

I cut off the meat, my hands shaky, body sweaty. One more peach would help. I gave myself a cut. I couldn't go on, I licked the sauce off my fingers and it made me sick, all greasy, nothing like the fruit. I wiped my fingers on my breeches and looked at the bread. I tore off half and threw it away. Was that good, was that enough? Did it look real? Maybe I should cut some more meat off. Oh Gods, I was so afraid, I needed some more fruit. Odin offered me wine. Was there a way I could sell him Horsey, then have her turn into Maya and announce the sale null and void, but keep the wine? There were slices of peach placed around the roast, I picked one, soaked with that sauce. It seemed to grow inside my mouth. I spat it out into my hand. I could eat peaches, I just had, just not those. The real ones. *No*, something whispered inside me, a strange voice that didn't seem to belong to me. *Those were the real ones.*

Oh Gods, my belly *hurt*. Like having eaten basalt. Like the fruit had become heavier, then stuck inside me somewhere. I had to act normal, force a smile. Some more fruit, maybe just a small... an apple. I would stop tomorrow. I wiped my mouth with my sleeve, then again. Was there juice in my beard? It kept feeling like there was juice in my beard, the longer I wiped, the more there seemed to be. I needed some fruit – but I had just eaten some.

I went into the bathing room and submerged myself in the hot tub that was mine alone. The water wasn't hot enough to wash the cold sweat off my skin or the juice out of my beard. I should get out and call Thjálfi to do the numbers. Just remember to get dressed first, so he wouldn't be shocked seeing me naked again. I was sitting on the bench, dripping water, my hand wrapped around the green shell, ready to crush it without bothering with a knife. No, I was still in the tub. Had I left enough meat on the bones, or too much? He must have known, he must have looked inside the basket. I just needed a tiny bit... it was all Odin's fault for coming and scaring me.

Horsey helped me place the columns and the crystals as far as the rock allowed me. To get any closer I would need to be blindfolded. Like normal horses, Odin said. Could goats be blindfolded? Absolutely not, I knew, I hoped, prayed. I felt the weight of the bag filled with food I got from Röskva, the smaller bag on my other hand with food I picked myself from the basket. I had to go into a forest and dispose of Röskva's food, but there was no forest here. Just open space with green grass and a golden beach, leading towards Heimdall, but also the wrong place.

"Trees," I said into space. "Let's go and find some trees. I need—" I paused, berating myself for explaining myself to a horse. She'd never know.

She wouldn't, would she? Slowly, trying to hide my head between my shoulders, I looked towards her, rather than at her.

Horsey was openly glaring at me, her eyes narrowed, teeth bared, as if she were a wolf. She already knew, for how long I couldn't tell. *You are a horse*, I nearly said, *you can't judge me, but please don't desert me, I need you and I need this too, you don't understand, how could you understand that there were times when Röskva had no face, just bone and blood and brain and that sometimes my hands dripped with blood and the forest I sat and watched was on fire?* I was so arrogant when I thought I'd do this on my own. I needed Horsey, Lady Freya, Thjálfi, Heimdall, even Röskva, the manservants whose names I didn't even ask, much less memorise. I stumbled, my legs, arms, even eyes tired. I was in so much pain. The visions, the dreams that were not dreams were scrambled, odd, muddy. I needed more and more fruit, I forgot things, I drank more and more just to make the visions lose their contours.

I thought I'd just stop once we were done. Now, for the first time, doubt appeared in my mind. Maya told me to only eat the fruit once every moon-turn and Lady Freya might have not wanted me to complete the wall and become her "owner". The unimaginable thought formed in my mind. She could have done this to me on purpose.

"I'm sorry," I said to Horsey in a little, broken voice, nearly expecting her to answer. "I have to go home." Without waiting, I began to drag my feet, slowly, my vision out of focus. She caught up and whinnied. I got in the chariot. I was sitting on a sharp tool of some sort. I was in bed and sun shone outside. I was alone, dressed, my dirty boots... I barely made it in time to pull off my breeches. This wasn't even shit anymore. It was... I threw the pot away again. When I was done the forest would be full of my waste. I felt so useless, worthless, so lonely. I just wanted a hug and for someone to tell me that it would all end well. I couldn't deny the fruit was making me sick. Here I was now, not having eaten any, and feeling even more sick. I had to stop eating it and I had to eat it, too.

The basalt slabs danced in front of my eyes. I didn't bother hiding from Horsey anymore, openly eating a few yellow thick-skinned things the names of which I had forgotten along with most of numbers I'd learned. I wrapped my arms around a basalt column, carried it, placed a crystal underneath, returned, tapped another crystal against Horsey's, *I want to die*, not even knowing whether I had to do that or not, unable to tell how much time had passed and how much I had left, lifting a column, *I wish I could fall asleep and not wake up*, carrying it, did I touch Horsey with this crystal? I placed it underneath anyway, how many had I done, how many were left? *I wish I could die. Please be over.*

I ordered Thjálfi to bring me dinner – small and light, I stipulated, no greasy meat, maybe some poultry. He watched darkly as I tore off a piece, put it in my mouth, chewed, but couldn't get myself to swallow it.

"I'm afraid," I muttered. I needed a friend so bad.

"My lord," he answered. I had no friends here.

"How long do I have left until Freyr is reborn?" My voice came from afar, foreign even to myself.

Thjálfi scratched the three hairs on his chin. "I am not sure. I think we've passed the midwinter by now, but it's so difficult to say here when all the days are the same. I could always take the chariot and check in Midgard—"

"No." I didn't want to hear that the chariot went missing, or, worse, that he'd found Thor. "I'm using it. So, what number of days would that be?"

"I really don't know, my lord."

"When does the winter end, how do you know?"

"When His Grace Freyr is reborn."

"When is he reborn?"

"When the winter ends."

I glared at him, incredulous, and Thjálfi blushed. "I'm sorry," he said, staring at his lap, "but that's just how it is."

"Where is he when he is, uh, not reborn?"

"He disappears. He becomes old, then very old, then the oldest man in the Nine. Only Her Grace Freya knows what happens then. The next day there's just some dust, I believe. Her Grace Freya then leaves Ásgard and goes to—"

"Mourn him," I said. "Thank you."

"My lord," Thjálfi started, looking at the nearly untouched food, then back at me.

"*Thank* you," I repeated, "that will be all."

No fruit. Not even the tiniest bit. I'd eat the dead bird he brought. It had black feathers, it was a raven. No, it didn't. It was chicken. A raven was watching me. I looked around, that cold sweat making my skin and clothes stick together. Where was the raven? I drank some water instead of mead, looked at the little brown breads that looked like tiny, delicious...bricks. They gave me bricks to eat. They were having fun at my expense. My skin was itchy, probably from the sweat, or something was biting me all over, like fire ants. Just a berry would help. Or two, they were so small. Odin drank wine every day and he seemed fine and he offered it to me for Horsey... no!

I grabbed the small brown bread bricks and threw them as far as I could. The bird carcass followed. I sent the plates and bowls flying as well. Then I stopped moving for a blink or two. I could jump and never feel like this again.

I was *so* tired.

I forced myself to go to bed. My feet kept itching and I couldn't stop moving them. The sweating made the touch of the soft furs unpleasant, scratchy. There might have been not enough time and I couldn't even tell. I should have been halfway through. *I want to die.* If Lady Freya were to stop helping me, if the wall would no longer keep growing on its own... I was so tired and I wanted to fall asleep and never wake up and I couldn't sleep at all. When I shut my eyes I saw faces, ever-changing faces, Heimdall's eyes in Pig's face, Herjólf, the remains of Hillevi's head that I had never seen clearly, so my mind provided me with the worst it could come up with, now her lips were Maya's and were moving, my eyes opened and oh *Gods*, I needed just some berries, straw or blue or red berries, just so the itching and the faces that made me feel sick would stop. Tomorrow, tomorrow I wouldn't touch any. Today I would just have very little, just to sleep.

I gave Horsey an apple the day after and watched her...straighten up. Her coat, mane, tail became shinier. I still felt the touch of the apple in my hand. The skin inside my hand itched, demanding one. I brought nothing with me except the apple Horsey already ate. I was strong. I didn't have to give it to her. I had. It's just that I wished I hadn't.

Work.

Something occurred to me that day as the endlessly repetitive work went on and on. I not only didn't know how much time I had left, but also how much of the wall still needed to be done. I just assumed that reaching Bifröst meant that half of the work was done. What if I was wrong? I had to ask Thjálfi to fly me around Ásgard.

Both of us were very silent on our way back. Even the goats seemed worried. If anything went wrong right now, if I had less time than I hoped I had, I could already start making a noose for myself instead of wasting time on the wall. My belly hurt really bad now, my skin itched, I needed some fruit, but didn't dare to eat it next to Thjálfi. He was busy with the goats, he wouldn't notice, something whispered inside me—

...not now, not in the air, dread Gods...!

"Thjálfi," I yelled, "I'm sick, land!"

The goats bleated and pulled up instead. I bent out and vomited, and it felt as if I made some space for the diarrhoea to stay inside for a bit longer.

I spat, then again. "It's fine," I said, or tried, unsure whether the sound came out. It wasn't. I fell on the bed and felt absolutely lousy, my body itchy, sore, shivering, sick. My mind was sick too, with worries, the visions that never left anymore, obscuring the real world where I seemed to do nothing but chop off basalt columns, carry basalt columns, place down basalt columns, *please end*, move on, carry basalt columns, place down basalt columns, shit green, liquid stuff, feel like I was going to drop into the reeking puddle, Herjólf's eyes, my hand lifting the white cloth, *I want to die.*

~

"I permitted myself to take the chariot and visit Midgard, my lord. The snows are melting. I would say there are maybe twenty days, if we're lucky."

I felt all blood drain from my face and my fingers began to move by themselves, as if convulsing. I needed some fruit right now, I couldn't take this. Twenty days. "Bring me...gin," I said, my voice choked.

"My lord, if there is anything..."

"Just gin."

Maybe twenty, if we were lucky. I now wished I hadn't learnt the numbers, that I didn't know what "twenty" was. I could delude myself into thinking that it was a lot. Thjálfi said "we". That was nice.

I sat in the tub fully dressed, waiting for the shivering to stop, praying that I wouldn't shit in the bubbling water. Thjálfi didn't even ask if I wanted to eat. Twenty days. Maybe.

I tried to feed Horsey another apple in the morning, groaning internally because of the headache and bellyache and simple fear, and she refused to take the apple.

"We need to..." I started and yelped when she tried to bite me. I felt terrible. I needed to eat that apple to stop feeling terrible. Her stare was so like a person's, so bitter that it made me want another apple. But she continued helping.

I put up another column. Then another. Then another. Then another. Then another. *I can't go on.* Then another. *I want to die.* I ate another apple. I put up another column. Then another. Then another. I was so tired that I had to take a break and just drop on the ground. My bowels kept spasming at unexpected moments. I cried in pain, curling, wrapping my arms around my knees. Teary-eyed I looked to see Horsey staring at me, chewing on the grass. She paused, then looked up and produced a sound between a neigh and a growl.

"It's going well," said Loki. "Congratulations. You might be *almost* done just in time."

"Almost isn't enough," I muttered, lifting myself up on my elbow.

"Ah, my dear boy, it's enough for us, because if you do almost all of the work, we will finish it ourselves in no time. Maybe you should actually work slower? Then we would have no choice but to beg you to finish. Who else could possibly do this? You're so strong and wise." Loki grinned. What had he seen, what did he know? Was that Lady Freya's plan from the start? To have the wall built, but not completed, like he had just said?

"I really like your horse," Loki remarked, petting Horsey's mane, jumping away with a giggle as she attempted to take him under her hooves. "She's a bit temperamental, but beautiful," he continued from a safe distance. "Would you be willing to sell her to me?"

"Absolutely not!"

"Even if I promised to help you finish the wall in time?"

"Even."

"Think about it. When you are dead, your horse will not be much use to you. Why wouldn't you sell her then if it would save your life?"

"Odin asked me first," I muttered.

"Whatever he offered, I'll give you twice as much."

It took me longer than I would have wished before I could answer. "I doubt it," I said. In front of my eyes stood two huge goblets full of blood. Wine. Not blood.

"Where does she come from? I don't recall ever seeing such a beauty here in Ásgard. And you are not allowed to have any outside help," mused Loki further. "I am probably missing something. Oh well, even my wisdom, second only to Odin's, although there are differing opinions on that, does not allow me to understand all that is happening..."

A column broke with a very loud crack.

"Go away," I spat, then tried to force my voice to sound more polite. "Please go away. I need to get back to work, as you can see."

"Think about my offer."

"I promise to think about it a lot," I muttered. I needed a little something after this, not a lot, an apple, but a smaller one. Horsey whinnied, alarmed. I ignored her.

The next day the wall grew even faster than usual and I walked

Horsey around until we reached the end, right after which we found a beautiful basalt cliff. To our left grew a tall forest. There was something familiar about it, I thought, then covered my eyes with my hand and tried to look above the trees. I saw a red, towering building, then colourful spires, thin like weeds. Bilskirnir and whatever Sif's hall was called. I gulped. We might just about finish in time. If we were lucky.

New strength seemed to enter my body, only to sap out within blinks, replaced by the cold sweat and gloomy thoughts about death. I had no fruit. I had to go back. I would finish early today.

"How many days?" I asked Thjálfi shortly in the evening, passing him a large cut of meat.

"I can't possibly eat this much, my lord. And neither can you. I – I noticed. I am worried, my lord, please forgive me for saying so..."

"But I've been throwing it away," I accidentally said. My hand shot up and covered my mouth, but it was too late.

"I know, my lord, I saw. The snows in Midgard are gone and the nights are getting warmer. Preparations for the feasts are underway. Freyr might be reborn any day now."

"Oh no," I groaned, an answer to all that he had said.

"I know, my lord. If there is any way I could help..."

"Thank you, Thjálfi," I said. I poked at the food. He ate slowly, gazing at me with concern. I just wished he'd go already.

Finally alone, I decided on Idunn's pineapple – which was neither a pine nor an apple. The sun was down, the fires burning. I had no patience, cut the fruit in half with one blow of the axe, making a mark in the table, then started to pick out bits of the pineapple with a knife, wolfing them down. I barely registered that I cut the corner of my mouth, just licked the blood off along with the juice. I was eating as fast as I could, trying to disconnect from the worry that was eating at me, making me sick. Any day now. I drank the gin now as if it were water. Any day now... how was it possible that the basket was nearly empty, yet the sweet, safe feeling seemed to be *just* out of my reach, *almost* there, as if with each bite I got slightly closer to a place I could never enter?

My hand blindly reached into the basket, searching. In disbelief, I looked. Then turned it upside down, stupidly, opening my mouth, as if something would pour out of it. The basket was empty.

My breathing was shallow. I gasped for air and it felt as if my lungs didn't want it. My vision was both sharp and blurry at once, everything changing shapes. I lifted myself from the bench and immediately fell to my knees, smashing my jaw against the iron railing. I was finally dying. There would be peace soon. It's just that I didn't know death would feel that horrible, with my whole body being pricked with cold and hot needles at once as I crawled towards the bed, hitting the doorframe with my head, falling on the floor, lifting myself back to all fours unsure where "up" and "down" were anymore, the sweet warmth's embrace turning into me being thrown into the forge fire and crushed with basalt columns that pushed me onto the sharp edges of the burning coals and also ice and I made it to bed and

−no

−not yet

−in the darkness Gunnar was screaming as he burned alive next to me. He tugged at my arm, first gently, then harder, the flames moving onto my arm now, it was not Gunnar, it was Ludo's red, feverish face, Dalebor's torch. "Don't touch me!" I screamed and punched him with all my might. The nightmare broke like a piece of glass thrown at the wall and my eyes opened just in time for me to see the back of Thjálfi's head slamming into the sharp bricks of the inglenook.

A piercing shriek of pain. A blurry figure, Röskva running towards her brother. She stood on the other side of my bed. They were watching me die. Was it real now? Röskva sent me just one brief glance that sobered me up like a bucket of ice water in the face.

I jumped out of bed... no, I rolled out of it and fell on the ground, darkness and lights dancing in front of my eyes until I could just about see again. I lifted myself to all fours and crawled towards Thjálfi. Röskva hit me with her little fists as I gently touched the back of his head and gasped. I not only felt blood, his skull felt soft. Cracked. I didn't understand, why did death get the wrong person?

"You killed him!" Röskva cried. "You killed him!"

"There is a Goddess of healing somewhere," a voice said, it was mine, "he is still breathing, can you take him to her?"

"She won't touch us, we're not Gods! You killed him!"

"She must," I hissed. "I can demand anything I want to finish the wall. I demand Thjálfi healed right now. Make her..." My grip loosened and I nearly dropped Thjálfi's body. Dread Gods. *Body.* I couldn't. Just some fruit– "Tell her the wall-builder demands... that Odin himself..."

Röskva lifted herself up slowly, the tears suddenly drying, her body radiating defeat. "She won't touch him," she said quietly, pulling the rope. "It's me you should have killed, Your Grace. My life is in your hands now."

"Wha—" I managed, before the door opened. "You... get some more... take him to... Röskva! What's her name?!"

"Eir."

"Tell her the wall-builder demands that Thjálfi is healed. There's an oath Odin made. To me. Hurry up..." I tried to lift myself up. I needed healing, too. My body was poisoned. The only thing that could help was the poison itself. *Please don't let Thjálfi die, I asked for me to die,* I had very little time... any day now. I ignored the commotion as Thjálfi was being taken outside. When I finally stood upright I felt something wet drip, then pour down my legs. Liquid diarrhoea. I was so tired. Did they see? Hear? It didn't matter. The basket, then... but the cloth on top wasn't so white, it was dirtied, as if I'd wiped my hands on it after forging.

I felt my heartbeat slow down rather than speed up. It filled my entire ribcage, as if there was someone inside me punching at it until my whole body vibrated. I gasped for breath. I knew before I knew. I took the cloth between two fingers and pulled it off.

The basket was full, but the fruit was rotten. Maggots crawled over it, in and out of it. I screamed and in a sudden outburst of strength I grabbed the basket and threw it into the abyss below. Lady Freya had cheated me. The Gods had conspired against me. It was exactly like Loki had said. The wall would be almost ready, with the gap just big enough for them to declare I failed. I wouldn't just die, I would die like this, scratching my skin until there was blood under my fingernails, shitting myself, in horrid pain, wishing only that Thjálfi would recover.

Why would Röskva say that I should have killed her, what could she have done? All I told her to do was take care of—

I dropped to my knees and vomited. I was shivering, cold, the red sunrise making me think of red apples. I needed to find something. My bag! Where was it? There could be something! I screamed, a roar that came out as a whimper, and thunder answered. Wind grabbed the trees and shook them violently, as if trying to tear them out of the ground.

Everything turned black and then I was wearing clean breeches with nothing underneath and a tunic. I was in bed, holding on to the empty bag. I cried; why did I throw the basket off? I had eaten worse things than maggots. Röskva said... All she had to do was take care of Horsey. Röskva... Horsey...

Yesterday I ran down the stairs, even with my innards in a knot that would unexpectedly untie itself every now and then. Today old age seemed to have caught me in its merciless vice. I was so weak I had to rest over the rail. Dizzy, stumbling, I took one shaky step after another. There was no rail to lean over as I headed for the stable. I seemed to black out, then return to see all wrong. The chariot wasn't there. Neither was anybody else. Only a black horse stood motionless outside, its back towards me. She looked like I felt. Broken.

"Horsey," I tried to yell, but it came out as a wheeze. My heart was fluttering. When I extended a hand to touch her, my knees suddenly just folded and I fell. My throat was blocked with unvoiced curses. I had to hold on to something. I couldn't use Horsey's leg, I needed something like a stick. Where would I find one? Darkness kept covering my eyes and I kept blinking, seeing something so odd I couldn't believe it was there. I extended a finger to touch it, then pulled at it, causing Horsey to move, let out a sound. Her hind legs were tied with a thin, silvery chain.

Someone lifted me into a sitting position.

"You don't look so good. Are you ill, my dear Módi?" Loki encircled me, squatting where I could see him.

"Go...away."

"I couldn't leave you like that! It would be horrible of me. But! In my infinite wisdom, second only to Odin's, although there are some who believe it to be the other way round... I thought of bringing you a little present. It is something that you have most probably never seen before, it is called Idunn's fruit." He paused.

My entire body and mind began to pay attention. Horsey, the stable, everything else disappeared. There was only Loki's hand resting on a basket covered with a white cloth. When I lifted my head, very slowly, Loki messed up my hair, chuckling. "You see, I found this lovely basket someone threw away. I had this feeling, it's hard to explain, I'd call it a gut feeling. How is your gut feeling? Never mind. I brought you some blueberries," he said, withdrawing a bit, then showing me one. My hand moved in a futile attempt to reach the basket. Loki pulled it further away from me and tsk-tsked. "Apples," he continued. "Grapes. They are a wonderful invention; did you know that Odin's wine..."

"Please," I groaned. "Give them to me. I beg."

"I hope Odin is not watching," said Loki, his voice full of concern. "He might be angry with me, very angry, for bringing you the fruit without his permission, or indeed even Idunn's permission. I am risking a lot for you. But, my dear Módi, I feel like you are angry with me, although I am here to help you. I'm a bit afraid of you, such a big, strong jötunn, one who might even take on my friend, Thor. Why don't I leave this basket here, so you can reach it in...a bit? When I am safe? Once you do, please remember that you owe me a lot, perhaps even your life. Or your beautiful, sad horse that you should have sold to me."

"What have...you done..."

Loki disappeared. Did I really see a black raven fly away? It didn't matter, the basket was there, out of my reach, filled with fruit.

Fruit.

I scratched the ground with my nails, as if I were climbing, pulling myself a bit closer to the basket, my head dropping and hitting the ground. It hurt. I was tearing my own fingernails off my fingers that turned into claws. Tears fell from my eyes, maybe. My feet, everything, useless. I'd use my teeth if I could. I blacked out for a blink or for a while. Maybe I fell asleep or I was asleep right now. I hated the fruit and I needed it and I loved it, but I mostly hated it, but I needed it and I touched the basket with the tip of one finger, then another, and I scratched and pulled at it until it toppled over. A yellow banana fell where I could reach it, berries rolling around. I ate the banana together with the bitter skin, my jaws at first refusing to move, then regaining their strength. I lifted myself up to my knees and picked the berries from the dust, swallowing them one by one. My stomach contracted violently. Cold sweat again. No vomiting, no waste. I had to keep it all inside.

I stood up, my legs a bit uncertain, whole body sweaty, itchy, sore. I needed to break that chain. When I pulled at it Horsey let out a cry of pain and so did I. I looked at my bleeding fingers in disbelief. The thin wire cut into my hands. I could break chains that were a hundred times as thick as this. This was something made of magic. She'd never be able to walk like this. That was what Röskva meant. She failed at the task I had given her, one she loved beyond everything else.

I offered Horsey an apple, feeling my whole body and mind protesting, hand shaking. *It's mine, she doesn't need it, I do.* I hated myself for the relief I felt when she turned her head away.

"Please," I cried. "You must help me."

Listless nothing.

I ate the apple, panting, my breaths quick, shallow. Despair. I would carry her over. I'd have to come back for the basket. What if someone steals it? Bugger it, I decided as I dove under Horsey and lifted her up in the air as if she were a giant sheep. She let out a grunt of pain and surprise. *I need you,* I thought, unable to speak, *for Hillevi, for Jötunheim, for you, Maya, for my life.* I'd felt like this once before. I was only moving out of habit by now.

When I put Horsey down, as gingerly as I could, she looked even more unhappy. Eleven columns waited for us and, from what I could tell, there was space for exactly eleven columns. I counted the crystals I had – sixteen, more than enough. The weakness again, the cold sweat pouring over me like rain. The crystals did not have the spells in them. Basket. My skin itched. I ran, then slowed down, feeling my body become heavier. Slower, faster. I could only try to get through the shits and the sweat and the itchiness and the nausea and the dizziness and oh Gods... Loki hadn't forced me to eat the fruit, he told me to eat as much as I wanted. It wasn't his fault that I wanted all of it. Everything black. Back at the shore. Eleven columns, sixteen crystals. Very soon.

"Horsey," I groaned, hugging her, petting her mane. I could as well hug a tree. "Please." I rubbed a crystal against hers. No reaction at all. I lifted one end of a column. It was heavy. I was still strong. I lifted it further. It broke with a loud crack. There would be no magic. No wall. So close.

I couldn't stand. My knees kept trying to fold, send me down. I dropped heavily on a pile of rocks. Too uncomfortable to sit. I lay on them and shut my eyes. Something sharp biting into my shoulder. Hurts. More fruit would help, something inside me whispered, a seductive, hissing voice, I would be stronger then. I would have laughed if I could. Stronger? I was but a golem that couldn't remember its name. It needed fruit to sleep, to wake up, to crawl. So incredibly weak—

Something seemed to shift uncomfortably inside me. As if I thought of something important. Weak... no. Fruit?

Golem.

When I sat up the dizziness made me half-blind. As if my head stayed behind. I couldn't wish for anything that wasn't there. But golems were just piles of rocks. I was sitting on a pile of rocks. I just needed fruit – needed to give the golem a name. Hope that it would work in this place with rules nobody would tell me.

I chewed on a kiwi, sucking in the juice that threatened to escape. The skin was disgusting. I was disgusting. What names were there? "Golem"... I ground my teeth. Why did I have to be so stupid? Thor. Maya. Herjólf. Pig. Golem-y. Something that nobody could come up with, not even a name, just a word.

I approached Horsey again, dropped on my knees in front of her, and wrapped my shaky hand around the crystal on her neck. Her head hung, lifeless, just at the right height.

"I don't know how to do magic," I whispered. "Dear Maya, dear Horsey, dear...Ásgard. Please give me a golem. His name—"

Horsey let out a sharp neigh, right next to my ear, deafening me. So I couldn't even say it to her. But how would the golem know what its name was then? *Hrungnir*. A brawler. A word I had never heard uttered outside Jomsborg.

I wished and wished and nothing happened. So that was it.

On my knees, I approached the gap in the wall and looked down at the sea. It was another cliff, less sharp and less tall than the first one. Perfect for the goats to launch into the air, low enough so they could return. Everything danced in front of my eyes as I withdrew, rolling to my back, mindlessly staring at the sky. Something appeared, maybe real, maybe not. A black raven landed on top of the wall, observing me.

My basket. Next to the pile of rocks. I crawled. Black and white, grey. Mind neither here nor there. Straw-berries. A groan. I hadn't noticed there was a large whetstone on top of this pile of rocks. I was so sick that I missed it when I sat on it—

I nearly bit off my fingers together with a strawberry.

"Stand up," I said.

Nothing happened.

I licked juice and dirt off my fingers. The golems in the Great Hall... nobody said anything to them, nobody said their names out loud, but they did what they were supposed to. Like they knew without words, but they didn't, because golems were not alive. They just responded to their names, which they knew. Even if my pile of rocks had an ear I could whisper into, I couldn't do it with the raven so near me.

Doubt overwhelmed me for a moment. Maybe I really just missed the whetstone and I was talking to rocks.

Stand up, Hrungnir.

The whetstone was the first to rise in the air. The raven shrieked and so did I. The whetstone turned into the golem's head as other rocks joined it building neck, shoulders, arms. The thing kept growing, taller than me, taller than the columns. Horsey didn't react, motionless, deaf and blind. Watching the golem come to life that wasn't life, smaller rocks forming its fingers, not quite connected, made me feel sick. No, the fruit made me feel sick. The lack of it. I swallowed a large plum, pit and all. Snot dripped down my face. I wiped my moustache with my hand, watching the golem still continue to build himself up until the rocks stopped moving.

For just a blink terror overwhelmed me until I understood. I only told him to stand up. The command had been executed. Hrungnir was now standing up.

Lift a column, Hrungnir, I instructed the golem in my mind.

He moved excruciatingly slowly, each small rock followed by a slightly larger one, hundreds and hundreds of them following each other. The golems that guarded the Great Hall were smooth and efficient, while some parts of Hrungnir were tiny pieces of gravel that nearly, but not completely touched each other. He squatted – a sight both terrifying and fascinating – and wrapped his "hands" around one end of a column, then began to straighten up. With a slow, loud, elongated crack the basalt broke. Hrungnir continued to lift the broken off piece of basalt in his "hands". Without Horsey's help I could have ten golems and achieve nothing but produce lots of small shards I could throw at the raven.

I bit into an orange and its skin tasted even worse than that of a banana. I craved the calm, restful tiredness so much, my mind dissolving into something a bit like happiness, or maybe just lack of unhappiness. Now my body demanded more as I was still chewing. I should be feeling youthful and calm. I just felt rotten, as if the maggots were consuming my insides. Maybe I was shitting maggots, I didn't even know.

There was no point to anything anymore. Hrungnir just stood there, expecting commands, but I had none for him. I ate from the basket, crushing nuts with my teeth, glaring at the pineapple – very funny, Loki. A new feeling overwhelmed me, like I was not here, neither here nor there, except I didn't know where there was. There was a gap in the wall. I was not there. Nothing was there.

There was an idea. One that I had a very long time ago, as I waited outside the Great Hall, drawing in the dirt.

Forgetting that I was not supposed to say it out loud I opened my mouth to issue the command. It was drowned out by a lengthy, piercing scream that shook the ground, made the sun shine brighter, butterflies appear around us out of nowhere. It was different from the piercing shriek that marked the beginning of winter; this one was filled with joy, triumph. Freyr was reborn.

Hrungnir heard me.

The bits of him, one by one, filled up the gap, the "knees" following the "calves" as the "toes" followed the "soles" of his feet. The sight made me drowsy. The scream broke my skull. The rocks inside my stomach exploded. When my eyes no longer saw, my ears no longer heard, and my body was no longer in pain I only felt grateful that I could *finally* stop existing.

CHAPTER 9
MAYA

I WASN'T JUST BEING RIPPED in half. My belly was erupting, veins turning into cracks. Bloodied fragments of my flesh, no longer held together by the skin, were being kicked out from the inside. I was either blind or writhing in the darkness. My scream was a voice that was neither that of a human nor a horse, its broken shards never stopping, like my agony. Loki's offspring was being born. Through the umbilical cord – there was an umbilical cord connecting the thing with *me* – it kept greedily sucking out the remains my strength, blood, anything it could steal before being cut off, finally removed from my body. Its greed was endless, stopping just short of killing me. The product of Loki's deed would be ruthless, cruel, fast, but never stupid. It might still need me. It wouldn't get me.

In one final push, or pull, or tear I felt the rest of the thing emerge from me and I immediately shifted back into my human self. I couldn't wait. I should have. The blinding pain became smelted iron ore being poured into my body, so powerful that it threw me out of the dream before I landed into another one. Here I was nothing but an observer. Odin rode an eight-legged horse, so grey it was nearly silver. The animal's name was Sleipnir, "slippery", like Loki's personality. No one but Odin could ride the creature, faster than the wind. I knew all that from the prophecy I had been forced to learn. I never expected to be a part of it.

I was in my bed, sunshine coming from the garden. I was my human self. I was awake. This was real, the room, the dull, heavy pain filled my abdomen, my insides. The removal of the thing from me hadn't happened yet. I still had that to look forward to, live the impossible dream, knowing I must survive so that I could drown afterwards.

I closed my eyes, my mouth full of ash, my body stolen from me.

"...his pain."

"It would mean a lot for Thor."

The door leading to the garden was open. Freya was conversing with another woman.

"Freya, I can't heal someone who is not a God. What kind of precedent would this make? Soon I would have lines of people demanding that I heal them..."

Eir. The healer. Of the Gods. And nobody else.

Were they talking about me? No, she said "his pain" and I meant nothing to Thor. Eir meant Magni, "just a jötunn" she wouldn't look at twice. *He* is *a God*, I wanted to shout, but I only managed to mumble. It *hurt*.

"Then I guess we should be thankful you're taking his pain away, Eir, you are too kind," said Freya. "And Magni?"

My mind went blank. Who was the "not a God" then?

"I don't have good news there either. Loki has apparently been shifting into you, stealing—"

"Into *me*?!"

"He was stealing the fruit from Idunn's garden, then giving it to Magni... I'm sorry, Módi..."

"Everyone knows, darling. Loki? Into *me*?! While I mourned Freyr's death? Wait till I lay my hands on that little—"

"The cook died," said Eir. "So will Magni, eventually. We've been feeding him a bit of apple mash every now and then. He regains his consciousness for long enough to tell us a bit of what happened, then drops back into... The fruit made him insane, Freya, he keeps pleading with me to leave him to die and help the boy instead. Then he stops breathing, Freya. He stops *breathing*. I have three men sitting there to breathe air into Magni's lungs. Then we put some mash on his tongue and his pain starts again. How long do you think this can continue?"

"He is a God and you know that. Surely..."

"He has been abusing the fruit and destroying his body through the entire winter. I'm sorry."

"So you can't do a thing for Magni and you won't do a thing for Thjálfi?"

I sat up too fast and the room spun. Thjálfi?

"Thor will find himself a new steward." I almost heard Eir's shrug.

"Thor loves that boy," said Freya coldly. "So does Magni."

"Then remove that love. Isn't that what you do?"

The first step was the hardest. Having only hind... two legs, needing to lean over anything I could reach with hands that I forgot how to use... I must have been as white as the wall I rested upon. Sweat was dripping from my face, as if someone had slowly poured water over my head. I could barely see the two Goddesses, one silently furious, one indifferent.

"Eir," I croaked.

"You need to be in bed...!" cried Freya. "Darling, please return to bed!"

I ignored her. "I used to think that you were good...Eir. I thought that you... couldn't help anybody but the Gods... turns out you're just lazy."

"How dare you!"

"Eir, I demand that you help him, and I will pay any price you want..." I paused. My knees were giving in. It was hard not to slip down as I rested against the wall, trying to will myself into remaining upright. "Wasn't Odin clear? Magni gets all he wants. Týr confirmed that... I know you'd never bother to spit at me. Thjálfi..." I ran out of breath. When Röskva was not with me, Thjálfi would come over, sit next to me heavily, quietly confessing that he was worried about

"Módi". There was kindness, sadness, love in his voice. Whatever happened to him, I wanted him healed.

"Honey," whispered Freya, "this is not appropriate..."

"Ásgard owes Magni," I said, snow and ash falling in front of my face. I would have waved them away if my hands weren't so heavy. "Get out of here. Eir. Don't come back. Until Thjálfi..." Something was crushing my lungs. The snow disappeared and ash turned into a dark void, in the middle of which a tiny blue flame made of ice kept burning.

"Your maid has lost her mind. Poor girl." The person speaking somewhere far away felt contempt towards the maid, I registered without emotion.

"She is in shock, but she is right. Odin, Týr, Magni, Thor would all want Thjálfi to recover. It will be kept a secret, to spare you from having to help anybody else. We wouldn't want you to get exhausted from too much work, would we? Name your price and I will ensure..."

$\sim$

The light returned and it took me a blink or two again to understand I was in bed again. Eir was gone. Freya sat next to me, her face sepulchral.

"I must get rid of this thing," I mumbled. Was it my own convulsion, or... again. I felt movement inside my belly. As if I had eaten a fish that was still alive. "Get Eir to remove it."

"Oh, petal," said Freya, reached for my other hand and began to caress it gently. "Eir will not help you."

"Um. Probably not," I admitted. "I should have been, um, nicer..." Freya's hand stopped moving. Neither of us blinked as our eyes locked for a moment, before hers dropped to our connected hands. One was smooth, long fingernails shining a colour I couldn't name; the other one dirty, common.

"Human," I said flatly. "It's because I'm human."

Freya was silent, still looking at my hand she held in hers. Thinking. I stopped breathing. *Tell me*, I begged in my thoughts. *Cry, scream, make it all about yourself. I might... I* want *to forgive you. Please, Mother.*

"Oh, darling, that too, but..." she finally started and my heart fell into a million crystal shards, each causing a wound that would never heal. Hope dies last, they say, and it did just then. I only felt exhaustion. If I couldn't change the past, I would find a way to alter the future. I wanted the thing gone.

Freya's grandchild.

"I tried to change her mind many times. Eir doesn't consider it healing. I had women coming to me since I first arrived here and word got around. They begged me to remove their pregnancies, some caused by Odin himself. I couldn't and Eir wouldn't."

Like she'd touch humans. I bet if a Goddess asked, Eir would suddenly change her mind.

"I worked with the greatest of human healers, tried all we could come up with. There were times when we succeeded, but half of the women, if not more, died together with the..." Freya gestured vaguely, looking genuinely sad. "Perhaps a day will come when Eir changes her mind or I find a safe way, but that day is not today. Oh, darling, if it were possible, do you think that I would have—"

Time stopped.

Back when the Nine were created, a legend said, the land of ice – Niflheim – and the land of fire – Müspelheim – were divided by the void, Ginnungagap. As the fire and the icebergs grew, they met and the resulting steam filled the void, leading to creation of all the life in the Nine.

In *my* void the blue flame that was also ice unexpectedly exploded, consuming me first before greedily devouring everything and everyone else. The end of it all, as predicted by the prophecy I carried. This fire and this ice would not create life; they would burn the worlds, then freeze its ashes until nothing else was left. I remembered this colour, this energy. It filled Harbard's blue orb.

"I... I wouldn't have lied to you," continued Freya, sounding a bit choked. "That's all I meant. You are too dear to me to risk your life." She paused. "Petal, it didn't have to happen. Why did you do that? Why did you decide to help him? He wanted *me* as his...payment, not that I know why, but, darling, why would you betray me like that? What have I done to you? Is it still about that cage? Did you want him to take me away, do you hate me so much?"

No, Mother. I would never want you to leave your beloved Sessrúmnir. You would make a wonderful skeleton covered in rags with tufts of tangled "hair". Brisingamen would hang off its neck, heavy enough to pull the skeleton down, too frail to beg for the fruit that destroyed Magni. Still alive in that windowless, door-less room when the final battle came to pass.

"It's never been about you, neither Magni nor I care for you," I said, letting just a drop of disdain colour my voice. "He chose you, because everyone knows that there is no man in the Nine who wouldn't want you and that is the kind of thinking that appeals to Odin. Why did I help him? Because he is one man in the Nine who I love, in a way you'll never understand. He has suffered a lot. He's broken. He's—"

"Dying," said Freya matter-of-factly. "If Eir can't help him, who can?"

One day Magni and I would find ourselves on a ship cast around freely by a storm. Both of us would be alive, if only to drown. There must have been a way to save him, I just had to figure it out. "You don't know that he will die," I muttered.

"It's happened before," said Freya. "A cook dared to drink Odin's wine, helped himself to it every day, stole more and more until he got sick. There was no need to punish him. He was just left alone until he stopped breathing."

"Magni is a God. He's immortal." I paused. "Those greatest human healers? What do they do?"

"Herbs, potions, incantations... Few of them get further than sleeping potions or poisons before they are burnt at the stake as witches. Only one has real power, so great that nobody dares to accuse her of having it. I suspect that she is a Goddess herself. She has been alive for many, many winters now. Nevertheless, Gróa's herbs won't do what you want, darling, we tried. I understand that you are very upset—"

We tried. "I'm not talking about myself. Get her over here, so she can help Magni."

"Gróa lives on top of a hill that seems to be built of mana and she won't leave it. Her husband is a shifter, he does all her errands. Hmm, I suppose we could capture him, then force her—"

"Send Magni over there."

"Darling, I understand you are in shock, but you are way more bossy than someone in your situation..."

"My *situation*?! Loki raped me! I am safe from any man or any woman, but not from a stallion! He tied my hind legs with a chain, then just did whatever he wanted, now I am carrying his..." My voice cracked, the dull pain in my abdomen nothing compared to the torture inflicted upon my mind. "I may die from this! I'm going to give birth to an eight-legged horse! Magni and I built a wall to protect Jjj...Ásgard, he's not going to touch you, don't you think he deserves..." I paused, my mouth open. "You want him to die," I whispered. "To make *sure* he doesn't get you."

Freya's lips were pressed so hard they almost disappeared. Only the red substance that she smeared on her lips, giving an impression her lips were bloodied, marked her mouth. "How do you know it's going to be an eight-legged horse?" she slowly asked.

"The prophecy," I said when I could breathe again. "Eight-legged horse, child of Loki and another shifter in horse form, what else? No, wait, I'm sorry, I made a mistake. I won't give birth to anything."

"Darling, I told you that it's not possi—"

"I am but a weak human," I hissed. "Nothing more than that. How could I possibly give birth to a horse? Wouldn't I have to be a Goddess of some sort?"

"Angrbóda was also—"

"Angrbóda died. I won't. I'm going to get my revenge." I pulled my hand out of hers, then crossed my hands on my chest. The pain in my abdomen turned into pressure, as if a fat cat had sat on me. The nauseating feeling of movement, again. "I'm going to shift into a mare and remain so until this thing is removed from me. In the meantime, Bragi will spread the truth far and wide. Loki was convinced that he managed to stop us, I mean, Magni and his horse, which was absolutely not me. In his excitement Loki turned into a mare, to have sex with a stallion, as nothing else satisfies him anymore." I paused. "With more than one stallion. A *herd*. He enjoyed it so much he let one of them, or more, I don't care, impregnate him, her, whatever. Loki will give birth to what I am just guessing will be an eight-legged horse named Sleipnir. I want every single person and God in the Universe to despise Loki, the most revolting abomination that ever lived. I want everyone to spit in disgust at the sound of Loki's name. Where even is he?!"

Freya's surprised expression turned into a grimace. "Nobody knows. He could be an eagle in Midgard, a fly in Svartálfheim... Even Odin's ravens won't be able to find him when they don't know what to search for. I will find him and take revenge for using *me*, can you believe his audacity...!"

"Audacity," I huffed. "He raped me, nearly killed Magni, but somehow it's about you?"

"Petal, you're exerting yourself too much."

"I'm just a maid, who was in so much shock she dared to talk down to Eir. Nothing happened. I just hit my head, or something."

"Sweetie, you shifted back into your normal self in front of people. You were seen."

"Then Bragi will tell his story to them first," I barked. "Why did Loki help us with the wall?"

"He never did."

I briefly forgot about everything that happened to me. "You...?"

"Darling. Please. Who else could it be but Odin? Despite his *wisdom* it never occurred to Odin to just fortify an entire world. He gave Magni impossible conditions, then made sure he would nearly succeed... oh no, honey, I just had a thought. It might have been Odin who sent Loki to Magni."

"Magni is his grandson," I said stupidly.

Freya dropped my hand and started nervously pacing around the room. "This is Odin we're talking about. He allowed Thor to go to Midgard and do whatever Thor is doing there. He got Magni to build a wall around Ásgard, but did not let him complete it. It was his plan all along and his grandson is an acceptable price. Oh, petal, doesn't it make you sick?" Freya shut the garden door, then the window that was always open for a reason. "I despise Odin," she hissed. "His wisdom, his plotting, his lack of any morals..."

Only the feeling of being choked stopped me from letting out a snort. I could absolutely breathe, I told myself. There was plenty of fresh air around me. I wasn't really suffocating.

"I can't wait to leave the Nine behind," she continued, spitting rather than speaking. "He can stay here behind his wall—"

My eyes opened wide as if someone poked me with a hot needle. "What did you just say?!"

Freya froze with her mouth open, hand mid-gesture, like a surprised statue.

"Darling," she finally said, "I think you should get some sleep. If you would like some milk of the poppy..."

"Swear to me that you will have Magni taken to Midgard, to Gróa. Now."

"It's not possible, sweetie. Don't forget you helped him build a wall around Ásgard, and if Thor can't cross Bifröst..."

I smiled sourly. "Magni is unconscious. He will not know he crossed it."

"What if Heimdall doesn't let him back in?"

"I think he might," I said. Horse or not, I'd noticed much more than Magni would have thought.

I inspected the stable in which I was going to spend Gods knew how much time. For a normal horse the moon would have to turn twelve times, but neither Loki nor I were normal horses. The thing was already moving—

I bent and vomited on the clean hay.

"Honey," said Freya, her voice tense. "You don't look good at all."

"How strange," I snapped. I seemed to only have two moods, anger and numb resignation. "I'm having the time of my life. Is anybody going to clean this place or will you just leave me here?"

"I will clean it," said Freya with determination. "I will leave Freyr every day this summer – for you. Only when the time comes for you to give birth..."

"Oh yes, thank you for the reminder. Bragi's saga won't be told before the – this thing is out of me." I bit my lip. *Birth.* "Don't tell Magni about any of this, or he'll want to avenge me, he's very... like that. I'll avenge myself. If Loki is caught before the end of this, you can play with him a bit, but I need him alive and well for what I've got planned." I swallowed and my voice lost its sharpness. I was almost certain Magni would survive. Almost. "Bring me news about Magni once there is any, please."

"I will let you know the moment I hear anything."

I slapped my buttocks with my tail a few times. I had gotten so used to this form during the winter that it felt like I finally got comfortable. The movement inside me seemed to stop. Were horses' wombs larger than human ones? Probably. I wasn't familiar with horses' insides, even when they were mine. I tried to sigh, but I neighed instead. I rolled my eyes, which worked, then tried to scratch my chin, which didn't. Shifting back and forth always confused me.

"I will come here every day," Freya said. I didn't believe her for even a blink. Unfortunately, she kept her word.

Every morning and evening, without a fail, she would arrive, alone, to clean the manure, soiling her blindingly white gowns. Both of us knew she could have worn something more reasonable, but she was making a *statement.* She attempted to braid my mane only once, even though I didn't actually manage to bite her. Brushing it was permitted. Once Freya decided that the ablutions were finished, she'd sit and talk for a bit, never too long, just enough for me not to try and kick her out.

"Darling, try to look at the bright side. You have discovered that you've got a new ability. You, personally, are contributing to the future of everything..." She retreated very fast, shouting something about kicking and anger being bad for future mothers. I only stopped seething once I destroyed a feeder under my hooves.

"I will admit that I kept deluding myself that maybe you just needed to meet the right human, the right jötunn, God even, to fall in love, find happiness. I thought I could make you happy. That's all I know... love. I apologise. I was wrong."

You're a cruel, cold, calculating monster that still *won't tell me*, I thought, grinding my teeth. *If there is one thing you know nothing about...* Sudden doubt overcame me. What if it was Harbard who lied? Just like my secret before, I couldn't ask without revealing that I already knew. Oh, and also because I was currently a horse.

"We can't talk about the you-know-what here," she informed me briefly, "there might be flies, perhaps even birds nearby." She left quickly and I wished I could ask for Röskva to attend to me, knowing it was impossible. How was Freya going to hide the event from everyone? I was pretty certain some sort of helpers would be necessary for the thing's removal. Bragi would be very busy.

The you-know-what involved Odin hiding behind his wall. Fenrir was already talking. Freya talked about leaving the Nine behind. Was it possible that whatever Týr was doing with his hand could happen without me being there, did it already happen? No, I'd have to witness it if I dreamt it. Hopefully.

"Loki can't be found. He changes his loyalties whenever he feels like it, unless he is too scared of the consequences. Either the... what he did..."

It's called rape, you dumb bint.

"...was more important than any consequences he imagined possible, or he was forced into it." She examined her fingernails and frowned. One of them probably wasn't perfectly blue or something. "Now he's got my wrath against him. Týr will not rule in his favour..." Freya paused, biting her lip in the exact same way I always did. I knew what she meant. I was only a human, as far as everyone was concerned. Týr would never favour me over a God of any sort.

The cold tentacles of doubt wrapped themselves around me again. Surely, knowing I could die during the event, she would tell me the truth, get Týr to listen to me? Would she watch her daughter struggle giving – during the event, knowing the thing could literally tear me into pieces, and still say nothing? Or was she so certain that I had to die in Midgard that she decided I'd survive this?

"Magni is being transported to Gróa tonight. There is nothing more that can be done for him here. Let's just hope that you are right and when he's unconscious he will not know that he is crossing the boundary between two worlds. Are you sure that will work?"

You're talking to a horse, I thought, rolling my eyes in answer. Nevertheless, she asked me a few more questions before she left me alone with my worries. There was something peculiar to her voice, something I didn't like. She wasn't lying. What was it, excitement, an accusation? Accomplishment. She sounded like she either had accomplished something, or was about to. I couldn't imagine her caring for Magni so much all of a sudden.

"Did you know that Loki is neither one of the Æsir nor Vanir? Nobody knows where he came from, possibly even he doesn't know. He represents chaos and destruction, but he is much more complicated than that. Destruction can be a good thing, like when a forest burns and is replaced by a fertile field, but while you are in that burning forest you don't think about how much better it is going to become one day." She put emphasis on "better".

You know nothing of burning forests, fertile fields, or being raped by "chaos and destruction", and then carrying a monster inside you. Mam.

"Gróa is doing her best. Her powers are nearly unlimited, but you see, sweetie, she doesn't believe in them. She casts spells, makes herbal mixtures, builds sacrificial fires and pours blood of freshly killed animals into the flames. She deludes herself into thinking that she is performing ritual magic that she learned from her mother or grandmother. Nevertheless, she might just save Magni. Might."

What if the fruit killed Magni, but left Módi alive? I thought, horrified. He swore to remain Magni until everything was over, but nearly dying changed things. A sudden idea popped up: I could probably use Módi for my revenge against Freya. The realisation that I was someone who could think that horrified me further. *Still*, my mind calmly continued, *he would definitely enjoy that.*

I wouldn't.

There was a time when I believed myself to be the Goddess of vengeance. I didn't seem to have it in me now though. The frosty fire waiting inside me didn't feel like vengeance. It was all-consuming, like the destiny of the Nine when the prophecy came to pass.

Perhaps there was some important reason why Freya wouldn't tell me that she was my mother, or Harbard really had lied to me. Freya and I shared some mannerisms, like biting the lower lip, but that could have come from me watching her as I grew up. Also, despite her penchant for drama, I knew that it cost Freya a lot to leave Freyr every morning and come over to clean horse manure, mine or not. I...didn't want to do bad things. Not any more than Magni. I would like to, one day, look back at my past and think "yes, this is who I wanted to be".

As if Freya could read my mind, the next morning she ruined everything.

"Darling, I know that this is going to change you forever, destroy your soul, crush your heart."

I whinnied in disbelief. Soul, heart? How did she think horses mated?

"I mean, because of Loki doing this horrible, horrible thing to you..."

It's called rape, *you stupid bint, come closer and I'll pull hair out of your head!*

"A woman never gets over it. It will make you suffer for many winters. I will do my best to help. I promise you." Freya sniffled. "I will try to restore your faith in love." Before I had a chance to react, she ran out, weeping demonstratively. I would have shifted into my human form just to yell at her if I didn't know there was no way I could survive that with an eight-legged colt growing inside me.

The rage blinded me, as if someone had covered my eyes with red fabric. I would have the thing removed from me, never see it again, turn Loki into minced meat, yes. My "soul" would not suffer once the process was over. I would get through this out of *spite*. I was a Goddess. I had no "faith in love", no heart. I *was* the blue fire that would end everything.

Hmm, though. If the prophecy were true, Loki had to live until the very end. Still, the prophecy didn't detail which body parts Loki would still have or not... ow! The thing kicked me! Inside! I cry-neighed in surprise rather than pain. Was it close, was I close to not having it in me?

A woman never gets over it. Come over next time and I'll give you a bite mark you'll never get over... The thing kicked again, moving inside me, making me feel sick. I would cry if I could. Remove it from me. Bugger Eir and her opinions on what did or didn't constitute healing.

"Nobody knows, I already took care of it," Freya informed me at the next opportunity, "and I'll take care that no others find out." She continued, but I stopped listening. I would have paled if I could. There was no way Granny Frigg didn't know all this would happen, yet she had told me nothing.

The anger was gone before it had a chance to really appear. Frigg never told anybody anything. She had left her husband in order to not to answer his questions. She wanted to be a mother so badly and she knew she would never be. I understood so clearly now why Frigg didn't want to know the future. If I had known any of this would happen, I would have never helped Magni. I was contributing to the future whether I wanted to or not. As Granny Frigg told me.

I kept waiting for the thing to give me my body back and it just wouldn't. It moved, it kicked, made me either urinate a lot or not at all. Did real horses just know somehow? The thought made me feel sick. Everything made me feel sick now.

"Let me tell you something about being a Goddess," Freya started one day and I nearly passed out. She was finally going to *tell me*. "A Goddess doesn't need any mana to do things that she was always destined to do. Anybody can learn magic, especially crystal magic, but nobody other than me can go to a place where there is no mana and make two beings fall in love with each other just like that. This is what Gróa fails to understand. She mixes her potions, sacrifices animals, uses their blood, refuses to leave her reservoir of mana. If she did, she might discover that she doesn't need any of this. She seems afraid of herself. Oh! Thanks to her Magni is going to be fine, darling. What an odd creature he is, a man and a child at once. You could mistake him for Thor if he didn't have that unfortunate face."

Why do you still have hair? I planned to tear it out of your skull, didn't I?

"There is something you should know. Magni went through horrible, horrible pains there in Gróa's house. He can never touch even the smallest seed of the smallest berry from Idunn's garden again.

Since he is immortal, he wouldn't die. He would simply suffer for an eternity." Another sigh. "He is going to age, my sweetness, until he turns into the oldest man that ever lived. Someone will have to kill him one day, a mercy killing, I am so sorry to say it. But for now, he is alive and that's what matters, right?"

A mercy killing. Harbard would love to hear that.

A few eternities later, Freya arrived as usual, but remained silent.

I stopped chewing, suspicious. She was staring at my belly, her hand covering her mouth. *Yes, Mother, my belly is enormous, I feel sick, I feel ready, get the thing out of me already and never talk to me about it!*

Powerless, restless, I lay down, then got back up clumsily, wondering whether doing that could speed up the process somehow.

"Oh, aren't you a beauty!" said a woman's voice. I winced in surprise at the interruption. Nobody but Freya ever visited me. "My name is Airi. I will take care of you."

She was a young elf, the black silk of her hair in complicated plaits. Freya would love me to look like that. Airi seemed to radiate peace and kindness, beaming, as if happy for me. I wished I could smile back, then wondered why she'd never come here until now. Just her presence calmed me down. I'd exchange a hundred Freyas for someone who felt so warm. Once all this was over, perhaps Airi could—

All my muscles, weak from barely moving, tensed at once. It hurt.

"Don't worry," said Airi warmly. "It will be alright."

Freya said she would "take care" that nobody would find out. I had never seen Airi before and I would never see her again. Elves weren't any more important to Freya than jötnar or humans. Airi was checking my belly and what I imagined was my udder.

"You seem ready," said Airi. Nicely. *Please say something nasty. Pinch me. Give me some reason to at least mildly dislike you.* "We'll be ready too." She kissed me. "Has anybody ever told you that you're a beauty? Because you are. I feel honoured that Her Grace Freya permitted me to be here for you. There will be four of us to make sure that everything goes well. We know how precious you are." She kissed me one more time and a tremor went through me. Four of them. I needed to lie down. I needed to get up. I needed to do something.

I might have been wrong, Freya might have meant... oh, for Gods' sake, I knew exactly what she meant. She had already "taken care" of those who had witnessed my previous shift. How many people had seen it? Good Gods, had Röskva, the sweet, loving Röskva been there?! No blood was ever spilled in Ásgard, which was why Ifing came useful every now and then. It wasn't accessible now. But there were many trees to hang people from and many poisons to give them.

If I were to shift right now and demand that Airi and the other helpers were kept alive, I would tear myself into bleeding chunks of meat. I had to shift into a human as soon as the thing was removed from me, I had to demand that they were kept alive, just locked somewhere until Bragi made them forget. I couldn't allow four people whose only wrongdoing was helping me get rid of the thing to die!

I cried, then again, in blind panic and in pain that suddenly arrived. I remembered the dream. I knew what would happen now. I wasn't ready, I thought, before losing any control over my mind and body. The thing was kicking its way out. *Help*, I screamed, no, I didn't, I let out a sound that I *remembered* as the pain I *remembered* began. Voices... *Please be over, please, it hurts*, I wanted to cry, *stop it, end it*! The sounds that came out of my mouth – was I even still a mare, did I shift by accident, please stop – my body was being torn – *someone inserted their hands into me*. Gods, Gods, please make it stop, stop *stop* stop, I was drowning in the pain, on the ship with Harbard who shook his head, Týr's absentminded smile turning into his usual bitter frown, Fenrir wolf's children swallowing the sun and the moon, the blue ice that was fire. I was blind, writhing in pain that just wouldn't end, so overwhelming that I didn't care whether I would even survive it, make it stop, Odin on Sleipnir, galloping, his spear up, flying in the air... spear, what, he had no spear, I was delirious, *now must I sink*, the prophecy ended, *now must I sink now must I sinknowmustIsinknowmustI*–

"It's a monster!" someone cried and I vaguely remembered that I had to shift into my human form for some reason, and once I did the pain ripped me in half before I truly sank in the darkness.

~

I didn't die. It was much worse.

My body had truly changed for the first time since I stopped growing. My nether parts were nothing but burning pain. My breasts, rock hard, hurt. Apparently my human body had readied itself to feed a horse. The skin over my abdomen felt loose and I neither dared nor wanted to examine what lay further down. It felt inflated, as if... shivers went through me and my underbelly reacted with convulsions. I could only hope that there was nothing left inside me. I felt *distorted*. I wanted my mind to just free itself from everything, to prove Freya wrong, but I myself served as a reminder that the event had happened. I was afraid of my body now that I knew what it was capable of. Treason. Torture. It disgusted me, I disgusted me. Even if it were to heal as fast as any other wound would, I would always know.

I nearly cried when another cramp squeezed my abdomen. The bracelet that I used to lovingly stroke would never let me forget. Normally, after such a long time in horse form, I would keep getting confused by having hands and missing my tail. Not now. The stretched skin made me cry, even though it didn't cause me pain so much as frustration and powerlessness. What if it just stayed like that? Who would do this willingly? Was this how women felt after giving birth?

It gave me a pause. No, normal women didn't feel like this. I'd shifted too fast, because...

Because...

I was going to do or say something. I had a task to fulfil once the thing was out of me. This body that no longer felt mine was distracting me from something important. Good Gods, it was driving me insane, what – who! It was Airi, the sweet, wonderful elf who made me feel loved, that's why I shifted too fast! I wanted to stop Freya from executing the four people who did everything to help me. "It's a monster," one of them yelled. There were two monsters, not just one, only one was prettier than the other.

I lifted myself with one hand, clenching my teeth. Sitting up caused me so much pain that I didn't pull the rope so much as hang from it with all my weight. I neighed, alarmed, afraid for a blink that the entire construction would fall and crush me. When I dropped on the bed, breathing heavily, I told myself that pain was good, it meant I was alive. I needed to stay alive for what I intended to do.

"Darling," panted Freya, bursting through the door instead of Thrud. "I was so worried about you."

"Airi," I just said, noting that her worry was not so great as to at least place a maid here.

"Oh, don't worry, petal. I took care of everything, nobody will know."

"You mean she's dead. They all are, aren't they?"

Freya's smile didn't waver. "The secret is safe, Bragi's saga is being spread, I refused to listen to it, because I want to remember. Everyone else—"

"Why couldn't Airi and the others be made to listen then, together with everyone else?"

"Darling, they were just elves. There are plenty where they came from. Now... shouldn't you wish to see..." Her voice broke, an unspoken question mark in the air.

I neighed with disdain, then coughed. "Eir mentioned that you can make a mash from Idunn's apple," I said.

I let Freya feed me with a spoon as if I were a baby myself. The fruit's soft warmth made me feel better. Still not good enough to forget about the deaths Sleipnir contributed to before he was even removed from my body. I wanted to ask questions and watch Freya's face as she'd squirm to answer them. When you gave birth to me, did you bleed a lot? Did it hurt to sit? Were your breasts sore, did your nether parts feel like someone tore them – I made myself feel sick instead of letting the apple mash soothe me.

Once I stopped fighting the sweet erasure of my body's broken-ness, my mind lazily drifted back to the stable. I lifted my hands and looked at them in amusement. There were fingers, rather than hooves. I was lying on my back and it was mostly comfortable. I closed my eyes, letting the warmth carry me into the half-sleep that still couldn't stop my mind from lazily wondering how many more people would die once Odin got his hands on the slippery monster.

I understood why Magni kept eating more and more fruit.

It took me a while to learn to walk on just two feet again, get used to the concept of plates and cutlery. My laughter sounded suspiciously similar to a whinny. My body gradually returned to what it used to be before the event. My mind didn't.

I wanted to get rid of the bracelet, which now constantly reminded me of Loki. I didn't think cutting off my hand would help me forget. I knew that I would never survive even approaching Surtr, much less his sword. I hated having to admit that Freya had a point. I should have thought about it longer. The younger me had been blinded with excitement, convinced about her safety. To be fair, the bracelet had saved me a few times. Until it really mattered.

Granny Frigg's words about the future being woven by the Norns and our deeds contributing to it, no matter what we chose to do, reverberated in my head. I wanted to feel proud once the time came to look back on the life I'd had. What memories did I collect? Watching Magni deteriorate as I continued to help him with the wall? "Röskva" telling me that Magni needed me, leading me out of the stable, then tying my hind legs with the chain as I stupidly let her, tired and trusting enough to not even notice "she" was a shifter? The process that led to the monster emerging from me? Airi's sweet voice, gentle touch, assurances that all would be okay? Nothing was okay. I should have continued lazing around. It was the only way to keep myself and others from getting hurt.

I was tempted to begin building a new dungeon inside my mind, even deeper, the cell's door thicker, the chest with too many locks to find keys to. Unfortunately, I knew now that it would never work. Instead, I would follow the example of Granny Frigg and stop trying to build my future, which was clearly building itself. I'd remain in bed forever. It was very comfortable and if there was a safer place, I couldn't think about it. All my needs were satisfied—

A memory made it through, as if pushing the others away with its elbows.

"Your Grace."

"There is an herb," I said. "It tastes like snow. No, like air on a winter day, when you turn it into tea it may be hot, but the taste is cold..."

"Do you mean mint tea, Your Grace?"

"Um, I don't know what it's called. Do we have it? Can you bring me some?"

I only needed a sniff to know that the maid had brought me what I'd hoped for. It would cleanse my mind and body, I told myself, then slowly sipped it. It tasted like the past; like betrayal and powerlessness. I wondered if Gróa had a potion that could make me forget, or whether Bragi could come up with a story that would make me forget my own past... no. I had to remember in order to take my revenge. Loki wouldn't get away with it. He was hiding somewhere nobody could find him, which right now I didn't mind too much. It meant there was no need for me to go anywhere or do anything.

"Petal," said Freya, once we finished our daily ritual where she tried to get me to leave the bed and I refused, "Magni is back. Gróa gave him a sleep potion and he was carried into Ásgard."

"Mhm," I answered.

"By Heimdall," she hissed in a conspiratorial whisper, then emitted a fake giggle. "Heimdall carried Magni in his arms."

"Mhm."

Freya looked rather taken aback. "You don't want to see Magni?"

"I'd love to," I said flatly.

"I knew it!" She clapped her hands enthusiastically.

I interrupted before she had a chance to say anything else. "Here," I said. "He can come here."

"B-but... darling... you can't stay here forever..."

"Stop me," I muttered.

I could see in her face that something was coming. I stiffened in anticipation. "Wouldn't you like to see your..." A nearly unnoticeable pause. "Sleipnir?"

I nearly shot up, rather than sat up, the rage almost enough to get me out of bed. "Get out of here," I hissed, "right now. Never mention that thing again. Never! Understood?"

With her mouth open, eyes wide with terror, Freya stepped away, walking backwards, until she found the door and shut it very quietly. I lay in my bed, shaking. Would I like to see "my Sleipnir"! Maybe I could even be cured of my inability to love once I saw my sweet eight-legged baby! *Bugger*, I thought, angry with myself. I had a chamber pot at hand. It was nearly empty, but still would have looked good smashing onto Freya's face.

I used the chamber pot, called to have it cleaned, accepted a mug of fresh mint, emptied it, and tried to go back to sleep. The anger kept eating at me, no matter how much I tried to pretend to myself that nothing special had happened. Every time I was about to doze off I felt a wave of itchy heat go through me, making my hair stand up, as if I were going to get attacked again. Would I like to see "my" buggered Sleipnir? All I wanted was to forget about the thing. Right after I got my revenge.

~

"Maya. Wake up."

I was missing Magni so much that I was hearing his voice in my dreams. I could even feel his hand on my arm. It felt very realistic. Was I witnessing the future again? I could tell I was in a bed of some sort, feeling exactly the same as when I was awake...

"Wake up! It's me!"

"Good Gods!" I cried. I jumped out of bed as if someone had poked me with a needle, more alive than any time since Loki's deed. Magni's arms made my ribs croak in alarm. "I missed you so much," I told his chest, my voice somewhat muffled, "I was so worried about you...!" My delight suddenly died out, my body stiffening, which he probably didn't notice. "Let me see your face!"

Magni loosened his embrace just enough for his beard to get into my eyes. I pulled at it, making him laugh. When he sat on the floor, cross-legged, beaming, my doubts evaporated. I had never seen anybody, not just Magni, smile like this, as if his entire body radiated happiness. His eyes shone, his face crinkled only by joy.

My grin froze, my stomach diving. Something was wrong and I knew exactly what. Someone had given him fruit.

"What happened?" I asked carefully, trying to sound natural and not at all terrified.

"That Gróa made me drink a horrible concoction. All the time. Day and night."

"That's all?" I needed to know more before deciding whether to feel relieved, frustrated, or to remain terrified for a bit longer.

"I was so sick," reported Magni cheerfully. "I couldn't eat and I was still throwing up. And worse. From the other end, you know."

My imagination cringed.

"I was sneezing, everything itched, it hurt, I kept getting cold, then hot," he continued, sounding strangely delighted. "Even my *hair* hurt. I couldn't sleep. But those herbs of hers were the worst. I swear I still smell them, even here. I had to drink that concoction *all* the time. When I threw up, she'd bring more. I begged, but they wouldn't even give me so much as the smallest grape..."

"Remember that sickness," I interrupted, "because that's what will happen if they give you that smallest grape, Magni. And it will never end, because you're immortal. Would you like that?"

"No," he admitted, "but it was worth it. Thor can never return to Bilskirnir again, he will never see his chariot or goats. Sif is gone, too. Do you know why they all act very strange when I ask about her?"

I shook my head, avoiding his eyes. If Magni could be carried to Midgard and back, and all that was needed was a sleeping potion, Thor could cross Bifröst the same way. I suggested it to Freya myself. She tried to question the horse-me before using Magni as an experiment.

I didn't even have to look at him to sense his happiness. I wanted it to last as long as possible. He'd find out soon enough. From someone else.

"Jötunheim is safe. I'm alive. So it's all good. I just wish I could..." A deep sigh that gave me goosebumps. Would he manage to stay away from the "smallest grapes" forever? "Gróa kept telling me twenty-five times a day how sick the fruit made me. As if I didn't notice. Did you know that two times twenty-five is fifty?"

"Everyone knows." Magni gave me a wounded look I didn't understand, as if I had said something wrong. "Ah," I remembered. "I

have good news for you, Thjálfi is fine... oh, you know that, silly me."
Magni's expression changed, but not into a smile. Bugger. There was
a chance that at least one of them wasn't too happy with the other's
company. "Is he, um, are you..." I gestured, searching for the right
words. "What happened to him in the first place?"

My right words wiped out the rest of that joy he'd brought along.

"Never mind," I sang, wishing I could slam my head repeatedly
against a wall without him noticing. "He's fine, so are you, nothing
else matters!" I almost added a cringe-worthy squeal of happiness. I
would say nothing more, just smile and nod.

"You matter. Lady Freya said you were doing great. So why are
you in bed? What happened to you, there at the end? You wouldn't
help me. Then I thought I would die. But I didn't." The excitement
lit up his eyes again, quickly replaced by concern. "Who put that
chain around your legs?"

I bit my lip. I never intended to tell Magni about it and it didn't
occur to me that he might simply ask. "I was..." I started, elongating
the words, "...cheated, by... um, Loki came to me... looking like
Röskva. I was very sleepy and didn't realise it was a shifter." Truth.
"He took me outside, placed that chain around my legs, I couldn't
kick him, I couldn't do any magic anymore, even walk." Truth. "And
then you found me." I nearly sighed with relief at having finished.
"May I have—"

"And what did you do after that? When I was gone?"

Oh bugger, I hadn't thought about that either. "I was on a
mission," I muttered. "A very special and secret one. I only just came
back and I'm very tired. So, um, may I ask a question?"

Magni nodded. His face remained serious, but his eyes were
smiling again.

"Do you..." I started, then bit my lip. How did I ask about the
fruit without giving him ideas? "Do you still miss..." My voice died
out again. I forgot how to speak to people.

That deep sigh again. "Sometimes. A bit. Not really, not like that,
just to... it's just that it made me feel so soft and warm. Like everything was fine, even if it wasn't. Like I could do anything."

I couldn't stop myself from nodding.

"At the end it wasn't fine at all. I thought I'd die, and she made me drink that concoction, and I was so sick—"

"Yes, I remember," I interrupted. I wasn't ready to hear about his both ends again.

"I don't miss that. I would just like to feel this nice feeling again. For a bit. So I wouldn't eat much, now that I know, just something small. Like a strawberry. I like them a lot," said Magni dreamily, before his tone suddenly changed. "No, I don't miss it at all."

I had never met a less convincing liar.

I was about to thank him for his visit and encourage him to come back once I had my regular three-day nap, when I remembered something. "Magni, how come you still dwell in Bilskirnir? Odin doesn't mind? Nobody said anything?"

"Ah," said Magni, rubbing his hands as if he were cold, staring at them. "Yes. That. I will be judged. Would you do me a favour? Just a very little one. Nobody would know."

I immediately bristled. I had to make sure everybody would know not to do him "very little favours".

"They say a part of the wall can be breached," he continued. "They mean my golem. There is no crystal anywhere there. So if you could tell the crystals what to do, then I'd put them under H—"

"Never say his name! Not even to me! Just think it. Even then think quietly."

"I'll try," Magni answered, his baffled expression suggesting he took me literally. "Will you help me? Please?"

The sigh that came all the way from my toes echoed his.

I would have to get out of bed. Maybe even bathe. True, I was sticky, but the bed didn't complain. All that to see the wall I never wished to see again, yet another reminder I didn't need. But they took away a broken, dying man whose body and mind were equally sick, and returned a kid with the stars in his eyes. "Did you say they will judge you?"

"At the Assembly," said Magni. "In two days. They were just waiting to see whether I returned alive."

I opened my mouth, then closed it with a loud "pop", like a fish. "Alright," I grumbled. "I'll go. I will need a crystal."

Beaming again, Magni opened his hand. Two. "Can we go now?"

"This was Freya's idea, wasn't it?" I said, suddenly irritated.

"Ooo, Lady Freya..."

"Good Gods. Never mind. Get out of here and wait in the drawing room. Have a drink, or something. I have to take a bath and get dressed, then we'll go." How did I not notice until now that I *reeked* of sweat? I swore to myself that Loki's actions wouldn't affect me, then I locked myself in my room and never left the bed.

I rang for a maid. Vanadís looked so excited when I asked her to change my smelly bedding and put fresh flowers in the vases, that I almost apologised. "Thank you," I said instead, then let out a deep, deep sigh. I had a wall to finish and lots of avenging to do. Just thinking about it made me want a nap. We'd go, stick the crystal under the golem, then I'd come back. Rest a bit, drink some mint tea. Make plans, prepare for various possibilities... I knew that was what I always promised myself to do and it never worked, but if there was one thing that was certain, it was that I had time. Loki wouldn't dare to show up in Ásgard anytime soon. I could afford a few more moon-turns of napping. I meant, preparation.

"I came up with a golem because of you," reported Magni, jumping around me excitedly like a happy puppy. I walked in weird spurts, slowing down because I didn't want to see that wall, then speeding up just to be done with it. I simultaneously wanted to return into the safety of my bed and kick myself in the shin for having wasted so much time. I sent a tired smile to the flame-haired ball of excitement that had enough energy for both of us and then some. "You told me that as a God I could wish for anything that wasn't alive. I should have wished for a golem earlier. If you were a Goddess, what would you want? I can wish for it for you."

An irregular, black line began to materialise in front of us. "To turn back time," I muttered. With the wall standing and Fenrir wolf now talking... oh, who was I kidding, he'd never been a wolf, no matter how hard Týr tried to convince us. I only had two dreams that suggested there was a future for me. In one I was about to drown, in the other I watched Odin ride Sleipnir into battle. I preferred the drowning.

"Can you turn back time?"

"No." I was dragging my feet, trying to stall again. As long as I didn't look—

"Maya, look!"

I braced myself, knowing that the memory was going to hurt. Reluctantly, I raised my head. Then I raised it further and further until I felt pain indeed. In my neck.

"Is..." I said, then spent some time looking for the next word that should follow. "Is..."

"This is my golem," said Magni. He sounded as if it was his first-born son.

I looked down again. Then up. "It's quite tall," I said weakly.

"That was his hand," Magni pointed. "That's his legs. And that between the legs... I'm not sure. It was just to fill the space. Why is it that the harder I try not to think his name, the more my head is trying to think it?"

"What's that whetstone on top for? Decoration?"

"It's his head," said Magni, sounding offended.

"Ah, of course, what else could it be. Won't it fall on us when wind blows?"

His face darkened. "You think it's stupid."

"No! Both of us are probably only alive because you came up with this." I sighed, but only on the inside, staring at the construction I could probably fell with a well-aimed kick. I could see why Odin didn't consider the wall finished. "Give me the crystals," I commanded, extending my hand, and when Magni's sweaty palm touched mine the golem exploded.

I was too surprised to scream. I just dropped to the ground, covering my head with my hands, instinctively sending all the mana I could access into the crystals I held, building a shield like the one I once used for *rain*. And rocks rained around us, some the size of boulders, smashing the ground hard enough to make Ásgard – or maybe just me – shake. Magni's yell coincided with the one blink of silence between the thuds.

"Hrungnir! Defend!"

I looked up just in time to see a huge, sharp chunk of rock, probably a piece of the whetstone, heading towards my face. I was so convinced it would kill me that I didn't even yelp, my breath taken away, until the rock bounced from my shield and flew back where it came from. Defend from what? I thought it was wind... or... thunder... I dared to glance just in time for an unmistakable hammer to strike the whetstone piece, sending small chunks all over the place, some of them back towards me again.

Now I screamed. There was no way my shield could stop Mjölnir. I didn't care about the golem's demise, I'd think about it once *I* didn't die.

The chariot shot through the newly created gap. It was completely out of control, nearly sideways, Thjálfi hanging down, holding on to the reins, probably screaming, his voice drowned out by the goats' bleating. He lost his grip just in time to send me into a panic right before he, too, bounced from the shield and his body flew away. The goats seemed to find a common ground, or common sky. The chariot disappeared before I had a chance to blink and sudden silence rang in my ears.

I dared to lift myself up to my knees. I couldn't see any more rocks flying around. No hammer either. Or his owner. Just a lot of golem.

"Father," cried Magni, throwing aside rocks that I seemed to recognise as Hrungnir's leg. Thor was very still and silent, as if he didn't even notice, or...

I took a sharp intake of breath. A huge piece of whetstone stuck out of Thor's forehead, blood trickling down his skull. Mjölnir lay next to his hand, which Magni grabbed, kissing it, sobbing. That was rather unexpected, a sober, cold thought inside me remarked. Who would have thought Magni would be so upset to see his hated father dead?

If I weren't on my knees I'd drop down now.

Impossible. He couldn't die. The prophecy made it very clear. Thor might have not been moving or breathing, there might have been a rock sticking out of his bleeding forehead, but he had to live. A few blinks earlier my shield had sent the whetstone back in the air and the hammer smashed through it, sending pieces everywhere. My stomach twisted. A meaningless human becoming an accidental Godslayer. If Thor were to die, despite the prophecy, I'd have to find that ship to drown on very fast.

"Father," mumbled another voice beside me and I nearly jumped out of my skin. Thjálfi, his face bloodied, was crawling over, dropping next to Thor's body to grab his other hand and join with Magni's weeping. My thoughts suddenly calmed down, as if they were both emotional enough, so I didn't have to be. Doing my best to ignore the cries and sobs, I examined Thor in search for signs of life. I couldn't tell whether his chest was moving as the two mourners pulled at his hands. I moved to his lips, nose, forehead – oh bugger – eyes...

Thor's eyelid briefly trembled, as if he was trying to blink.

"Away!" I shouted, then cast Thjálfi and Magni away like pebbles. "He's alive!"

"Father," groaned Magni, "don't die. Please don't die."

I glanced towards Thjálfi. He sat up, rubbed the back of his head, rolled his head around, his eyes glazed. I would be more gentle with non-Gods the next time we all tried to kill Thor.

"Eir—" I started. Both my voice and Magni's sobs stopped as if cut. Thor's lips moved in a soundless groan. He was attempting to say something important, something that could still turn out to be his last words.

"I killed the troll."

Magni dropped Thor's hand. His eyes wandered between the rock in Thor's forehead, the rubble, and me.

I was just going to exhale, but accidentally yelled instead. "It wasn't a troll! It was a golem!" I barely managed to keep "you halfwit" on the inside.

"My head hurts," complained Thor. "Be quiet, woman. Where is the troll then... danger..."

"Um," I said nervously, looking around in case he wasn't completely delirious. If there was a troll coming, we had to close the gap in the wall right now.

Thuds of what sounded like a whole band of attackers made it clear that we were late. All our heads, except Thor's, turned. I bit my lip so hard that it hurt. I would have preferred a troll.

The moon had turned perhaps once since Sleipnir was born, yet the thing was large enough for Odin to ride. Its coat was silver, shining in the sun as if it were oiled. Greasy. Slippery. Like its father and its owner. Odin slid off the horse and patted its neck. I wanted to look away from the thing, but I couldn't tear my gaze off it. Now that it was no longer running, its eight legs began to twist around each other. It had problems remaining upright. I didn't want to see it being cute.

I couldn't believe I got out of bed for this.

"I see the wall is not as safe as we were promised," said Odin.

I was about to end my life by answering the All-Father when the scream I readied turned into a gulp that nearly choked me. Something else flew through the hole left by Hrungnir. A sharp, deafening sound that made ravens' shrill shrieks sound melodious, felt as if someone threw a rock at my forehead as well.

"My head hurts," complained Thor, unaware of an unnaturally large bald vulture hovering over him. The grotesque bird landed, making me recoil in both fear and disgust even before it shifted into naked, mostly bald Sif. The bird was prettier.

"My love!" she wailed, dropping on her knees, rocking back and forth, her voice still a high-pitched shriek. "My one and only love!"

"After your hair," said Odin. He seemed calm as a rock... or maybe some other object. I looked at him, baffled, and saw a little smirk. He was *enjoying* the situation.

"I want my reward, Odin, now! Thor is back! I want my hair, I want the jötunn and that maid!"

"Someone stop this racket," mumbled Thor, "bring me to the troll. Or is this the troll?"

"What is all this talk about a troll?" asked Odin.

"His head..." I started.

"I'm afraid I mentioned a troll to His Grace."

Thjálfi's face was white, except for the droplets of blood. "A big and scary troll, wanting to marry his daughter. I didn't know how else, didn't expect... My life is in your hands, Your Graces."

Sif let out a shriek so high-pitched my teeth loosened in the jaw. Thjálfi stumbled on his feet.

"The troll," muttered Thor. He opened his hand and Mjölnir placed itself in it. "I hear it."

"There is no troll!" I yelled. "Can someone get Eir over here? Right now?"

Sif's head turned on her neck exactly like a bird's would, her eyes bulging. Her hair had never grown back, messy tufts of it sticking out of red, raw skin. Her eyes were completely black, as if the pupils had expanded to the entire eyeball. "I'll kill you," she hissed. "Slowly. Your life belongs to me. And the jötunn's."

For a blink fear paralysed me, until I remembered the solstice feast a long time ago. Sif's pearly laughter, so different from the vulture's screeching. A dark elf's hand on her leg. "Later," I said. "We're busy. Thor, don't move until Eir comes here. Odin, I mean – O All-Father, where is Eir?"

"Eir, my child, is on her journey."

"What?" I said flatly, trying to look at Thor with one eye – his fingers kept moving around the handle of Mjölnir – and at Odin with the other.

"She left Ásgard not long ago, disguised as an old woman, wearing a hood and cloak, chased by the guilt of having been called, I believe, 'lazy', or perhaps it was 'a monster', or even 'egoistic'. It made her very upset. She wants to spend a year and a day carrying her help to others who are not as fortunate as most of us here..."

"Gróa!" cried Magni. "Get him to Gróa!"

"Hmm," said Odin.

I snapped my fingers, exhaling very slowly, making sure not to accidentally scream in someone's face again. "Gróa. Thjálfi, find the chariot. I'll try to keep him in it. Gods, what a mess."

Sif continued to cackle and croak in the background, slamming Magni's shoulder with her fists, which Magni didn't notice.

Odin's sigh seemed to come from the ground under his feet. "The Assembly has already been called," he announced. "It shall be postponed, until it is determined who is responsible for Thor's death."

"I'll take part in that," said Thor, clearly and loudly, before his eyes closed.

I swallowed something that grew inside my throat. Magni still held Thor's hand, staring at his father as if he had never seen...his father before. Odin seemed more concerned about the inconvenience of postponing the Assembly than his son's life. "He's breathing," I said, coolly surprised at how calm I sounded. "If you don't want to bring Eir back, better get him over to Gróa, or take responsibility for his death yourself. As long as he remains unconscious..." I wished I could stop Magni from hearing me. "...we can just transport him over Bifröst. Magni and I will go and—"

"The jötunn is not leaving Ásgard until the Assembly's decision is made."

"He's got a name and he's your grandson, you old bastard!"

Odin looked rather taken aback by my tone. Even Sleipnir neighed disapprovingly.

"Your Grace," I quickly added. "Your Grace old bastard."

Instead of striking me with his staff, he smiled. "He has to stay, but you can go. Sif, you will stop this spectacle right now, then join me in Valhalla."

"In Valhalla?! What am I supposed to do there? Don't I have a hall anymore?!"

"You will sit with me, *quietly*, and watch the warriors, let their deaths soothe your nerves. You will need to find your calm before the Assembly decides your fate as well. True, today marks a year and a day since your departure, but you did not bring Thor back. Thjálfi did." He glanced at her. "You might want to put something on."

I had to look away, unable to deal with what I was seeing in the deep, green lakes of Magni's eyes. Thor had to reach Gróa as fast as possible and I had to return before Magni used the only way he knew to feel better.

"Go to Sessrúmnir," I said to Magni. "Wait there for me."

"Why can't I—"

I silenced him with a quick gesture. Thor's manservants might be convinced to serve His Grace Magni Idunn's fruit. In Sessrúmnir he had no chance of getting any without either Freya's or my permission.

As angry as I was with Eir for deciding to have a conscience at an inconvenient time, with Sif for being Sif, with myself for getting out of bed, with Thjálfi for inventing a troll, I had no time. I told Thjálfi to give the goats some valerian root and take some himself, then sent him away. As gently as I could I placed Thor in the chariot, sat in it myself, then used my powers to transport us both over Bifröst under Heimdall's baffled gaze. I headed straight to Gróa, where I barely introduced myself, winced at the sight of an imposing bear that turned out to be her husband, thanked her in advance and flew back so fast that the chariot nearly beheaded Heimdall. I had to find Magni and make sure he hadn't eaten anything.

"What was that?" he asked, staring at me weirdly, when I found him in the garden.

A silver mug stood in front of him and I almost nodded in approval. I needed a drink too, although probably not the same one. I pulled at the rope. "Which that?" I asked, pushing away the thought that I did a much better job than the goats ever could and maybe I found my calling after all. Especially since I'd found Gróa's dwelling just like that, never having been there or even having seen her before.

"When you just laughed at me? Just now?"

"Wine," I said to Gefn or Höfn. "White. Thank you so much. What do you mean, just now? I took your father to Gróa. I mean, Thor. I mean, I took Thor to her, not..."

He waved away my unspoken apology. "You came in and it was as if you couldn't see me. You went to your bedroom, came out with a wooden box, then left. I was shouting to you and you just laughed—"

I grabbed his mug with both hands, took a gulp and some of the liquid fire inside came out of my nose. I coughed, sneezed, and cursed at the same time, ignoring Magni's concerned questions.

The box contained the thin silver chain that Loki had used to bind my legs. The one that Magni had tried and failed to break, never noticing it was tied with the simplest of knots. Loki had predicted that once Magni had returned I would finally leave my bed to go and "finish" the golem. He had probably helped Thjálfi find Thor, his timing impeccable. Vanadís, the maid that was so happy and excited about me going out, was another shifter I had failed to recognise.

I now knew what Loki would be holding in his hands once the time came for Fenrir wolf to take Týr's hand between his jaws. I had been right all this time. I should have stayed in bed. Really, the Nine would be a much nicer Universe if all of us just stayed in bed.

CHAPTER 10
MAGNI

I THOUGHT I HAD DIED, but I hadn't.

I had been here, in bed, then somewhere else, also in bed, then in Gróa's dwelling, in bed. My body had been twisting and tossing around, out of my control, or anybody else's, breaking the chains used to tie me down. I remembered feeling as if I was staring into the white light of the Great Hall. Then I would slip under a black surface and see Thjálfi flying through the air again, hit by me, his head exploding into bone and blood and meat. I kept returning to life for more of the white pain, more vomit and shit and itching, blood under my fingernails as nobody was strong enough to stop me from scratching my skin. They asked me things and I only answered so that I could plead with whoever was near me to save Thjálfi. I could live with the other visions and memories, but not that one.

A different vision: a pale, fair-haired woman with white and yellow flowers in her hair, kissing me on the forehead. Deep, dark, sweet sleep. When I had woken up I felt rested and happy. I asked Gróa about Thjálfi again and this time, when she assured me as always that he was perfectly fine, I had believed her. A strange feeling: I remembered seeing the image of his body flying through the air, but I couldn't recall it.

The unbearable everything had been replaced by something like resigned peace, then hope, then belief that I would live on and not like this. The wounds I had caused myself with the scratching had healed and disappeared. I was spending more time awake now, my body starting to listen to me again. I told Gróa that I was thirsty and she had nodded, gloomily reminded me of how sick the fruit had made me, then brought me more of her bitter concoction. I should have kept quiet.

Gróa watched me as I ate my first meal in what seemed to be many moon-turns; watery porridge. The spoon I was using stopped mid-way. Porridge. The word seemed to scratch at some sort of memory. Bad dreams. I used to have bad dreams. About porridge? I couldn't see why that would be... I had eaten all of it, slightly baffled by the taste, as if my mind or stomach had been expecting something else. Gróa had reminded me a few more times how sick the fruit made me, then brought *more* of that bitter mixture. It had clearly taken my taste away together with the bad dreams.

I still stayed in bed most of the time, but I had begun to walk now, at first leaning on a thick stick like an old man until I felt stronger. It was during those walks that I realised my memory was full of gaps. I couldn't even tell how many and how long there were. Only the face of my lover, Herjólf, seemed clear to me. His eyes, voice, hands. His lips. He had given me a beautiful dagger as a present. I would find him and bring him here, to Ásgard. We would be happy together.

On a night no different from the others I emptied my tenth mug of the "tea". It had seemed even more bitter than usual. When I closed my eyes I saw Herjólf's playful half-smile. I fell asleep smiling back and woke up in Thor's bed. Thjálfi sat next to me and I cried with happiness that he was alive. He cried too. That made me cry more, as if the tears were imprisoned and only let out now. Thjálfi guessed what I couldn't say and left me alone. The tears rolled down my face, even though I was grinning. Life had been so good to me. Maybe I couldn't remember much, but all I could recall filled me with hope and happiness. And Thjálfi was alive, too.

Lady Freya came to visit. She said a lot of things about Loki, then demanded that I examine Brisingamen, her golden necklace. I did as instructed, blushing slightly from being so close to the Goddess herself. If Brisingamen was missing, Lady Freya said, I could be certain it was somebody else. I had a feeling that I would recognise her now, Brisingamen or not. Her presence felt different from Loki's falsehood. When Loki visited, in the guise of Lady Freya, I felt like I was talking to a friend, another proof that I was stupid. The real Goddess felt like a real Goddess.

Before she left, Lady Freya asked to look at the inside of my hand. Surprised, I let her. The tip of her fingernail gently traced one of the lines marking it. The line disappeared, as if it had never been there. Lady Freya smiled at me, then winked, as if we shared a secret, and asked about my first lover.

I felt like I found a way to pale and blush at the same time. He was... I remembered thinking about him just the night before, or was it two nights? The Goddess of love was asking me about him and all I could recall was the sight of a naked man's body – but not the face. Not even the name. All of it just gone, like the other memories I was missing.

Lady Freya left me with my shame, telling me that Maya was feeling tremendously well, missed me very, very much and couldn't wait to see me. The door had barely shut behind her when a raven landed on the railing. It dropped a rolled piece of parchment on the floor of the balcony, immediately departing. I unwrapped the parchment and my first instinct was to throw it out. It was covered with runes. A spell.

I had no intention of touching magical things ever again, except for the ones I liked. I could only hope that since I couldn't read, the spell wouldn't work, but I wanted to know what it said. I called for Thjálfi and told him to be careful. His face darkened. There would be an Assembly in three days, he said, to decide my fate. One that would decide whether the wall was or was not finished. It took me a blink or two to recall what wall he was talking about.

More memories unfolded in front of me. I recalled Horsey, or Maya, unable or unwilling to help me with the crystal, her hind legs tied with a silver chain. The golem that was just a golem, a pile of rocks, neither unbreakable nor unmovable. I'd named him Hrungnir, "brawler", a weird choice of word for something that was supposed to stay in one position forever and never do any brawling. Where would I get a name like that from? I tried to recall the events. We were building the wall, Horsey the horse's legs were tied, I created the golem, I got very sick, the lady kissed me on the forehead, Thjálfi was fine. I shrugged. It was a better name than, say, "Golemy". The fruit and Gróa's poison brew did something with my memory, but it didn't matter.

Everything was great. I just had to see Maya – a wave of happiness washed over me, she was doing well too, she missed me – and ask her help one more time. Then even Týr would have to say that we succeeded. I would now live in Bilskirnir, work at the forge, knowing that I had saved Jötunheim from a horrible war and that it was now safe forever. I still didn't know what had happened to Sif and nobody would tell me, but I guessed she went to join Thor in Midgard.

This gave me a pause again. Midgard... I couldn't remember much at all. Laughing with some people, sitting by a fire, drinking together. Who were they? Maya finding me and asking me to come to Ásgard. Working at a forge at a small town or settlement surrounded by a wooden palisade, which had given me the idea for the wall. A beautiful, endless summer. The rest seemed to be hiding right next to the edge of my consciousness. A dream undreamt.

I might have forgotten the name and face of my lover, but I remembered his gift.

I looked around before opening a small, unassuming chest that stood in the corner. It contained my old belongings – a rag that still smelled of wood smoke, a leather belt, a pair of trousers. Not a lot. I shut the chest. Between the chest and the wall hid a pair of worn-out leather boots with something like pockets sewn into them. I pulled a silver, sharp dagger out of one. The handle of the knife was small and undecorated, almost the same colour as the boots. I would never fight again, I knew, but my lover's idea was very smart.

His name began with K. Or maybe P. The complete lack of recollection was more bewildering than shameful. *Maybe he wasn't that good then*, an odd, cynical voice inside me remarked. I blushed. There was undressing together for the first time, my embarrassment at the sight of a naked man, the discovery that I was not the only one who felt like... I just didn't remember the man.

It was hard not to notice as I ate dinner that there were no decorative slices of peaches, berry sauces, or even a very small grape anywhere. Did they think it would tempt me? That would never happen. It was just fake fruit, no, *real* fruit, and it wasn't even here, yet I could almost smell it. I could *taste* it as I tore off a chunk of meat and put it in my mouth. The bitter ale seemed sweeter than I remembered it.

Maybe it really was good that they kept any and all fruit away from me.

I couldn't understand what had happened, or why. The first time I ate the real fruit it felt so good. The second – almost as good. Then – almost almost. Then...

I shook my head, pushed the plate aside, filled my tankard with mead, played with the dagger. The inability to recall either the face or the name of my first lover was almost painful. H... He... *Heimdall.*

I blushed so hard that he could probably hear it from the Rainbow Bridge. I remembered Heimdall. Vividly. He carried me in his arms, I'd been told more than once, and I wished I could remember *that.* The image of his face under my eyelids was sharp and clear. I knew I should feel shame that my first, forgotten lover's name and face were replaced with a God with eyes like dark lakes of danger and desire, but I didn't. He joined me in my dreams, too, but my first thought when I woke up, happy, rested, had nothing to do with Heimdall. I would see Maya.

I had never felt like this before, excited about every day that came, wondering what it would bring. It was the beginning of happiness, I thought. It would just get better and better.

Then it all fell apart.

How could I have not realised that if it was possible to make me unconscious and carry me back and forth to Bifröst, the same applied to my father? Odin got what he wanted and didn't even have to cheat me out. I'd done it to myself.

My father. I had cried. I had said that I loved him and I had meant it. I didn't want to think about him. He could still die, I thought, but instead of hope I felt the nausea that accompanied raw terror.

If only I could stop thinking. A little something... even just half a peach, just one grape. Maybe there was one somewhere, something that fell to the ground. Something that didn't go bad, like a nut. I would be extremely sick, they all told me. It's just that *I couldn't stop thinking* that if we had walked a bit faster, if I had left Bilskirnir in the morning just a bit earlier, the hammer would have just bounced. If I hadn't shouted "defend"... if, if. Nothing good had ever come out of me thinking.

I dropped on my father's seat on my father's balcony, poured myself some of his mead. It used to dampen the pain, mess up the thoughts. Now it just made me want to smash my stupid head against the table in anger and frustration. How could I explain to them all that I'd rather have the sickness than this?

"Her Grace Maya," announced Thjálfi, already out the door when I shouted his name.

"What's going on?" asked Maya as I extricated myself from behind the table. Thjálfi's face was white. Even his freckles paled as I approached him.

"My l- Your Grace – let me—" he managed, then let out a terrified squeal when I grabbed him and gave him a bear hug. His muscles relaxed so suddenly that he would have fallen on the floor if I weren't holding him. Maybe I shouldn't have patted his back.

"It's 'brother'," I said, "and thank you. Can you stand on your own now?"

"I – I think. Yes. My sincere apologies, my lord. Thank you, my lord."

I had to smile sadly. I was going to be mylorded for the rest of my life, but that only meant one more day anyway. In the meantime, there were cold meats and baked potatoes and no fruit at all.

"Mint tea," said Maya shortly. I winced, having already forgotten she was here. "Do you have it?"

Thjálfi swallowed, his throat apple bobbing up and down, a hint of grimace on his face. "I believe Her Grace Sif finds it tasty."

"Great. Bring me some."

"Do it," I confirmed, curious.

"Yes..." he tried, looking right next to me rather than at me. "Yes, m-my lord." His lips formed an uncertain smile, one of a dog not wanting to get kicked, and then something fell into both my eyes at once and I had to wave him away before rubbing them for a while.

Maya waited, drumming her fingers on the table and saying nothing, as I turned my tankard around in my hands, examining the decoration. She'd probably come to tell me how I would be executed. Hopefully not by that horrible Sif.

"Your Grace." Röskva bowed to Maya, behaving as if I weren't there. She brought a jug and two horn cups. The jug was transparent, made of crystal, filled with green leaves and steaming water. My eyes popped out and my stomach growled in terror. I managed to keep quiet until the door shut behind Röskva.

"It's that stink! Where does it come from?! I smelled it in your sleeping room too!"

Maya shifted uncomfortably. "I... I washed myself..."

"This, this... this is that concoction from Gróa! The poison, that mixture! Are you sick too?"

"Magni, this is mint. It's delicious. It's very refreshing."

I tried to hide my nose in my tankard and breathe in the aroma of the mead. "I'm refreshed for the rest of my life," I wheezed, once I finished sneezing and coughing at once, having nearly drowned myself. "Keep it away from me. Sit here, so I can't smell it. Dread Gods. I mean, good Gods. How did it go with Gróa? Will she give Thor the refreshing tea too? He'll kill her if she does."

"Many things can kill him first. The goats try every time. Did you know they were afraid of heights? Now that I've seen what they can do I'm also afraid of heights. I'm surprised there is anything left of that chariot."

"It can't be destroyed," I muttered.

She ignored me. "I'm sure this could be done in a more efficient way. So, I asked Thjálfi how he found Thor. He said he had a little birdie on his shoulder, telling him where to go."

My hand tightened on the tankard, bending it out of shape a bit.

"No, no," Maya said quickly, "a literal little birdie. Named, I would assume, Loki. The birdie instructed Thjálfi to tell Thor a troll had arrived to marry Thrud."

Troll. That word seemed to cause something in my memory to open for a blink and immediately close. Troll...

"Thjálfi blames himself," sighed Maya. "Poor kid."

"It's my fault. I told Hrungnir to defend."

"Actually, I used my crystal shield."

"Mhm, good." I scowled at her bragging.

"The one that reflected Hillevi's arrow and that man's knife. I think it reflected some chunks of the whetstone."

"Good for you." Hillevi's arrow... Troll...

"Onto Thor's *head*," she specified, sounding angry for some reason. "Could you listen to me? He threw his hammer at the golem, then my shield reflected the whetstone back at him and now I will stand accused of killing a God."

"But you did nothing wrong."

"I had a shield," said Maya shortly taking a sip of the poisonous brew. She looked like she was really enjoying it. Maybe it was a woman thing. "As you *know*, I'm just human. He is a God, so are you. Thjálfi is Thor's favourite. I'm – I'm nothing. Who do you think will be blamed? It's all about rules and hierarchy, Magni. That is why I have to call Odin His Grace or All-Father and he calls me 'child'."

"That's unfair."

She rolled her eyes. "Would you kill a boar?"

"No," I immediately answered, "because they are holy to Lady Freya."

"Oh, for Gods' – deer then?"

"Sure," I said. "I did that many times. You just have to know where to hit. I can show you if you want."

"Thanks, but no thanks. What I mean is that even you have two sets of rules. You say you wouldn't kill. You also don't think killing deer is killing."

"But... but that's food."

"So imagine that you are you and I am the deer. Which one would you keep alive?"

"That's stupid," I huffed. "People talk and deer don't."

"Cats don't talk. Do you eat them?"

"No, because they're holy to—"

"Leave it, leave it! All you need to know is that somebody will die for all this and it won't be you." She sounded oddly cheerful.

"The wall," I reminded her. "I'll die for that."

"You won't," said Maya, waving my concerns away. She looked around, then leaned towards me. I did the same, excited despite not knowing why. Before she had a chance to say a word, Röskva appeared in the doorway.

"Your Grace, Your Grace. Her Grace Freya has arrived."

The first yourgrace sounded much more polite than the second one.

"Pink wine," said Freya, pushing past Röskva. "Lots of it. And a blindfold, this place is hideous. I can't understand how anybody can live like this. It looks like some sort of fortress."

"It does," I livened up, "doesn't it?"

"A...blindfold, Your Grace?"

"It was a joke, honey, which means I was not serious. Pink wine will do. And not in one of those things. I'm sure Sif has crystal goblets like civilised Gods and not some..." She glared at me, then my tankard and I blushed, although I didn't know why. "Some others. Are you still here?"

"Someone sat on a bee," muttered Maya to no one in particular as Röskva confusedly yourgraced, seeming unsure who to hate the most for the time being, then sprinted away.

"Pumpkin, don't irrrrrrritate me."

Now both of them were drumming on the table in the exact identical manner. I refilled my tankard from the barrel simply because looking at them made me nervous. The cold meats were still tempting, but now with Lady Freya around I didn't dare to touch anything.

"Your Grace," said Röskva. "Should I stand here and refill your goblet?"

"Get out," said Freya, "and take your attitude with you. Shut this door, then shut the next one, then the one after that, and when you run out of doors to shut, go to Sif's basement and take all the other servants with you. We need absolute privacy."

"Your G-graces," Röskva whispered and disappeared.

"I'm here on an important mission," said Freya once the door shut.

"I am not in the mood for any more important missions, thank you."

"I'm not here to ask about your mood. Loki?"

Maya grimaced like someone who just drank refreshing tea. "No shifters, apart from you."

"Oo," I remembered. "Brisingamen?"

Freya pointed at her neck and I quieted. Good Gods, what a masterpiece. Perhaps one day I might dare to ask her to take it off and let me examine every tiniest ring and weld. If it was even called a "weld" when you couldn't see it. I realised I was staring and withdrew, my blush so hot that it probably even made my hair redder. Freya kind of squinted at me, poured herself a goblet of wine, emptied it in one gulp, then immediately refilled it. "Maya, darling, you might have forgotten this. It was a quite emotional time. After you returned from your mission, I mentioned leaving the Nine to you. It is time to learn more. What are you doing, Magni?"

"I'm going away, so you can talk."

"Oh, for my sake. If I just wanted to talk to her, I wouldn't have come to this place, would I? I have an offer for you both. I will ensure that your lives are spared at the Assembly if you take an oath to help me."

"Help with what?" I asked.

"I will tell you once you take that oath."

"Then we're not doing it," said Maya, "because you are going to ask for something we shouldn't do. I know you."

"What I tell you must remain only between the three of us and absolutely nobody else."

"Ravens," I muttered.

"One is in Jötunheim, watching the army there, one is watching the gap in the wall. Loki..." She gestured vaguely and Maya seemed annoyed, but said nothing. "As you will know, he's given birth to Odin's horse..."

"Sleipnir," I nodded. "How did Loki do that?"

"With great pleasure," hissed Maya. I'd swear she sounded jealous. As if it were Loki's fault that she was not a Goddess and couldn't do things like birthing magical horses. "What do you want?"

"Language, petal, language. I'm still your—"

"Yes?"

My gaze kept moving between the two of them. I could hear what they were saying, but I had no idea what they were talking about.

"Thor declared his will to participate in the Assembly and Odin can't pretend it didn't happen, because there were witnesses," said Freya drily. "Therefore, if Thor lives, the Assembly cannot take place until three days after his return. Some of the Gods have already arrived, since Magni's fate was going to be decided tomorrow. Which means that Odin will have Sif screeching at him until Thor recovers and I'm not sure who is going to get the blame for that."

"Probably me," said Maya, "since I am nothing but a mere human." She emphasised the last word and Freya pursed her lips, looking to the left, meeting my eyes, averting her gaze as fast as she could. I hadn't done anything to her! Apart from when I said I wanted to sell her to the highest bidder. But other than that, nothing.

"You will take that oath," Freya said. "The outcome of it all will depend on what happens to Thor." She paused. "Luckily it was his head, not some vital organ. Nevertheless, there is still Sif and the gap in the wall. I will have to be very persuasive. Oath, honeys, oath. You will never share a single word said here with anybody else. Ever. Torture, blackmail, bribery, I don't care, not a word."

"That depends on what it is," insisted Maya.

"Oath."

"Tell us first."

"Oath or I go away and very soon you die."

"Fine, fine. Do I swear on Odin's staff?"

The corners of Freya's mouth went up, showing just a bit of her teeth. I felt as if a horse had kicked me in the gut. I'd seen that expression before. Many times. But where, when? Who was it? The image remained on the edge of my memory, as I kept trying to pull it out and it stubbornly refused. There was something wrong with me. I closed my eyes and the featureless face was replaced by a big, juicy peach. I could almost smell it...

"Magni," urged Freya.

"Ah, yes, I swear on all that is dear to me that I will not say a word about what will be said here. This is my oath and I make it freely."

"See, Maya," said Freya triumphantly, "this is how one takes an oath, not a 'whatever, I swear then'. You better keep that oath, both of you, or you *will* lose everything that you have ever held dear."

"I don't have anything," I said.

She nodded towards Maya. "You have her, Thor, Heimdall, Thjálfi. Everyone has something or someone. Still no Loki?"

Maya shook her head, her lips pursed. She seemed to be Freya's complete opposite, then she'd make a move or make a face and they'd nearly look like sisters.

Freya exhaled slowly. "There are two Universes. One is ours, the Nine Worlds as we know them. The other one has...separated." She produced a branch. "I brought special devices to explain it, especially to you, Magni. This is a branch."

I looked at it closely just in case it wasn't.

"Here, at this end," Freya pointed, "it is just one branch. Then at one point it splits into two. One of them goes left, one goes right. This is what happened. There was one Universe, and then it split into two."

"Nonsense," shrugged Maya.

"Darling, don't make me slap you. So, one branch, and then, all of a sudden – two. They grow from the same stem, split evenly, which is not exactly what happened, but that's the branch I found. This one is the Nine. This one is the Tenth, which contains all of the Nine and more."

"That's not how branches work," I pointed out and Freya rolled her eyes before emptying her goblet.

"It's a metaphor, son of your father. It means that I am trying to explain something to you using examples, because otherwise you wouldn't understand it."

"I don't either," said Maya.

"I've got a second presentation. This," said Freya, "is an apple."

"We can see that," Maya answered. I gawked. Was it an apple or an *apple*? Freya grabbed a perfectly fine, sharp iron knife, glared at it with her lips pursed, cut off the top part of the apple, put the knife down, looked around for something, didn't find it and wiped her hands in her gown. I sniffed the air, trying to look inconspicuous. It was just an apple.

"Thor doesn't believe in napkins, I think," said Maya.

"There's a cloth," I said, offended. Both of them looked at it as if I was offering them a dead rat.

"Soldiers live in better conditions," scoffed Freya. "We should go into Sif's wing, it's a bit on the frumpy side, but at least reasonably clean. As I was saying..."

"My father picked all this," I interrupted, "and I love it like it is."

"Lips moving, still talking. When I put the parts of the apple together, they look like one again. Once I start pulling them away from each other, they become two. One of them is smaller, one is larger. The smaller one is our Universe, the Nine. The larger is the Tenth."

"There is one world bigger than all Nine?" asked Maya, her eyebrows wandering up her forehead. Now she and I must have looked identical. Except the beard. And everything else.

Freya sighed. "They call it Earth, all of it. Let me show you..." She produced more apples and started cutting them, taking breaks to glower at the knife, then at my cloth, which I had only used a few times. "We have nine apples now. The tips are our worlds. The table is the other world." She removed the tips and piled them up together. "This, for instance, is Midgard. It is a part of what they call

'Europe'. Midgard is huge, but Europe is bigger. Now, the interesting thing is that Jötunheim is a part of what they call Norway, and apparently Norway is somehow also a part of Europe..." She pushed away the apples, produced another one and cut two chunks from it. "Like this. Who makes a hole in the table? Do you throw bones in there? Midgard, Jötunheim, both come from one apple called Europe."

My eyes kept moving between apples that were also other worlds that were one and had Jötunheim in Midgard. "Do we have to remember all this?" I groaned.

"Not at all, I can write it down for you later." Her smirk made me wonder whether she could see through my moustache that I also knew how to purse my lips. The sun was starting to go down. She would find out very soon what the hole in the table was for.

"You said they all split," interrupted Maya. "Who went where, then?"

"Oh, this is the strangest thing, pumpkin. The lives of people split as well. The same person became two, one of them in the Nine, one in the Tenth. But! Not the Gods. I am only here, there is no other Freya anywhere, and if someone mentions Loki, I'll stab them with this...thing."

"This knife is art," I muttered. I was waiting.

"You'd better get me some light, not your art," huffed Freya and a blink later her wish came true. Her chair hit the ground as flames burst out from the cut-out in the middle of the table. "That is dangerous!" she shrieked, pointing the knife at me. "I could have burned my hair, my dress! Is this your idea of a joke?!"

"It's Thor's," I said politely, "and it's actually very simple crystal magic."

Maya snorted.

Freya ostentatiously checked her sleeves for burn marks. "Candles," she said to Maya, "torches, even a fire pit, but a fire table? How long ago did Thor get hit on the head and how many times? What was I saying, darling?"

"Lives of all people split and there is one world that holds all of the Nine and more than that. How do you know all this?"

Freya picked the knife, stared at the fire, then inserted the tip of the blade into the flames, turning it around lazily. The tip turned cherry red, then brighter. It was a thin knife and I watched, fascinated, waiting. "The Norns," she just said.

"The Norns are concepts. They are time itself. You can't speak to time."

"What's the point in asking if you're just going to be a contrarian?"

"I'm not a contrarian!"

"The Norns are a concept or representation, yes, but so are all of us Gods. What do I represent, what does Freyr represent?"

I missed Maya's answer, fascinated, watching the tip becoming orange and the dull, cherry red crawling towards the handle. I'd have to fix this knife later.

"What price did you pay for that?" asked Maya and I began to listen again.

"The prophecy."

"Hearing I ask from the—"

"No, not now! Not in front of him! The prophecy was the price. It must be shared with Odin whether I want it to or – this is hot!" Freya cried out and dropped the knife on the table.

"That's how fire works," I said, picking up the knife with two calloused fingers, dropping it on the ground before the oak started smoking. "It's hot. I can explain it to you one day."

"Stop," begged Maya, "both of you, we don't need any more wars between Gods!"

"I should have tied you up and gagged," said Freya. "Then I could talk without interruptions. In some other place that doesn't set itself on fire. As I was saying, there had always been one Universe, the Nine Worlds, until suddenly there were two. I believe this might be the reason why Frigg no longer looks into the future at all. Because, you see, if you look at this branch... it splits, too. But one part is shorter."

"Which part is that?" asked Maya, her voice tense.

"Ask Frigg and see if she answers. I have an idea, though. You once noticed that the prophecy didn't mention me. I believe there is a reason for that. Maya?"

"No shifters."

"I found out..." Freya lowered her voice. "I found out how to travel from our Universe into the other one."

"And?"

"And I intend to leave the Nine to Odin and his wisdom, taking the Tenth for myself, or rather for us. Myself, Freyr, you two, Idunn of course, Thrud, Vanadís, the twins, you know, everyone we will need and everyone I trust."

"Why me?" I asked.

"Because you look enough like your father to make them believe again."

"Again?"

Freya picked a slice of an apple and began to fiddle with it instead of eating it. I couldn't stop staring, saliva gathering in my mouth. Those apples couldn't have possibly been Idunn's, but what if they grew near and... "When the worlds split, the Gods remained here, in the Nine. The people know that we walk around them, talk to them, sometimes marry them or—"

"Rape them," Maya said.

"Have encounters with them, darling. Thor kept attacking Jötunheim, but not the Norway place, obviously. Odin walked around Midgard, having encounters, but not in the Europe. And so on. Those who remembered us there have died, passing the stories to their children, who then passed them to their own. Those stories changed over time, but the saddest thing is that they began to see them as just that. Stories, Sagas, songs. Entertainment. Eventually they came up with a new God. Named God." Freya's eyes, when she rolled them, shone red, like Odin's. "That's how imaginative that God is. And there's only one, arrogant enough to say he can do everything. Who has that kind of time? His believers are starting to spread like a disease. We must stop that. Once Thor here, I, and our... uhm... you..."

"Just checking," I said. "Have you been inhaling herbs?"

"Son of Thor, you may be a God, but I've got more experience at it. Don't irritate me." She returned her attention to Maya. "You will notice, honey, that I have not named one world. Ásgard."

A strange, tickling thought – once, long ago, there had been someone somewhere who called me "Thor".

"Or Müspelheim."

"Why would I want to travel to Müspelheim? It's even worse than this place. I believe Ásgard is an exception. It is not a part of Europe or Norway or other – I don't know everything yet. But I believe that Ásgard there is like Ásgard here. Only the new one is empty, awaiting us. Ready."

"Yes," said Maya, "that's great. How did you learn about the Europe, the Norway, the new Ásgard? The new God?"

"Remember your oath, petal," muttered Freya. "Petals. I found a passage a while ago. It's possible to use it to travel back and forth between the Universes. It's in Jötunheim *and* in Norway. They build ships and travel like that, since they can't shift; only Gods can shift, and they don't have us there."

"They have that new one," I said.

"I tried on my own already," said Freya, ignoring me. "I have obtained the favour of men in the Tenth..."

"She slept with them," Maya explained to the fire.

"...then sent them on journeys in search of the new Ásgard. The first one forgot about me the moment he found it, returned to tell me that he gave it a name of his own and that he would gather men and women to live there under his command. He died in an unfortunate accident soon after. I sent another one, who returned to tell me it was possible to sail around the entire world, that he had stayed all winter, that he gave it *his own* name, and yes, guess what, that he would gather men and women who would live there under his command. He, too, had an unfortunate accident. I began to get excited, though. What power does the new Ásgard have to make those men forget about *me*?!"

Maya snorted.

"Your lack of respect for me is very disconcerting, pumpkin. Don't make me regret telling you all this. Clearly, I cannot trust mortals. Imagine what would happen if we let humans come over here and see Ásgard for themselves! First, you will build another wall around the new Ásgard. Then and only then we can start allowing people inside. Ones I choose."

"Jötnar would build you a wall for one glimpse of Brisingamen," said Maya.

"There are no jötnar anymore, darling, only humans."

"What—" I started and ran out of words.

"No, no, I misspoke. You see, in their one world Thor no longer attacked anybody. Therefore, as the stories were passed down, Norwayans started believing that the jötnar, the real ice giants, lived elsewhere. The dark elves began to mix with the jötnar and the humans. Since they were to be found in the same world and didn't live under the ground forging..."

"That's not what they do..."

"Petal, stop interrupting me. The ones who still believe are convinced they all live in Midgard, while the real jötnar are being slain by Thor in some other place they can't see. The real dark elves, ones that forged my Brisingamen, must live in some other place they can't see." Freya turned silent for a while. "Stories. Bragi can change reality, but—"

"I knew it!"

"Sweetie," hissed Freya, "be quiet, or else you'll find out what 'or else' means. Bragi can't create that reality. If they can't see Thor in a wedding gown getting married to a jötunn king or an eight-legged horse that Loki gave birth to, that's all it's going to be. Stories, very memorable ones, but still. Entertainment. They know Thor has a son named Magni, that he saved Thor from the mighty troll Hrungnir—"

"Already?" interrupted Maya.

"Saved?" I interrupted.

"—so what? Stories. We will travel there in the guise of 'humans' ourselves. We will assume new names. Once we have settled in the new Ásgard, once the wall and our halls stand ready, we will bring over Idunn and give her a garden ten times as big as that patch she has here. We will bring my Freyr when I am certain of his safety. There will be no Odin, no 'wisdom', no Loki, no Týr babbling about just and unjust. I will decide what is or isn't just." Freya cleared her throat. "This calls for a toast. Skál, my darlings, for the new Ásgard where nobody but me rules!"

None of us moved.

"What is it? Have you forgotten how to drink? Surely not you, Magni. You must agree this calls for a toast."

"We haven't agreed to anything," said Maya quietly.

Only the whisper of the wind and the subdued hiss of the flames cut through the silence until Freya's goblet landed on the floor, breaking into sharp shards of glass. "But it's – it's obvious," she stammered, "it's – you will die otherwise. Magni...? You don't want her to die?"

"Her?"

"If she disagrees, then she must die," sighed Freya. "It's a shame, but she knows too much."

"Then I also disagree!"

"That would mean both of you must die. Double shame. And just when you've found happiness again."

"Have I?"

"What happiness?" croaked Maya. "He's haunted by those memories, this – I don't even know what it is—"

"Magni, dear," cooed Freya. "Tell us about your dreams."

I wished I could refill my tankard without her seeing. "I don't know. I don't really have any."

"You do," insisted Maya, "and they are horrible."

"Your first lover," said Freya softly, touching my hand. "I'm sorry you had to split."

Maya let out an indeterminate sound. I reached for a chunk of meat just to gain a bit of time. All this had suddenly become very strange. "It's okay," I muttered. "I don't remember him. Eh, since you're the Goddess of love, do you..."

"It was meant to end, petal. It ended right when it had to and the way it had to. It's perfectly fine not to remember. There will be others."

"Oh?" I cheered up.

"In the tenth world," Freya specified. "So many others!"

I didn't know what to answer to that. "So many" seemed like an awful lot of work, especially when I had a wall to build. But if Heimdall... I meant, if someone were to...

"You've taken it all away," said Maya icily. "Gone. He doesn't remember."

"There is a lot awaiting you there," said Freya to me. "Happy life, filled with love. I imagine there will be sex in it as well. Poor Maya will never understand it, but I know you do. Or would you prefer to die?"

"N-no, I wouldn't."

"I'm glad to hear that, since if Maya were to betray me, you would be the one to die. The other way round, too. So maybe you should try to convince her not to break her oath and to follow us to the tenth world, where we can all be happy."

"Would I get to say something about the new Ásgard and all?" I asked.

"Obviously," Freya said after a thoughtful pause. "You are a God after all. Once we got rid of the impersonator."

I would make sure the fruit of Idunn's garden was shared, giving away all that went to waste here. All of the "humans" would be equal. Except for the ones who fought for Odin. They would stop anyway, because we would share everything. Maybe not my red brick hall with crystal magic and a table just like this one. And not the forge. But apart from that, everything.

"Don't trust her," hissed Maya, interrupting my reverie, "she's nothing but—"

"Maya, darling, those memories Eir and I have taken away? They can be brought back."

It would be so wonderful if she could keep us alive and then take us away from here. She said that thing that was so alien. "Other lovers." Because, even though that was here and not in the other place, I'd had a lot of dreams recently. Just not ones I'd want Maya to know about. I knew I should feel ashamed of them, but I wasn't and I only felt a bit ashamed that I wasn't feeling ashamed. Maybe Heimdall could come with us, too.

"Deal?"

"Deal," I said, hoping that in the light of the fire they couldn't see how red my face was and that they definitely couldn't read minds. I had no idea what I just agreed to.

"I guess we're going, then," said Maya, resigned, lifting herself up.

"Not tonight," said Freya. "Tonight get some rest. Don't forget you've made an oath."

I didn't even say goodbye when they left. My head was full of future. Bits of what had been said kept bouncing inside my head. Memories taken away... the new world where everyone would be equal, I would make sure of that... all of them naming themselves humans when humans were the worst, why would they not name themselves something normal, like jötnar... the son of my father, Freya called me, it felt so odd, so good... *please let him survive this*. The new Ásgard, free from Odin the Murderer, Sif the – the Sif, Thor himself. I would find the God named God and talk to him, explain that we didn't have to fight. Maybe he could just join us in the new Ásgard. I would be Magni the Protector, Magni the Peaceful. No Valhalla, no armies that keep slaying each other for Odin's amusement. Other lovers. If Lady Freya said so it had to be true.

Halfway through my Gods-knew-which tankard of mead I decided to go to bed when I set my tunic on fire, even if only a bit and by accident.

"Your Grace," said Röskva, sounding triumphant. "His Grace Thor is back. We are afraid that you will have to leave."

It was way too early for important news. One of my eyes didn't really want to open, the headache thumping. It took me a while to understand what she'd just said and suddenly I was completely awake. "He is alive! Is that what you mean? He is? Is everything alright, is he well? Of course I will leave, can I just see him for a blink and... and see him?"

Röskva looked taken aback. "There are guest chambers," she said, oddly uncertain. "He is..." She paused. "Alive, yes. Please follow me, Your Grace."

She led me to chambers almost as big as Thor's, only missing the view, the balcony, the bench, the bed, and the fireplace with benches inside it. Thjálfi, she explained, would come to pick me up once it was possible to visit Thor. I kept grinning and thanking her, which seemed to upset her. Still, she produced an apologetic half-smile that shocked me after the previous displays of hatred. I was even offered something to break my fast with.

I ate, drinking nothing but water, promising myself to never even look at a tankard or a barrel again. Thjálfi kept not appearing. My headache was almost gone and I decided that I wouldn't anyone stop me, even Röskva. I marched towards what used to be my bedroom this very morning, opened the door as quietly as I could and gasped together with Thjálfi.

"My lord," he said, looking under my arm, then over my shoulder, "I was just on my way to... coming for..."

He was searching for an escape so clearly that I felt goosebumps. "How is he?" I asked, almost angry.

"Hard to say," muttered Thjálfi, eyeing the space between my legs.

"I hope he's not dead?"

"N-no. He's... Perhaps you should see for yourself, my lord." He bolted away at speed that sent my heart right into my throat.

Expecting the worst, I tiptoed towards the pile of furs. A giant, red-haired man lay stretched on the bed, a grimace of pain on his face, the rock sticking out of his forehead exactly like it had been before.

I inhaled sharply.

"Thjálfi," muttered Thor. "Leave me."

"It's not Thjálfi," I said.

Thor's head slowly turned towards me. His eyes were red, as was the scar tissue around the rock. The wound had healed as fast as mine would. Just not the way I expected. Mjölnir was at his belt, but he didn't look as if he'd be able to lift it. I grabbed a heavy wooden stool and sat next to him. The sound made him grimace and turn away again.

I wouldn't take Thor's hand. He'd killed my kin. My mother. He was the only "family" I had left. I hated loving him, I couldn't explain where it came from, I would ask Freya to take that away from me, but not now, because now I *had* to reach for his hand, hoping he would protest, hoping he wouldn't.

"Does it hurt?" I asked quietly.

"Only when I breathe," he rumbled, a voice that came from somewhere deep below the ground. "When I speak and when I don't. When I move and when I don't. All through the day and all through the night. But otherwise it's fine. Just a surface wound."

"I'm sorry."

"Mhhmm. You're my son."

"I am."

"What's your name?"

It took me a blink or two to really hear his words. I dropped his hand. "I guess I'll be going. Good luck with your recovery," I said. My eyes must have become as red as his. My legs refused to cooperate, my feet so heavy that not even I could lift them.

Thor grumbled, turning, his feverish eyes searching for me. Grimacing in pain he felt with his hand until he found my knee. "Son. It's not like that. I don't remember... this thing took a lot away from me. So I was told. I don't even know what I don't know. I know you are my son, because Thjálfi told me my son was here and because I can see what you look like. I've been told I've got a wife somewhere. This is my hall. My hammer can destroy almost anything. It almost destroyed me. I don't know how any of this happened. Can you sit closer to me?"

I knew how it felt not to remember.

I sat on the bed and took his hand again. I wouldn't cry. "Do you...remember your name?"

"Sure I do. Odin." I gasped and the corners of his mouth went up, just a bit, dropping immediately, as if even that exhausted him. "Nah. Kidding. I'm Thor. Always have been, always will." His eyes seemed to close and open on their own, as if he was trying to see, but couldn't stand the light. "Son, what do you drink? Because that woman has been giving me some sort of bitter poison all this time..."

I scowled. Gróa was trying to refresh him. No wonder he'd lost memories. "There's mead," I said. "Ale. I meant, water."

"Mmhm. Mead. There's a barrel outside, you will find some brass tankards..."

I stifled a slightly hysterical, inappropriate chuckle. He'd forgotten his wife's name, but not where the mead barrel was. I helped him sit up. Sweat ran down his white face surrounded by orange, flame-like hair, the long beard. Like mine.

"Tell me about yourself, son," he rumbled once he was sitting down, equipped with a tankard. "Skál. Tell me all I should know."

My mind immediately went blank. I lost even the few memories I had left. "So, I'm your son. My mother, eh, died. She was not your wife. Her name is Sif, by the way. Your wife's." I paused. I was talking rubbish. "I've built a wall around Ásgard. You broke through it, so now I'm going to die."

"No."

"I took an oath."

"Good. Anyone who tries to hurt you will die as well. This is my oath, so now there are two. What is your name?"

"M—"

It wasn't my body that froze, but my mind, time, space.

Módi. Our name is Módi.

But I am Magni.

You are too weak. You've already forgiven everything and he never said he was sorry.

What – who is this? Go away.

I'm not going anywhere. Go to sleep, child. You've been up for too long.

Leave me alone! What are you?! Leave me alone!

A vision flickered in front of me, a terrible one. Blood. My fingers entwined with someone's hair. Fire, lots of fire. Odin's red eye. Maya's angry face. One of the missing memories.

I didn't want them back.

I gulped some mead and it nearly came out through my nose. "Magni," I said, forcing my lips and tongue to move and the air to come through my throat. "That is my name. Magni."

"I like it."

"You... you chose it."

The mead tasted bitter. You called me "Mighty", because you felt your son should have a big name, but I found that out from Mother, because you never spoke to me. I learned to forge to be more like you. I forged myself a hammer, proud that I could use my tools to make more tools, like magic, but real. I wanted to show the hammer to you, but you threw me out, because you were busy. Having sex with my mother. You destroyed everything that I had ever known and killed the few people who cared about me. I should remember how to hate you. I didn't.

"Good choice. It fits you," he muttered and now my throat felt strange, as though someone were choking me, and that pressure inside my eyes was back. As if they were swelling. "Magni, my son, I don't care who tries to harm you, even if it's Odin himself and his entire army. Anyone who so much as threatens to put their finger on you is going to speak to Mjölnir first."

"You can't," I said. "You're the protector of Ásgard. Blood has never been spilled here. Except from your forehead, I guess."

"My forehead? Ah, that forehead. Rrrummm. Do you have a wife? I'd like to meet her."

"Ummm. No. I don't have a wife."

"A lover?"

"Not anymore."

"Mmhmm. Did I... I'm sorry. I really don't remember things. Did I used to know her?"

I stiffened.

Thor was friends with Loki, who could be a man or a woman, who had sex with a horse, then gave birth to Sleipnir. Thor's fury at the idea of marrying King Thrymr had turned a whole City into dust. In Jötunheim there were men who had sex with other men, but they did not love each other, or at least never said it. Once a man and a woman had children, the more the better, so we wouldn't become extinct, he and she could do anything they felt like. In Midgard there had been a woman. Had she been my lover? No. Not even if there was nobody left in the Nine.

Why was it so hard to say to my father? What would he think? Why did I care about what he would think?

"Hmm?"

"It was a man," I said, my body rigid, preparing for I didn't know what.

Thor was silent for a while. "I'm sorry," he finally growled, "but I thought you said it was a man."

I felt the hairs on my arms stand up. It was coming. "Y-yes. It was a man."

"And then?"

My eyes opened wider. "And then, uh, nothing. No wife, no woman. I'm not..." I swallowed. "I—"

"And before?"

I had no idea what to say. I just let out something of a grunt.

"So there was only 'a' man? Just one?" He didn't sound disgusted. Just surprised. "Are you sure you are my son? I'm sorry, that wasn't funny. I need more mead to be funny. How old are you?"

I took his tankard and went to refill it, together with mine. I had a feeling I was still drunk from last night. I had completely lost track of my own age by now, even though now I could count. Too many memories had left me. Sixteen? Twenty? Something in between? "Old enough," I said, handing him the tankard. "Skál."

"Just one man," he mused. "When there are so many in the Nine. My son can have anything and anybody you want. Just take it."

My emotions were all over the place. That was what had happened. He'd found Járnsaxa, wanted her, so he just took her. Sif didn't like that. The City fell, because Thor wanted Mother and took her.

"Son," said Thor, turning to face me again. His red eyes and the rock in his forehead made me shiver. "You can find beauty every-where. Every woman, old, young, human, Goddess. The jötunn women are special, it's like they are different even from all the others that are different. What I want to say is that your mother was special. I may not know her name, but she was special to me. You are proof."

I couldn't talk, couldn't remember how to.

"You don't have to go to Jötunheim, though. You could look here, in Ásgard."

I quickly got rid of the vision of Heimdall's eyes, shaded by those eyelashes, those lips, which in my dream— "I haven't got time. I will either die in three days, and then there's no point, or I won't, and then I will have plenty of time."

"Three days is time aplenty. What else will you do? Sit here with me? Why is it three days?"

Now that his eyes sought mine, I felt myself blushing and stared at my tankard. I could just drink for three days. Two and a half by now. "The Assembly is in three days," I muttered.

"*My* son can get a man in three days. Or two. Men, not days. Or a whole hand. That's four."

"Five," I muttered, feeling my face trying to smile.

"Even better. See? Now go and have a good time."

"Not before you tell me why that rock is still in your head. She couldn't do it?"

Thor groaned. "I'm very thirsty. Skál."

"Skál. Mead is dripping down your beard."

"And yours."

His eyesight seemed unaffected. He was also right. "I thought Gróa could do anything."

"Eh. She probably could. I am not proud of this, rrrrrrummmm. Just so you know. Her witchery..."

"It's herbal and ritual magic." Gods knew I've been told that enough times while I sat there vomiting the refreshing tea.

"I call it witchery and you would too if you could see it. She was mumbling some spells and grinding some herbs and whatnot into a paste. Then she made me drink those leaves with hot water. Rrrrrummmm. Only a witch would make a man drink that."

I quickly took a gulp from my tankard.

"She was massaging this paste into my forehead, chanting something like witches do, like my head wasn't aching already. She said she was out of something or other and sent her husband away. It became dark and he still didn't return. She stopped with her paste and chanting, even with the poison brew. All worried. Some women are like that, you go away for a moment and they're crying. I promised her that his death would be avenged. I was being nice. It made her cry harder."

I wanted to hide my face in my hands and cry, too.

"I promised her that once he died, he would go straight to Valhalla, he looked like a great fighter. She lost it. Can you believe it? She just cried and cried, ran outside, then returned, instead of taking the rock out. I yelled and she didn't seem to hear me, just kept repeating his name, whatever it was. I'm bad with names. So... I am not happy about this, you understand? It was an accident." He paused.

My grip on the tankard tightened until I bent it. "What did you do to her?"

"I grabbed her arm," he continued, sadly, "and it broke."

I gasped.

"I couldn't help it."

"You couldn't help breaking her arm? How?!"

"I didn't know it would be so fragile! I just wanted to stop her from the crying and the running, remind her that she had a God with a rock sticking out of his head, and she just kept repeating 'where is my husband', like anybody cared where he was when I had a rock—" He groaned. "Hurts."

"Like anybody cared? Did you just say that?"

"You can get a new husband," said Thor, "but you can't get a new me. Or a new head."

"Asshole."

"Why would I want a new asshole? Son, I know you wanted to save Ásgard, but you made a big mistake with that wall. We couldn't fly back inside until Thjálfi pointed out that golem. That was very lucky, or I would have had to stay in Midgard forever. You should have thought of that. Good job otherwise. Son, tell me something. Loki, he's my best friend, I remember him. Where is Loki? I'd like to see him. He's good fun."

I crushed the tankard and some remaining mead tricked down my trousers. "He's away."

"Aaah. Shame. You'd like him." He rrrummm-ed again. "Magni, son, what is that Assembly?"

∾

I woke up with a headache. The place where I was both seemed familiar and wasn't. It took me a while to recall that these were the guest chambers. It was the bed that was smaller, not me having grown larger overnight.

The light hurt my eyes when I took a peek outside. No balcony, no forest. The view was on the courtyard and I could see people working outside. Not bad, just not as nice. Unlike my dreams, which were very nice. Very entertaining. Inspiring. Recently my dreams had been getting more and more—

The grin awakening on my face disappeared abruptly when I remembered how the evening ended. I had told Thor about the wedding gown and King Thrymr. He had insisted it never happened. The more I told him about it, the more he had insisted it was all a lie. I didn't want to make him too upset, so instead I told him about Loki giving birth to Sleipnir. My father turned green and told me to leave him alone for a while, like for instance three days.

My father.

He fell for women and took them, just like that, because they had something special. What could have ever been special about Sif? She looked and sounded like a vulture both before and after she shifted. Maybe she was very good in bed... My stomach protested, still half-full of mead. I drank some water, then more, until the jug was empty. If my head was hurting, his must have felt like Mjölnir struck it, with the piece of whetstone seemingly there to stay.

I wouldn't "take" anyone. How could I do that? Did Thor just go to women and say "I'm going to take you"?! My eyes opened wide when an unwanted image of – of Niedomira came back to me, a memory hidden until just now. I could never behave like that! Although if the visitor turned out to be someone else, wearing armour that he needed help with, a sword that needed some care, then... then what? He wouldn't even look at me, I thought, before remembering that he had. He smiled and called me "Sire". Like nobody else before or after. Was it some sort of hint that I didn't understand?

I must have been puce and could only thank the Gods and the

key in the lock that nobody could see me right now. How did people and Gods just know those things? The taking?

Freyr, the God of ecstasy and fertility and sex. He would know. I couldn't just demand a God to come over here to explain to me how to take someone, but nicely. Also, Freyr was a monster, the Crop-Destroyer, I reminded myself sternly. I would never talk to him. Anyway, if everyone else had managed without his help, so would I. Thor said there were many others who were also special. It's just that I didn't care about anybody else and this one was...working. I couldn't just go and interrupt him. By Freya, *how* did people ever arrange anything?!

Miserably glad to have something that distracted me from my diminishing, yet still present headache and dark thoughts about the Assembly, I broke my fast before heading towards Sessrúmnir. Maya sat in the garden, staring into space and fiddling with something red. My feet seemed to grow roots for just a blink. A straw-berry. I remembered those. A straw-berry.

"The Assembly is coming in two days," she said, swallowed the fruit, then smiled. I had no idea how she even noticed me. "I can't wait for it to be over."

"You can't wait to die?"

"We won't die. Granny Frigg knows the future, all of it. I don't, but I have dreams, premonitions. I had one last night. You and I were in a small tent. There was a brazier and two beds. I sat on one of the beds and you sat on the other one, holding another man's hand. He was a dark elf." Maya paused and finally looked my way. "I think that's it. It wasn't much of a dream, really. Aha, you seemed quite nervous."

I felt myself blush, getting nervous from just hearing it, wondering what dark elves were like and if maybe Heimdall was one.

"I don't believe there's ever been a single brazier in Ásgard. We will live long enough for this to happen, it won't be in the coming two days, and it won't be here."

"The tenth world?" I whispered.

"I don't know. A place with tents and braziers and dark elves."

"Are you sure that's really the future? That we will live?"

Maya's dark eyes met mine. She wasn't smiling. "No," she said. "I'm not sure. That was a very handsome dark elf, for your information. Have you eaten yet?"

Processing all those sentences next to each other took me long enough that she repeated the question with a little frown. "Yes," I said, "I mean, no. I mean, a-actually I wanted to ask you what it means when someone calls you 'Sire'."

She shrugged. "Nobody has ever called *me* that. Why?"

"Anyway, Heimdall," I said innocently after a pause long enough to divert her attention. "What is he like?"

Maya gave me a very particular look. "What is he like? Heimdall stands at the crossing of the worlds, guarding it from those who understand how it works and know where it is. That's all he does, day and night. What can he be like?"

"You don't like him?"

"I hate people who are pretty and they know it," she huffed. "He's just like Freyr and Freya, don't get me star – oh no! Magni! He called you 'Sire'! Was it in...? Was he...? Don't tell me you and Heimdall...!" Her hand flew towards her mouth, her eyes open in shock.

I almost managed not to respond, but "how...?" somehow made it out.

"I can't believe it," she groaned. "I just can't. When was that?"

"Uh... you were there."

Maya seemed to redden somewhat, her mouth silently opened.

"At the Rainbow Bridge," I reminded. "You were there. Ah, no, that was later, when Odin came..."

"That's not what I mean, I mean the, the you know what!"

I shook my head.

"When did you two," she hissed, "you know?"

"I have no idea what you mean."

She rewarded me with a dark look. "I'm sure you don't."

I barely said my goodbyes before seeing myself out.

It wasn't so far from Sessrúmnir to the Great Hall. Or Bifröst. Just in case I wanted to make sure I remembered where it was. I could just walk past my wall, checking how it was doing, until I would approach... uh...

What did Maya mean with all that? "You know what"? I didn't, that was the problem, and nobody would tell me. Although maybe they would if I dared to ask right before dying of shame. She said I'd be holding a dark elf's hand and be nervous. The only hand I had held in a very long time was Thor's. A brazier? Svartálfheim was hot, that was why all the dwarves were blacksmiths, the last thing it would need was a brazier. I would prefer if the dream I had had last night foretold the future. It should. I was a real God, after all, even if I didn't feel like I was very good at it. Maya was just a talented human.

I walked in a strange pattern, closer to the wall, then further from it again, hiding from the surprising number of people working around me, drawn towards Bifröst, then remembering everyone would see me there. Not that I was not allowed to be there, at least from what I knew. How come I couldn't remember anything about my ex-lover? Clearly, one of us must have said or done the right thing and I couldn't even recall his name. It must have been the fruit, I reluctantly admitted. I ate it, because memories kept haunting me day and night. They didn't anymore. I ate and ate and ate until I just wiped my own mind clean.

When I sat with Thor and he asked me about my name something had happened. I didn't want to think about it. It's just that those memories seemed to still be somewhere and what if they'd come back when I least expected it? There was a *Niedomira*. I thought I didn't know anybody with a name like that.

I was so lost in my thoughts that I didn't notice that I'd returned to Bilskirnir until I got stopped. A manservant politely yet firmly redirected me around the hall, explaining that a few of the other Gods were feasting together with Thor and – he looked down in embarrassment – I was not invited. It felt like a punch in the gut. I told myself that those were just some Gods I didn't know. They came here to judge me. He was probably telling them to spare me.

I was not invited.

I went to the forge, pulled at the blower, and grabbed the largest sledgehammer and a thick chunk of iron. Sweat poured off me as I slammed the iron, not waiting for it to get hot enough, producing something I would pay for Thor not to see. I angrily threw the "result" at a wall, causing it to crack, leaving a large indent.

I just wanted to do good things and to help everyone and to see what Heimdall looked like without this armour on and to stop a war. Loki had tried to kill me. I had had to drink that poison brew of Gróa – I hoped she and her husband would be fine. Thor had destroyed my golem. My only reward was the faint hope that Lady Freya would somehow keep me alive. They wouldn't even give me any fruit. I had to just go on feeling and thinking and not being invited.

It just felt so *unfair*. If I were to survive this and get to that tenth world, I would make sure everything would turn out fine and fair for everybody. In the meantime, there was mead.

"Your Grace," said a man clad in chainmail and leather.

I looked up from my breakfast. He hadn't knocked. "Hmm?"

"I must request that you accompany me to the Great Hall."

"Aha," I said with my mouth full. I quickly swallowed, then wiped my mouth with my sleeve. "You must be one of the, eh, other Gods. I'll show you where it is."

The man gulped, visibly uncomfortable. "Perhaps I haven't been clear. My companions and I will take you there." He cast a look at me and flinched. I was as tall sitting down as he was standing up. "For the Assembly," he finished, his voice slightly shaky.

Four nervous men flanked me as we walked towards the Great Hall. I tried to appear calm, reminding myself that Lady Freya would save us, Thor would probably help, unless he was still angry about the wedding dress, and I had to hold a dwarf's hand in a tent. A dark elf's. So it had to end well. It's just that I was afraid that it wouldn't.

Maya was already waiting outside, accompanied only by one of Lady Freya's maids. Her lips produced a smile, but her eyes were open a bit too wide. Maya was afraid too and now I regretted having eaten.

At least I knew what to expect now, I reminded myself. A blink later the door opened, we were led inside, left standing in that circle of light and it was all I could do not to drop to my knees and plead for mercy. The other Gods, obscured by the void, whispered something to themselves, the sounds creating one unsettling hush. Odin cleared his throat and silence fell over the Hall.

My memory of the first time I had stood here was at best hazy, one of those that the fruit had taken away, but I couldn't remember being so afraid. And nothing had even happened yet. *Say something,* I prayed, when nothing continued to happen. I'd never been good with silences. Odin just sat on his throne, motionless, the tiny red pinprick of light in his one eye.

"Here we are," I said when the wait became torture.

"I can see that," answered Odin. A woman's tinkly laughter sounded, bouncing from the walls, surrounding us, making me wince. When the silence returned, it seemed to also echo around the walls, sucking in the sounds, so absolute it made my ears hurt, too.

"We have a few things to discuss today," said Odin. "Why don't we start with Maya? Step forward, child."

He sounded kind. Maybe it wouldn't be so bad.

"You are accused of failing in a mission to bring Thor back to Ásgard. You are accused of helping build a wall that would forever keep Thor outside. You are accused of using magic to throw a whetstone at Thor in an attempt to kill him. What do you have to say for yourself?"

Maya shrugged. "Nothing."

Both Odin and I were taken aback by that. "Really?" he asked after a brief pause.

"Really. I'm just a human, wipe me off the ground, let's be done."

"Hum. Go up and sit next to Freya."

It was Maya's turn now to pause, then ask "really?" Odin nodded. She glanced at me, then disappeared in the darkness and I was on my own again.

"Step forward, Módi," said Odin, "or perhaps Magni, which do you prefer?"

"Doesn't matter, Grandfather." Not a single gasp of shock or at least hushed surprise. *Everybody* knew and nobody had said anything.

"You have made an oath on my staff to build a wall around all of

Ásgard except Bifröst, a wall tall enough to make jötnar unable to attack. You have made an oath to do so within one winter, starting after the death of Freyr and ending with his rebirth. You have made an oath to neither accept nor demand any help that would come from outside Ásgard. You have been provided everything you wanted and more…"

"Loki—"

"Do not talk unless you are asked a question. The gap in the wall is such a size that Thor's chariot can get in and out. You have failed to fulfil your task. What do you have to say for yourself?"

"What about me?" screamed a woman. "What about the hurt he caused me? Surely…"

"Silence! It is not your turn to speak, Sif. What do you have to say for yourself, Magni?"

"Nothing!" I had a lot to say, but none of it mattered. It was clear that the decisions had been made already. Maya and I could only hope that Freya hadn't changed her mind. *Lady* Freya.

"Very well. Go up and sit next to Freya."

I swallowed, then looked at the darkness around me.

"To your left," said Odin. "Take a few steps and you will notice stairs. Ascend the stairs."

I strained my eyes. Nothing, just the black void. I stepped a bit closer to the edge of the light circle and noticed a change. The light that shone on me seemed to dim as the darkness became less dark. Encouraged, I took one more step and suddenly I could see. When I turned back, the circle of blinding light was gone. I told myself that they'd simply covered it, then saw the stairs that somehow led both forward and straight up, towards a wall that was also the ceiling.

My stomach seemed to curl and beg for mercy. The breakfast wanted out.

"Close your eyes," whispered Maya, grabbing my arm. I squealed in surprise. She was standing on the wall, horizontally, her head nearly touching mine, while she was also below me on the stairs that led up. As if I weren't nauseous enough. With my eyes shut so hard I could see stars I felt as if I were walking *up* completely normal stairs. A few more steps. A warm hand grabbed my cold and clammy one, and I was gently pulled down to my new seat.

I covered my eyes with my hand, then peeked between my fingers. The Great Hall was now narrow and long. The seats, most of them unoccupied, formed a circle, even though the Hall was not circle-shaped. Odin sat exactly opposite me, his throne at the same level as my seat, even though I had just walked up the stairs. Or maybe sideways the stairs.

I felt like I was already being punished.

"I'm going to be sick," I whispered.

"Keep your eyes closed," answered Maya, also in a whisper. "Thor—"

"Before we get to the main item in the agenda," said Odin, and his voice sounded very different from here, as if he were just another man sitting in the circle, which he was, except the circle was also narrow and long and straight... I covered my eyes with my hand and tried to breathe. "There is a matter that should have been settled many winters ago. A girl was born from two divine parents, a God and a Goddess. That girl has never been given the place in the Assembly that she deserved, instead serving Freya..."

Maya let out a little squeal.

"...fulfilling her whims and demands..."

"This is some sort of mistake," said Freya, sounding as if she was being choked.

"She was used," continued Odin louder, "to serve, when she should have been served. She has worked, when she should have had others working for her. She was living in Freya's hall, when she deserved a hall of her own. Each of us, together and separately owes her. I believe Týr will have no qualms when I invite her to join us."

"No," whispered Maya. "No, no, no."

"Please step in front of me," said Odin, then paused for what seemed to be a very long time, "Thrud."

Maya and Freya simultaneously let out sounds so weird that I forgot I wasn't looking and tried to lean and take a look at both. They must have either liked or disliked Thrud very much. I accidentally paid attention when Thrud entered the circle of light, except now it wasn't really so light, just as we were not surrounded by dark-ness, and it wasn't a circle and she was growing as she walked forward and also upwards and—

"Magni," I heard from somewhere very far away. "Magni, are you okay? You passed out."

"Oh no," exclaimed Thrud from above or below or front or to the side of me, "I'm going to get His Grace some water…"

"No," barked Odin. "No more."

"Sire," someone whispered, handing me a brass cup and a cloth so white it shone its own light. "A blindfold. Should I help?"

I gulped, my mouth even drier right now. "Please."

Maya let out a snort as I held on to the cup as if it could save me, letting Heimdall tie the cloth around my eyes. It helped a lot. Not just because I couldn't see the unnatural everything. Also because I felt his fingers touch my temples, ears, hair, and it might not have been a lot, but suddenly it didn't matter whether the Great Hall was an upside down straight line that was a circle with Thrud in the middle of it.

"Is this calamity over?" ensured Odin. "Step closer, my lady. In the name of most of us gathered here, but not in the name of your parents, I apologise. Sif, Thor, you will apologise in person and I suggest you don't wait too long before…"

"It's not necessary," said Thrud. Her gentle voice silenced Odin. "I neither want nor need apologies."

"You are owed by everyone in here who never protested or tried to help you," Odin insisted. He sounded irritated. "Everyone who treated you as a lowly servant is indebted to you."

"I withdraw all the claims I didn't even make."

"Surely," he nearly pleaded, "you would like a hall of your own?"

"No, thank you, Your Grace," said Thrud. "If I may wish for anything, I would like to remain in the service of Her Grace, Freya. I am happy."

"Why would anybody be happy to be a maid…?" cried Maya.

"Her Grace has never once screamed at me, hit me, nor treated me badly. If I have any divine abilities, I don't know them, and I don't want to. Like Her Grace Frigg, I am very pleased with a domestic life. I have no responsibilities of any sort. You, All-Father, have to...be the All-Father. Her Grace Freya, His Grace Freyr, Her Grace Eir, His Grace..."

The hisgracing and hergracing continued forever until she mercifully ran out of Gods. She hadn't mentioned Loki and somehow this made me feel both better and worse, as if his absence made him more present.

"...they all have responsibilities, tasks. If I may choose anything, then I choose to remain in Her Grace Freya's service." Steel sounded in her polite voice. I thought only Odin could do that. "I wish for things to remain the same."

"It is just," a low voice announced. Týr, I guessed. I heard a sharp intake of breath from Lady Freya's direction. Her maid just told her what to do and Her Grace had to listen. This was so oddly entertaining that I nearly forgot why I was here. Týr would be announcing my fate soon.

"Very well," said Odin. He sounded like he needed a drink. "Very well. Thank you, Thrud. Let us move on. Sif, please step forw—"

"I want his head!" yelled Sif. "And that girl's head! I have done what I was supposed to do, Thor is here! I want him to stay here and never leave again! He has duties, Thrud just said, he is the protector of Ásgard, not some sort of...man who gets to run around and fondle other women. I demand—"

"Stop," said Odin. Not only did Sif's voice die out, but its echoes were silenced as well. "Before you continue, which you will not, I am going to tell you what this looks like from my perspective. You sent Mjölnir away, causing great danger to Ásgard and unnecessary destruction of a jötunn city, nearly killing the son of Thor, whose head you demand, and Maya, Freya's" – he paused – "maid, whose head you also demand. Why would I, or anybody else, listen to you?"

I understood that pause. Maya, a human who had to do what Lady Freya told her to, was being served by an actual maid, Thrud, who was a Goddess and I had no idea who would be telling whom what to do now.

"You put Loki and Thor themselves in danger."

Sif screeched, bird-like, and I carefully I lifted the blindfold. All I saw was a cloak that covered her completely. Was it hiding a person or a vulture?

"I strongly suggest you keep quiet. Thor left Ásgard because of you. When he returned, it was out of love, but not for you. Thor has also made it clear before the Assembly that he would leave Ásgard forever if a single hair were to fall off—"

"Hair!!! My hair!!!"

I scowled. Listening to Sif felt like having someone scratch my skull with a rusty nail.

"Silence! If a single hair falls off *Magni's* head, Thor will leave and not return this time. If you remain in Ásgard, he will do the same. Thor does not wish for you to be his wife anymore. There is a war brewing, the army of jötnar grows with each day, led by a mage whose powers we neither know nor understand. We need Thor more than ever. Much more than we need you. What do you have to say for yourself?"

This silence was more deafening than the shrieks.

A noise of fabric. "All-Father. May I speak?"

"Freya."

"I can resolve every single of those problems. Before I do so, I will name my conditions. I would like Maya to remain in my service – alive and untouched. I would like Magni to join me, if that is his wish – alive and untouched."

"The girl hurt Thor," said Odin shortly.

"Nay," rumbled thunder above. The Great Hall seemed to shake a bit. "My own fault. I have no claims."

"I do!" shrieked Sif and the echoes of her voice carried for just a blink before I heard a little *pop.* Complete silence followed. I had a feeling that she'd remain quiet for a while now.

"If you would like to claim that Magni had help he shouldn't have had, I demand that *you* are put on trial," continued Freya as if nothing had happened. "Maya and I have resolved the matter of her failed quest between us. It was I who gave the task to her and it is up to me to decide what is owed."

"The wall is not completed."

"I should be very happy about that, since Magni demanded me as his reward. Yet. if I were to judge, he has succeeded. When Freyr was reborn, the wall was complete."

"Mjölnir—"

"If there is something Mjölnir can't break, I would very much like to see it. As far as I know, Thor is not an enemy of Ásgard who needed to be kept away."

"Which was Magni's intention."

"Prove it," said Freya, slightly louder. I instinctively flinched when I felt her hand rest on my shoulder. At least I thought it was hers, unable to check, since I was wearing a blindfold and there was something about it that – "The oath did not ask for a wall that would not fall under the blow of Mjölnir. Thor was not mentioned in it either. Magni hasn't failed. I suggest that his reward, which is *me*, be exchanged for his life, to ensure that everyone is satisfied."

"That is a lie, all of this is a lie! He is mine, mine, he ruined my beauty forever, ended our love, Thor's and mine, he destroyed everything I ever held dear...!"

"Shut your mouth!" roared Odin and this time the Great Hall really shook. Something fell to the ground, probably a piece of basalt, breaking again and again as the echoes bounced from the walls, turning louder, forcing me to stick fingers in my ears as I nearly cried from the intensity. How could they take all this noise?! Freya's grip on my shoulder tightened. Only now did I realise that I was rocking back and forth. This was all too much. Sif was accusing me of "ruining her beauty" even though she hardly had any when I saw her that one time when Thor "fought" Hrungnir.

It seemed like the silence had returned. I was still afraid when I took my fingers out of my ears. I wasn't sure whether my life had already been spared or not.

"Sif," said Freya, "remove your cloak."

"I refuse! You will not humiliate me again!"

"Do it," said Odin, "or Magni will help you, like he did before."

It had happened and I didn't remember, I still didn't, but it had.

Unclear visions flickered in front of my eyes, unsettling ones that I could only hope were not real. They scared me more than the

Great Hall. I lifted the blindfold. I felt like I owed it to Sif to see what I had done to her.

When she let the cloak fall down from her shoulders, I stopped breathing. The visions inside my head seemed to wobble, then disappear.

A mass of gold dropped nearly to Sif's waist. Her locks looked like each of the golden hairs was lit from the inside. Her hands wandered up to touch the hair, as if she couldn't believe it was real. When she shook her head the golden silk floated in the air as if in slow motion. I blinked when the reflections of the light blinded me. The Great Hall seemed to disappear. The waves of gold made everything else irrelevant.

"I don't understand," said Sif, her voice suddenly soft, breaking. "How... is this... for me?"

"Thor," said Freya, "won't you speak to your wife?"

The answer was something between a grunt and a rumble.

"But you love her so much," Freya said softly. "I know you do. And she loves you too. Why dwell on the past?"

I snorted, then gasped.

Thor was running sideways and also from under the ground, his arms already extended. I dropped the cup in my hurry to pull the blindfold back on. "My love!" he cried.

"My love!"

"Oh, my love!"

"Get a hall," Maya muttered as the sounds of sloppy kisses followed, then stopped. Brief silence. Crack of the basalt. Thor's rumble, this time oddly joyful. Sif's giggle. I couldn't resist taking a quick peek just in time to see him running outside with Sif in his arms. All he could lift a few days ago was his tankard.

I was starting to feel like I would probably survive.

"Crystal magic is very simple," muttered Freya under her breath, then raised her voice again. "I am not done, All-Father."

"Still. You have been working very hard, my lady."

"Anything for the great Ásgard. I was convinced that now we are defended by the wall, the jötunn army would disperse. This is not the case, as it keeps growing, gathering not just the jötnar, but also elves, dark elves, humans. In the guise of a maid, I have approached their queen, for their great mage is in fact a woman, whose name is Járnsaxa..."

I must have made some really strange sound, because someone tapped me on the shoulder, then wrapped my shaky fingers around a mug. I emptied it greedily, burning my tongue, before realising it was refreshing mint. It didn't matter. My mother was alive.

"I believe her to possess magic greater than perhaps any of us," continued Freya once I quieted. "I have no proof, but I believe that it is true that she can control weather, the sun, the moon, the clouds even. She is absolutely convinced that her army can cross Ifing."

My mother was a great mage.

"It's not possible," someone said dismissively.

"Mjölnir crossed Ifing," said Freya. "I don't know whether Járnsaxa is lying or telling the truth. She seems very certain, though."

My mother was a queen.

"What do you suggest?" Odin's voice had changed back to that of an old man. I could almost see him leaning forward, holding on to his staff so as not to fall on his face.

"I would like to take Magni and Maya and send them to talk to Járnsaxa. She knows them both." I felt the grip on my shoulder again.

"What will they talk about?" I could barely hear Odin. I would get to see Mother again. She was alive, she was a great queen and possessed magic.

"They will offer their help," said Freya, "and find out what she can do. She has a young maid who can be easily persuaded to get some rest and let someone else take over her duties for one evening."

"Magni looks like Thor. He's the last person—"

"Not when his head and beard are shaven."

I'd shave it three times a day if it meant seeing my mother again.

"Granted," said Odin. "You have worked very hard. You deserve all that you ask for."

"Is nobody going to ask my opinion?" complained Týr.

Odin seemed to consider this, deep in thought. "No," he finally said.

Týr harrumphed and Heimdall chuckled softly. I wouldn't be able to say how I knew it was Heimdall. I just did. I would survive this, so would Maya, Mother was alive and a *queen*. I would see her. Then we would go to the tenth world, where I would be Thor and everyone would be equal. Lady Freya truly resolved all the problems. It almost stopped me from thinking about how peculiar it felt to have Heimdall blindfold me.

"...Loki," I heard and started paying attention again.

"Loki, who is unfortunately absent, has been helping Magni with his work," said Odin, "while simultaneously stealing from Idunn's garden. Magni's greed is not Loki's fault; the thievery is. Loki has given birth to my stallion Sleipnir, a process that I hear he greatly enjoyed, and that is a gift beyond all others, a horse nobody else can touch or take away from me. He has done some of my bidding, yet refused or lied when I asked him for other things. Týr, now is your turn to decide what is right, what, if any, punishment he deserves."

They were calling me greedy and it wasn't Loki's fault and Týr would decide *if* he deserved punishment?!

"I—" started Týr, then stopped to clear his throat. "I need a drink. Is this mint? I despise mint. Please give me some wine."

Týr was the God of justice. It was clear as day what was just. What was there to think about?

"No opinion."

I could almost hear Odin's eyebrows wander up. "Now that I ask, you have no opinion?"

"No."

"But you are the judge of what is and isn't just. It's your purpose. If you don't know what is just, then who is supposed to know?"

"There is one more who has a claim on Loki's head. Until that one raises their hand to tell us their story, or until things develop further, I cannot declare what is just."

In the ensuing silence I heard the unmistakable sound of grinding teeth, although with how sound carried here it could have even been from me.

My mother is alive and a queen with magical powers and I will get to see her.

420

"Very well," said Odin. "Very well. Well. Very well. I say. This is unexpected. Do you have any explanation as to what you mean by things developing further?"

"Since I cannot see the future, no."

Odin's sigh was long and heavy. "Is there anything else," he said, rather than asked. He sounded like he was ready to lie down with a lot of his magical wine. I could relate.

Nobody spoke.

"The Assembly is over," he said.

"You can take your blindfold off," Maya said. Her voice remained stilted. "It all looks normal now."

I peeked to check. It did. Like a very big – well – hall. Just a few long tables; chairs, one of which I sat at. "What happens now?"

"Drinks and snacks," Maya muttered. I was trying to figure out which God was which, but the tone of her voice made me pay attention. She looked like a thunderstorm waiting to happen. "Go, try Granny Frigg's cookies."

"What did I do to Sif's hair?" I asked, suddenly remembering that I'd forgotten.

"Oh, Magni, honey," said Freya. "I convinced her that the necklace I sent was a gift from Thor that he had forgotten about after he got hit with that rock."

"It's fake?"

"Of course it's fake," growled Maya. "Like everything Freya does."

"Are we really going to see my mother?" I asked. Maya seemed really upset by Thrud's... whatever it was.

Freya nodded, a strange smile playing on her lips.

"And she is a queen?"

"*The* queen. A very powerful one, too."

I would get to see her. Talk to her. I'd convince her there was need for a war, for an army. Thor wouldn't attack anymore, I was certain of it. They could get busy rebuilding the cities, castles, villages, farms. Ruled by my mother, *the* queen.

"Grandson."

It suddenly became very empty around me when Odin handed me a goblet of wine. He smiled. "Skál."

I turned into stone.

Idunn's wine, made especially for Odin, the one I wanted so bad. Made from her grapes. Wine that kept him immortal, if not really young.

The desire, the warmth, the happiness, the relief. That feeling when I first ate a peach and everything became more than I had words for. I hadn't tried the fruit for such a long time now. I recovered. The wine would be safe, it had to be. Probably.

Not even the smallest bit, said Gróa, over and over and over again. Maya said the same. Not even a bit, but there were no bits in wine. Wine was not really fruit, it was just made of it, just a drink. Odin would not hand it to me if he thought I could be in danger.

There was some saliva in the corner of my mouth.

My eyes met his one eye that still shone red. The smile was kind, encouraging. This was not a face of someone who would try to make his grandson sick by fulfilling his dream, wish, desire.

It was Odin's face.

"I'm afraid I can't drink it," I said, putting the goblet down. "I would love to drink anything else with you, All-Father. Just not this wine."

"It is an offence to refuse a toast."

"I know. I can't drink your wine."

"Smell it."

I would never be able to stop myself from drinking it once I smelled the magic. At the same time, refusing a toast from Odin out of all... all everyone could end with a fate worse than just death. He had me again and all he needed to do was give me what I asked for.

I lifted the goblet again and very carefully sniffed it.

"Skál," I said and drank with my grandfather. "May I ask you one question?"

"You may."

"Why did you help?"

The way his eyebrows wandered up, but the missing eye remained hidden by a shadow that wasn't cast by any light, was very disconcerting. "Help?"

"With the wall," I said. "You must know what I mean."

Odin slowly shook his head. "I did not help with your wall. I interrupted you. My ravens watched you. That was all."

"All-Father," interrupted Maya. "Are you okay? You answered a question directly, without a riddle."

"Dear Maya, I was just about to search for you. I believe you might answer some of my questions regarding Sleipnir."

Maya probably said something, or maybe coughed or choked or cried, but she disappeared. So did everyone else, the Great Hall, all of the Nine. There was only one man left, his tunic and trousers so white that they looked as if he was dressed in light. The belt was golden, like Sif's hair, only useful.

"I have your blindfold," I remembered, then felt most of the blood in my body rush towards my face, except some that went somewhere else. "Eh. Sire."

Heimdall's smile, the teeth shining on his brass... bronze... golden-skinned face, was as dazzling as the white he wore. "We might still need it."

My mind seemed to get stuck. I understood each of the words, but not the whole sentence.

"Heimdall, be a darling," cooed Freya, "I need just a blink or two with Magni, then he's all yours."

"All mine," repeated Heimdall, then his tongue made an incredibly brief appearance, like I remembered, like it did in my dreams, before he turned away. The disappointment, the *pain* I felt was brutal.

"Magni, petal, you will not fall in love."

"What," I groaned.

"It's a promise, not a threat."

"Consequences," hissed Maya, her face possibly redder than mine. I really needed to find out why Thrud being a Goddess made her so upset. Just not now. "What about the consequences of just making Thor love Sif and—"

"Petal, you've made an oath."

"It had nothing—"

"This is neither the time nor place to talk."

"It's winter, shouldn't you be grieving?"

"Darling, you *will* allow me to grieve whenever I feel like it, won't you? Now let's go and find you something useful to do."

Maya continued hissing angrily as Freya grabbed her arm and pulled her away. I gawked, still crumpling the white cloth in my hand. As if by magic, the sort that I had never known before, but welcomed, Heimdall appeared in front of me. He wasn't there, then before I had a chance to blink he was standing so near that I could feel his breath move the hairs of my beard.

"Sire," he said.

"What does that mean," I groaned. "I know the yourgrace and the mylord..."

"That's what I call those I respect and consider my equals. Until I get to know them better."

"Know better," I repeated, the only words I remembered from the entire language.

"I can't stay away from Bifröst for long. It is my task to guard Ásgard, even right now. Still, it's been a long time since I have visited my hall, Himinbjörg. I don't believe you have seen it before?"

I had no thoughts left at all. Maybe there just wasn't enough blood in my body for my mind to work at the same time as the rest.

"I was wondering if you would like to take a quick look," he murmured. He stood so close our lips were *almost* touching. "I should see whether it is being kept in good order."

For the first time in my life, I heard clearly what he didn't say.

"Sire," I managed.

Thank you for reading *Children*! The stories of the Ten Worlds continue in *Land*, coming in 2021.

I hope you enjoyed the book. I would be very grateful for a short comment or rating on Goodreads, Amazon, or any other website of your choice.

Subscribe to my newsletter at www.bjornlarssen.com/newsletter for advance information, book reviews, notifications about promotional events, photos of Iceland, free e-books and short stories, and anything else I can possibly come up with.

Feel free to contact me any time at bjorn@bjornlarssen.com

www.bjornlarssen.com
www.twitter.com/bjornlarssen
www.faccbook.com/bjornlarssenwriter
www.instagram.com/bjorn_larssen

ACKNOWLEDGMENTS

Sixteen months and twenty-three days after starting work on this book, I can finally declare it finished thanks to many patient and kind people... don't believe anybody who suggests writing is a solitary job.

First and foremost, I'd like to thank my wonderful editor and friend, Megan Dickman-Renard. Without you this book would have been very different...and not in a good way. Thank you for sprinkling your magic all over it.

Thank you so much to my ever-patient, kind, helpful beta-readers – Izabela, Queen Timy, Justine, Krystle, Marian, Angela. *waves vigorously towards the Murderous and Fancy Cheesers*

Terry Tyler has been a mentor and friend, sharing her knowledge for no other reason than just because she could, same as Debbie Young. Thank you for your kindness and patience. I'm trying to repay it by helping others.

Penni – thank you so, so much for your constant support, and for pointing out the Old Norse translation (OMG) had potential to accidentally offend lots of people. You're my saviour!

Marian – you are one of the most wonderful people I have ever had the pleasure of meeting. I am proud to be your friend and to have the privilege of working together. (And to be a little Marai boy! Can't wait to see what happens to me next.)

100% Pure Love for Anna, Gerardo, Ewa, Casper, Georg + Benjamin, Marieke, aaaaand the Beeps! KKMF and thanks for letting me stay around.

Thank you so much for sharing your stories with me – you know who you are and I am both proud and grateful that you have trusted me. I hope I've done a job good enough to do you justice.

Massive thanks to all the book bloggers for all that you do for the indie community, for your time, passion, hard work.

This book (or this life) would have never happened without my wonderful husband. Kocham Cię i dziękuję za Ciebie codziennie.

ABOUT THE AUTHOR

Bjørn Larssen is a Norse heathen made in Poland, but mostly located in a Dutch suburb, except for his heart which he lost in Iceland. Born in 1977, he self-published his first graphic novel at the age of seven in a limited edition of one, following this achievement several decades later with his first book containing multiple sentences and winning awards he didn't design himself. His writing is described as 'dark' and 'literary', but he remains incapable of taking anything seriously for more than 60 seconds.

Bjørn has a degree in mathematics and has worked as a graphic designer, a model, a bartender, and a blacksmith (not all at the same time). His hobbies include sitting by open fires, dressing like an extra from Vikings, installing operating systems, and dreaming about living in a log cabin in the north of Iceland. He owns one (1) husband and is owned by one (1) neighbourhood cat.